What Reviewers Say About
The Elite Operatives Series:

"*Missing Lynx* puts the thrill in thriller. In true thriller style, Baldwin and Alexiou take their women around the globe…from Vienna, all around the U.S. Southwest, on to New York, down to some of the most dangerous parts of Mexico, on to China and Vietnam and back to the Southwest. Quite the wild ride. But that's what lends verisimilitude to this tale of the traffic in human beings. Lynx hooks up with a mercenary during her journey and that relationship sends a sizzle through the story that is palpable. Heroine and anti-heroine. Quite the chemistry. A dark, edgy, often grisly tale, Missing Lynx has the grit and pacing of a Bourne saga, but with highly engaging and thoroughly challenging female characters. Not for the faint hearted."—*Lambdaliterary.org*

"Kim Baldwin & Xenia Alexiou just get better and better at coming up with tightly written thrillers with plenty of 'seat of the pants' action. *Missing Lynx* is a roller coaster ride into the seamier side of life and the bonds which bind humans into trying to better the world. This is a book which grips the reader until the final page!"
—*Just About Write*

"Unexpected twists and turns, deadly action, complex characters and multiple subplots converge to make this book a gripping page turner. *Lethal Affairs* mixes political intrigue with romance, giving the reader an easy flowing and fast-moving story that never lets up. A must-read, even though it has been out for a while. *Thief of Always*, the duo's second, and equally good book in the Elite Operatives series, came out earlier this year."—*Curve Magazine*

By the Authors

Dying to Live

Lethal Affairs

Thief of Always

Missing Lynx

By Kim Baldwin

Hunter's Pursuit

Force of Nature

Whitewater Rendezvous

Flight Risk

Focus of Desire

Breaking the Ice

DYING TO LIVE

by

Kim Baldwin
and Xenia Alexiou

2011

DYING TO LIVE

ISBN 10: 1-60282-200-X
ISBN 13: 978-1-60282-200-9

This Trade Paperback Original Is Published By
Bold Strokes Books, Inc.
P.O. Box 249
Valley Falls, NY 12185

First Edition: February 2011

CREDITS
EDITOR: SHELLEY THRASHER
PRODUCTION DESIGN: SUSAN RAMUNDO
COVER DESIGN BY SHERI (GRAPHICARTIST2020@HOTMAIL.COM)

Acknowledgments

The authors wish to thank all the talented women at Bold Strokes Books for making this book possible. Radclyffe, for her vision, faith in us, and example. Editor Shelley Thrasher, your insightful editing of this book is deeply appreciated. Senior Consulting Editor Jennifer Knight, for invaluable insights into how to craft a series. Graphic artist Sheri for another amazing cover. Connie Ward, BSB publicist and first-reader extraordinaire, and all of the other support staff who work behind the scenes to make each BSB book an exceptional read.

We'd also like to thank our dear friend and first-reader Jenny Harmon, for your invaluable feedback and insights. And finally, to the readers who encourage us by buying our books, showing up for personal appearances, and for taking the time to e-mail us. Thank you so much.

My cherished friend Xenia, we're more than halfway through the series and I can't tell you how much I'll miss the joyous task of co-authoring your stories. Writing with you has been a most welcome distraction during some troubled times, and you manage to make me laugh every day. I'm honored and deeply touched by your faith in me and hold you close to my heart.

For Marty, for everything. Forty years of friendship and so much more. Your encouragement started me on this path, and I'm forever grateful.

Mom and Dad, I miss you both so much and know you're watching out for me. And for my brother Tom, for always saying yes when I need a ride to the airport.

I also have to thank a wonderful bunch of friends who provide unwavering support for all my endeavors. Linda and Vicki, Kat and Ed, Felicity, Claudia and Esther, Karen and Pattie. You are family, and near or far, I hold you always close to my heart.

Kim Baldwin, February 2011

❖

As always, a very big thank you to my wonderfully supportive friends.

Claudia, Esther, May, Nicki, Steven, Georgia, thank you for putting up with me and for your constant encouragement.

Mom, Dad, and Sis. You are my biggest reward and comfort. Thank you for everything.

Of course and always, my gratitude and respect to my invaluable friend Kim. Thank you for pointing me in this direction and for being there every step of the way. I am always there for you, no matter what.

And last but not least, a big bow of appreciation to all the readers out there who make writing one of the most rewarding things I've ever done. YOU ALL ROCK.

Xenia Alexiou, February 2011

Dedication

For my father
You raised me as your equal, gave me wings,
and let me use them.
Because of you, I'm not afraid.
I love you.

Xenia

"Corruption eats away at the public's trust in the medical community. People have a right to expect that the drugs they depend on are real. They have a right to think that doctors place a patient's interests above profits. And most of all, they have a right to believe that the health care industry is there to cure, not to kill."

—David Nussbaum

PROLOGUE

Fossa del Lupo, Italy

"When the Lamb opened the fourth seal, I heard the voice of the fourth living creature say, 'Come!' I looked, and there before me was a pale horse! Its rider was named Death, and Hades was following close behind him."

The surgical mask muffled his words, so the elderly priest overenunciated the passage from the Book of Revelations. Once a rotund man with boundless energy and unflappable optimism, he was barely recognizable now. The violet vestments of sorrow and penance the padre wore hung loosely about his shoulders and waist as he raised his arms beseechingly and turned to face his sparse congregation. Tears streamed down his face as he fell to his knees, and the undercurrent of terror in his tone was unmistakable. "They were given power over a fourth of the earth to kill by sword, famine and plague," he said, his voice breaking, "and by the wild beasts of the earth."

Alone in the last pew, a thirty-three-year-old bachelor glanced up at the first of the fourteen Stations of the Cross that ringed the tiny chapel. A gilt-etched rendering of the Savior in chains, the caption beneath it read: *Gesù è Condannato a Morte*—Jesus is Condemned to Death. He'd never been a religious man and his recent visits to the house of God made him feel like an imposter. But now was not the time for misplaced guilt. Not when the future seemed so grim and death was everywhere. The church was one of the few places still considered safe from the virus, because everyone with symptoms had been banned from public gatherings, and religious services were no exception. How ironic, he thought, not for the first time, and how hypocritical. The one place where the dying feel the need to visit for solace and hope, forgiveness and redemption, was now closed to them. The so-called men of God were only interested in preserving their own lives. The bachelor wiped at the sheen of perspiration that drenched his brow.

"Let us pray," the priest cried out.

The man shut his burning eyes and joined the others in their loud prayers for God's mercy and forgiveness.

Only a handful of the village's one hundred and twenty inhabitants dared this rare gathering. Those with families would not risk venturing out, but the forced isolation and growing despondency over the situation had driven those who lived alone to seek the companionship and the consolation of the church. Like him, each parishioner covered his face with a scarf or mask and sat well apart from his nearest neighbor.

The horrible sickness had so far not touched their small community. When the first cases reached Italy along the southern coast, the village administrator had taken early and extreme precautions, barricading the pair of two-lane roads leading in and out, closing the school and businesses, and advising residents to remain in their homes until further notice. But the scourge now surrounded them. Towns and hamlets in every direction had been hit hard, the death toll rising exponentially by the day, and it seemed only a miracle could spare them.

That morning, he had awakened with a headache and queasy stomach, but he'd managed to convince himself the *pesce crudo* he'd prepared the night before was to blame. A stupid choice, he thought in retrospect, since the last delivery of fresh seafood to the village had been more than two weeks earlier.

When he stepped before the mirror to shave, it was more difficult to reassure himself that the raw fish was also responsible for his gray pallor and the dark circles beneath his eyes. Less than a week ago, he had defied the ban on travel, so desperate for cigarettes that he'd walked two miles cross-country to Camucia. There'd been no reported cases there, so he'd felt it worth the risk. But in the intervening days, the relentless menace had killed a dozen people in the very neighborhood where he'd shopped.

The short trek to the chapel winded him, and the fever that had accelerated with each step now made him want to discard his heavy coat, but he didn't dare draw any undue attention to himself. As he prayed, he got a sudden urge to cough and fought to suppress it, his heartbeat accelerating as he recalled the stark news video of the dying, in hospitals unable to cope with the pandemic.

He grappled for his handkerchief when he could no longer contain the violent compulsion and hacked loudly into the white linen. Recoiling in horror when he saw the thick glob of bloody mucus he'd expelled, it took a long moment to realize the chapel had fallen silent. The priest and all the congregants were staring at him, fear and accusation in their eyes.

He bolted from the chapel and into the dark night, his chest constricting with another urgent spasm of coughing. Despair washed over him as he ran, unmindful of any particular destination. He couldn't bear the thought that he might be the agent of death to his beloved village, nor could he endure the certain agony of his fate.

Falling to his knees, he screamed a prayer for guidance, and the distant whistle of a train blared his answer. Passenger traffic had ceased days ago, but freight lines were still carrying medical supplies and essential provisions to devastated areas.

The rail was a half mile from where he knelt. As though in a trance, he walked to the tracks and arrived before the locomotive came into view. Waiting patiently, he recited the Act of Contrition and thought of his parents, long dead. The roar of the nearing engine filled his ears, and he gathered his courage, made the Sign of the Cross, and stepped forward. *Dio se ci sei, ti prego di avere pietá della mia anima!* Lord, if you are there, please have mercy on my soul.

CHAPTER ONE

Northwest of Budapest, Hungary
Three weeks earlier, October 1

Viewed from above, the secret complex, tucked into a remote forest in the foothills of the Carpathian Mountains, looked somewhat like a giant V. One wing contained the research labs and the numerous prison-like cells where the human trials were conducted. The other housed a large kitchen, dining room, and dormitory where many of the employees lived. In the space between the wings was a courtyard, where workers could enjoy some sunshine when the weather cooperated. A high wire fence, surveillance cameras, and a small team of security guards prevented unwanted outsiders from intruding.

The facility, less than two years old, contained a state-of-the-art BioLab, level 4. It was here that research had been conducted on some of the most virulent and incurable biological agents known to humankind, so extraordinary precautions had to be taken. The lab was air-locked and required a palm print and retinal scan to access it, and the scientists who worked inside with the infectious materials wore Hazmat suits with individual oxygen supplies.

The complex had been built for a single purpose: to develop viruses that would kill quickly and spread rapidly. The lab manufactured several biological agents, but concentrated on one in particular; this one contained a stealth component, one that would disappear quickly after infection, so that efforts to isolate and identify it would be time-consuming and almost impossible to achieve.

It took the handpicked team of scientists at the lab four months to develop the formula. The man in charge, Doctor Andor Rózsa, named it the Charon virus, after the mythological ferryman to Hades. A chimera of the H1N1 virus and pneumonic-plague bacteria, it was highly virulent and had a near 100 percent mortality rate.

When the virus was perfected, the team moved on to phase two of the secret project: to develop an antivirus vaccine that would both prevent and cure the lethal contagion. That was more difficult and took them another eight months to perfect.

For the last half year, they'd been conducting human trials at the complex, to both ensure that Charon did its job without mutating and that its cure worked quickly, with 100 percent effectiveness.

On this night, the man behind it all was to evaluate the final results of those trials. If everything was in order, he would finally be able to launch the scheme that would make him a billionaire several times over.

Doctor Andor Rózsa was well positioned to cash in on the windfall without fear of being linked to the pandemic he was about to launch, as long as his meticulous planning went off without a hitch. Charon was his secret pet project; he had a legitimate career as well, as a top virologist with Pharmamediq, Incorporated, a major pharmaceutical company in Budapest. As such, when the time was right he could announce he'd come up with the formula for the antivirus, and no one would suspect him.

As Andor navigated the seventy-minute drive from his office at Pharmamediq to the complex, he reviewed every detail of his plan. He had spent years making it, so he wasn't worried that he'd missed something. However, he was meticulous and took great satisfaction in recalling how he'd put it all together.

He'd had a few great challenges to overcome. First was where to obtain the numerous individuals needed for the human trials, since none of them could survive to tell about the experiments. He solved that by using orphans, runaways, and homeless adults from the streets of Budapest, lured into social-service vans by promises of food, shelter, and jobs. Also, he bribed a warden at a remote prison to release a number of prisoners to his custody: all forgotten men, lifers with no families who would not be missed.

The other major obstacle was to find the perfect individuals to take Charon out into the world and release it. Andor needed three people capable of killing without hesitation if the price was right and experienced in tracking and isolating their targets. They'd all have fake IDs that would pass close inspection, but one had to have no criminal history that might impede his ability to cross international borders. He'd be bound for the U.S., which now did facial and fingerprint identifications of travelers, often chosen at random. It took time to make the right connections, but Andor was confident he had the people he needed.

He parked beside the wing that housed the human-trial cells, and went inside. His chief aide, Patrik, who oversaw the project while he put in his hours at Pharmamediq, was waiting for him. "Everything in order?" Andor asked.

"Yes, sir," Patrik replied. "Two more of the virus test group expired overnight, exactly as anticipated."

"Excellent. Let's make our final walk-through."

The two men visited the first of the two dozen rooms that lined the hallway, starting on the left side. This was the Charon group: the men, women, and children who were infected with the virus and closely monitored until they died. Several people had been housed in each room during the six months of trials, the rooms thoroughly disinfected between occupants. The team now had extensive knowledge of what the virus did to the human body and an accurate progression timeline: they knew precisely how long it took from date of infection, to first symptoms, to death.

Only two patients remained in the Charon group. Both had only hours to live, at most. Further viral trials were unnecessary, and it was time to begin eliminating all traces that Charon had been developed here.

Each small room in the hallway looked very much like a prison cell, with a single cot, sink, and toilet. The occupants had no televisions, radios, books, or view to the outside. These were only lab animals to Andor; he viewed them with clinical detachment, as every good scientist should.

The only window in each room was a thick Plexiglas one in the door that allowed the staff to monitor the patient's condition as he or she deteriorated. Communication was carried on through an intercom, and meals were delivered through a self-contained slot beneath the window. The precautions had been necessary when the complex was built, but weren't now. Everyone who worked there had been inoculated with the antivirus.

Andor removed the patient's medical file from a holder beside the first door he came to and scanned it. Group 1 patient #87 was a thirteen-year-old runaway, infected seven days earlier. He stepped in front of the window and peered inside. The girl was hunched in one corner, her eyes closed. She was pale and shaking violently. Spatters of blood and crusted vomit marred most of the room's beige walls, the bedding on the cot, and the litter of used meal trays and water bottles scattered around the floor. Fetid brown evidence of the girl's chronic diarrhea could be seen in a wide circle around the toilet.

Andor curled his lips in disgust, imagining the stench in the room, before moving on to the next cell.

The remaining virus patient was a thirty-eight-year-old homeless woman. She was in virtually the same wretched condition as her neighbor, though still conscious. She lay on her cot, soaked with sweat, eyes wide open and mumbling incoherently. Not all of their patients hallucinated before they died, but many did. Her room was only marginally cleaner than the girl's.

The rest of the rooms on that side were vacant, so Andor moved to the cells that contained the subjects who'd been infected and then injected with the antivirus.

He peered through the first window at the fifty-two-year-old convict inside. When the man—a hulking brute with tattoos on his arms and neck—realized he was being watched, he stormed the door and began to bang on it, screaming obscenities. The doctor pulled the man's chart from the wall and studied the latest entries. "Remarkable. BP, temp, CBC, Chem 7, U/A, electrolytes—all within normal range. Viral cultures negative. It's hard to believe he was hours from death just three days ago."

"All subjects have made the same progression," Patrik replied.

Andor perfunctorily checked the rest of the patients on that side of the hallway to see for himself. Satisfied that all the subjects had completely recovered, he turned to his aide. "We've no further use for them beyond extracting whatever organs we have orders for. I'll take care of that before I leave. Prep the patients we need and destroy the rest."

Patrik nodded. "So you concur we can proceed as scheduled?"

"Yes. Give the go-ahead."

The three emissaries who would unleash Charon had all been injected with the antivirus vaccine two weeks earlier, to ensure they would return for payment without infecting anyone beyond their targets. Of course, Andor didn't intend to give them anything beyond their travel costs. When their missions were completed, they had to be eliminated, because once the pandemic started spreading, they would realize they hadn't been after a single target, or two, as they'd been told; they were part of the world's greatest biological nightmare.

He'd done everything he could to ensure the three would never be able to link him to the pandemic, should they be caught or decide to try to use their knowledge as leverage to demand more money. He never dealt with them directly. And even the intermediary who did, didn't know who he was. This employee received his instructions from Patrik, who used disposable prepaid cell phones for each communication. The antivirus syringes that the intermediary injected into the trio, as well as the materials they'd need for their missions, were left for him in a train station locker across the border, in Vienna.

Andor had also carefully selected the targets who would be infected. They were a diverse group, seemingly random victims with nothing in common except that all held jobs that put them in daily contact with a large number of people. Authorities would have to work harder to track down the "patient zeros," who would be infecting many others within a day of being infected themselves.

Andor's three deadly emissaries had already received detailed files about their targets to memorize, along with fake passports and cash for their plane tickets and other incidentals. They'd also been given stainless-steel capsules containing the deadly virus, which they would swallow before their flights. Once the capsules had been excreted from their intestinal tracts, the contents would be mixed with water and placed in lipstick-sized refillable atomizers. All that remained was for the intermediary to give them the go-ahead.

Later that night, Agent X would drive to Germany for the first part of her assignment, then fly to the Democratic Republic of the Congo. Agent Y had a single target, in China. Agent Z was destined for Colombia and the United States.

Andor headed back to his car for the drive back to Budapest, buoyed by the imminent launch of his long-awaited plan. He had no concern for the millions who had to die to make it happen. After all, he was certainly not alone in his quest to seek profit from genetically manufactured biological agents. Several governments were purportedly concocting bioweapons using the variola virus, the agent of smallpox, including the U.S., Russia, and China. SARS, anthrax, Ebola, and botulinum neurotoxins were other popular pathogens rumored to be in play in labs worldwide, in both the public and private sectors. One lab in the Ukraine had called it an "accident" when it was discovered their seasonal flu vaccine contained a deadly avian-flu virus that killed hundreds. But Andor knew it had been a deliberate act for human trial and profit, just as this was. The difference would be in the planning. No one would be able to connect the upcoming pandemic to him. He would only reap the rewards for having discovered the antivirus.

Within a few weeks, Andor would be heralded as the most brilliant scientist of the century and the savior of humankind. Certainly a Nobel Prize would follow. That prospect was almost as satisfying as the fact that he'd soon be one of the richest men in the world.

❖

Munich, Germany
October 2

"Guten Abend, Professor."

"You're early," the professor mumbled, without looking up from his papers.

"Would you like me to come back later?" Agent X asked.

The man didn't answer, but waved at her absently to come in, still intent on the pile of student essays he was correcting.

She pushed the cleaning cart into the office, grateful the file she'd been provided had everything she needed to ensure a smooth completion of the first half of her assignment. As expected, Gunther Zimmerman was working late, a reliable habit after his thrice-weekly botany lectures, according to his bio. The file also had all the relevant information she needed about the University of Munich Biocenter, including a complex blueprint that incorporated the location of the janitorial closet, security cameras, and restrooms nearest the target's office. She'd waited there, dressed in the cleaning coveralls she'd been given, until everyone but Zimmerman had gone home.

She moved about the office with a can of furniture polish and rag, dusting every surface. When she reached the bookcase behind the professor, she pulled the small atomizer from her pocket and sprayed it in his direction. Another minute or two of cleaning and she was done. She smiled to herself as she pushed the cart out of the office. The man had never even looked up.

But she was only a step or two into the hallway when the professor's voice rang out. "Hey!"

Agent X snapped her head around to look at him as her heart started to pound.

"You forgot to empty the wastebasket," he said with annoyance.

She went back inside with a look of apology and dumped the overflowing bin into her cart.

Once outside in the parking lot, she fished the prepaid cell phone from her pocket and dialed the number she'd memorized. "Germany complete," she reported. She removed the SIM card and torched it with a lighter before tossing it into a trash bin, then crushed the phone with her boot before disposing of that as well. She also got rid of the atomizer—it had only contained enough for the single spray. She had a vial to swallow and another atomizer for phase two. Four hours later, she arrived at the airport in Frankfurt to catch her flight to Kinshasa.

When she arrived in the Democratic Republic of the Congo, she was to check into the Hotel Membling, feign illness, and ask to have a doctor sent to her room. The physician on call for the hotel was also on staff at Kinshasa General, one of the largest hospitals in Africa.

❖

Beijing, China
October 2

Agent Y traveled by train from the airport in Hong Kong to Beijing, then took a cab to the Forbidden City, looking every bit a tourist with a camera around his neck. He had a picture of his target, along with a snapshot of the taxi he drove, distinctively adorned with a large Chan Chu figurine hanging from the rearview mirror. The talisman, a frog with a coin in its mouth, was supposed to drive away evil and increase wealth.

The agent waited patiently for more than an hour until he saw the targeted taxi pull up at the stand. He got inside and told the driver to take him to Emperor Wanli's tomb outside Changlingzhen. Once the airborne virus was sprayed, it remained virulent for up to an hour, so the thirty-eight-mile drive each way would ensure that only his target would be infected.

❖

Cali, Colombia
October 3

Agent Z shoved his hand into the pocket of his coat to reassure himself the smooth steel atomizer was still there as he entered the

Centro Cultural de Cali, headquarters of the municipal secretaries of tourism and culture. The nine-hour bus ride from the airport in Quito, Ecuador had exhausted him, and he was anxious to complete the first part of his mission. Ten minutes before closing, most of the workers had already departed for the day, but a lone clerk remained at the information desk.

From a distance, the agent checked the clerk against the photo in his pocket. The information he'd been provided was correct. The newest man hired was the only one who had to stay until the end of the shift.

Agent Z asked the man for a list of area hotels and sprayed him when he turned his back to retrieve the information from a rack behind him.

By this time tomorrow the agent would be in Dallas, stalking a twenty-two-year-old woman. As assistant manager of a McDonald's restaurant on Lemmon Avenue, her duties included the unfortunate task of closing up for the night.

❖

London
October 7

"Stop looking so bored and smile, honey."

Zoe Anderson-Howe automatically complied as she faced her father, who looked particularly handsome this evening in his favorite navy Savile Row suit and cream silk tie. The tie matched the low-cut cocktail dress she'd chosen for the occasion. Her long, dark brown hair was swept up in a fashionable chignon, and the delicate sapphire necklace that added a splash of color to her ensemble matched the deep blue of her eyes.

"That might be easier if it weren't the third time we've done this in as many weeks, Daddy. And from what you say, it's gotten us nothing. Why should tonight be any different? I really don't have much to smile about."

"Perhaps," Derrick said, scanning the well-heeled guests assembled in the private banquet room at the Loose Cannon, one of London's premiere staging grounds for corporate gatherings. The food was exceptional and the ambience of the arched brick walls and understatedly elegant décor set the place apart. "But we have about twenty reasons to try, all of them handpicked to be here tonight."

Zoe sipped her champagne and considered her options. Many of the hundred or so guests were unfamiliar. "Do I need to dazzle anyone in particular?"

Her father tilted his head toward a couple in their late forties, an Internet-made millionaire with a bad hair transplant and his newly Botoxed companion. "Why don't you start with Van Haren and his wife?"

Zoe sighed, but her faux smile never faltered. She knew her job as PR Director of Skye Lines, her father's airline, required a certain amount of after-hours schmoozing, but this recent need to aggressively court new investors was demeaning. Not to mention terminally boring and rarely effective. The tight economy had everyone watching their wallets.

"Ah, yes, the nouveau riche and their scent of eau de despair. Forever angsting about their inferior beginnings and constantly desperate to fit in. I don't think I have the energy to deal with boring stories about their above-all-odds and beyond-everyone's-expectations catalogue of achievements."

Derrick Anderson-Howe waved to acknowledge a well-known local realtor who was looking their way as he leaned toward Zoe and lowered his voice. "Although your appraisal of them is accurate, tonight is about being productive. Unless you want to start cooking your own meals, making your own bed, and getting your beautiful hair done at WeSnippit, we need their money. We need everyone here to like us and we need them to trust us."

"And what better way than by showing them what a wonderfully united team we make," she said drolly.

"That's right." His hazel eyes beseeched her to turn on the charm. Zoe looked nothing like her fair-haired, chiseled-jaw father;

she had her mother's coloring and softer features. "Can you do that for me, for us?"

This time her smile was genuine and heartfelt. "You know I'd do anything for you, Daddy."

Derrick grinned back and squeezed her elbow in appreciation before returning his attention to the crowd. "I see our reinforcements have arrived." He gestured with his head toward the door, and Zoe followed his gaze.

"You didn't tell me Uncle Eddie was coming." The evening was definitely looking up. Her father's older brother had a wonderfully dry sense of humor, and she always loved hearing him relive his latest adventures. A bachelor physician/virologist, he taught at Cambridge but was often out of the country, taking jobs as a private consultant.

"You know him," Derrick replied, motioning his brother to join them. "Never one to make commitments. I didn't want to get your hopes up."

"Zoe, darling, don't you look luscious." Edward embraced her warmly and kissed both cheeks.

"Wonderful to see you," Zoe replied. "Got some stories for me?"

"Indeed I do." He winked at her. "But later. I've apparently been drafted to use my considerable charms to empty some wallets tonight." Edward turned to his brother.

"Derrick," he said with mock seriousness, sticking out his hand.

"Edward," Derrick replied with a straight face as they grasped hands and shook.

Zoe giggled. Her father never got it when his brother poked fun at him. Derrick was British to the core, but Edward had definitely loosened up from his frequent trips abroad.

"Who shall I woo first?" Edward asked.

Derrick surveyed the room. "Madeleine Beaubien, I think." He indicated a middle-aged redhead who'd just arrived with a younger woman. "She's CEO of a large French banking firm that's recently opened a new branch in the financial district."

"Great dress, bad accessories," Zoe commented. "And I don't just mean the purse, which is still less offensive than the daughter she has draped permanently on her arm."

Edward laughed and headed off toward the woman.

"Play nice, Zoe," Derrick said, his voice more pleading than reproachful. He had such a soft spot for her he'd never been much of a disciplinarian. "You are not to provoke her tonight."

She glanced about for a waiter to refill her glass and spotted an unfamiliar woman near the bar. The tall, lean beauty, dressed in a Vera Wang pantsuit, had olive skin and classically sculpted features.

"Zoe, did you hear me?"

Her father squeezed her elbow again. "Huh? Yes, of course." The dark-haired stunner across the room was so distracting it took Zoe a few seconds to remember what they'd been talking about. "Besides, it was just that one time," she said defensively. "She actually slapped the waiter for petting her pedigree Chihuahua and then called him a third-class citizen, not worthy of touching her baby. I just hid the pooch in the coatroom for a few hours. How was I supposed to know her mental meltdown would include getting down on all fours and emitting a special come-hither bark in front of two hundred people?"

She returned her attention to the woman near the bar as her father chuckled. "Who's the cute butch?"

He followed her gaze. "I think you mean Eleni Skouras. The man to her left is her husband. He's a Greek ship owner."

"And she's a closeted dyke."

"You are to refrain from—"

"I believe my interest in tonight's event has been resurrected." Zoe set her empty champagne glass on a passing waiter's tray and grabbed two full ones. "And so has my curiosity about the Mediterranean. Go be productive, Dad. I'll talk to you later."

As he dutifully headed off toward one of the well-heeled guests, Zoe hesitated, watching him go. She couldn't help but be concerned about him, given the changes she'd witnessed in recent months. Like many other CEOs in the aviation industry, he'd been worried about the future of the company and in rather bad spirits for the past year. He was tense all the time now, and his sense of humor had evaporated. He kept reminding her how much they needed to find financiers, with an increasing sense of desperation in both his voice and attitude.

To the best of her knowledge, her father had had nothing but brief, purely physical relationships since her mother passed away. None of them were noteworthy enough to require introductions, but he seemed to always have some stunner on his arm, especially for occasions like this. Derrick was certainly prime material for the legions of British socialites seeking a mate. Tall and slender, ruggedly handsome, with just the right amount of distinguished gray at his temples. From all outward appearances, anyway, financially secure and endowed with all the qualities that women most admire in long-term companions—wit, charm, kindness, eloquence, and a deep respect for the feminine gender. But in recent months, he'd been spending more time alone, and he'd asked Zoe to be his companion for this affair, and many others.

Zoe had mixed feelings about the prospect of her father ever remarrying. Certainly she wanted him to be happy, but she couldn't shake the feeling that such an event would be somehow disloyal to her mother. Ten years had passed since she had succumbed to acute lymphoblastic leukemia, but not a day had gone by without Zoe whispering a morning greeting to her mother and a good night as she retired.

The first years had been hard for both her and her father. Derrick had coped by burying himself in his empire and showering Zoe with gifts and attention. But they were not what she needed. There were things only a mother could give a daughter. Her example had provided Zoe with a disciplined direction to her life and a desire to put others' welfare ahead of her own. When she died, so did Zoe's motivation and inspiration. Gone with her mother were her adolescent dreams of studying medicine to join Doctors Without Borders, to actively do something about the poverty and disease-stricken people her mother had felt for and donated to for years.

Instead, Zoe ignored her classes and embraced hedonism. Vowing to take life less seriously, she partied her way through

Oxford. She got in because of her father's financial persuasion, not her own academic abilities, and three years later had a BA in economics and management.

At the age of twenty-three, when her indiscretions and promiscuous behavior started to make the tabloids, her father forced her to join the company. He said it would give her a sense of direction and help her put her energy into something more productive than women and alcohol. She fought until her father threatened to cut her off financially. Although she doubted he'd ever make good on the promise, she also needed something to keep herself busy until the later hours of the day when she could start partying again.

It took Zoe another three years to realize that no amount of women and alcohol would bring her mother back, and yet another three to find herself in a compromising yet less restless life. She did her job, even enjoyed it occasionally, but she was comfortably numb. Even her one-night stands had become so routine she was now looking for ways to up the excitement by taking risks with married women. She enjoyed seeing how far she could get them to go, and this evening was no exception.

Zoe slowly approached the Greek couple. The husband was in what seemed a serious discussion with an Arab, while his beautiful wife looked about as interested in the gathering as she was.

Donning her most charming smile, she stopped in front of the striking woman and offered her one of the glasses of champagne. "A couple of these and you might actually make it through tonight."

The woman laughed. "Thank you. Is it that obvious?" She accepted the offering and downed the contents.

"Only to someone who's looking closely. I'm Zoe Anderson-Howe."

"Eleni—"

"Skouras," Zoe said. When the woman lifted one eyebrow in surprise, she explained. "I inquired. It was hard not to."

"Because?"

Zoe positioned herself at the woman's side and slid her hand down Eleni's back.

"Because you're the most attractive woman here." This could

backfire but she didn't care, and she could tell by the way the woman was looking at her that she was mentally already on second base.

"I'm here with my husband," Eleni said in a low voice, implying they needed to be careful.

"So I hear. Technicalities don't deter me," Zoe replied, and her companion laughed again. "Can I get you another drink?" she whispered in Eleni's ear.

The woman glanced around nervously and set her empty glass on the bar. "Can you find us a place to drink in private?"

Zoe moved closer. "I'm sure I can arrange that," she said before discreetly nipping at Eleni's earlobe. "Follow me."

CHAPTER TWO

Munich, Germany
October 7

At the University of Munich, Professor Gunther Zimmerman glanced up from the notes he'd prepared for his evening botany lecture as the three-hundred-seat auditorium began to fill with students. He had a wretched headache and considered calling in sick, but this was the vital first class of the winter semester.

Halfway through the lecture, a bout of dizziness seized him and he had to leave the podium and give the rest of his remarks from a chair. By the time he departed for the night, he was sweating profusely and felt sick to his stomach. A few weeks prior, flu had swept across the campus, as it always did this time of year. But it had been relatively mild, so Gunther wasn't concerned. He just hoped he could shake it off quickly. It'd be murder trying to reschedule his packed curriculum.

❖

London, England
October 7

Zoe was so close to climax she didn't register the sound at first.

She'd found an empty conference room near the party that was perfect for their needs and scored a bottle of champagne and two glasses from a passing waiter. But Eleni had been so delightfully eager that the bottle remained unopened, precariously balanced on the edge of the long table a few feet away.

Zoe reclined on top of the smooth mahogany surface, resting on her elbows, her dress hiked up to her waist. Eleni sat before her in a cushioned chair, positioned so Zoe's legs were draped across her shoulders. Zoe had a perfect vantage point to watch the woman go down on her, and the visual, combined with the Greek's talented tongue, were enough to send her rapidly toward the precipice.

Her mind was so hazy with lust and arousal it took too long for her to realize she had heard a knock on the door. Before she had the chance to reply or react, Eleni's husband stood there, knuckles stark white as he clenched the doorknob.

"What the hell is going on?" he demanded in a thick accent. His angry glare was fixed on his wife, who'd bolted upright from her chair. Shame darkened Eleni's features as she wiped at her mouth, smearing her lipstick.

Zoe never flinched and felt no compulsion to immediately adjust the dress still pooled about her waist. "If I have to explain, then surely the Greeks have been overestimated."

Eleni's husband moved into the room, leaving the door ajar, and the couple launched into a heated debate in their native language. Zoe had eased off the table and adjusted her dress when noise from the hallway alerted her they were about to have more company. But before she could make a discreet exit, her father joined them.

"Zoe?" Derrick's tone was accusatory as he took in her dress, Eleni's lipstick, her husband's outrage, and the champagne bottle.

"Hi, Daddy," she replied, nonplussed. This was nothing compared to some of her previous indiscretions. "Eleni and I were getting to know each other when her husband walked in."

At this, the angry Greek ceased the tirade with Eleni and turned his attention toward Derrick. "Your daughter corrupted my wife."

"Zoe?" her father said again, his expression extolling her to explain and apologize.

"Oh, please." She pivoted to face Eleni's husband. "Any woman displaying this much vigor and talent was 'corrupted' long before I came along."

A burst of light from behind them made all four turn in the direction of the door. Several people had been drawn to the doorway by the shouting. Most were curious partygoers, but in the front was a well-known tabloid photographer who'd caught Zoe misbehaving on several previous occasions. Grinning at them, the man got a second shot of their startled expressions before anyone could react.

Derrick spoke first. "Get the hell out of here, you damn vulture."

"Shit," the Greek couple said in unison as they hurried out of the room.

The photographer ducked away, but several other voyeurs stood their ground. "The peep show's over," Zoe announced as she shut the door.

Derrick ran his hands through his hair. "How could you be so—"

"Bored and horny? Easy. The first usually precedes the latter." As she always did in such circumstances, she tried to make light of the situation, and her blunt response was not unusual. Since her mother's death, she and Derrick had always spoken frankly with each other.

But he was clearly in no mood for it tonight. "This is not the time for your customary flippancy," he snapped, and began to pace.

"Don't be dramatic, Dad," she replied tiredly.

He stopped and glared at her. "This will be all over the tabloids by tomorrow."

"It's not like the paparazzi caught us in the act," she said. "All he has is a snapshot of us talking. The rest is hearsay."

"Which I'm sure some of the onlookers will verify." Derrick sank into the chair Eleni had vacated and loosened his tie. "Christ, Zoe. Is it so difficult for you to stay out of trouble? To abstain from getting on your back?"

"Don't make it sound like I'm some kind of nympho. Besides, I've been on my best behavior for—"

"Over a whole year." Derrick was clearly infuriated and Zoe was beginning to regret her decision to mix business with pleasure tonight. "Give my daughter a trophy for staying out of the tabloids for three hundred and sixty-five days."

"Look, I'm sorry. I was sure she had locked the door."

"I'm sorry?" he repeated, shaking his head. "Aside from the fact that you sound disingenuous, I'm sure a part of you finds all this amusing."

She frowned and took a tentative step in his direction. "That's not true."

"You're a twenty-nine-year-old woman working for a multimillion-pound company, and all you have to say for yourself is that you're sorry?"

Zoe couldn't blame him for being angry. He'd bailed her out of trouble more times than she could count, always with little complaint. Everyone, she supposed, had their breaking point.

"The fact that you're sorry does not change a damn thing," her father said. Derrick rarely raised his voice at her and never cursed, so she began to grasp the seriousness of the situation. "Listen to me, Zoe, and listen carefully. I have spent the past year trying to save this company. I'll never be able to do that if you keep putting our names—and the airline's—in the scandal sheets. I love you, and you know and count on that, but I will not throw away a lifetime of hard work and sacrifice because you refuse to grow up." He cradled his head between his hands tiredly and didn't speak for several seconds. "Maybe we need to reconsider your involvement in this company."

That got her attention. "What are you saying?" she asked carefully.

"It's too late to find a replacement for the Colombian launch the day after tomorrow, and perhaps it's a good idea to get you out of the country as this shit hits the tabloids. But after you get back… maybe it would do you good to…" He looked up at her.

"Can we skip the faux buildup?" she asked, her heartbeat accelerating. "What are you saying?"

"I'm about to do something I should have done a long time ago. Honey, it's time you grew up, and it's time I started acting like a father rather than a friend. Maybe if you have to worry about putting food on your table, you'll have less time to get into trouble."

Zoe gasped. "You're cutting me off?"

"Only until you grow up." He rose and put his hand over hers. "I'm also firing you."

"You wouldn't."

"I just did."

She knew that look on his face. He was determined to see this through. "You must be joking."

"I'll have the limo pick you up for the airport the day after tomorrow at six p.m. sharp. Please be ready." He headed for the door.

"What if I refuse to go?" she called after him.

He had his hand on the doorknob but turned back to face her. "That would be a poor decision. This will be your last decent paycheck for a while, after all."

"Bloody hell," she whispered, still in shock.

"Welcome to the real world, honey." He shut the door between them, leaving Zoe alone to contemplate her predicament.

❖

Beijing, China
October 7

Three sharp raps on the window of his cab roused the driver from his nap. Outside, looking at him expectantly, stood three older white women, all rotund and with hair dyed the same unnatural shade of red.

"Are you for hire?" one of them asked.

He nodded and started the meter as one of the trio hefted her bulk into the passenger seat while the other two piled in back. He had parked in the lot next to the Forbidden City and not at the taxi stand in front because he needed a break. He shouldn't be working today at all; he'd been up sick all night with vomiting and diarrhea, but he had to have the money.

Fate, however, was apparently not going to allow him rest any time soon. The Palace Museum was unusually crowded, and the taxi stand was absent any other vehicles.

"We'd like to go to the Ming Tombs," the woman in front told him, before turning her attention to her companions. "This was such a great idea. Can you imagine how much our husbands are missing us right now?"

They were halfway to their destination when a sudden coughing spasm hit him. He managed to snatch a tissue from the box on the dash just in time.

"Oh, my God," the woman beside him said, as she shrank back against the glass on her side. "Is that blood?"

Chapter Three

San José del Guaviare, Colombia
October 9

EOO Operative Gianna Truman, code name Fetch, hoisted the backpack of medical supplies onto her shoulders with a groan and departed through the side door of the warehouse into an alley strewn with trash. The sun was so bright she winced and fumbled for her sunglasses. The tedious journeys to town from the remote FARC encampments in the mountains always drained her, and this one was no exception.

It was moments like this she missed the drugs the military and the EOO provided her. Provigil could make her go on for endless nights without sleep, giving her a constant energy boost and awareness that fatigue would normally never allow. Performance enhancers, nootropics. Beta-blockers, particularly propranolol, to regulate her heart and block out panic and fear. Electroporation and biafine to make her heal faster. She and a few other ops were given the right blend of meds to create the perfect soldier, but coming down from them was always time-consuming and even painful.

Fetch had brought a supply with her to the jungle, but her mission had lasted much longer than expected. Though she'd run out weeks ago, she still often felt the effects of withdrawal: headaches, nerve pain, sensitivity to light, mood swings, and even aggression. Right now, she was feeling them all.

When she reached the street, she paused, surveying her surroundings to ensure she wasn't being watched. Satisfied, she started off toward the rendezvous point five blocks away. The pickup had taken less time than anticipated, so she didn't hurry. The FARC guerrilla who would drive her back to the camp trail wasn't due for a half hour.

As she passed a newsstand, she paused to read the headlines of the various newspapers and magazines, to catch up on what had been happening elsewhere since her last foray from the jungle two weeks earlier.

This was exactly what was wrong with the world. Fetch stared at the cover of *Tatler*, a British import gossip rag. What people like this needed was a dose of life. Real life. Maybe they'd have a little less time to worry about what they were going to wear and who they were going to screw next, mentally or physically, and more time to look around and see how ridiculous their polished lives were.

She wasn't sure what irritated her more, the caption—ZOE SHAGS TYCOON'S WIFE AT POSH PARTY—or the flippant, uninterested look on the subject's face. Wealthy British socialite Zoe Anderson-Howe had been caught seducing the wife of Greek shipping mogul Nikos Skouras.

It was bad enough that the privileged often felt they had somehow earned the right to whatever acts of debauchery necessary to keep them entertained. But what bothered Fetch in particular about the article was the look on the spoiled brat's face, the bored look of, "I've been down this road before, and I don't care what anyone thinks or what the repercussions may be on anyone's life, including my own."

Rich people like this Zoe Anderson-Howe didn't consider whether their impulses might destroy someone else's career, home, family, or psyche because they could afford to reinvent themselves and move on. The Brit had probably found the tabloid attention unfair and a complete invasion of her privacy, but deep down—or at least as deep as someone like her was capable of—she'd likely have thought it amusing.

They were the same age, Fetch noted—twenty-nine—but that was apparently all they had in common.

Zoe Anderson-Howe lived a life of excess, surrounded by every materialistic luxury that caught her whim, while Fetch didn't need to hold on to anything. Civilians or even other ops talked about their favorite friend or film, sweater or pictures, souvenirs or cars. Her life's possessions were minimal, and easily replaceable. She had no attachments at all; she even avoided keeping her own apartment or house. When she wasn't away on a job, she stayed at the Hotel Vertigo in San Francisco, surrounded by impersonal furnishings and decorations. It wasn't one of the city's more upscale establishments, but it was centrally located and the beds were comfortable. And, as with anywhere she stayed, as long as it was clean and aesthetically pleasing she was satisfied. She required only a duffel bag with clean clothes.

While Zoe lived a life of indulgent debauchery, Fetch had chosen a life of battle, one that meant defending the rights and lives of innocents, rich and poor. She felt privileged to be in that position and would do whatever was necessary, including infiltrating the FARC by living in the jungle for months alongside ruthless fanatics. But she couldn't help feeling frustrated when she saw articles like this, chronicling the careless depravity of some of those she was putting her life on the line for. She seemed at times to care more about these people's lives than they did. They had so many reasons to want to invest in the future of the planet, but instead chose to invest in their self-indulgent lives.

Don't be so hard on them, sweetheart. They haven't seen what we have. They don't feel the need to fight because they don't even know they have to.

Fetch could hear Samantha's voice as though she were standing next to her. Sam was always the voice of reason, the one person who could take away her fears and doubts and make her believe the world contained more than corruption and war. God, how she missed her.

Fetch thought of Sam every day. She kept waiting for the pain to subside, hoping the adage was true that time could heal all and any pain. But although three years had managed to numb her, it hadn't done anything for the ache in her heart, still as fresh today as that day in Iraq when her world crumbled beneath her. She and Samantha were taking cover behind the remains of what had once been a house. It had been quiet all morning; the insurgents they were sent to eradicate were apparently lying low, plotting their next move.

Samantha was standing beside her, looking out at the ruined buildings around them with a wistful expression. She'd taken off her helmet because of the heat, and her shoulder-length blond hair was tousled and badly in need of a wash. But Fetch couldn't imagine a more beautiful sight.

When she was sure no other soldiers were in sight, she got down on one knee and withdrew the ring from the thigh pocket of her fatigues. "Marry me."

"What?" Samantha looked down at the two-carat diamond in its platinum setting and then scanned their surroundings.

"I want you to marry me when we get back next month."

"Do you realize that someone could see us?" Samantha sat beside her on the dusty ground, her expression one of shock and bewilderment. Homosexuality was not tolerated in the army and the current "Don't ask, don't tell" policy was a sad attempt at quasi-acceptance. Sam's ass would be on the line if she were outed. She ran her fingers through her sweaty hair and rested her head against the stone wall, quiet as she stared up at the ceiling. "What are you doing?" Sam finally asked, squinting against the sun that came through the holes and cracks overhead.

"I'm asking you to spend the rest of your life with me."

"In the middle of a desert, hiding behind a wall?" she asked as she turned to stare at Fetch.

Fetch looked around at their surroundings. "I think it's original. Don't you?"

Samantha smiled. "You're crazy."

"About you. Say yes."

"Why are you asking me now, and here of all places?"

Fetch shrugged. "I know it's not very romantic but it just feels right. It's how we met, after all."

Though she made no move to take the ring from Fetch's hand, Sam's eyes were moist with emotion and the proposal clearly pleased her. "But there's so much I don't know about you. I've known you for almost a year, and you still refuse to talk about your life."

"You know I love you, don't you?" *Fetch placed her hand on Sam's thigh.* "You know that, right?"

"I do," *Samantha replied gently.* "But I don't know who you really are."

"What do you mean?"

"You come and go as you please, and you won't tell me how that's even possible. You're privy to information and asked to attend meetings that the rest of us aren't. I've seen you make phone calls in town, then deny that you have. Sometimes I...if you've been privately contracted, why won't you just tell me?"

"Someday we'll talk about all that." *Fetch squeezed Sam's thigh to reassure her.* "But right now you need to trust me. Trust that no matter who I am and what I do, it doesn't change what I feel for you." *Though she lived and worked with the army battalion that Samantha was assigned to, Fetch was part of an elite and covert counterterrorism squad, whose objective was to capture and kill leaders of Al Qaeda. She passed on emerging EOO intelligence to the unit and headed up all hostage rescue efforts.*

"Can you answer this one question?" *Sam asked.*

"I will if I can."

Samantha cupped Fetch's face. "Please don't lie to me."

"I've never lied to..." *The look on Samantha's face told her she knew—or at least suspected—better. This woman meant the world to her, and Fetch wanted nothing more than to tell her the truth about everything. But now was not the time. They both had to remain focused, and she had to finish this mission. After that, all bets were off. Samantha was due for release next month, and once they were both back in the States, she'd confess as much as she possibly could about her identity.* "I hope I won't have to," *she finally replied.*

"Please. It's important."

"I'll try." *Hopefully the desperation in her voice would make it clear that she had no control over what she could say.*

Samantha was watching her closely, as though studying her for signs of deceit. "I want to know your name."

"What? You already know it."

"No, I don't. You're not who you say you are. I'm willing to wait until we get back to find out the rest. No longer than that," Sam said. "But I want your name now."

Fetch bit the inside of her lip as she considered the consequences. "Does it really matter that much?"

"It does to me."

She took a deep breath and let it out. "Gianna."

Samantha smiled. "That's beautiful."

"If you say so."

"Gianna." Samantha cupped her face again gently between her hands and looked deep into her eyes. "I look forward to getting to know you as your wife."

Fetch's heartbeat suddenly accelerated until it was booming in her chest. "So that's a yes."

"Absolutely."

She'd barely placed the ring on Samantha's finger when the rat-a-tat of machine guns broke the quiet. Insurgents were moving in on them, firing their AK-47s, and the U.S. forces in the surrounding ruins began to fire back. She and Sam immediately jerked on their helmets, grabbed their M4 rifles, and took up their positions, joining the exchange of gunfire.

The sound was deafening, but over the cacophony Fetch heard a shout for help and turned to her right. One of the U.S. troops firing an RPG from behind the wall of an adjacent ruined building yelled that his partner had been hit, but he couldn't leave to help him because a barrage of gunfire had him pinned down from all sides.

Fetch could see the injured soldier on the ground between the two buildings. Half of his right leg was missing, but adrenaline kept him conscious and alert as he continued to launch grenades from his M203. He finally collapsed and tried to crawl to cover. It would be only seconds before the rebels finished him off.

The wounded man scanned the area, desperate for a way out. "Fuck, I'm hit!" he screamed, and tried to get up. "I can't move. Fuck, I can't move."

Apaches were gunning down insurgents from above. Fetch half turned to Samantha. "Man down. I'm going out."

"Go." Sam's attention was still focused on the rebels firing at them. "I've got you."

"See you in a sec." Fetch peeked around the wall. Several of the insurgents had taken up positions in the building across the street.

"Hey, soldier," Samantha shouted over the din as she laid down a barrage of cover fire from her rifle. "I love you."

"Yeah, me too." Fetch raced in a crouch toward the injured man, firing as she ran.

Just as she reached him, a soldier nearby shouted, "Shit, it's a missile! Get down!"

Instinctively, she dropped, her body covering the injured man, as the distinctive roar of incoming heavy ordnance blotted out all other sound. She looked up in time to see the small house they'd been taking cover in—the place where Samantha still was—be blown to pieces.

In the chaos of dust and noise, three soldiers materialized from behind her and dragged her and the injured man to a ditch protected by a low wall. Though momentarily blinded by the blast and blowing sand, she fought against them, screaming Samantha's name and trying to break free.

But a brute of a GI held her down, half-sitting on her chest. "She's gone, Soldier. I'm sorry. She's gone."

Not long after, Fetch was back in the U.S., but part of her never returned. Watching Samantha die before her eyes had cost her sanity the first few months. EOO Chief Montgomery Pierce must have seen the hollowness in her eyes, because the few assignments he gave her were trivial. Sleep deprivation had caused hallucinations. She couldn't stop replaying those moments when her future with Sam, the hope of a normal or at least as normal a life as she could have, died.

Somewhere in her subconscious she realized her slow but steady deterioration and turned to over-the-counter drugs to help her sleep. But then the nightmares and cold sweats started. Too tired to get out of bed, she refused to answer the phone even though she knew the organization would be pissed at her. She got up only for the toilet and occasional food delivery. Pierce and Joanne Grant, another member of the EOO governing trio, showed up at her doorstep one afternoon. She expected them to go ballistic on her and she didn't care. She opened the door and went back to bed without a word. The organization forced her to get counseling within their facilities. For a year, she was assigned to desk duty and research.

At first, she thought herself weak, and if it hadn't been for Grant's comforting words, she would have pretended recovery just to get out of her mundane existence. But as it was, she found solace in the routine.

The EOO had taught her to succeed by any means necessary, but she always sought perfection. For Fetch, failure was not an option, and the rigid rules she had implemented for herself and lived by meant that she was forever unsatisfied. Her world lacked any gray areas, and Samantha had given her those. Now that she was gone, Fetch had reverted to black or white, right or wrong, saint or sinner, good or bad, and nothing in between was even a possibility.

Part of her wanted to fight back the nature of her inner beast and deal with life differently, now that she knew she was capable of a middle ground. But she mostly felt like she had to struggle to jumpstart a new belief, and she didn't have any fight left. When any emotions returned, they were anger and frustration. Anger at Samantha's death and frustration at herself for letting herself get close to someone and compromising them both. If Samantha hadn't been covering her back, maybe she would have seen the missile. She would have gotten out of there.

Samantha had insisted that she learn to see with her heart, but her death had proved that Fetch was right all along. The heart was no different from any other organ. It, too, was a puppet, waiting for the brain to pull its strings and give it orders. As far as Fetch was concerned, what others referred to as passion was nothing but another word for irrational. And she was anything but.

Fetch rebooted to her default settings, once again content and comfortable on the emotional sidelines of life and, soon after, when field work finally seemed feasible, the EOO once again assigned her to SAR missions. If she concentrated on getting the job done, did what she loved and saved lives, she'd eventually reclaim command of her own life. In war-stricken countries, when faced with the injustice done to poor people, she could put her own pain into perspective more easily.

This time she was assigned to Operation Boomerang, a search-and-rescue mission in Colombia. Specializing in infiltration operations, she quickly gained numerous contacts in the region. For this reason she was given her current assignment: penetrate the FARC, locate a group of Western hostages, and pass on the intel to a covert team of U.S. special ops. The leftist rebels of the so-called Revolutionary Armed Forces of Colombia—the People's Army—currently held some nine hundred hostages in small encampments throughout the jungle interior that were constantly on the move. Many of the hostages were police, members of the Colombian military, and others seized as bargaining chips in the rebels' negotiations with the government for political leverage. But a few were foreigners, snatched for large ransoms that helped fund some of the FARC's activities, like narcotics trafficking—including taxation, cultivation, and distribution.

Three Italians—a telecommunications-firm executive, his wife, and daughter—had been kidnapped more than a year earlier and were believed to be held somewhere in the massive Guaviare jungle southeast of Bogota. The Italian government had asked the U.S. for assistance when negotiations to free the family had stalled at an impossible sixty-million-dollar ransom, but Washington felt that any "official" rescue efforts might compromise its own interests in the area. So arrangements were made to contract the intelligence-gathering mission to the EOO, who would be paid by the Italian telecommunications firm.

Not long after she was dispatched to the region, Fetch had two more kidnap victims added to her mission: a pair of Australian humanitarian-aid workers who'd spent more than two years in captivity. They were believed to be in the same camp as the Italians, and prospects for their release through negotiations were grim. The

FARC wanted to exchange the pair for a group of rebels held in a Bogota jail, and the Colombian government flatly refused.

Previous attempts at an armed rescue of kidnap victims had almost all ended in disaster. The rebels would execute their prisoners at the first sign of an approaching helicopter, which was usually the only way to get close to the remote camps. Along with pinpointing where the Westerners were being held, Fetch was supposed to advise the covert extraction team on the best way to get the hostages out without bloodshed.

She spoke fluent Spanish, and with her olive skin, brown eyes, and dark hair, she passed easily as a native. Using the legend of a disillusioned paramilitary medic, she enlisted in the FARC with a group of villagers too poor to have any other means to support their families.

In keeping with its quasi-Marxist philosophy, internal FARC regulations gave female fighters equal status with men, and that was the reality in some of the bigger encampments. Men and women shared cooking duties, washed their own clothes, and both sexes did guard duty and went on patrol. In the smaller camps, it was sometimes a very different matter, more of a reflection of the society at large. Women there were often relegated to the menial jobs: cooking, gathering wood, and tending to the crops and animals.

Fetch's background as an ex-soldier and her tough, unemotional demeanor, however, quickly set her apart. Her intolerance for sexual advances, a common occurrence for women within these groups, had been met with attempts at rape. But her combat training soon made it clear she was not to be messed with. She'd broken the arms and legs of those who tried to take sexual advantage, and in return they had called her *pervertita*.

Her medical skills also helped her establish an equal position among the male guerrillas. She wasn't a doctor but, like all EOO ops, had received extensive medical training so she could treat her own wounds and injuries in the field. Her nickname became La Medica.

After six months in the Guaviare jungle, she'd reached a critical point in her mission. All FARC guerrillas were routinely rotated to new camps, but because of her medical expertise, Fetch got moved around more than most. Often she was sent to tend to a senior officer or valuable hostage, and other times to train other guerrillas in basic wound care and other procedures. When she returned to the jungle after this foray to replenish her medical supplies, she was to finally be sent to the camp that held the Italian and Australian hostages she'd been assigned to locate.

In anticipation of that, she'd made a detour on this trip to San José del Guaviare. Before replenishing her medical supplies, she'd retrieved her cell phone from the bus station locker where she kept her EOO gear. With any luck, she would soon be able to accomplish what she'd come here for and return home.

❖

Cali, Colombia
October 9

Two long lines of locals and tourists stretched out before the information desk in the massive Centro Cultural de Cali, so when one of two men behind it put the Cerrado/Closed sign at his station and disappeared through a door behind him, a collective groan went up.

The departing clerk had only had the job for four months. He knew he risked losing it by taking yet another break, but he was feeling so miserable he had to lie down for a while. His head was about to explode, and though he'd downed at least two liters of water since morning, he still felt severely dehydrated. He chalked it up to the fever he'd been trying to shake since the night before. Though he'd taken three aspirin before bedtime, the fever had only gotten worse. When he'd awakened after a restless night, the sheets had been soaked with sweat.

He had barely stretched out on the couch in the employee lounge when his supervisor walked in, frowning. Before the man could speak, the clerk bolted to his feet and headed back to work. No matter how rotten he felt, he had to force himself to finish the day.

Chapter Four

Aeropuerto Internacional El Dorado
Bogota, Colombia
October 10

Zoe Anderson-Howe ducked into a ladies' room on the way to customs and immigration, to freshen up and allow the other first-class passengers to get well ahead of her. She'd fulfilled her duty, hosting the gala in-flight party to celebrate the launch of Skye Line's London-to-Bogota route, but the trip had been ghastly. The special "guests" that Derrick had invited for the premiere flight were mostly nouveau-riche Brits more interested in gossip about *her* than in investing in the airline. Several had brought along copies of *Tatler, The Sun*, and *The Daily Mail*, all of which had her name and image splashed across the cover.

She hadn't slept properly since the Loose Cannon party three nights earlier, too engrossed with her father's announcement he was cutting her off and firing her. In her opinion, she hadn't done anything that warranted such extreme measures. She'd bedded the wives of business partners before, and although her father hadn't caught her in the act, he had surely read about it in those stupid rags. Zoe simply couldn't see what was wrong about two, or sometimes three, consenting adults partaking in a few hours of sexual expression. Although her decision to "live a little" during the benefit hadn't been ideal, it definitely did not justify her father's reaction.

He couldn't possibly mean it. He was just upset the paparazzi were there and caught them. In time, he'd come to see...

But something told her he intended to make good on his promise this time. And if so, her life was about to radically change. She had saved nothing of her salary. She had no reason to. She spent it on clothes and jewelry, spas, champagne, and entertainment—virtually anything and anyone that caught her fancy. When she ran out of funds, her father had always been there with his checkbook, albeit much more reluctantly in recent months.

Without employment and her father's largesse, she could no longer afford her lavish penthouse apartment in Soho, the payments on her Bentley, her weekend getaways. Could it possibly get any worse?

Once she was through customs, she began to search the sparse crowd gathered to welcome incoming flights for the local her father had hired to serve as her escort, driver, and bodyguard. Although news reports indicated a sharp decline in violence and kidnappings in Colombia in recent months, Derrick was always overly prudent where her safety was concerned.

She spotted her name on a placard, held aloft by a tall, dark-skinned man in his thirties, appropriately dressed to greet her in a black suit, starched white shirt and gray silk tie, and polished boots.

He bowed courteously when she approached and immediately reached for her carry-on. "Welcome to Bogota, Miss Howe. My name is Enrique."

"I hope the car is nearby," she said tiredly. "I'd like to be taken to the hotel straightaway."

"Certainly. May I have your baggage-claim tickets?"

Once they'd retrieved her luggage, Enrique led her to a newer-model Renault Megane, a four-door sedan, and Zoe collapsed into the backseat. The sun was just coming up. After a nap at the hotel, she intended to go on a lengthy shopping expedition with her company credit card, probably her last for a long while. And she refused to feel any guilt about it. After all, technically she was still an employee of the company, at least until that evening. Her final duty would be to host a party for Colombian aviation officials and other VIPs. Then she was on her own.

The driver of the Jeep-like Lada Bronto tossed his cigarette out the window and pulled away from the curb, careful to keep at least three vehicles between him and the black Renault Megane. At the first traffic light, a short distance from the airport, he pulled out his cell. *"El Paquete ha llegado,"* he reported. The package had arrived.

❖

Kinshasa, Democratic Republic of the Congo
October 10

Kinshasa General Hospital, with two-thousand beds and more than twenty-two hundred employees, was one of the largest such facilities in Africa. But in a country devastated by years of civil war, where forty-five thousand people still died every month from disease, starvation, and violence, the facility still had trouble keeping up with even the routine daily cases.

Though one of its leading doctors was so dedicated to his patients he rarely missed a day's work, he decided to call in sick for his afternoon shift. He'd awakened with a fever and chills, aching all over. But just as he reached for the phone, it rang. The chief resident asked him to report to the emergency room ASAP. Casualties were pouring from an overnight battle between the army and opposition groups.

Stifling a groan, he told the man he'd be there in twenty minutes.

❖

Bogota, Colombia
October 10

"So where can a girl who likes girls go to get a drink?" Zoe asked Enrique as they left the Marriott. Her final stint as Skye Lines' PR Director had been a successful, if tedious, affair. The Colombian VIPs had seemed enthusiastic about her father's decision to begin the first direct flight from Britain to Bogota, and one of the local bankers he'd invited had promised to contact the home office about investing in the company. She'd managed to forego much of the usual leering and unwanted propositions from the men in attendance by choosing a more sedate and conservative ensemble than normal. Instead of her usual low-cut cocktail dress and stilettos, she wore a navy pantsuit with a beige silk blouse and pumps. Now all she wanted was to forget about business—and her future—for as long as possible.

"I don't understand," her bodyguard answered, keeping pace with her as she headed away from the building and toward a cluster of shops, restaurants, and bars farther down the block.

"A lesbian establishment."

"I don't know, Miss." If Enrique was shocked he didn't show it. He continued to walk beside her, seemingly engrossed in the mass of pedestrians around them.

She paused and glared at him. Why did so many people have to have everything spelled out for them? "Then why don't you make some phone calls and find out?"

"Of course, Miss Howe." He flipped open his cell and, after a brief conversation, turned to her. "There is a club called Margarita's. This way, Madam," he added, gesturing toward a street ahead that veered off to the left.

"Is your gender allowed?" Zoe asked. "Or is it for women only?" The bodyguard was necessary even if Colombia was much safer than in the past, but having to be shadowed throughout the duration of this visit seemed a bit of an exaggeration. Especially with her nerves on edge as far as her future was concerned. The last thing she needed was someone to inhibit the remains of her plush existence.

"I was told it was a 'mixed' environment."

"Very well, then." Zoe sighed. They walked in silence until Enrique pointed out an alley.

"It's in here," he said.

"You are to stay out of my way and be as discreet as possible," she instructed him, brushing back her hair with a sweep of her hand.

"I'm here to enjoy an hour of local entertainment and I don't want you in my face. I don't even want you in my peripheral vision."

"I understand." He paused outside the door, allowing her to enter alone.

Despite its less than auspicious exterior, Margarita's was a lively and welcoming place. Brightly painted murals of musicians and dancers decorated the walls, and the booths and tables were comfortable-looking, a cut above many of the gay bars she'd frequented outside Europe. Salsa music boomed from the speakers, and the dance floor was crowded with gyrating bodies, mostly male.

A long oak bar lined the wall to her left. Behind it, three dark-skinned men were busily pouring drinks for the crowd. Zoe claimed one of the high padded barstools and ordered a gin and tonic. She considered trying something local, but decided she wasn't in the mood for cultural experimentations. Right now she needed to hold on to whatever reminded her of better days.

Once she had her drink, she swiveled to watch the dancers. Many of the women present were dressed provocatively, in bright-colored dresses with slits up the side and plunging necklines. Most of the male couples were content to rub up against each other, gyrating in sync to the booming beat, but a few showed off their salsa moves in well-choreographed displays that looked like something out of a TV ballroom contest. Though she enjoyed watching them, Zoe had never been much of a dancer.

When she scanned the room for Enrique to make sure he wasn't being obvious, she spotted a very cute woman about her age, alone at the end of the bar. Her eyes were dark, her hair long and wavy. Brunette, but then again, it was Colombia. Most, if not all, women here were dark. That suited her fine.

Zoe smiled at her in a way that nearly always got results, and before long the woman got up and came to stand beside her. Close up, the view did not disappoint. The stranger wore a bright yellow shift that hugged her soft curves, and the short hemline showed off long, shapely legs. "Habla Inglés?" she asked the woman.

"Yes," the stranger replied, offering her hand. "My name is Jasele."

She accepted it, caressing the woman's hand with her thumb before letting go. "Zoe."

Jasele shifted her weight from one foot to the other, as though not entirely comfortable. "You come here much?"

"You apparently don't," Zoe replied, smiling. Probably married, she guessed. "Or you'd otherwise know the answer."

The woman laughed nervously.

"Unless, of course, it was merely an attempt at conversation," Zoe added.

"Pardon?" Jasele moved closer, a quizzical look on her face. "I don't understand."

"I guess profound discussion is out of the question for tonight," she mumbled, more to herself than her attractive companion. "But you know what? I'm not really in the mood for chatting anyway."

Almost mechanically, the woman put her hand on Zoe's thigh. "Do you want to dance?"

"I'm afraid I'm rhythmically challenged."

Confusion once again darkened Jasele's expression. "What?"

Oh, sod it. "No, I don't dance." She answered slowly and deliberately, as though talking to someone mentally challenged. Her mood had deteriorated within seconds and all she wanted now was a hot bath and a bed. It wasn't until this draining exchange that she realized how tired and jetlagged she was.

Jasele's face brightened. "No problem. I can show you." She took Zoe's hand and turned toward the dance floor.

"Thank you, but no." Zoe resisted the gentle tug and remained where she was. "I think I'll retire for the night."

She thought the stranger would let go, but to her surprise, Jasele only tugged harder, practically pulling her off the stool. "Come. It will be fun."

Zoe scanned the crowd and caught the concerned look on Enrique's face. She dreaded him having to step in. "Okay. One dance."

Jasele led her to the middle of the thick crowd of dancers, then looked at her curiously for a moment as though sizing her up. They were still holding hands. Very timidly, the stranger rested her other hand lightly on Zoe's waist and began to move to the music.

It was awkward from the start. Despite her insistence they dance, Jasele kept Zoe at arm's length as though she felt almost uncomfortable touching her, and she rarely met her eyes. There was none of the ease and open flirtation evident in all the couples around them. And despite her initial enthusiasm about showing Zoe some moves, Jasele danced almost perfunctorily. Something wasn't right. Though Zoe tried to follow the stranger's steps, their interaction was more an unbearable ordeal than fun. When the song was finally over, she quickly pulled away. "Thanks for the dance," she said, turning to leave.

But once again, the woman grabbed her hand. "Drink with me."

"Maybe another time. I'm really quite tired."

"One drink. Please."

Zoe checked her watch. It was eleven thirty. A nightcap might relax her enough to shut out the negative thoughts of her near future and get some sleep. "Sure, okay. One drink." She started to head to the bar, but Jasele, who still held her hand, tugged her instead toward the rear of the club.

"This way. Better drinks in the back."

Zoe allowed the woman to take the lead. "I hadn't realized there was another bar there."

"Bar, yes. This way." Jasele maintained a firm grip on her as she led Zoe through the throng of dancers, down a hall past the toilets and into a dark, musty room. Once inside, her companion shut the door and switched on the lights. They were in the club's storage room. The long, rectangular space was crowded with spare stools and tables, and boxes of liquor were stacked floor to ceiling with narrow aisles between.

Zoe was a bit surprised since Jasele had seemed so distant on the dance floor. "I'm flattered. But I think you've got the wrong idea," she said, not unkindly. "I'm not interested."

She started toward the door but the stranger blocked it by putting her body against it. Jasele had an odd expression—more challenge than seduction. Zoe wasn't in the mood for this. "Please get out of the way." Just as she was about to pull the woman to the side, someone from behind covered Zoe's head with a black sack and roughly hugged her against them, pinning her arms at her sides.

"What the bloody hell? Let go of me," she shouted, struggling to break loose. Whoever held her only gripped her tighter, nearly lifting her off her feet. He was incredibly strong. She fought against a rising panic.

A sharp rapping at the door broke the quiet. Then, Enrique's voice: "Is that you, Miss Howe?" The most beautiful voice she'd ever heard.

"Help!" she screamed.

The sound of the door crashing open filled her ears, followed a millisecond later by a single gunshot.

As she was dragged away by her captor, she heard Jasele say, "*Vamonos. Esta muerto.*"

Zoe knew enough Spanish to understand that Enrique was dead.

CHAPTER FIVE

London
October 11

Derrick Anderson-Howe reached for the photo of Zoe that sat on his desk, taken when the two of them had gone skiing one winter in the Swiss Alps. He'd reconsidered, several times, his decision to fire his daughter and cut off her funds. But now he knew he'd done the right thing. His bank had called this morning because of a number of extraordinarily large out-of-country charges to the company credit card, a routine check to guard against identity theft.

In one day in Bogota, Zoe had racked up nearly twelve-thousand pounds in purchases at several boutiques. Christ, she must have purchased a whole new wardrobe just to spite him. He'd immediately told the bank to cancel the card and send him a new one. Zoe's hotel had been prepaid, so she was on her own to come up with funds for any further spending sprees in Colombia.

The buzzer on his intercom sounded; his secretary needed him for something. "Yes?"

"A call for you on line one, sir. The gentleman wouldn't give his name, but he said it was urgent."

"All right, Mrs. Winters. Thank you, I'll take it." He reached tiredly for the phone. "This is Derrick Anderson-Howe."

"Listen carefully, Mister Howe. I represent the Revolutionary Armed Forces of Colombia. We have your daughter in our custody. The price for her safe return is fifty million U.S. dollars."

Derrick sat upright in his chair. "What? Who is this?"

"We will be in further touch with you regarding the location for the exchange," the caller instructed him.

"Wait!" Derrick shouted into the phone. "Let me talk to my daughter."

As though the man expected the request, Zoe's voice, angry and defiant, came on the line a few seconds later. "Just contact my father. He will give you whatever money you ask for." Though obviously a recording, it was enough for Derrick to know the call was authentic.

After another moment, the caller came back on the line. "I hope for her sake your daughter is right. Her life depends on it. Like I said, Mister Howe, we will contact you soon."

"Wait! I can't raise fifty million dollars," Derrick shouted, "that's—"

The line went dead.

"Wait!" he yelled again, clicking the button several times to make sure the call had really disconnected. "Jesus Christ!" He slammed the phone down, his heart booming.

Think. Stay calm. But the image of Zoe, surrounded by armed men ready to take her life if he couldn't raise an impossible sum of cash, was overwhelming. He knew The Revolutionary Armed Forces of Colombia was another name for the FARC, the guerrilla group notorious for taking hostages, and often killing them when their demands weren't met or when rescue operations were attempted. *Dear God.*

"Mrs. Winters," he barked into his intercom. "Cancel all my appointments for the rest of the day."

Derrick pulled out his BlackBerry and dialed the entry number for Chez Maurice. He used the name to cover the identity of an old school friend, Collier Morris, who worked for British intelligence.

❖

Parkland Hospital
Dallas, Texas
October 11

"Six more people are in the waiting room with similar symptoms," the triage nurse told the chief attending of the ER. "What the hell do we have here? Any news from the lab?"

"Nothing conclusive," he reported. "Looks like a mutation of the H1N1 virus, but it's different from any strain we've seen and it's not responding to Tamiflu or anything we throw at it. We need to get the CDC on this and start putting these people in isolation."

The first half-dozen cases, admitted a day earlier, had one common factor. All the patients worked at or had visited the same fast-food restaurant, and some of the symptoms—diarrhea, vomiting, and dehydration—made them initially suspect E. coli or botulism was to blame. But the patients quickly developed high fevers, headaches, chest pain, and racking coughs with bloody sputum. They went downhill alarmingly fast—two were now near death—and since that time, an additional fifty-eight people, most with no connection to the restaurant, had been admitted with apparently the same mysterious illness.

❖

Southwestern Colorado
October 11

Montgomery Pierce, Chief Administrator of the Elite Operatives Organization, set the stack of current case files on the small conference table in his office and went to the window to stand beside Director of Academics Joanne Grant. The other member of the governing trio, Director of Training David Arthur, was due any moment for their weekly ETF status briefing.

"Beautiful," Joanne murmured, gazing out at the Rocky Mountains and the nearly half-million-acre Weminuche Wilderness area that adjoined the EOO's sixty-three-acre campus. Winter had come early this year, already bringing a foot of snow. She put her hand on his back and caressed it lightly through his charcoal suit coat. "Want to do a little cross-country skiing after lunch?"

"Whatever you like, honey." It was another of her subtle attempts to get him to exercise more regularly, take off some of the flab around his middle that he'd developed in recent years from sitting behind a desk. Since they'd become romantically involved, she'd also changed his eating habits, bringing well-balanced brunches to his office and cooking vegetables and lean meats and fish for dinner. He had more energy these days and adored how Joanne fussed over him.

Two sharp raps at the door announced Arthur's arrival.

"Come in," Pierce said.

As Arthur entered, his copper-colored crew cut a vivid contrast to his winter white fatigues, Pierce drew the blinds, a habit whenever they were to discuss anything important. The chances anyone could observe them were practically nil; the office was on the top floor of the neo-Gothic administration building, the highest structure in the secure compound. But Pierce had been an EOO operative for nearly all his sixty-one years—he'd been one of its first students—and he still always took extraordinary precautions.

The remote and covert campus, which operated under the guise of a private boarding school, housed and trained an elite fighting force assigned to missions outside the reach of normal law enforcement. The best of these were the ETFs—the agents of the Elite Tactical Force. Hand-selected from orphanages worldwide and raised within the compound, they could deal with any situation.

They took seats at the table, but before they began, Pierce turned down the volume slightly on his large screen TV. It was always on, usually tuned to CNN. On more than one occasion, the news media had been the first to alert them to a global crisis that would require their services.

"We currently have seven ETFs in the field, soon to be five," Pierce said. "Domino just wrapped up Operation Crush and is expected to arrive tomorrow for her debriefing." He opened the first two folders, glanced at the top pages of each, then set them aside.

"No new developments with Viper or Cameo. Both are still in the initial phase of their missions. So far, everything's going smoothly."

The third folder said Operation Fortune/Allegro at the top. "Allegro retrieved the codes and is en route to Izmir Air Force base in Turkey, where a plane is standing by to take her to the Pentagon. I talked to her this morning. She got a little banged up getting out of the building—sprained her ankle badly jumping from a second-story balcony—but says she'll be fine in a few days."

He set that file aside and reached for the next in the pile. "Reno is in London, as you know, working with MI5 to help retrieve and decipher the encrypted e-mails sent between those suspects they arrested last week connected with the kidnap threat against the Royal Family. He expects to be done there in another day or two."

The next folder was headed Operation Clarity/Badger. "There were three new bombings today in Peshawar—" Pierce went silent when the TV newscast broadcast the familiar tone of an important news bulletin, and all three of them turned to watch.

"Hospitals in Dallas, Texas have asked the Centers for Disease Control for help in identifying a mysterious flu-like illness spreading through the city with alarming speed. So far, three people have died, and a total of one hundred and twenty-eight others have been admitted with symptoms that include headache, fever, body aches, chest pain, and a bloody cough," the newscaster reported, over video of a nurse taking the temperature of a young black man, whose hospital gown was stained with small specks of red. "The CEO of Parkland Hospital says patients are not responding to any known treatments, including antiflu medicines like Tamiflu."

"Joanne," Pierce said. "Remind every op to make sure they're fully up to date on all their vaccinations." Along with the standard vaccines, the EOO had access to new ones not yet approved by the FDA, since its ops traveled worldwide and were exposed to every conceivable kind of disease.

"Of course, Monty."

"Where was I?" He glanced back down at the file he'd just opened. "Oh, right. Badger reported yesterday that he's following up a lead that indicates a former Pakistani military officer is orchestrating the attacks in Peshawar. He's hoping to get a name within a day or two. Blade's standing by as backup, if necessary." He closed that folder and stacked it neatly with the others, then opened the final file.

"Fetch made contact this morning," he told them, and both Grant and Arthur turned to him with their full attention. The other updates had been fairly routine. Fetch had been in the field a long time, working in deplorable and dangerous conditions, and was rarely able to report her progress. "She's being moved again and is relatively certain it's finally to the camp with our targets."

"Great news," Joanne said.

"How's she holding up?" Arthur asked. Of the three of them, he was the least likely to show any kind of emotional attachment to any of his former students. But he had a soft spot for Fetch. Like Arthur, she was a soldier to the bone. Pierce had rarely seen either of them dressed in anything but fatigues.

"She sounded understandably tired. She's also out of meds," Pierce said. "But she's confident she'll have some good intel for us before long. At her last camp, she befriended the communications officer and was able to overhear reports that indicate all the hostages are still alive, although one of the women—we don't know which— has a bad infection. They're transferring Fetch there to treat her." The FARC had an elaborate radio network and communicated through codes based on algebraic algorithms. Fetch had memorized the complicated codes before she'd left and apparently had been able to use that knowledge to her advantage.

"I hate these long gaps between her reports," Arthur groused as he got to his feet. "We through?"

"That's all I have."

"Before you go, David," Joanne said, "on an unrelated matter, Lynx called me this morning and invited us all to her concert the day after tomorrow in Philadelphia. She has a solo."

"I'll have to send my regrets," Arthur said. "I'm taking the senior class out for a three-day winter-survival excursion in the morning."

"I'd like to go, Joanne," Pierce said, unable to suppress a smile. "Will you make the flight arrangements?"

"Certainly."

Arthur had started to leave, but paused at the door to look back at him with a curious expression. "What's going on with you lately, Monty? You've been unusually chipper the last few months. And since when are you a fan of classical music?"

Pierce considered how to answer. "Lynx did an extraordinary job in Operation Face," he replied, remembering how she'd almost become a victim of the serial killer called the Headhunter when she'd chased him down in Vietnam on her first solo assignment. There was more to it, but that was all he planned to volunteer, even to David. "I think we can do more to show our ops how much we appreciate how they put their lives on the line. Call this a first step."

CHAPTER SIX

Guaviare Jungle, Colombia
October 11

The new FARC camp where she'd been transferred was bigger than all the others Fetch had been rotated through. Some of the smaller ones were extremely primitive—merely a bivouac of two-man tents that moved to a new location nearly every other day. Because this one held the most valuable of the hostages, it had a semi-permanent look. Crude, frond-covered huts, with walls made of stout tree limbs and boards cut by chainsaws, dotted the encampment, along with a few dozen small tents made of camouflage material. Wood planks had been laid as walkways through the ever-present mud. The large kitchen tent, open on one side, was well stocked with small crates of canned goods and bags of rice. Beside it was a large fire pit for cooking.

There were other resources she hadn't seen elsewhere. A small divided pen to one side held some thirty pigs and a pair of donkeys, and the ground had been tilled in the small patch where sun penetrated the thick jungle canopy. Several rows of seedlings poked their heads from the rich brown earth.

The importance of the camp was underscored by the fact that nearly one hundred guerrillas were here, and the person in charge was Chief Diego Barriga, one of the Secretariat—the FARC's seven-man Central Command. Outside his large tent was a small satellite dish and gasoline-powered generator, which provided power for his laptop, electric lights, and sophisticated communications equipment.

On her first tour of the camp, Fetch took note of the multitude of booby traps that had been placed around the perimeter. Well-concealed stake pits, trip wires connected to grenades and land mines, bear traps, and spring-loaded snares and nets were positioned on more than half the crude trails leading into the camp. These were supplemented with regular patrols of guerrillas armed with AK-47s, M16 rifles, and M60 machine guns. Guards were also positioned near the huts that housed the hostages.

The location of the camp itself was an additional deterrent to any potential surprise attack. Fetch and her escort had to travel two hours by Jeep from the nearest town, most of it over rough terrain, then hike for several hours to reach the high mountain campsite. There were no clearings anywhere within a reasonable distance large enough to land a chopper, and the guerrillas had been careful to pick a site so dense with lush trees it would be difficult to spot from the air.

Orchestrating a rescue mission in this remote and well-guarded camp would be perhaps the greatest challenge of Fetch's illustrious career in the EOO.

❖

London, England
October 11

Derrick Anderson-Howe sipped his seventeen-year-old Glenfarclas single-malt Scotch and forced himself to remain calm, as he waited for Collier Morris to pull up outside his eighteenth-century brick residence in the exclusive Mayfair district, just three blocks from the U.S. Embassy. He'd explained the little he knew about Zoe's kidnapping to Collier on the phone, and his old friend had said he'd make a few calls and meet with him later that evening to chart a course of action.

In the interim, Derrick had spent much of his time surfing the Internet for information on the FARC, and what he'd learned had only added to his distress. The guerrilla group was well-organized, well-armed, and nearly impossible to locate. Their hostages were often held for years in deplorable conditions. Rescue efforts usually ended in the death of the kidnap victims. The few rare exceptions— notably the 2008 rescue of fifteen high-profile hostages—included Colombian presidential candidate Ingrid Betancourt, who'd been in captivity more than six years. But that mission took months to plan and had involved both the Colombian and U.S. military.

The sound of tires on the gravel outside alerted him to Collier's arrival, and Derrick went to the front door to admit him. He'd sent his housekeeper home early, telling her he'd fix his own dinner tonight. Until Collier advised him otherwise, he was keeping the crisis quiet, fearful that any misstep on his part might further endanger Zoe.

"Hello, Derrick," Morris said, offering his hand. "How are you holding up?"

"How bad is this?"

"We'll get her back. But you have to be patient."

"Where do we start?" He gestured toward his den.

"How about one of those," his friend replied, glancing at the drink in Derrick's hand. "Put mine on the rocks." Morris settled into one of a pair of high-backed padded chairs set before the fireplace. As he took the Scotch, he loosened the perfectly formed Windsor knot in his red silk tie and unbuttoned his double-breasted suit jacket. Morris looked several years older since they'd run into each other at the club. In the past eighteen months, Collier's hair had thinned considerably, and his face was etched with wrinkles. No doubt the result of his stressful job.

"I've contacted one of the foremost experts at this sort of thing," Morris said. "A few private companies specialize in conducting the lengthy negotiations required for the release of hostages, and Jaime Farnsworth has agreed to take your case. He's had extensive experience in dealing with the FARC." Morris pulled one of his business cards from the breast pocket of his suit and wrote a number on the back. "This is his cell. He'll drop by later tonight and meet with you en route to the airport. He's booked on your evening flight to Bogota."

"That's excellent news," Derrick said. "You said lengthy negotiations. What are we talking about here? Days? Weeks?"

"Probably months, Derrick. These things take a great deal of back-and-forth. That's why I told you on the phone you mustn't be alarmed by their initial fifty-million-dollar demand. They always begin with an outrageous figure. It's Jaime's job to negotiate it down to something more reasonable."

Derrick ran his hand through his hair. "Months?" he repeated, unsure how Zoe might contend with such a long imprisonment. Nothing in her pampered life had prepared her for this. She was a strong, independent woman, but months in captivity would certainly break even her indomitable spirit, not to mention the unspeakable things those bastards might do to her, and the threat of disease and who knew what else.

"There will be some very tough moments, Derrick," Morris warned him. "Typically they'll say they'll torture or even kill her in the early stages of the negotiations. They'll want a large down payment to guarantee her safety, which you mustn't give them. If you pay too much, too soon, they will conclude they can ask for the moon. The negotiator will guide you through all this."

"How can we be certain they won't just kill her right away?" Derrick asked.

"She's too valuable to them," Morris explained. "During the negotiations, Jaime will ask periodically for proof she's still alive and well. They expect that. Often that proof will come as a video or photograph that can be dated—she'll be holding a current newspaper or something. But it's never pretty. The pictures are meant to shock the families into complying with their demands."

Derrick took a long swallow of his whiskey. "Does this Jaime have any idea what the final figure will be?"

"He estimated, based on his experience and your position, that the negotiated ransom will be somewhere between ten- and twenty-million U.S. in cash."

Jesus. Derrick had mortgaged most of his considerable assets to keep the airline going. He could raise ten, maybe, by shutting down the company, and solicit another million or two at most from friends, but he could never meet a twenty-million demand.

"I'm pursuing some other avenues that may be of help." Morris downed the last of his drink and got to his feet. "Contacts within the intelligence community that may be useful. I'll be in touch."

❖

Seattle, Washington
October 12

The man in Seattle had barely fallen asleep when the bedside phone jangled beside his head. The digital clock said 1:30 a.m., so it had to be the hospital and the news couldn't be good. He'd kept a vigil beside his wife's bedside for forty-eight hours and had only reluctantly agreed to his daughter's demands that he get some rest and allow her to sit with her mother overnight.

"Yes, hello," he answered, trying to control the tremor of uncertainty and fear in his voice.

"Daddy..." It was his daughter, and she was crying. He gripped the phone tighter. "Daddy...Mom's...Mom's *gone.* She..." More crying. He was crying too, now. "She started coughing up blood. It was everywhere, and they couldn't stop it. They tried..."

He was already out of bed, reaching for his pants. "I'll be right there, honey," he said, his voice breaking. *Damn it to hell. Oh, God.* She couldn't be dead. It couldn't be true. He shouldn't have left her side. No, he should never have allowed her to go to China with her sisters. But he'd never refused her anything in thirty-two years of marriage.

All three of the women had come back ill. His wife's sisters really shouldn't have continued to their homes in Chicago and Cincinnati after staying overnight here. They already had fever and headaches. But they were eager to see their husbands and said they'd rather consult their own doctors. He wasn't particularly fond of either of them. But he'd call them in the morning. They'd have to be notified. And warned that whatever this flu was they'd all come back with, they should take it seriously.

❖

Cali, Colombia
October 12

"You feeling okay, man? You look like shit."

The driver took two more aspirin, chewing them so they'd work faster, and slumped back in the seat of the truck. He hoped this damn flu he'd gotten would blow over soon. He and his cousin had a full day ahead of them, the long drive to San José del Guaviare followed by three dozen deliveries to small groceries scattered throughout the city. His cousin didn't know the route, and it took both of them to unload the heavy crates of produce.

❖

Kinshasa, Democratic Republic of the Congo
October 13

"Try the doctor's number again," the chief resident at Kinshasa General Hospital told the nursing supervisor. "We need every available body here. I don't care how he's feeling."

"I've tried five times already," she replied. "He's not answering. Should I send someone to his house?"

"We don't have anyone to spare," he replied, surveying the bustle of activity around the ER. The hallways were lined with patients, in cots and chairs and some even on the floor. The waiting room was jammed as well, and they couldn't send the overflow elsewhere. Every hospital and every private clinic in Kinshasa had been overrun with patients suffering from this damn illness, and half the medical staff had caught it as well. Two of their best physicians were among the more than five-hundred known dead. Bodies in the morgue downstairs were stacked like cordwood, their relatives too sick or too afraid to claim them.

He thought he'd seen everything in his four decades at the hospital. It had been the first in the world to deal with an outbreak of AIDS, and they'd suffered through Ebola, typhus, Lassa fever, cholera, and other diseases not seen in most of the West. But he'd never experienced anything that killed so many, so fast. Nothing they had tried had been effective against it.

As bad as the situation was, he knew it could only get worse.

❖

The Kimmel Center for the Performing Arts, Philadelphia
October 13

Jaclyn Norris looked out at the patrons filing into the twenty-five-hundred-seat Verizon Hall, a cello-shaped auditorium especially built and designed for the Philadelphia Orchestra. This was her first time to see Cassady perform without having to hide in the shadows, and she had a wonderful vantage point. She was positioned in the middle of the first-tier balcony, in the choice Conductor's Circle seats just behind and above the stage. From here, she could look directly down onto the musicians and beyond, to the audience. She had declined Cassady's offer of a front-row seat on the main floor. Though it would have given her a better view of her lover, she would also risk running into one of the governing trio of the EOO.

Cassady had frequently invited Montgomery Pierce, Joanne Grant, and David Arthur to attend her concerts, but they had declined all except her first big performance after graduation. Jack had deliberately avoided that one performance, not wanting to chance being seen. Although it was well after she had faked her death and had facial reconstruction, she always feared one of the big three would make her. And she knew what they did to ops who deserted.

She still didn't know why Pierce had withdrawn the order to have her killed when the EOO learned she was still alive and working with Cassady, aka Lynx, in Vietnam. So far, Pierce had made no move to contact her, and he was aware that she and Cassady were now living together. Even stranger, he had not summoned Cassady for an assignment since Operation Face.

The musicians emerged from the wings to take their places, and when Cassady settled into her seat among the second violins, Jack, as always, thought she would burst with pride. Her silky blond hair shone under the lights, and the formfitting black gown she'd chosen for tonight was one of Jack's favorites.

Everything about Cassady filled her with pride. She was bright, determined, brave, and so full of hope for the world, and more important, for Jack. They had been inseparable for months, spending most of their time at her apartment in New York, with the occasional long weekend at Cassady's place in Colorado.

Jack hadn't felt this happy since…well, *ever.* For the first time in her life, she felt free to just *be.* She didn't feel like she had to run, or hide, always looking over her shoulder, trying to struggle through another day. On the contrary, she looked forward to each new morning. It meant one more day she could spend with Cassady, one more night of holding her in her arms while they talked or simply watched a flick. One more glorious chance to make love to her and share a dinner or walk in the park.

It also meant another day to share her dreams for the children she was now once again counseling, in New York's Center for Troubled Youth. Jack was finally living the dream she'd never dared dream and hoped to never have to wake from.

As the orchestra warmed up, she lifted her compact binoculars to scope out the area directly in front of the stage. Were they there? She was curious about how her ex-bosses would look after all these years. She slowly scanned the front row seats, searching faces with the powerful lenses, and suddenly froze. Her breath caught in her throat. There, staring right back at her through his own binoculars, was Montgomery Pierce.

They both remained motionless for several seconds, apparently neither wanting to be the first to back off. Could Pierce see the challenge in her posture since her eyes were covered? She didn't know what she expected to see in his face, but it was difficult to read his expression. His lips were tight. Finally, he lowered his binoculars but continued to look at her. Sadness. That's what Jack saw. Raw, almost uninhibited sadness. Joanne Grant glanced up, following his gaze, and Jack saw her lips move, forming her name. Jaclyn. *That's right*, Jack thought. He'd never called her Jack, never anything but her full name.

She studied them both. Pierce's once-blond hair was now completely gray, and the wrinkles around his mouth were deeper, but the intense look in his eyes was still there. Grant had gained a few pounds in the nearly nine years since Jack had seen her, and her formerly ebony hair was white and shorter than ever.

Grant put her arm on Pierce's, leaned close to his ear, and said something. Pierce reacted with an uncharacteristically sad, almost melancholic smile, then looked up at Jack and slightly nodded just as the lights dimmed.

She should've been happy to see him out of sorts like that, with an almost guilty look on his face for a moment, but she simply felt devoid of emotions. If pressed to admit to anything, she'd probably have said she was almost a bit sad herself. She put the binoculars away and turned her attention to Cassady as the conductor raised his baton.

❖

"Are you all right, honey?" Joanne asked in a low voice.

"I don't know," Monty replied distractedly.

"How did she look?"

"Like she hates me. And why wouldn't she?"

"We can talk about all that later. We're here for Cassady tonight. Please try to enjoy the evening." She squeezed his hand.

"Of course," he said. "You're right."

"I told Cassady we wanted to meet with her after the concert."

"Did she ask why?"

"She didn't have to. She's bright. She just said this virus had to be stopped."

"She's always been fearless." Monty tried for a smile, but Joanne would see through it. His mind was still on Jaclyn and the bittersweet feeling of seeing her. Even from this distance he could ignore the facial reconstruction enough to recognize her. And though her eyes were obscured, that familiar air of confidence and daring had never changed. The body language that spoke of cool, controlled intensity. She had a presence that mirrored only one other he had ever known.

"Will you ever talk to her?" Joanne asked casually.

"I don't think she's interested."

"But it's in *your* best interest. This is eating you up."

"I have it under control, Joanne," he said, a bit irritated. More by the truth of the statement than her persistence.

"You don't have to put up that cool and controlled façade for me."

"What?" Monty was surprised. Had she been reading his mind? Just then, the orchestra started to play.

❖

Centers for Disease Control
Atlanta, Georgia
October 14

"Two more reports on Epi-X, from Chicago and Cincinnati," the emergency-response coordinator said as she set the latest faxes in front of the CDC director. Epi-X, the Epidemic Information Exchange, was the encrypted Internet-based reporting network that allowed public-health agencies to share information about emergencies and threats. "They're sending blood samples, but it appears to be the same strain of H1N6 as Seattle and Dallas."

The CDC had determined that the new virus that was causing outbreaks worldwide was closely related to H1N5—the swine-flu strain that had swept through the Ukraine two years earlier. Like the N5 variation, this mutation caused pulmonary hemorrhaging and cardiopulmonary failure, but with a much higher mortality rate.

It also killed indiscriminately, targeting all ages, races, and health profiles, and did not respond to any known treatments, so they'd given it a new designation.

Their technicians, along with the lab at USAMRIID, the military's facility at Fort Detrick, Maryland, were working to isolate the variant, so far without success.

Outbreaks had now been reported on five continents. The initial ground-zero cases apparently occurred almost simultaneously in Colombia, Germany, China, the Congo, and the U.S., but the virus had spread rapidly from those countries to neighboring ones. The confirmed death toll, now topping twenty-eight thousand, was rising by the hour.

"Call WHO and tell them we recommend a global alert," the CDC director instructed. The World Health Organization had helped establish GOARN, the Global Outbreak Alert & Response Network, an early warning, instant-transmission service intended to combat the international spread of dangerous outbreaks such as H1N6. "And get the secretary of health and human services on the line."

"Right away, sir."

❖

Washington, DC
October 14

The health-and-human-services secretary was briefing representatives from several other government agencies about the virus when the CDC director's call came in. He put the director on speakerphone. "Perfect timing. I'm meeting with reps from the White House, Congress, FEMA, the FDA and FBI, among others. What do you have for us?"

"Confirmed cases now in seventeen countries," he replied. "You want the list?"

The FBI director spoke up. "Yes, please."

The secretary knew the agency was investigating whether the outbreak had resulted from a biochemical weapon because the virus had appeared simultaneously in five locations thousands of miles apart. The FBI chief was particularly interested if any cases had occurred in the countries that topped their list of known terrorism threats.

"In Europe: Germany, France, Italy, and the Netherlands," the CDC director said. "In Asia: China, Russia, Mongolia, Japan. North and South Korea."

The secretary of health and human services was taking notes, as were most of the others at the large conference table.

"In Africa: the Democratic Republic of the Congo, Sudan, Chad, and Egypt," the CDC director continued. "In South America: Colombia and Ecuador. So far, the confirmed cases in North America have been confined to the U.S., but we have unverified reports of a few cases in Toronto."

"No cases in the Middle East?" the FBI director asked.

"None confirmed."

"The death toll?" the secretary inquired.

"Twenty-eight thousand, six hundred forty-two," the CDC chief replied. "But it's increasing by a few hundred every hour, and there may be thousands more cases out there that haven't been confirmed yet. Doctors in many of these countries have limited experience distinguishing this from other variations of H1N1."

"Anything new from the labs about what we're dealing with?"

"Negative. We've been unable to isolate the mutation," the CDC director said. "We may be dealing with a stealth component."

"What does that mean?" the FEMA director asked.

"We could be looking at a genetically engineered strain," he explained, "a chimera of different viruses, where one of the components is designed to go dormant after a certain period or when exposed to specific stimuli. If that's the case, we may not be able to trace the effective component by the time we get the blood samples."

"So you're saying we're definitely looking at biowarfare?" the FBI director asked.

"It's possible, but I can't confirm that."

❖

Budapest, Hungary
October 14

Doctor Andor Rózsa left his office at Pharmamediq, Incorporated and pulled out his cell phone as he walked to his car. Everything was proceeding exactly as he'd planned. The World Health Organization had just issued a global alert about the pandemic on GOARN, and the statistics they'd reported confirmed that all his emissaries had performed their missions to perfection. Now it was time to tie up a few loose ends.

The intermediary had already confirmed that all three agents had arrived back in Europe without incident and were awaiting their payments.

Andor got his aide Patrik on the phone and told him, "Call our intermediary. It's time to take care of our emissaries. Make sure they're all made to look like accidents."

"Yes, sir," Patrik replied. "And of course I'll ensure that's done before I perform my part."

Andor hadn't initially felt it necessary to eliminate the intermediary as well, but Patrik, the one man he trusted, had wanted his own guarantee that he couldn't be linked to the crisis. *He's learned well from me.*

CHAPTER SEVEN

Guaviare Jungle, Colombia
October 14

Zoe cursed as her left foot sank ankle-deep into the thick mud and struggled to find the energy to extricate herself and continue. The absolute terror that had seized her when they set off on the trek three days ago had faded. Now she could feel nothing but exhaustion.

They'd hustled her out of the Bogota bar and thrown her in the back of what she thought was a van, never removing the dark bag from her head. Jacolo and the man who had taken her remained with her, she on the floor of the vehicle and they on either side within arm's reach. The male driver always spoke in what was either an angry or irritated tone.

She'd tried to ask her captors who they were and where they were taking her. She knew they'd never answer, but it was the only way to deal with her helplessness. Every time she spoke, they either told her to shut up or ignored her altogether. She'd undoubtedly been kidnapped. Socialist guerrilla groups had once threatened visitors and locals alike in Colombia, but matters had gotten much better in recent years. They now advertised the country as a safe, beautiful haven that everyone could visit.

My arse. Zoe tripped and fell for what seemed the thousandth time. Her navy pantsuit was covered in mud and she was freezing. She pictured her warm, wool Roberto Cavelli trench coat, still hanging in the coat check at the bar. Or more likely now wrapped around one of the waitresses, since it had remained unclaimed so long.

Every time she fell, it took her longer to stand again. She wasn't acclimating well to the change in elevation as they rose higher into the mountains. Every breath was an effort, even when she was allowed brief rests.

And her feet were a mess. The rubber boots she'd been given two nights ago to replace her ruined pumps were much too big, and the trails were steep. The constant up and down in the sweaty footwear was excruciating. She'd dared to take the boots off only once and found her entire feet were rubbed raw with blisters, the toenails black. Who knew what kind of dreadful infections one could develop in such a godforsaken environment.

A short, stout man probed her ribs from behind with his rifle. "*Levántate,*" he barked. She knew after having heard the word nonstop for three days that it meant get up.

"Wait. Please," she pleaded tiredly. "I just need a minute."

"No. *Vamonos.*" The soldier kicked her thigh.

Zoe lifted herself to all fours and contemplated biting his leg. He was so close. But her satisfaction would be very short-lived. He would seriously hurt her, she had no doubt.

The night of her abduction, the van had left the paved road after a long drive and bounced over rough terrain for several more minutes before finally stopping. Someone had dragged her out and removed the sack from her head. They were in the jungle. It was pitch black and ominously quiet except for a low, distant buzz of insects, but she could sense people around her. And up ahead, dim light through canvas told her they had reached a camp of sorts. Someone shoved her from behind and told her to walk.

She headed toward the encampment, a guerrilla walking behind her. As they neared, her guard pushed her toward the largest tent and told her to enter. Inside, a bearded man in fatigues sat in a chair, looking down at maps by the light of a lantern. Zoe stood there waiting for him to look up, but he ignored her.

"Where am I?" she asked.

"No questions," he said, his attention still fixed on the maps.

"If it's money you want—"

He looked up at her, clearly irritated. "I said no questions," he barked, as he pushed a button on a tape recorder by his elbow.

"It was a statement, not a question," she shouted back.

He got up and smacked her across the face. "That was a statement, too."

Shocked, she rubbed her cheek. No one had ever hit her, not even her parents. This was undignified, uncivilized, and un-bloody-believable. She wanted to slug him back, tell him to go to hell, but common sense and self-preservation prevailed. Instead, she stared at him with all the menace she could manage.

Unfazed, he motioned to the guerrilla behind her, and the man came forward with Zoe's purse and laid it on the table. She'd forgotten all about it.

The bearded man opened the bag upside-down and spilled out its contents but, before he'd even glanced at her passport, declared, "I know who you are. You are going to stay with us until we get what we need."

Zoe raised her hand. Asking for permission to talk like she was back in primary school was ridiculous. But she wasn't in the mood for another show of macho bullshit.

"Speak," he said.

"Just contact my father. He will give you whatever money you ask for." God, she hoped she hadn't overestimated her father's account. She had no idea what she'd be worth to these people, but she'd heard and read enough to know that bargaining was part of the deal. Her father would sacrifice anything to get her out of there. "I can tell you how to reach him."

"Not necessary," the guerrilla replied, sitting back in his chair. "We have information."

"Then please call him now."

He put up his hand, warning her. "Enough."

But Zoe would not be put off. This was obviously the man in charge, and at least he spoke fluent English. She had to know what she was in for. "How long will I be here?"

"No more questions." He said something in Spanish to the man who'd brought her in, and the rebel immediately grabbed her arm and pushed her out into the night again.

"Where are we going?" she asked, trying to keep her balance as he practically dragged her along.

"Now you sleep," he replied. "Soon, we leave."

"For where?"

He didn't answer. Instead, he shoved her to the ground outside a small pup tent. From the light provided by a campfire a few yards away, she could see the tent was filthy.

Her captor knelt beside her and retrieved a thick metal collar from the tent. *A dog collar?* His intention was clear.

"What the hell are you doing?" She shrank away as he reached for her.

The man grabbed her roughly by the hair, and she struggled to break free, but he overpowered her easily. He pinned her, belly down, by sitting on her back, and placed the iron collar around her neck. Then he padlocked it to a heavy chain about six feet long that was somehow fixed firmly in the ground.

"I'm not a dog, you son of a bitch," she yelled as he finally released her and got to his feet. She rose as well and pulled at the collar. The metal was lined with leather, but it was so tight it rubbed against her neck. "Get this off of me," she demanded, though she realized the futility of such a request.

He laughed and made a barking sound, "*Guau, guau,*" then walked away.

She didn't sleep at all during the scant hour or so until dawn. The blanket in the tent didn't cover her, and every time she tried to get warm, the rattling of the chain and the choking around her neck reminded her of her predicament. Her emotions kept shifting between anger and fear. As long as she was worth money to them, they probably wouldn't harm her, but what they might be capable of in the meantime terrified her.

Four guerrillas came to get her at sunrise and they'd been walking ever since. Three days now of endless marching, all day and all night, slogging through the mud and over tenuous, slippery logs placed across streams. It had rained much of the time, drenching downpours that kept her soaked and miserably cold. And when it wasn't raining, mosquitoes and horseflies bigger than any she'd ever seen deluged them. Everywhere they traveled, everything looked the same, all dense jungle with a maze of faint paths. How could they possibly know where they were going?

Except for the sporadic five-minute pause to eat stale bread and drink from a dirty flask that was eventually passed to her, all she got from these men was an occasional grumble or order to levántate—get up—when she fell. No one had tried to communicate with her. Though they seemed to understand much of what she was saying, they obviously had a limited command of English.

Her escorts were a ragtag bunch. Two were older, probably close to her age, and actually resembled soldiers in their faded camouflage fatigues and loaded ammunition belts crisscrossed over their shoulders. The other two wore T-shirts and sweatpants and looked to be only in their mid-teens. All were armed with rifles or machine guns. Most odd was their diverse assortment of hats: a beret, a straw fedora, a colorful peasant chullo with ear flaps, and a New York Yankees baseball cap.

Zoe wanted desperately to ask where they were taking her, why all this walking, and had someone contacted her father? Surely they must have asked for a ransom by now, and her father most certainly would have complied. So why bother moving her around and not simply take her back to Bogota? She tried to console herself by concentrating on the knowledge that such transactions took time. Maybe just a few more days and she'd be on her way back to London.

As the sun began to set on the third day of their march, Zoe wrapped herself in the blanket they'd given her. She must look like a mud-gray ghost from all of her falls. Her once-navy pantsuit clung to her, damp with grime and sweat, and she'd snagged it so frequently on the thick undergrowth it looked like Swiss cheese. Her hair was matted, her skin filthy. She dreaded having to live through another cold night trekking through the impenetrable jungle. Years of Pilates and yoga had not prepared her body for this kind of physical exertion. "Don't you creeps ever sleep?" she asked out loud to no one in particular.

"Walk," one of them said from behind her.

"I am, plonker," she mumbled. Every muscle in her body ached, and she was so weak and exhausted she was having trouble thinking clearly. Already pushed so far beyond what she'd ever thought herself capable of, she knew that the next time she fell, she might not be able to get back up on her own.

They were marching across a clearing high in the mountains when all at once the men broke out in a frenzy of shouting and whistling. It took Zoe a moment to realize they were sounds of happiness and greeting. Below them, in the distance, she saw smoke and tents, huts, and farm animals. Men and women were waving back at them. Did this mean they could finally stop walking?

The guerrillas hurried her down the steep slope, no doubt eager to see their friends. The four men were so excited and distracted, Zoe considered running for it. It was twilight and would be full dark soon. Maybe she had a chance. The jungle was only twenty feet to her left. But before she could decide what to do, one of the men kicked her feet from beneath her and she was face-down again on the muddy ground.

Someone dug a knee into her back and placed another metal collar around her neck, similar to the one she had on the first night. She didn't struggle this time. She didn't have the strength and knew it was useless. One of the men attached a section of chain to the collar, then pulled her to her feet, choking her.

The man with the other end was the short, stocky guerrilla who'd been with her the whole while. "Next time I kill you," he warned. He must have seen her looking toward the jungle.

When they finally reached the new camp, men and women ran to greet them, so excited they seemed on the verge of throwing a party. It was hard to tell in the dark, but Zoe reckoned there must be at least twenty of them. Most ignored her, but a few studied her with a varied range of emotions. The women looked like they were sizing her up, and the men were practically peeling her clothes off with their eyes.

One of them, a scrawny youth in his late teens, stood directly in front of her, ogling her and licking his lips, alcohol on his breath. Though she wanted to break eye contact, she forced herself not to, glaring back at him to show she wasn't afraid.

The smile on his face broadened, and he licked her cheek. Zoe, determined not to break, didn't react, but the smelly soldier took this as an invitation. He neared her again, but this time the menacing voice of another man stopped him. Everyone parted to let him through.

If the guy had bothered to shave, he could have been attractive. He was tall, and fit, with skin the color of caramel, dark eyes, and a strong chin. He said something in Spanish and everyone returned to their tent or campfire.

All Zoe wanted was a place to sit and rest. Although she was afraid and hungry, her exhaustion was more powerful. Apart from the short guy holding her by the chain, the only man to remain was the one who'd sent everyone away. A chief of sorts, she guessed. He studied her face. "Hungry?" he asked.

Zoe looked him straight in the eye. "I don't want your stinking food. I don't want anything from you."

The chief gave her a charming smile and motioned to the other man with his head. Again, the man jerked the chain, so brutally hard she gagged. She grabbed the collar to relieve the pressure, but the short guerrilla only tugged her away even more fiercely.

When they stopped near a tent, she was relieved—she could breathe again—and welcomed the opportunity to get off her feet and into a somewhat warmer environment. As the man attached the end of the chain to a steel ring embedded in a heavy block of concrete, Zoe, without being asked, stooped to enter the tent. She was almost inside when he yanked her back out and dragged her by the throat through the mud to the side of the tent.

"Tent for me," the short guerrilla said. "You sleep here."

"Are you bloody mad? It's freezing," she shouted.

"You say you want nothing from us, *sí*? So..." He shrugged. "You get nothing."

Zoe found the driest place she could to sit and wrapped herself tight in her blanket. It did little to ward off the freezing temperatures. She had nothing to lean against, so she sat Indian style. Through the canvas of the tent, she could hear the loathsome fraggle snoring and wanted nothing more than to sneak in there, grab his rifle, and put more holes in him than a colander.

She'd never physically hurt anyone, had never even contemplated such a thing. But her hatred for these people had begun to consume her. How much longer would she be here? How much worse could it get? And, most of all, where the hell was her father?

A small group of rebels hunched around a blazing fire several feet away. The warmth beckoned her. She tried to calculate how close the chain would allow her to get and decided it was worth trying. But just as she got wearily to her feet, one of the men—the scrawny youth who reeked of alcohol—turned in her direction. When he saw her looking at him, he gestured lewdly with his tongue.

"In your dreams, you son of a bitch." She sat back down as he laughed and turned his attention back to the others.

An hour or two or three passed, it was impossible to tell. Time was meaningless here. She nodded off, but only for a few minutes. Her legs went numb from sitting in the same position. God, she'd never been more tired and hungry and dirty, had never felt more miserable in all her life. She told herself to concentrate on the future, think of a better time, when all this would be nothing but a despondent memory.

Images flashed through her mind: vacations, holidays, friends, parties. She called up every pleasant recollection she could, desperate to distract herself and help her make it through the night. She rocked herself to keep her blood moving.

"I want my mother," she said aloud. "She'd keep me warm. She always knew how to make me feel better." Great. Now she was talking to herself. Was this the first sign of madness? The possibility terrified her.

But thinking of her mother made her feel less alone. As she pulled the blanket even tighter around herself, she imagined her mom was tucking her into bed, just so, the coverlet up to her chin. Then she began to hum the lullaby her mother always sang to her before she kissed her good night.

A dull probe to her shoulder roused her. For an instant, before she came fully awake, she was back home in her cozy Soho penthouse. But the cold and her aching body reminded her of the awful truth too soon. With a groan, she opened her eyes to the sight of a combat boot. Looking up, she saw the chief.

"Hungry?" he asked, in the same placid tone as the night before.

Zoe wanted to kick the smug smile off his face. Fight back. Scream. Run. But she wasn't capable of much of anything at the moment. "Yes. I'm hungry now."

CHAPTER EIGHT

Southwestern Colorado
October 15

EOO Chief Montgomery Pierce turned up the volume on his television when a graphic came on highlighting the countries reporting outbreaks of the mysterious H1N6 virus.

"Officials at the CDC are refusing comment on unconfirmed reports the deadly virus may be a biologically created weapon of mass destruction," the newscaster reported. "Sources at the White House tell CNN that scientists have been unable to isolate the mutation that distinguishes H1N6 from other varieties of swine flu, possibly because it was genetically engineered to evade detection. The fact that the outbreak began in several countries almost the same day, with no apparent commonality between the first patients, reinforces suspicions that this new strain was created in a lab and deliberately released. The sources would not speculate on who might be behind such a well-orchestrated threat."

Pierce turned down the volume. The report contained nothing new. He'd been briefed two days earlier by his contact at DOD, the deputy director of the military intelligence service, who had called to solicit the EOO's help to track down the origin of the virus. Pierce had immediately recalled Reno, their computer expert, to see what he could uncover by hacking into the databases of known biotechnological and pharmaceutical companies. Their resident biochemist and virologist, meanwhile, would be provided a sample of the virus and workspace within the Bio Safety Level 4 section of the U.S. AMRIID facility.

Pierce didn't think either move would be of much benefit. Their biochemist was an exceptional scientist, but why could he come up with anything faster than any other expert currently trying to analyze the virus. And Reno's chore could involve months, even years, of work. Scores of known labs existed worldwide, and countless covert ones as well, and most of the databases were encrypted to guard against corporate espionage.

He absentmindedly tapped the smooth surface of his desk. He hated feeling powerless against such a threat. The EOO was used to getting results. Its motto was "Failure is not an option." But they needed a lead. He expected one government or another would ask them for additional help soon, so he'd put three more of his top ops—Allegro, Domino, and Lynx—on standby.

A knock at his door signaled the arrival of Joanne and David Arthur, whom he had summoned. At least they might be able to do something about this other matter. "Come in."

They entered and headed for the two cushioned armchairs opposite his desk.

"What's this about, Monty?" Arthur asked. "You pulled me out of a jujitsu class."

"You don't say," Monty couldn't help remarking, and Joanne laughed. It was rare to ever see Arthur without his fatigues, but he'd arrived in his well-worn *gi*, the thick white robe-like uniform he used when teaching martial arts.

Arthur frowned and looked at his watch.

"Point taken, David, this won't take long," Pierce said. "I just got a call from a London contact at SIS. The FARC kidnapped Derrick Anderson-Howe's daughter Zoe five days ago. They're starting the usual negotiations, but asked for our help in getting her out. Apparently they heard rumors we have someone in place down there."

"How did that happen?" Joanne asked, concern deepening the crow's feet at the edges of her vivid green eyes. "Surely no one here would compromise Fetch."

"I'm certain that's not the case," Pierce replied. "I'd be willing to bet someone at MIS dropped that little tidbit. I'd liked to have kept them out of this, but Fetch needed those FARC codes before she went in, and we couldn't get them anywhere else. I didn't trust asking anyone in the Colombian government or military. There's too much corruption down there."

"Fetch already has a lot on her plate right now," Arthur said. "And it's taken her half a year to finally be in position to get good intel on the hostages she went in there for."

"Agreed," Pierce said. "But we can ask her to see if she can find out anything about Zoe Anderson-Howe as well."

"When she calls again, which probably won't be for another two or three weeks at least," Joanne reminded them.

"Perhaps she'll contact us sooner, if she can find a quick way to get them out of there," Pierce said. "In any case, I'm adding this woman's dossier to the Operation Boomerang case file. It never hurts to have SIS owe us a favor."

❖

Guaviare Jungle, Colombia
October 16

Fetch spent most of her first days in the new camp familiarizing herself with the layout, security, the hierarchy of the guerrillas assigned there, and especially with the condition of the hostages targeted for extraction, all of whom had been in captivity more than a year.

She was familiar with hardship, having been stationed in Iraq, Iran, Afghanistan, and many other war zones, and had managed to keep her sanity to survive in the most brutal terrains and circumstances. But she had never become used to seeing civilians and soldiers suffer and did everything possible to prevent it. Giving up was never an alternative. An organization that didn't take no for an answer assigned her missions. Not having signed up or volunteered for this life, she had to do what she was trained to or run. And the latter wasn't an alternative. Not because she feared the consequences, but because she truly felt the world needed her. Unlike most of the operatives, Fetch was a full-time ETF. She didn't have a professional life outside the organization because her specialty required long-term, deep-cover missions.

Fetch was a born soldier and would sacrifice everything to protect and serve. She didn't do it for country, for she, like all the other ops, didn't pledge her allegiance to any flag, religion, or political party. She was trained to protect or eliminate whoever posed a threat to humanity. But she knew, like every soldier, that the day would come when she had seen too much suffering to be able to categorize and consign her emotions tidily.

She had nightmares too often about mutilated and tortured bodies. Visions of mother and child, still clutching each other after death, haunted her. It was the only time she saw peace etched in their faces, the kind of peace Sam was deprived of. Her body, or what was left of it, would always be lost in that ghost town. If Sam had never loved her, maybe Sam would be alive.

She'd sworn to herself to defend and save as many as she could, but never get emotionally involved. It wasn't easy, but it was necessary in order to survive and succeed. After Sam's death, her oath and convictions were stronger than ever before. If she was to rescue these innocent people, stuck in this merciless jungle, she would have to close herself off to their present pain and focus on securing their future.

The captive she'd been transferred to treat—one of the Australian humanitarian workers—was deteriorating rapidly. Thirty-one-year-old Kylee Robinson had been living under wretched conditions for almost two years, and Fetch could see her struggle to get through every hour of every day. Most of the time, Kylee sat on a flat stone beside her hut, rocking back and forth like an autistic child. She'd lost so much weight she barely resembled the photo Fetch had studied, taken before her abduction. Her hair was a matted mess that could have housed birds, and her clothes were filthy and threadbare. But Kylee's foot was the gravest concern. She'd developed a serious infection from a cut, and the whole foot and ankle were swollen and purple.

If they didn't get her to a hospital soon Kylee would lose her leg, at the very least, to gangrene. But the rebels would never agree. All Fetch could do was give the Aussie broad-spectrum antibiotics and keep the wound clean.

Though she had to have been in excruciating pain, Kylee never flinched when Fetch had debrided the cut a few days ago, shortly after her arrival at the camp. Nor had Kylee reacted when the bandages were changed yesterday. She was giving up. Her eyes were lifeless, and though others said the girl used to talk to herself—probably for comfort—she had now gone eerily silent. It didn't help that she was housed apart from the other hostages. The aid worker who'd been kidnapped with her, a fifty-three-year-old man named Willy White, was being held in a hut on the other side of the camp, near the Italians.

From her cot in a nearby tent, Fetch watched Kylee rock back and forth, vowing to sneak half of her meal into the woman's hut again tonight. She'd done so the night before, and to her surprise, the Aussie had eaten it. She'd continue to feed her as long as she could; she just had to make sure neither the guerrillas nor Kylee ever saw her doing it.

Fetch got up and grabbed the dirty pile of clothes from beside her cot. It was laundry day and she desperately needed a clean T-shirt.

From outside, the voice of the chief, Diego Barriga, beckoned her. "Oye, Medica."

She peeled back the tent flap and poked her head out. The chief, four guerrillas, and a woman she didn't recognize were standing in front of Barriga's tent. The woman, in profile, had to be a new hostage; she was obviously not a rebel. Her long, dark brown hair had been fashionably cut in layers in a salon. Her clothes—a navy pantsuit and beige silk blouse—were filthy and torn but expensive-looking. And she wore rubber boots obviously much too large for her.

Fetch grabbed her khaki ball cap, the intense daylight still too painful on her eyes, and headed toward the group. One of the men suddenly grabbed the woman's hair and pulled her head sharply back.

"Get your hands off me," the hostage yelled as she tried to break free.

Fetch could tell by the fight in the Brit that she hadn't been a captive long. Just as she reached the group, another rebel—short and fat and unfamiliar—grabbed the woman and backhanded her across the face. The hostage lost her balance and was about to fall when Fetch caught her from behind. The woman struggled to get away, but Fetch, a head taller and with the strength to match most men there, contained her with minimum effort.

"Let go," the Brit screamed.

Fetch wanted to. She understood the woman's fear, but as long as she kept her constrained the others wouldn't hit her again. "Stop fighting me, and I'll let you go," she said calmly, her English heavily accented. She smiled at Barriga as though she was enjoying the woman's struggle.

"Okay. Fine," the woman said. "Your death grip has stopped my circulation." She relaxed and stood motionless in Fetch's arms, and Fetch loosed her grip.

Probably too exhausted from the trip to fight any longer, Fetch thought. "Who is she?" she asked Barriga in Spanish.

As though she understood, the hostage turned to face her for the first time and opened her mouth to answer. But she gaped at Fetch for several long seconds before speaking. "You're a woman."

Fetch stared back at her. Even through all the mud, the woman was stunningly beautiful. And familiar. "What?" she mumbled, as realization and recognition sunk in.

Surprise still clear on her face, the hostage said, "I'm Zoe Anderson-Howe."

Zoe, spoiled brat and tabloid queen, Anderson-Howe. Fetch wasn't sure who looked more shocked.

Barriga broke the silence. "The medica will look at your feet. After that, we will take pictures."

"Pictures?" Zoe repeated.

"Proof of life," Fetch explained. "Your family demanded proof that you are alive. We need to give them that if we are to get the money."

The surprise on Zoe's face turned to horror. "My father hasn't paid yet?"

"Maybe your father doesn't love you," the short rebel who had hit her replied, then laughed.

Zoe lunged forward to hit him, but Fetch held her back. "At least I know who my father is," she screamed.

Fetch had to break this up right now. The rebel looked like he might hurt Zoe for the affront, and she was sure Barriga wouldn't stop him. Insulting someone's family was reason enough for murder in some parts of the world, and Colombia was one of them.

Fetch dragged the struggling Brit away as another soldier held back the short rebel. "If you want to stay alive long enough to get out of here, you have to learn to keep your mouth shut," she told Zoe when they were out of earshot.

"And how exactly will they get the ransom with me dead?" Zoe asked. "They need me."

Fetch tightened her grip and whirled Zoe around to face her. "But they can make you wish you were dead." She glared at the woman for several seconds so the words would sink in. Then she released her and turned toward her tent. "Let's go look at your feet."

Zoe followed dutifully, but her almost cavalier response made it clear she still wasn't getting the message. "I don't break that easily."

Being brave and optimistic under these circumstances was imperative for a hostage's survival and sanity, but this woman was bordering on foolish pride and ignorance. Two very dangerous qualities when at the mercy of mostly uneducated, trigger-happy soldiers. She stopped abruptly and Zoe collided with her. After turning slowly to face her, Fetch roughly grabbed her shoulders. "Do not for a second think they won't kill you." Her tone was ominous. "If you do anything to risk their safety, or become more of a problem than you're worth, they will end your existence without a second thought."

Fetch searched Zoe's face for signs of fear, but found none. "It happens all the time," she added casually.

Zoe heard the warning, but for whatever reason she couldn't explain, the words and the tone didn't jibe with the plea in the woman's dark eyes. This rebel also sounded like she herself was not the immediate threat, that it was the others Zoe needed to look out for. Was this a new intimidation tactic? "Get your hands off me," she replied.

"Did you hear what I just said?" the soldier asked, shaking her roughly.

Zoe rolled her eyes, determined to show the rebel she would not be cowed. "I'm sure you can make my life a living hell. You've all been doing an exemplary job so far, but I'm worth too much to you alive. So spare me the scary movie." She pulled free of the woman's grip. "Now, can we clean me up for the money shot?"

Surprisingly the female rebel didn't react at all to her words. Her attention had shifted and was fixed on something off to their right. Zoe turned to follow her gaze and realized they had an audience. The camp's chief, flanked by two subordinates, was observing them. "God, you're all voyeuristic freaks," she said to herself, positive no one had heard. Zoe pushed the woman away and walked past her.

She'd almost reached the tent they'd been headed for when a blow at the back of her knee landed her face-down in the mud. Again. She cried out as pain shot through her elbows.

"You move when I tell you to," the woman said sharply.

Zoe was so surprised she froze. Why had she done that? Just a moment ago, this rebel's threats had clearly contained subtle signs of concern. Her tone had been beseeching, not menacing. Were they all deranged?

"Get up," her guardian said.

But Zoe stayed where she was, splayed in the mud. She was so angry, if she moved right now, she'd do something irrational. Something that would have her be tied up like a dog again. She was too tired and hungry to risk going without food and a warm place to sleep for another night.

The female soldier stood over her. "Get up," she repeated, more forcefully.

Zoe mentally ran through a catalogue of ways the soldier could go fuck herself while she slowly got to her feet.

CHAPTER NINE

As the rebel busied herself pouring water into a large bowl and laying out her medical supplies, Zoe studied the woman and her surroundings. The cot she was sitting on was low to the floor and consisted of a thick sleeping bag over hard wood planks, but it was still more luxurious than the cold ground she'd been sleeping on since her abduction. The makeshift nightstand was an old wooden crate set on its side. On top were a pair of candles, in crudely carved wooden candlesticks, and a clear plastic box of assorted toiletries—toothpaste and toothbrush, shampoo, bar of soap, and a tube of insect repellent. Inside the crate were a well-worn olive cap with brim, three pairs of socks, and a pair of camouflage pants, all neatly folded. Beside it sat a well-polished pair of combat boots. How strange. None of the other soldiers seemed to give a damn about their footwear. A pile of dirty clothes was dumped on the end of the cot.

On the other side of the rectangular tent space a small wood table with a warped top held a chipped ceramic pitcher and bowl. On the floor beside it, a newer-looking backpack. The rebel was on her knees, rummaging through the pack for gauze, tape, ointment, and pills.

Zoe tried to reconcile the conflicting signals the woman was giving out. She seemed to have more in common with the male guerrillas than her female compatriots, which is why Zoe had first mistaken her for a man. She had a low voice and was tall—five foot eight or so—with an almost gender-neutral build: firmly muscled thighs, calves, and arms, a flat stomach, and small breasts. While the other female rebels outside clearly strove to maintain their femininity—they were braiding each other's hair and sharing makeup—this one seemed far removed from such concerns. Her dark brown hair had been cut quite short, in a style more suited for convenience than fashion. She wore no jewelry. And her overall demeanor was cool and businesslike, the professional soldier personified.

Only her face gave away that she was all woman. Her dark brown eyes were doe-soft, and her olive skin was smooth and unblemished. She had a thin, slightly upturned nose and full, pouty lips.

When the woman removed Zoe's mud-encrusted boots to look at her feet, she worked slowly and carefully, obviously trying to be as gentle as possible.

Zoe couldn't bear to look. "How bad is it?"

"How bad do they feel?" the woman asked as she painstakingly peeled shredded panty hose from her open wounds.

Zoe winced and bit her lip. "Like someone's taken a razor to them."

The rebel stood to retrieve the bowl from the table and a large plastic bag of cotton. "I'll get them cleaned up and apply some antibiotic. They should feel better in a couple of days." She sat cross-legged on the floor in front of Zoe and began to wash the blood and mud from her wounds.

"How long will I be here?"

"Can't say," the rebel replied without looking up from her task. "Maybe a week, maybe two."

"Just two more weeks before I'm out of this hellish nightmare?" Zoe repeated, more to herself than the woman tending her cuts. A couple more weeks she could do in her sleep, especially if they weren't marching her through the jungle all day and all night. The news was such a welcome surprise she felt almost giddy. But the euphoria was short-lived.

The woman paused and looked up at her. Zoe sensed from the regret and sadness in her eyes that bad news was coming. "Before they move you to another camp."

Her heart sank all the way to her painful feet. "But surely all this will be resolved by then."

"No, it won't."

"How can you know? I'm certain my father is already in the process of transferring you the money."

The rebel continued to gently bathe her wounds. "It's not that simple." Her responses were detached and cool, but not unkind. At least she was answering Zoe's questions, while the other rebels had all ignored her.

"What do you mean?"

She paused again to regard Zoe carefully. "That it takes time."

"Why? How much?" None of this made sense. The process seemed simple and straightforward. Ask for ransom, get ransom, and everyone moves on.

"Can't tell."

Zoe gripped the edge of the cot to stem her frustration. "Why is everyone being so bloody evasive?"

The woman ignored her question. "Does this hurt?" she asked as she smoothed antibiotic ointment over Zoe's tortured feet.

"No." The salve stung like hell, but she refused to admit it. "So, you're the..." What had the rebel chief called her? "The medica?"

"Yes."

That probably explained why the woman seemed brighter than most of her confederates, also why she treated the hostages with more dignity and caring. "Have you studied medicine?"

"You could say that."

The cagey answer piqued her curiosity. Why would a licensed physician choose to spend her life in such extreme, deplorable conditions? "To what do you owe your fluent English?"

The doctor looked up at her. "You ask too many questions."

Zoe sighed. "It doesn't seem to make a shite of a difference, since no one answers them."

To her surprise, the doctor said, "I studied general medicine in the States."

That tidbit was even more intriguing. Zoe had a hard time picturing this woman sitting in a classroom in a U.S. medical school, chatting casually with colleagues, then deciding to set up a practice in a jungle guerrilla camp. Something was fishy. "How did you end up here?"

"Circumstances," the doctor replied, as she unfurled a length of gauze and began to wrap Zoe's feet. "And the cause," she added.

"What *cause* are you talking about?" she snapped. "Kidnapping, torturing, and robbing people of their hard-earned money? Have you lot ever considered the option of *decent* hard work like the rest of us?"

"Is that what you call what you do for a living, Zoe?" There was challenge in the doctor's voice, and it was the first time she'd called her by name. "Because I don't think partying qualifies as hard work."

The remark, and the realization this backwoods doctor dropout had any clue about who she was, stunned Zoe. "You don't know anything about me."

"I know what I see and read," the woman said. "Maybe the next time you decide to vacation in this part of the world, you should avoid making headlines."

Zoe tried to mask her shock at hearing that the damn tabloids had made it halfway around the planet, to the Colombian interior, no less. It was bad enough that she had to deal with condemnation and scorn from her so-called peers, but to have a bloody terrorist dress her down like this? *Unbelievable.* "How I choose to live is my own damn business."

"Sad, yet true," the doctor replied in that same infuriatingly accusatory tone. "But if acting like a sex-deprived debutante is your idea of hard work, don't act surprised when people are alerted to your *decent* existence."

"How dare you presume to…to…" Zoe stuttered. She was furious. "And even if that were true, it still doesn't give you the right to abduct me. You…you—"

"Call me Doc," the rebel interjected, as she finished taping the gauze around Zoe's feet.

But Zoe wouldn't be stopped from telling this woman exactly what she thought of her, consequences be damned. "You… presumptuous, money-grabbing, filthy…*baboon.*"

"I would opt for the first," the doctor calmly suggested. "It's easier." She threw a pair of socks at Zoe and set her spare combat boots beside her on the cot. "These should be closer to your size."

Zoe was still so boiling over with outrage she refused to move. As she tried furiously to come up with some clever comeback, the doctor stood and drew back the tent flap at the entrance. Two guerrillas with rifles were waiting outside.

"Hop to, princess," the doc said. "We need the daylight for your *photo shoot*."

As she waited for Zoe to emerge from the tent, Fetch tried to reconcile their exchange with her assessment of the Brit from the media.

Her resolve to dislike the pampered, self-indulgent heiress was softening. She felt sorry for Zoe, even respected her a little. Though her feet would heal without permanent damage, they were bad enough to cause a lot of discomfort. But when Zoe strode out with her boots on, head held high, she did an excellent job of concealing how much pain she most certainly was enduring. Maybe, Fetch considered, there was more to the princess than met the tabloids.

But that didn't change the fact that Zoe presumed herself untouchable. Like Daddy's money would fix any trouble she got in to. She had an air of this all being just a temporary setback, rather than the dire situation it was. So be it. Fetch hadn't been hired to put up with rich-bitch tantrums. Zoe wasn't even one of the hostages assigned to her rescue mission. All she could do was to try to subtly advise her on how to act so that she might stay alive long enough to get out of here. How she was treated in the meantime would be entirely up to her.

The pair of armed guerrillas led them back to the chief's tent. Barriga emerged and pointed to a large rock and told Zoe to sit on it. To Fetch's relief, Zoe did as she was told. Barriga handed the woman a copy of *USA Today*, dated the previous day, and told her to hold it up. Then he walked over to Fetch and handed her a Polaroid camera.

Fetch positioned herself about three feet away and carefully framed the photo to make sure the newspaper was legible. Just as she snapped the picture, Zoe's expression changed from serious to arrogant. Not the look Barriga wanted. The hostages were supposed to look terrified to get the desired reaction from their families. Barriga stood behind Fetch and patiently waited for the picture to appear.

"Did you get my good side?" Zoe asked.

Barriga cursed under his breath when the picture finally cleared.

"Damn it," Fetch whispered under her breath, knowing what was about to happen.

Barriga stomped angrily over to Zoe and smacked her hard across the face. Then he grabbed her hair and yanked her head back. He leaned over so his mouth was almost on hers. "Maybe I have been too good," he said in English. "Maybe you are not worth my time." He straightened, took a rifle from one of his aides, and pointed it at her temple. "Maybe I should kill you. Or tie you to a tree for a week." He cocked the weapon and glanced over at Fetch. "What do you think, Medica?"

Fetch pursed her lips, as though considering the possibilities, and forced herself to wait a few seconds before answering. "I think she gets one more chance," she replied, trying to sound casual.

"Last chance, bitch." Barriga kept the rifle aimed at Zoe's temple, but retreated a few steps to be out of camera range.

Fetch snapped another picture and pulled it out of the camera. Several seconds later, the image of a terrified and bedraggled Zoe slowly started to appear.

Barriga gave the rifle back to his aide and came over to look at the picture. "*Muy buena.*" He took the camera and photo and glanced over at Zoe, whose expression hadn't changed. "Give her some food," he told Fetch in Spanish, before retreating back inside his tent.

Zoe got up, a bit unsteadily, and Fetch went to her. She felt sympathy for the Brit, but she had to be put in her place. Did she really think these people would let her get away with her juvenile, recalcitrant behavior? They'd shot hostages for a lot less. The only reason Zoe was still alive was the promise of a fast, fat ransom. Fetch hoped she'd been scared into submission, because she was already getting tired of Zoe's misplaced sense of entitlement.

She was encouraged when Zoe fell wordlessly into step beside her as she headed toward the cook tent. "Are you all right?" she asked.

"What do you think?" Zoe shot back.

Fetch stopped and turned to her. They were far enough away so no one would hear them. "That you should learn when to keep your mouth shut," she said in a low voice. "Your attitude will make being here a lot harder."

"Maybe you were born to take orders, be a good little soldier and do as you're told," Zoe said angrily. "But I—"

"You what? Listen to nothing but your self-absorbed self?" Although Zoe had no idea who Fetch really was, she'd hit the nail on the head, and that bothered her. In a sense, she *had* been born to be a soldier. Though it hadn't been her choice initially, she was a good one because she believed in what she did. At least she fought for ideals, not a good slot for her weekly manicure.

"What is your problem?" Zoe snapped. "Does my privileged background offend your collective beliefs that much? Are you blaming me for having money? I work for it, you know."

"Your father works for it."

"And I work for him," Zoe insisted. A flush of pink colored her pale, mud-stained cheeks, but Fetch couldn't tell whether it was from anger or embarrassment.

Fetch crossed her arms across her chest. "Let me guess. He's put you in a comfortable office and given you some comfortable task to justify your comfortable, overpriced existence."

"Do you realize how absurd this conversation is? And have you any idea how tired I am of having to justify myself, when you don't know a good God damn thing about me?" Zoe laughed, a condescending snicker of disapproval. "I mean, look at you. You steal, kidnap, and maybe even kill. Yet somehow, you've convinced your twisted self that you're better than me." She laughed again. "You probably fancy yourself some kind of bleeding Robin Hood, when everyone knows you're all nothing but a bunch of cocaine dealers."

It was an accurate assessment of the FARC, and probably the first thing out of Zoe's mouth that she agreed with. But Fetch could say nothing to set her straight about her own motivation without exposing her real identity. If Zoe had said this to any of the real guerrillas, particularly the men, they'd have been so offended they'd probably have hit her, or worse. So to make her role believable, Fetch couldn't remain silent. As much as she hated it, she had to defend the rebels and their lifestyle. "That's the world's misconception about who we are and what we fight for. All we want is equality. We are tired of watching the majority of our people live in poverty while the few live like kings. Our children die of hunger in the streets every day, and our politicians, together with the Colombian army, make us look like amateurs." Fetch hated every lousy excuse coming from her mouth.

"Oh, cry me a river," Zoe said. "Yes, your country is poor and your government corrupt. But trafficking in cocaine and hurting innocent people is still not right. What kind of animals kidnap and kill not only foreigners, but even their own?"

Fetch knew she was right. She had no rebel-textbook answer to reasonably justify these radical groups. "I can see how it would be impossible for someone like you to comprehend," she said. "Carmen is giving manicures after dinner. Go join them. I'm sure that's something you *do* understand."

"You know, I'd rather have you think I'm a superficial twit than a homicidal drug dealer," Zoe said, "which is exactly what I think of you."

Fetch wasn't sure why, but the description hurt. She had spent her life protecting people from exactly the sort of injustices she'd just been accused of. She would never be recognized for her deeds, since all assignments were covert and all accomplished missions credited to governments and official agencies. But to be accused of such atrocities, even if out of ignorance, felt painfully unfair.

Though she'd never really talked at length to any of the hostages she'd interacted with during her time in the FARC, she was rather certain that all of them felt the same as Zoe. She'd gone out of her way and risked her cover on many occasions to keep them safe, but always secretly—sneaking food to them while they slept, or an extra blanket. They couldn't know who was helping them, because they might use that information as a bargaining chip with the chiefs.

But even if all the hostages did view her the same, Fetch probably would've had an easier time taking criticism from any one of them but Zoe. The others were mostly humanitarians—people giving back to the world. Or policemen, or honest judges and politicians—all of whom risked their lives to protect and help those too poor to have a voice in their future. But, no, she had to be put down by a self-important, overindulgent hedonist. Someone so far removed from her own reality and values it was almost surreal. "You wouldn't understand any cause that didn't include party decorations," she told Zoe. "Because you don't understand—"

"Because I don't know the real you? The deep and profound makeup of the complicated existence that led you to your choices? No, I don't. But screw you for judging me when you don't have those insights into my life either." Zoe turned to walk away, but she'd taken only a couple of steps when she pivoted to face Fetch again. Her face was red from fury. "I may be everything you despise," she said, closing the distance between them again. "But *I*," she pointed her thumb at herself, "contrary to *you*," she pointed at Fetch, "have never tortured or killed *anyone*."

There was fire in Zoe's clear blue eyes, and they were standing so close to each other, Fetch couldn't look away.

"How about you, *soldier*?" Zoe said, the last word dripping sarcasm. "Have you ever killed? Or stood by, watching while it happened? How did it feel to look down at that innocent, lifeless body? Was it a woman like me? Did you look her family in the face to tell them you were responsible for their daughter's death? More important, did it help your *cause*?"

Fetch knew this woman had no idea what she was talking about, but she'd just touched a sensitive place. A place she hadn't chosen to visit in a long time. In a matter of seconds, she was back in that dreadful dilapidated house, taking cover behind a wall while she proposed to Sam. Again she was caught in that horrible limbo between present and past. That painful place where she was aware of the tragedy to come but helpless to change it.

She was so far away she'd forgotten her present surroundings until she felt someone's breath on her neck. Zoe's face was mere inches from hers.

"I didn't think so," Zoe said. "So don't make my existence sound so wrong. At least I don't rob anyone of theirs."

CHAPTER TEN

Zoe pushed against the doctor's chest to walk past her. "Do I have permission to eat now, or are you not through analyzing my life?"

The doctor led Zoe toward the cook tent, where a fire was blazing in the open pit. Men and women, most dressed in fatigues, clustered around it, standing in line or sitting cross-legged on the ground or on rocks. Others were eating at makeshift tables nearby. Several stared at her as she approached.

Only a handful of people sat at one of the tables: three guerrillas and two women and a man in torn, threadbare civilian clothes. There were other hostages here. One of the women—blond and painfully thin—seemed to be about her age. The other, a brunette with olive skin, was younger, perhaps still in her teens. The brunette sat close to a man Zoe guessed was her father—they had similar coloring and the same sharp features, and as she watched, the man put his arm around the girl protectively and squeezed her shoulder. She headed toward them and sat nearby on a dry patch of ground.

"If you're waiting to place your order, you'll starve," said someone behind her. "The food is over there." Zoe looked up to see the doctor, pointing to a large metal pot placed on stones beside the fire pit. "Get it while it lasts."

Zoe got in line behind a couple of rebels and two more people who looked like hostages: a tall, skinny blond man and a petite, dark-haired woman, both of whom looked to be in their forties or fifties. Everyone seemed to be serving themselves, but a woman with a filthy apron stood next to the pot, apparently monitoring portions. Following the example of the others, Zoe fished a tin plate and spoon out of a crate to one side and waited her turn. When the blond man reached the pot, he carefully scooped out one ladle full of food and emptied it onto his plate. It looked like gooey rice, with black objects floating it in. At first, Zoe thought the black bits must be insects, maybe small cockroaches or flies. Her stomach recoiled.

"How do you eat that stuff?" she asked no one in particular. She didn't even know if either of the hostages or any of the rebels nearby spoke English.

The blond man answered without looking at her. "You'd be surprised at what you can eat when you're starving." His accent was distinctly Australian.

"At least today we eat," the petite, dark-haired woman in front of her said. "You're the new one. I'm Marcella, from Italy."

"Zoe, from England. How long have you been here?"

"Almost a year...I think," Marcella said. "It becomes hard to remember. Willy there has been here longer, maybe two."

"Years?" Zoe practically shouted the word. "Can't your family or someone get you out?"

The blond man, who had started to leave to find a seat, paused to look at her and shook his head dolefully. "You're about to find out how screwed up these fuckers are," he whispered, and went to sit near the blond woman.

Marcella stepped up to the pot and carefully ladled out a portion for herself.

"What did he mean by that?" Zoe asked.

"Even if the guerrillas get the money they ask for," Marcella said, "they don't free you. They keep you here and ask for more."

A chill ran through her. "What? That's bloody insane."

"Everything here is," Marcella replied, and walked away.

It was her turn to get dinner, but though she hadn't had a decent meal since her abduction, she had lost her appetite. What if the same happened to her? What if she too was stuck here for a year, or two, or forever? The dreary prognosis made her stomach churn, and she dry-heaved, unsteady on her feet. As she tossed her plate and spoon to the side, the stocky cook said something in Spanish, but she ignored the woman and went to sit by the fire, almost in a daze. The rabid hunger she'd suffered for days had disappeared as fast as her hope.

The doctor was seated on the other side of the fire pit, looking in her direction. But she appeared to be distracted, lost in her own thoughts. How could this woman try to justify what was going on here? How did she and all these other fanatics have the right to take away her life?

She would not resign herself to an endless future here, in the jungle, constantly on the run and continuously guarded by Neanderthals. She'd take a sharp object and stick it through her eye all the way to her brain before she'd let that happen. *No,* she resolved. *I'll find a way out of here.* Although she didn't have anything or anyone to go back to, except her father, she refused to give up on life. Zoe was determined to figure out a way to escape, or at least die trying. She needed to be alone, to think and plan. These people, everything about her environment, were adding to her nausea. But where? She got up and walked over to the doctor, to ask where she was to sleep.

"I thought you were hungry," the woman said.

"I lost my appetite."

"You should eat," the doctor said. "You probably haven't had a meal in days."

"Is that what you call this crap?" Zoe glanced over at the blond hostage who'd been ahead of her in line. He'd already wolfed down his portion and was meticulously licking his plate.

"If they see you turn down food," the doctor said in a low voice, "which I'm sure they have, it might be a long time before they let you eat again."

But food was the least of her concerns. "Is it true? Do you keep the hostages here and ask for more after you receive the ransom?"

The doctor shrugged. "It depends."

"On what?"

The doctor looked around before answering. "On the negotiator I'm sure your father has hired. If they pay too fast or don't negotiate a considerably lower amount, then yes, they will ask for more."

"Because you think they can afford it."

The doctor nodded. "Yes."

"It doesn't even cross your deranged minds that these people may have just spent and mortgaged everything they own and simply don't have anything left to offer?" Several of the rebels standing close by were openly staring at her now, but Zoe didn't care.

"Get some food," the doctor said sternly, without looking up at her.

"Is that your answer?"

"No, it's a damn order," the doctor said, much more sharply, her jaw muscles tightening. "Go get some damn food. *Now.*"

"I just said—"

"I refuse to drag you around and nurse your ass because of deliberate malnutrition. If you won't do it yourself..." The doctor stared up at her, unflinching, her mouth firmly set. "I'll tie you down and force-feed you."

Was this woman out of her mind? Who the hell did she think she was to *order* her around? She wasn't a child. She didn't need to be told when to eat. "Can you point me to my quarters?" Zoe said angrily.

The doctor jumped up, grabbed Zoe by the wrist, and dragged her over to the food. Zoe tried to resist, but the woman was much too strong, and any attempt to dig in her heels only sent shooting pains through her raw, tender feet.

As the cook looked on with a bemused smile, the doctor jerked the ladle from the pot and dumped its contents on a plate. She shoved a spoon into the dubious concoction, picked it up, and pulled Zoe off to the side of the camp. Soldiers sitting by the fire started to hoot and whistle, shouting what Zoe was sure were obscenities.

They stopped by a tree, and the doctor dropped the plate on a low, crude table set beneath its branches. "I'll give you one more chance. You either feed yourself or I do it."

"You can't be serious."

The doctor pushed her up against the tree and pinned her by the throat. She reached down with her free hand, grabbed a heaping spoonful of the foul goop, and held it in front of Zoe's face. "Dead serious."

Zoe couldn't move. Damn, the woman was strong. The fire in the doctor's eyes made it clear she wouldn't stop until she got her way. Her hand was still tight around Zoe's neck. It was the first time the doctor actually scared her.

"Okay, I'll eat," Zoe managed to choke out.

When the doctor released her, Zoe coughed and tried to fill her lungs with air. When she could breathe again she picked up the plate and shoveled the slop in, taking huge, deliberate mouthfuls for the doctor's benefit, and finished in seconds. It tasted even worse than it looked. "Happy?" she asked, her voice hoarse, as the goop dribbled down her chin.

The doctor smiled. "Ecstatic. Let me show you to your quarters."

Zoe was led to a small hut in the center of the camp, constructed of rough planks with a roof of thatched fronds. It was dark inside, but the wide spaces between the boards in the walls provided enough light that she could immediately make out a hammock and a long, thick chain that stretched across the dirt floor. Without a word, the doctor picked up the small metal collar attached to one end of the chain, unlaced Zoe's left boot, and secured the collar around her ankle. She departed, leaving Zoe alone.

She stared down at the restraint. It didn't cut into her ankle, but with only a thin sock as padding between the metal and her flesh, it would leave some bad bruises as soon as she moved around very much. At least the damn contraption wasn't around her neck. She'd expected the worst after having to endure being chained like a dog.

As her eyes adjusted to the dim light, she explored the rest of her roughly ten-by-ten foot living space, holding the heavy chain in one hand to lessen the friction against her ankle. Her rope hammock bed had no pillow, but at least she had two blankets—the same one she'd had for the long march here, crusted with dried mud, and a thicker one made of wool. To her dismay, the only other item in the hut was a bucket in the corner that reeked of urine.

No clothes. No water. Nothing to clean herself with. No light of any kind, not even a candle. The idea of spending a year or more in this fetid prison was unthinkable. Unimaginable.

Twilight was fast approaching. Zoe wrapped herself in both blankets like a cocoon and stared out at the camp through a wide gap in the boards. The rebels were lighting fires in open pits scattered here and there. One was only a few yards away, but too far to give her any warmth. The night was fairly mild, but exhaustion had left her cold and empty. Only one thought gave her any hope right now—finding a way out.

She took off her boots, wincing at her sore feet, and carefully got into the hammock. She kept the blankets tightly coiled around herself to provide some padding between her body and the rough rope, but it was still horribly uncomfortable. Her raw feet were pinched where the ends of the hammock came together, and she was afraid she'd fall out if she moved much.

Living under these circumstances was not an option. Not because she was spoiled, an assumption the doctor seemed convinced of, but because she missed her life. No. It wasn't her *life* she missed. No one, not even a pet, depended on her. She'd even managed to kill the one plant her father had brought to liven up her apartment, because she forgot to water it. Responsibility had never been her strongest suit.

But Zoe did miss her father, the only person who, until recently, never judged her and always believed in her. She wasn't angry with him for firing her. He just wanted her to get her life together, but she was disappointed that her career had to suffer. She was good at her job. Maybe her heart wasn't in it, but she gave her best to the company. Not for herself, but for her father. She wanted him to be proud.

She regretted that he thought the stupid tabloids could undermine and disprove her abilities. It wasn't fair. She couldn't anticipate when and where the paparazzi might pop up to commemorate her lifestyle with their cameras, but they always seemed to be there to catch every unfortunate moment. The bastards never made a big deal out of her charity donations or fundraisers, however. Those always ended up buried on the last page of the rags, if they were covered at all.

"Opportunistic leeches," she said out loud. And the bimbos she was often caught with didn't help. They were anything but disappointed to be seen with her or accused of being her playmate. Some were even straight or married women who'd pop into the picture and kiss her at the last second. It didn't matter to them what the headline read the next day, as long as their mug and name were immortalized for a week. Regardless, what people thought of her rarely mattered, unless or until she had to endure her father's disapproving silent stare.

Zoe shivered. She should have been warm under the cocoon of blankets but she couldn't stop shaking. Her arm had started to tingle. It was going numb from laying on it. Though she wanted to shift position, she was afraid to rock the hammock and risk falling out. She had never been this tired, but sleep eluded her. Fear of being trapped in this jungle for an indefinite period overrode all other senses.

Even if she did escape, how long would she last, alone in the jungle? She didn't know the first thing about survival and had not been gifted with an internal compass. She had a hard enough time reading maps, never mind blind navigation. If only she'd watched those survival programs on *National Geographic* instead of using them to lull her to sleep. Maybe more of it had sunk in than she realized, like listening to foreign language tapes while you slept. Was it foolish to hope that some strange sort of telepathic osmosis had taken place, and she'd instinctively know what to do?

Laughter from outside only added to her misery. More than a dozen rebels were gathered around the campfire just outside her hut, talking in Spanish and passing around a bottle of something. Even if she could possibly extricate herself from the chain, which was secured to a heavy block of concrete, she wouldn't be able to slip away during the night if she was always so heavily guarded.

The glow of the fire shone through the gaps in the boards, painting the ceiling and opposite wall with strips of amber light. She was almost enjoying the display when movement caught her eye—something, thick and black, scurried up one of the light strips toward the ceiling.

Sweet God, was that a spider? And no mere house spider, for when it came into view again and she got a better look at it she knew it had to be a bleedin' tarantula. She screamed and shot straight up, so suddenly she was dumped ass over teakettle onto the dirt floor, the chain tangled around the now twisted hammock. "Bloody fucking spiders!" she screamed.

It took her five minutes to add a few new vulgarities to the English vocabulary and free herself from the Gordian knot. She picked up her blankets and propped herself up in a corner of the room, far from the hairy creature. She scanned the light strips, but she'd lost sight of it. That was it. She'd never go to sleep again.

"I bet you'd just love this," she said aloud, thinking of the doctor. Fight for the cause. Did the doctor really think she could convince Zoe of the righteousness of their ridiculous war? Oh sure, they wanted to use her life to make a half-assed pseudo attempt to overthrow their government, and pocket a few million for personal benefit in the process. Why, no problem. Be her guest. She was thrilled and privileged to be here.

"Gun-toting maniacs!" she yelled out into the night.

When she got out of here, *when* not *if*, she vowed to herself, she intended to do everything in her power to hurt these people. Yeah, right. Like what? No one could touch them. But it was probably normal to have thoughts of revenge, and force-feeding that overinflated doctor was high on her list.

She was so tired. But she wouldn't be able to shut her eyes until she spotted the spider again. When she finally did, it was scurrying toward the top of the door. "That's right. Keep going, you furry mutant." Relaxing a little, she reached up to run her hand through her hair and quickly found it was an impossible task. She ruffled it and enough dried mud to build another hut fell off and onto her blanket. Just bloody magic.

Shifting to position herself near one of the wide gaps so she could get a good look at herself by the firelight, she examined her clothes for the first time in days. Everything was torn and caked with muck. Her nails were broken and jagged, and her hands were badly scratched from the thorns and branches of the jungle. She had itchy bug bites everywhere, but her feet were the worst problem. She gingerly peeled off the socks the doctor had given her. They were still bandaged, but the gauze was thin, and when the cool air hit them her misery increased. As she pulled the socks back on, tears started to form at the corners of her eyes. She shut them tight and, wrapping herself up again in the blankets, started to hum her mother's lullaby.

Chapter Eleven

After she'd secured the chain to Zoe's ankle, Fetch returned to the fire. Most of the rebels had gone to bed, while the evening shift took their lookout positions around the camp. It would be her turn tomorrow, so she hoped to get a good night's sleep.

Though she'd been rough with the Brit, she was left with little to no alternative. She had enough on her plate keeping the hostages she was appointed to safe, without having to add the wild Brit to the mix. Zoe was not her problem, Fetch kept repeating to herself. And that irritating delinquent had no right to make her feel guiltier about Sam's death than she already did. Fetch had lived with those torturous ghosts since that dreadful day, and no amount of therapy had helped her find redemption. She would sacrifice her own life if it meant bringing Sam back, so who was this woman to judge her? Fetch didn't know why the Brit had gotten to her so much. It was like everything that came out of her mouth was an inaccurate truth.

She was lost in her thoughts when she heard Zoe yell, "Bloody fucking spiders!" from her nearby hut. Fetch had to smile, but not long after, Zoe shouted again. "Gun-toting maniacs!" At this, a soldier sitting on the other side of the fire pit jumped up, rifle at the ready. Fetch defused the situation by laughing and shaking it off with her hand. She told him to go get some rest and forget about the crazy hostage.

The Brit had no idea what thin ice she was skating on. New hostages usually rebelled in some way against their predicament, and many exhibited unpredictable behavior, varying from outrage to catatonic sadness. But Zoe's recklessness was something she hadn't encountered yet. Granted, they had pushed and smacked her around. The rebel who'd brought her in even boasted he'd chained her like a dog out in the cold. They'd given her ample reason to feel terrified. Nonetheless, this woman refused to show any signs of submission or even caution.

Fetch didn't know if she should be annoyed by or applaud Zoe's tenacity. Sure, the woman was gambling with her life, even after Fetch had warned her about how irrelevant her existence was to these people. But Zoe became even more arrogant, instead of afraid. She was either spoiled to the point of dim-witted denial or had a very twisted code of survival, one Fetch was not familiar or comfortable with.

Her own code consisted of strict military conduct. Fetch never swayed, rewrote, or argued her orders. The Brit's remark about her being a good obedient soldier was spot-on. It was not Fetch's place to question what was expected of her. Her strategy for survival was to endure long enough to get the job done. And that was fine with her.

It wasn't like she didn't care if she lived or died, but her own life was irrelevant when compared to saving hundreds or thousands of others. For a brief moment in her controlled life, Sam had made her feel that she was just as necessary to one individual as she was to one thousand, that it wasn't selfish to put her life first if that meant making someone she loved look forward to tomorrow.

But Sam was no more. No one waited for Fetch at the end of the day, but plenty depended on her to do her job. She would never let herself become necessary to one person again. For whatever reason, which she couldn't understand and was against everything she'd been taught, losing one person hurt more than the loss of many. If that was what love was about, it was no longer an option.

Fetch looked up at the sky to find the brightest star, as she always did when the memory of Sam was inescapable. The brightness of that star could be Sam's doing, telling her that she wasn't alone. But it was cloudy and dark and not one star was visible.

She sighed and stood up. After extinguishing the fire with a bucket of water, she stood listening. The camp was quiet except for the guards, who were congregated, sharing a bottle. Fetch went to her tent and retrieved her cell phone and hand-crank charger, then snuck outside the perimeter a good distance to check in with headquarters.

"Fetch," she said in a low voice as soon as Montgomery Pierce came on the line.

"What's your status?" he asked.

"Finally at ground zero," she replied. "All targets are alive, but one is very ill. Still gathering intel. Not going to be easy, but I should have something for you within a week or two."

"Roger. I have an amendment, if possible," Pierce said. "Assess location and status of Zoe Anderson-Howe. British."

"She's here as well," Fetch said. "Just arrived. Good condition."

"Excellent. Add her to Boomerang," Pierce said. "Check back when you can."

"Yes, sir." Fetch disconnected. So Zoe's father had been pulling some strings and somehow got the EOO involved. Not that she would have left Zoe behind on any rescue mission, but it might complicate things a bit to include the combative, unpredictable Brit.

She headed back to her tent, but paused just outside Zoe's hut when she heard a noise. Zoe was humming what sounded like a lullaby.

Fetch stood there for a while, listening. She was about to move on when the humming turned to crying. Though she didn't even know this woman, she did recognize the sound of hope being ripped away. It didn't matter who you were, where you'd been, or where you were going. No one was equipped to deal with the loss of hope.

"Good night, Zoe," Fetch whispered, before departing.

❖

San José del Guaviare, Colombia
October 17

Alejandro Trujillo forced himself not to look too frequently at the street outside the post office, where two Colombian soldiers armed with M50 submachine guns had stopped for a smoke and to watch passersby. The military and police presence in the city had been beefed up considerably since the last time he'd been out of the jungle two months earlier, no doubt a reaction to the FARC's bombing of several public buses last week.

Alejandro had swapped his guerrilla fatigues for plain tan trousers, a worn black shirt, and a straw hat, but he was aware he still stuck out. The clothes weren't his, but belonged to a farmer who had enlisted in the FARC some months ago, and they didn't fit well. The pants were several inches too long so he had to roll them up, and the black shirt was a few sizes too large. He was just fifteen, one of the smaller rebels in the camp.

He glanced down at the manila envelope in his hand, addressed to Derrick Anderson-Howe in London, England. The fact that he'd been given this prestigious assignment reflected the trust his commander had in him. Quite an achievement, he told himself. He couldn't wait to get back to camp to lord it over his best friend, Mateo.

Alejandro had chosen one of the smaller post offices to minimize the chance of being scrutinized by police or paramilitary, but that might have been a mistake. Only one worker was at the desk and the line was already long when he arrived, so he would have a long wait.

That wouldn't have mattered so much—he was used to standing around for many hours when on guard duty at the camp—but he had to remain inconspicuous here, which was becoming more difficult. He wanted to knock in the teeth of the man standing behind him. The bastard had a persistent racking cough and kept spraying his foul spittle against the back of Alejandro's neck. But the man was a lot bigger than he was, and any confrontation would certainly draw attention from authorities.

He couldn't wait to get out of here and back to his compadres. He'd have the rebel who'd driven him here make a brief stop at the corner grocery to load up on sodas and candy. Another reason to make Mateo envious.

❖

London, England
October 18

Though it was only ten a.m., Derrick Anderson-Howe took a long swig of Scotch to steady his nerves as Collier Morris pulled on a thin pair of latex gloves. They were in his study, seated side by side on a plush leather couch. Before them, on the coffee table, lay a manila envelope, which an express shipping company had just hand delivered.

"I don't expect there will be fingerprints," Morris remarked as he carefully peeled off the clear tape sealing the missive. "And if there are, they'll likely not be in any database. But I'll take it back to the office anyway to see what we can get from it."

After the initial notification call from the kidnappers, Derrick had received a brief second phone call two days later, in which he provided the FARC with the cell number of the negotiator, Jaime Farnsworth. Farnsworth had set up shop in a rented apartment in Bogota, outfitted with recording equipment and a short-wave radio. He'd spent a good ninety minutes before leaving London briefing Derrick on how things worked in such cases, and so far things seemed to be progressing as expected. The kidnappers had immediately called Farnsworth and given him a radio frequency for the negotiations, which would be conducted every three days, at ten thirty p.m.

The first official radio exchange lasted just ten minutes. The FARC representative demanded an immediate down payment of two million dollars to ensure Zoe's safety and provide that she was well cared for. Farnsworth rejected the demand and said that further ransom negotiations could not proceed until they received proof that Zoe was still alive.

Morris carefully extracted the Polaroid photograph from the manila envelope, holding the corner between two gloved fingertips, and glanced at the back before laying it on the coffee table.

Derrick steeled himself with another gulp from his tumbler before bending forward to look. Morris and Farnsworth had both warned him that pictures of hostages were always meant to shock the recipients into paying quickly. Zoe, however, had only been missing eight days, so he didn't expect this first "proof of life" would reflect as much change in her as later photos likely would. The glass slipped from his hand and landed with a thud on the heavy carpet as the Scotch burned in his stomach. He had to force back a sudden urge to vomit.

Zoe sat on a large rock, surrounded by dense, impenetrable jungle. Her clothes were torn and filthy, and she was wearing a pair of combat boots. So much dried mud covered her fair skin and dark hair she was almost unrecognizable. A light-gray ghost of herself. But the look in her eyes undid Derrick. Pure, stark terror. Dear God. What had he done to his baby girl, sending her there? This was all his fault.

He broke down, sobbing, burying his face in his hands. After several seconds, he felt a hand on his shoulder.

"I know it's difficult to see, Derrick," Morris said soothingly. "But this is encouraging. She has no visible bruises or injuries. And I recognize that front page. It's from just three days ago."

CHAPTER TWELVE

Washington, DC
October 18

Dawn was still an hour away, but the White House Situation Room, a massive conference room and hi-tech communications center located in the basement of the West Wing, had standing room only. When the president arrived, senior military personnel from all branches of the armed forces as well as MIS and the national guard were congregated in one corner, talking in low voices, while high-level intelligence officers from the NSC, State Department, CIA, FBI, NSA, Homeland Security, and Secret Service clustered together in another to exchange notes. All fifteen cabinet secretaries and the vice president were there, along with key congressional leaders, the Federal Reserve chairman, and a handful of the president's top scientific and medical advisors.

The six massive flat-screen televisions used for videoconferencing were currently tuned to the major news networks and several foreign media outlets. CNN was running video of angry people lined up outside a hospital in Nairobi that had closed to new patients. Fox News was covering a looting spree in Hamburg caused by food shortages. MSNBC was running a piece on the history of similar disasters, and the BBC was hosting a round-table discussion by experts trying to project the spread of the pandemic.

When the president was announced, the scattered groups dispersed and individuals almost comically jockeyed for the limited number of plush leather chairs. As the president lingered in the doorway, getting a whispered update from his chief of staff, he glanced around the room, studying the faces of the Washington elite gathered around the long conference table. The crisis was clearly taking its toll on all of them, affecting them personally even if they did their best to give the impression of being in control of the situation. When faced with one's own mortality, and especially that of loved ones, it was impossible not to let panic seep through the cracks.

None was more visibly affected, however, than his secretary of homeland security, a middle-aged brute of a man who had exuded nothing but calm self-assurance when they'd crossed paths in this room six days ago. But as the secretary now rubbed tiredly at his temples, the president was struck by his gray pallor and deep creases of concern.

The secretary of defense noticed, too, and said, "You look tired," his voice tinged with concern.

The homeland security secretary immediately jerked his head up and let the hands that had been cradling his temples fall to his sides. "If you're implying that I'm sick—"

"Not at all," the defense secretary replied. "You just seem tired."

"It's a migraine," he snapped in a low voice. "Nothing but a God damned glorified headache. That's all."

The president watched several of those standing near the homeland security secretary retreat a step or two, and two seated close to him gave up their precious chairs. Anxious murmurs spread through the room.

"Let's not panic, ladies and gentlemen," he said, raising his hand to ease the tension and restore order as he took his seat. Fixing his attention on the homeland security chief, he added in a quieter tone, "Are you sure you're well?"

"Everyone in this room is being constantly monitored, including you, Mr. President," the secretary reminded him. "I would've never made it past the gate if I hadn't checked out. It's been a rough week."

"That it has," the president said. "I can see how a situation like this might cause us all a headache or two." He smiled to lighten the atmosphere, and most everyone in the room either nodded or at least attempted to smile.

He shuffled some papers to mark the beginning of the meeting. "Nothing discussed here leaves this room," he said solemnly, before addressing his homeland security chief. "What do we have so far?"

"We have no evidence yet that this originated at any single point of origin, though it's clear it's no random occurrence. The instigating force has impressive resources to draw upon to have made this happen. Creating this virus must have involved months or years of research. And the logistics involved in such a well-orchestrated and untraceable global attack…" The secretary cleared his throat. "But despite our best efforts and an unprecedented information-sharing," he acknowledged the intelligence officials gathered with a nod, "we're still no closer to identifying who's behind this or why. We have people in all the points of origin trying to track down the patient zeros, but not all the countries involved are cooperating. It's a politically sensitive situation. If we press too hard, we may seem to be accusing them of complicity."

One of the military officers grumbled, "Everyone is dancing around each other, afraid of stepping on each other's dick. Especially if whoever's responsible is in their own backyard."

The head of homeland security glanced down at his notes, as though searching for some positive news to report. "We've set up a three-pronged approach to deal with this. While the intel specialists continue to track the cause, and several labs, including AMRIID, work to isolate the virus, FEMA and the national guard are setting up a plan to deal with the domestic repercussions. Widespread hoarding is already creating shortages of food, fuel, and emergency supplies in some regions, and gun sales are at an all-time high."

"I'm not hearing anything I don't already know." The president turned to the head of the FBI. "What have you come up with at Langley?"

"We're investigating all possibilities and monitoring recent activities of the well-established terrorist groups that target the

West. But we believe this is most likely state-sponsored, because of the complexity of the virus and scope of the attack. So we're focusing on the usual suspects. Iran. Pakistan. North Korea. Russia's at the top of the list, because of their long history with biological weapons. Sure, they've signed treaties to end their bioweapons program and close their nuclear-warfare facilities. But we have no way to accurately assess their compliance. We know Biopreprat has engineered other chimera viruses similar to this one. But if it is them, is Moscow acting deliberately or have some discontented virologists gone amok, hoping to profit somehow? At one point, they had fifty-thousand people involved in bioweapons research and production, in more than fifty facilities."

"What's been their official response?" The president directed the question to his secretary of state.

"We've heard little from them, beyond statistical reports of infection and mortality rates," the man replied. "Our embassy in Moscow has been digging for more, but we're doing so very judiciously. The current administration doesn't take well to accusations and no one wants to rock that boat."

The president turned to his chief of staff. "Set up a videoconference with the Russian president as soon as possible. I'll see what I can learn, maybe get him to agree to a neutral inspection of the labs we know about."

Glancing about the room, he next turned his attention to one of his invited guests. "Thank you for coming, Doctor. For those of you who don't know him, our visitor is an assistant director-general with the World Health Organization. Doctor, what can you tell us about the current state of affairs?"

The man consulted his notes before he addressed the group with a heavy French accent. "The WHO has just raised its pandemic alert level to six, the highest possible, which indicates an increasing and sustained transmission among the global general population. Forty countries now have confirmed cases, and seven others are awaiting the results of lab tests to be added to the list. In the past twenty-four hours, the first infections have been reported in Australia, the Middle East, and the Indian subcontinent. Probably the result of air travel."

"Do you have overall casualty figures?" the president asked.

"More than half a million people have been infected, and about one-fifth of those have died." The doctor frowned. "Hundreds of new deaths are being reported every hour. And those are just confirmed cases. Most likely tens of thousands more are infected, at least. People who are isolated, third-world countries mostly, or misdiagnosed, or who have yet to exhibit symptoms. The incubation rate, from time of infection to death, seems to be only a week or so, on average."

"Jesus Christ," one of the men standing behind the doctor said under his breath.

"Hospitals and clinics in the worst-hit areas are overwhelmed to the breaking point, especially as physicians and nurses are falling ill," the visitor said. "We're coordinating with several health organizations, including the International Red Cross and Doctors Without Borders, to set up field hospitals in those regions."

The president nodded toward the chairman of the joint chiefs of staff. "See what we can contribute in the way of tents, cots, and so forth. While reserving adequate supplies for our domestic needs, of course."

"Yes, sir," the admiral replied.

The president was quiet for several seconds as he scanned the room. "Can anyone here provide any positive news at all?"

No one stepped forward.

"That's all then, ladies and gentlemen. For now."

Later that morning, the president called a press conference, his first since the outbreak, though his close advisors weren't happy about the idea. He compromised with them by giving the media very little notice, which might mitigate attendance. The White House press corps would be there, of course; they had a workspace in the West Wing next to the press briefing room. But it might be difficult for some of the more radically leaning media to get their reporters there in time.

When he paused outside the briefing room so a makeup artist could apply concealer to cover the dark circles under his eyes, he realized that tactic had been in vain. He could tell from the din on the other side of the door that the room was packed with reporters, and they were coiled tight.

Though it was risky to hold a press conference right now, he thought it vital to maintain a veil of normalcy. Anything to forestall the level of public panic he knew was inevitable. So far, the U.S. had largely escaped the looting and riots that were breaking out elsewhere because of hoarding and shortages. But armed homeowners were reportedly threatening to kill anyone who came onto their property.

"Are you certain you want to do this, Mr. President?" his press secretary asked. "We can't adequately brief you on what might come up."

"I appreciate your concern, but this is necessary. Go ahead and announce me."

He took a deep breath and let it out as his aide entered the room. He'd run for office on the simple platform Honest Integrity, and so far, he'd managed to uphold that vow. But he doubted he would get through the next twenty minutes without having to lie. The Internet was abuzz with the rumor that his family had been relocated to a sealed underground bunker somewhere in Washington, stockpiled with supplies to last a year or more. He certainly couldn't confirm that rumor; it would validate the kind of panic that could ruin the country. Lying in this case was for the greater good.

As he steeled himself and stepped toward the podium, the room erupted in a chaos of shouted questions.

❖

Southwestern Colorado
October 18

The governing trio of the Elite Operatives Organization was seated at Montgomery Pierce's conference table with an array of personnel files before them and a list of the current whereabouts and status of all ninety-five members of their Elite Tactical Force. They were sipping coffee, as daybreak was still hours away.

"We'll be spread very thin," Montgomery Pierce mused aloud. "Thirteen countries have forwarded requests for assistance so far, and that number will explode in the coming days."

"I hate putting all our best resources into such a tenuous situation," David Arthur replied. "We can't adequately protect them. MIS says the experimental antiflu serum they sent us isn't guaranteed to have any effect whatsoever on this thing. It was developed six months ago."

"I agree," Joanne Grant added, looking down at the requests. "Some of these have much risk with very little possibility of success. This situation will only get worse, and we need to reserve our people for missions where they have some reasonable chance of making a difference."

Monty loosened his tie and stretched back in his chair. As he often did when he was mulling over a difficult decision, he tapped one finger on the tabletop. "I don't want to needlessly sacrifice our ops any more than you do," he said quietly. "I wish to hell someone would come up with an antivirus. But, barring that, we need to limit our involvement for now to this urgent missive from MIS." He reached for the decoded transmission that had been sent overnight from the Military Intelligence Service.

"All the bullshit involved in gaining access to confidential medical records is bogging down official efforts to track down the patient zeros. That's where we come in. We'll send two ops to each of the five hospitals that reported the first cases—in Beijing, Munich, Cali, Kinshasa, and Dallas—and have Reno standing by here to hack into databases as needed." He selected ten personnel files from the stack and split them into five piles. "We need to determine the patient zeros, see if there's any commonality, and try to determine how, when, where, and by whom they were infected."

"I'll start working on the logistics while you contact them," Joanne said. "And make sure all the teams get this experimental serum."

"They'll also need high-quality respirator masks and latex gloves," Monty said. "The best you can get. Even that crappy shit is probably long sold out where most of these people are. And issue orders they're to always wear them when in contact with others. No exceptions." He leaned back and went quiet for a moment, only vaguely aware of the muted cadence of his tap-tap-tap against the smooth surface of the polished wood beneath his finger. "I hope to God that after all these people have been through we don't lose any of them to this damned bug."

❖

Baltimore, Maryland
October 18

Luka Madison carefully set the breakfast tray on the nightstand and sat on the edge of the bed, instinctively matching her breathing to the slow rise and fall of Hayley Ward's chest. Their nearly three years together had been the most blissful she'd ever known, and with any luck, they'd soon have a new reason to celebrate their union.

"Time to get up, honey." She gently brushed a lock of strawberry blond hair away from Hayley's face. She wished they could spend the day together, but Hayley had to cover an important congressional committee meeting for the *Baltimore Dispatch* in a couple of hours.

Hayley groaned and snuggled deeper under the plush comforter. "Ten more minutes."

"Your pancakes will get cold."

Hayley cracked open one eye and spotted the breakfast tray. Yawning, she pulled herself up to a sitting position and rested her back against the headboard. "You're just too good to me. I can't wait to see how you spoil me when—"

The jarring ring of Luka's cell phone startled them both. Hayley frowned when Luka checked the caller ID and nodded. They'd talked about the likelihood that the EOO would summon her again, though she'd only been home a few days from her last mission. The news was full of the growing pandemic, and Hayley had written several virus-related stories for the paper. But both had hoped it wouldn't happen this soon.

"Sorry, honey." Luka grabbed the phone and kissed Hayley's forehead before heading toward the living room to take the call. She trusted Hayley totally, but the secrecy was for Hayley's own safety. She flipped open the phone. "Domino," she answered, relaying her operative code number as required.

Montgomery Pierce was his usual succinct self. That man wasted no words on occasions like this. "Andrews. Tomorrow. Oh-seven-hundred hours." Andrews Air Force Base, just an hour away from Hayley's two-bedroom apartment, was Luka's most frequent jumping-off point for missions, especially overseas.

"Are we protected against this?" she asked.

"Not completely."

"Didn't think so." She was silent for several moments, and to her surprise, Pierce waited patiently. Finally, she said, "I'll be there."

"Domino?"

"Sir?"

"Take care of…matters." Montgomery Pierce seldom if ever sounded worried. If he was asking her to 'take care of matters,' he wanted her to let Hayley know that this was a high-risk operation with less than usual guarantees.

"I intend to." She flipped the cell closed and turned to find Hayley poised at the doorway, watching her. Her heart broke at Hayley's worried expression. Luka went to her, and they embraced without words for several long moments.

"How long will you be gone?" Hayley whispered.

"However long it takes. Too long."

❖

Venice, Italy

"Must you?"

"I must," Mishael Taylor told her lover, Kristine Marie-Louise van der Jagt, who was comfortably sprawled on a lounge chair on their villa balcony. "You know how cranky I get when I don't get my horsepower fix. I won't be long."

"If you get another ticket, they'll confiscate the boat," Kris reminded her unnecessarily. "And I don't like you taking such risks right now."

Kris's protective attitude warmed Misha; it had blossomed into near-paranoia as the virus swept toward them from all directions. She understood the feeling all too well because she was just as determined that Kris stay safe. They hadn't ventured outside since she'd returned from her last mission four days ago and were having their groceries delivered.

She looked out over the canal in front of the villa. This time of day, it should be crowded with gondolas, delivery barges, and private vessels of every description. But in the last hour, they'd seen only two wood-trimmed water taxis, a lone floating greengrocer, and a police boat on patrol.

"Hardly anyone's on the water. Just a few ripples, I promise." Kris was right. She'd ignored the canal speed limit too often. The local cops knew her Lancia speedboat on sight now and she refused to give them any reason to confiscate it. She'd force herself to drive slowly until she got beyond the city limits and out on the open water. As she bent down to kiss her lover good-bye, her cell phone rang.

Kris sat up abruptly, her features darkening. "Is it…?"

Reluctantly, Misha checked the caller ID and nodded. Retreating into the house out of earshot, she flipped open the phone and sighed loudly into the receiver before identifying herself. "Allegro 020508. So, has the plague put a damper on your love life?" In truth, she thought it was wonderful that Monty Pierce and Joanne Grant had finally gotten together after who knew how many years of denying their attraction because of EOO rules that banned fraternization. But she enjoyed poking fun at her straight-laced boss.

"Are you fully mobile?" he replied.

She'd sprained her ankle a week earlier jumping off a second-story balcony in Turkey. But she'd been taking it easy since her return home, lounging in bed or on the terrace, and was almost back to normal. "No. Right now a beautiful woman is pinning me to a vertical position."

"Allegro—"

"Oh, you mean have I recovered? Yeah, sure."

"Be at Aviano by nineteen-hundred hours tomorrow," Pierce said. The nearest U.S. Air Force base to their Venice home was roughly sixty-five miles away, a ninety-minute drive for most people. But Misha routinely covered the distance in half the time in the Bugatti Veyron she kept garaged on the mainland.

"Let me guess," she said cheekily.

"No."

"I'm about to live dangerously, not that that's a challenge, and ignore that," Misha replied. "So, the excrement made physical contact with a hydroelectric-powered, oscillating-air-current distribution device. In other words, the shit's hit the fan regarding a certain deadly virus and you want me to find out who put it out there?"

"Be there."

The man had no sense of humor at all.

"Yes, master. I hear and obey."

CHAPTER THIRTEEN

Guaviare Jungle, Colombia
October 18

Zoe's stomach rumbled as she peered out through the gap between the boards of her hut, watching the other hostages line up at the kitchen tent. Her hunger and thirst had become so acute that she'd pay anything for a simple glass of water and gladly suffer another plate of the gooey beans and rice she'd eaten two days prior. She'd been furious at the rebel doctor for nearly force-feeding her, but the woman had done her a huge favor. Without that nourishment, her only real meal in days, she'd probably have been too weak by now to even attend to her most basic needs.

As the doctor had predicted, her initial refusal to eat had repercussions. The whole next day she'd been ignored. No one had come near her hut or even acknowledged her screams and curses of protest. Besides denying her food and water, they hadn't come to empty her waste bucket so the hut reeked of her own excrement. And the bandages on her feet badly needed changing. For a short while, after the doctor's treatment, they'd begun to feel a little better. But she'd moved around so much the day before they'd begun to bleed again, and the restraint had rubbed her left ankle raw. Now she could barely stand without excruciating pain.

"Please!" she shouted, to no one in particular. Her tongue was swollen, her mouth parched. "This is inhumane! I need food and water!"

No one answered or even looked her way. If they ignored her for another day, she would be in serious trouble.

The doctor might have helped. Though judgmental, she seemed more compassionate than the rest of these animals. And other things set her apart from the other rebels Zoe had come in contact with since her kidnapping. The medic was definitely less coarse and crude, and more intelligent—her English was quite fluent. But Zoe hadn't seen the woman since the night before last. Perhaps she'd been sent to another camp. If so, Zoe had no one to turn to.

The line for food got shorter, and still no one came to get her. She had about given up hope when the rebel chief gestured her way while talking to another guerrilla, a stocky, bearded man. The second man nodded and headed toward her hut.

"About time," she murmured under her breath as the rebel entered and bent to release her from her ankle cuff. He yanked the chain violently, which pulled her off her feet and sent her crashing to the dirt. Pain shot up her shoulder when she hit the hard ground, but she said nothing, refusing to give him the satisfaction of knowing he'd hurt her.

He smiled anyway and unlocked the restraint, then jerked her to her feet with an iron grip around one bicep. Pushing her along, he shoved her through the doorway and she fell again. The man only leered down at her with a laugh, and the rebels watching them joined in, amused at her plight.

She wanted to scream at them but held her tongue, knowing any further protests would only abort any chance she had at food and water. She got shakily to her knees, but before she could get to her feet the rebel again clamped his hand around her arm, this time dragging her toward the kitchen fire pit.

Once there, he released her and returned to his companions.

Zoe gathered her remaining strength and struggled to stand. Her hand shook as it reached into the wooden crate for a bowl and spoon. Three rebels were ahead of her in line. Could she stay upright long enough to get to the cooking pot? When she did, the same cook in her filthy apron watched Zoe as she scooped out a ladle of foul-smelling soup for herself. Her bowl was only half full, so she reached for another, but the cook barked something in Spanish and grabbed the ladle. Zoe held back a retort, then greedily downed a big gulp of the greasy concoction before making her way unsteadily toward a nearby stump to sit.

She had to get out of here. The rebels obviously didn't care whether their hostages lived or died. The prospect of spending months, maybe years in these conditions, suffering under this brutality, was inconceivable. When she finished her soup, she staggered toward a makeshift table where four of the other hostages were huddled, talking in low voices. Marcella, the Italian woman she'd met; Willy, the tall blond Australian; and the dark-haired man and young woman she guessed were father and daughter.

"How are you?" Marcella asked gently as she joined them.

"Not so great."

The Italian woman held out her flask of water, and Zoe drank from it greedily. "Thanks."

"In the beginning, they are very hard on new people," Marcella said. "They want to break you so you will be quiet. Not cause trouble or try to escape. It is best to go along, or you will only make things more difficult for yourself." She turned to the dark-haired strangers sharing her bench. "This is my husband, Tino, and my daughter Octavia." Both acknowledged Zoe with sympathetic smiles.

"These people are animals." Zoe drained the meager remnants of her soup. "I had no idea people could be so cruel."

Willy, the blond Aussie, snorted. "Doubt you have any real idea yet of what these whackers are capable of. Cut your throat if ya look at 'em wrong." He had a bit of soup left in his bowl, as did Tino, and both men silently pushed them toward Zoe. She accepted the offerings with a smile of thanks and gulped those down, too.

"Some are worse than others," Marcella said. "That one there…" She nodded toward a brutish hulking rebel with a pot belly. "Don't be alone with him if you can help it. Or him." She indicated another man with a subtle glance left. "They are the worst. They will hurt you if you do not let them…do things."

The implication was clear. The threat of rape was something Zoe hadn't dared consider. She shuddered. "Have you…did they…?" How did you ask someone such a thing?

"Not me. Or my daughter. I think because Tino is here. But Kylee…she has suffered much."

"I can't protect her." Willy's hands tightened into fists. "They keep her isolated most of the time on the other side of camp."

"Kylee?" Zoe remembered the painfully thin blond woman she'd seen when she arrived.

"Kylee and I were working for a humanitarian-aid group when we were taken," Willy said. "She's in a bad way. Doesn't talk much now and might lose her leg, I think, if they don't get her out of here soon. Bad infection."

"Where is the doctor?" Zoe asked. "Why isn't she taking care of her?"

"I heard one of the rebels say she was sent to another camp to treat someone. She's done what she can, I reckon," Willy replied. "She's really just a medic, and she doesn't have a lot in the way of supplies. Kylee needs to be in a hospital."

"Is the doctor coming back?" Despite her irritation with the woman, Zoe fervently wished she were still here.

"*Non lo so…* I don't know," Marcella said. "Everyone—rebels and hostages—we all get moved. No one says to us when or to where."

Zoe scanned the camp, noting the positions of the guards at the perimeter. "Has anyone ever escaped from here?"

"It is suicide to try," Tino said in a thick Italian accent. "There are traps and guards everywhere, and they will track you easily. If they do not shoot you on the spot, they will make things even worse for you. They had two Colombian policemen here when I arrived, and they tried to escape. One was killed, the other was starved to death. Besides, even if you made it away, where would you go? There is nothing here but jungle. You would not survive. Believe me, if I could get my family out of here, I would."

Zoe's depression deepened. Until she was released or found a way to escape, she would have to make the best of it. "I'll go crazy being cooped up all day, chained like a dog, without even the bare necessities. And I'm so filthy I can't stand myself."

"That will change once you stop fighting them. You'll be given work to do—find wood, work with crops and animals, keep the fire going. It will pass the time and get you out of your hut," Marcella replied. "And they do take us to the river to wash now and then."

"If you want things like a comb, toothbrush, or candle," Willy said, "you can usually get them. But they're special favors for those who work hard and don't complain or make trouble. Sometimes you have to give something in return," he added vaguely, looking uncomfortable. "At another camp I was at, a few even got books, pillows, and radios. The radios were a real luxury, because sometimes we could hear messages from family and friends. They play 'em on a station in Bogota."

To hear her father's voice saying that he loved her and was working to get her free would certainly help keep her sane. But was she willing to become a docile sheep?

She stared at two ants, making their way to the few crumbs on the table. Probably left over from the night before, since she hadn't seen any bread served this morning. She gently coaxed one onto her finger and watched the disoriented struggle as it tried to make its way back to the familiar surface of warm wood. Her skin was probably just as foreign to the creature as this environment was for her.

Did the bug realize that whether it got to eat, live, or die was up to the human holding it? Strange how their lives were on a disturbingly similar path.

Zoe rested her hand on the table and the ant ran toward the morsel. It was almost there when a big hand came down from behind her and crushed it.

The soldier grabbed her roughly by the arm. "You get wood now."

Zoe didn't move. She was so upset by the bug's brutal end, the sad finality of its fate, after it struggled so hard to get to the food that would sustain it, that she didn't register the pain in her arm. She looked up at the soldier hovering over her and wanted to hurt him, scream, and run. She wanted to be put back down too, so that she could return to her life. But she feared that if she tried to fight she would end in the same crushing manner. She wasn't prepared to die, and just like that little ant, she'd do anything to get back on her own path.

Zoe stood up. "Of course," she said, and the soldier poked her toward the jungle with his rifle. If bowing to these men was what it took to hear her father's voice over the radio, to help her stay focused on her own morsel of hope, that's exactly what she'd do.

❖

London, England
October 19

As the clock on his mantel chimed the half hour, Derrick stared out the window of his den at the darkness beyond. Dawn was still two hours away. He'd tried to catch some sleep, but whenever he shut his eyes he could only picture Zoe and imagine the worst. Her terrified expression in the proof-of-life photo was burned into his brain. Colombia was six hours behind London, so it was eleven-thirty p.m. there now. He prayed that Zoe was sleeping soundly, finding some brief escape from her real-life nightmare in a pleasant dream.

He paced, full of restless energy, waiting for the phone to ring with an update from the negotiator Jamie Farnsworth. Something was wrong. He could feel it. If the scheduled radio contact with the FARC had happened as planned, surely there would be some news to relate by now.

When the phone finally pealed, Derrick snatched it up before the second ring. "I'm here. How is she?"

"Sorry, Derrick." It was Collier Morris. "Farnsworth hasn't called you, then, I take it?"

"No. Not yet. Is this a bad sign? It's been an hour since they were supposed to make contact, and Jaime said the rebels usually keep these things fairly brief for security reasons."

"I wouldn't worry until there's reason to, Derrick. It could be any number of things. Radio interference. Maybe they're doing a back-and-forth every few minutes, which could be a positive sign. Or perhaps the rebel negotiator deliberately missed the appointed time. They do that sometimes, to make the families sweat. Make them more anxious so they'll pay the asking price."

"I feel so helpless just sitting around here." He'd wanted to go to Bogota, but Morris and Farnsworth both had advised against it. "Can't I do something to speed this up? I mean, of course I'm trying everything possible to raise as much as I can for the ransom, but surely I can do something."

"I know it's difficult, but try to be patient. These things take time. Your focus is right where it needs to be, on raising the money." There was a long pause on the other end of the line. "I don't want to get your hopes up, Derrick," Morris finally said. "And I can't go into specifics. But let's just say I know of some contacts who are trying to help. Contacts well-positioned to find out exactly where Zoe's being held. And perhaps ensure she's kept safe and looked after, as much as possible, until her release."

"What are you saying? That these contacts are actually with her, right now?"

"No. I don't know that," he replied. "Like I said, I don't want to get your hopes up. But just know more's going on than just Jamie's negotiations. Speaking of which, we'd better keep this line free so he can reach you. I'll ring you later. Stay strong."

Derrick was relieved that Collier's high-level position in the intelligence community was getting them expert behind-the-scenes help to keep Zoe safe. But it didn't lessen his anxiety about why he hadn't heard from his man in Bogota.

To pass the time, Derrick switched on the television and tuned to the BBC. This global pandemic was worrisome. His airline was suffering staggering losses as the virus spread and people stopped flying. He'd have trouble finding a buyer if he had to sell Skye Lines to pay the ransom, and the value of the company was shrinking by the day. Some of his own employees had been infected.

Most troubling, the virus was racing through Colombia. It was far worse there than in Britain, and Zoe might become infected. However, Farnsworth had said she was most likely being held in a remote mountain location, many miles from the hard-hit cities. That should lessen her chances of becoming a victim. Of course she would be far from any adequate medical help, not that doctors anywhere seemed to be able to keep people from dying.

He tried not to picture Zoe lying on some godforsaken filthy cot in the jungle, wretchedly sick and coughing up blood like the victims on television. And perhaps even dying there, alone, her body dumped into an unmarked shallow grave. But the images persisted, driving him nearly mad.

When the phone rang again, he nearly jumped out of his skin.

Jamie Farnsworth got straight to the point. "They've reduced the ransom demand from fifty million to forty. It's only a token concession, and about what I expected at this early stage. They're still demanding two million immediately to ensure her safety. I countered with a quarter of a million; they're considering that and will call me back in an hour. We should give them something in return for the proof of life, but it has to be a fraction of what they're asking. As I told you before, if we give them too much too soon, the FARC will drag this out for months or years. And they'll be much less willing to come down on the final number."

Farnsworth's counteroffer was roughly one hundred sixty-five thousand pounds. Derrick had stretched himself so thin to keep the company going that even this initial down payment would nearly empty his bank account. But he'd call his bank when it opened and ask a few friends for some short-term loans, if the rebels demanded more. "Did they say any more about Zoe's condition?"

"I'm afraid not," Farnsworth replied. "Nothing beyond the usual bullshit that a quick payment will ensure her safety. I told them we'd require another proof of life when we wire the money, and further proof every week until this situation is resolved."

"I need her out of there, Jaime. Time is critical with this damn virus sweeping through Colombia."

"I know that, Derrick. I'm seeing it all around me." Derrick detected the first hint of worry in Farnsworth's normally placid tone. "At least I got them to agree to a contact every twenty-four hours, instead of every three days," he said. "That's something. I'll call you when I know more."

Derrick hung up and went to his desk drawer to withdraw the proof-of-life photo. Slumping into the chair, he traced his fingertips lightly over Zoe's image, stroking her face. Then he broke down, wailing aloud and slamming his fist against the desk so hard that a loud knock soon sounded on the door. His housekeeper, awakened in her room one floor above.

"Mister Howe? Are you all right, sir?"

No, I'm not all right, he wanted to scream. Nothing will ever be right until she's safe at home with me again.

CHAPTER FOURTEEN

Munich, Germany
October 19

The EOO booked Allegro and Domino into adjoining suites at the Hotel Regent, a four-star establishment centrally located near the city's main railway station. As Luka surveyed her plush room, automatically checking for listening devices, she nodded approvingly when she noticed the double-soundproofed windows. It was dark outside, so she could see herself clearly in the glass. As usual, her medium brown hair badly needed cutting. It fell well below her shoulders and her bangs kept getting in her eyes. She had no obsession with her looks, none of the preoccupation with hair and makeup that most women did. And during her home time between assignments, she much preferred to spend every minute with Hayley than in a salon.

She had been informed en route only that she would be teamed with Misha and that one of their European contacts would brief them at twenty-three hundred hours. She was given a duffel bag that contained several respiratory masks, latex gloves, and the weapons and high-tech equipment they might need for their assignment. It also held two syringes containing an experimental antiflu vaccine. She'd injected herself with one when the military jet took off from Andrews. The other was for Misha.

Luka sat on the edge of the bed and switched on the TV. Even that simple act made her think of Hayley. Before they met, she'd preferred to distract herself by listening to music and setting up dominos—her *bones*—in elaborate layouts that covered the polished wood floor of her sparsely furnished suburban Washington condo. She hadn't even owned a television.

But falling in love had changed all that. She'd given up the condo, moving into Hayley's warmly cluttered apartment; and snuggling together on the couch, sharing popcorn over the latest Netflix film, gave her immense joy.

As Luka flipped through the channels, she happened upon a news bulletin and paused to listen. The German reporter was relaying the country's latest death toll. A recap of the "temporary" restrictions the government had enacted to deal with the growing pandemic followed. An eleven p.m. curfew had been imposed in the major cities. Only emergency personnel and health-care workers were exempt. Strict fines were being levied against citizens found stockpiling an unusual quantity of food and those who were profiteering from the crisis.

The grim situation here had been brought home to her when she'd landed at ten p.m. Normally the city center would have been bustling with people headed to and from bars, restaurants, and movie theaters. But the streets were virtually empty. All the cafes were closed, and the few pedestrians who dared venture out were wearing medical masks.

Luka was desperate to call home to check on Hayley, but private phone calls while on a job were prohibited. Just as well. Hayley had the day off, and it was four in the afternoon in Baltimore, a time when she often liked to indulge in a nap.

Luka had picked up the TV remote to seek something more positive to distract herself, when she heard footsteps in the hall, followed by the slamming of a door nearby. She smiled to herself even before she heard the all-too-familiar voice through the thin walls.

"Hi, honey, I'm hoooome."

She went to the adjoining door and opened it. Mishael stood on the other side. They were dressed alike, in dark jeans and black, long-sleeved T-shirts. The outfit was almost de rigueur for ops on the job. Misha, at five-eight, was two inches taller, but the thick rubber soles of Luka's black boots nearly made up the difference.

Hands on hips, Misha silently studied Luka as well, from behind a pale green surgical mask. Only the glint in her soft caramel eyes told Luka she was smiling.

"You plan to keep that on?" Luka smiled back.

"Yup, I'm accessorizing."

"And keeping your lame mug from the world at the same time. Win, win."

"Freak," Misha said, and took a step forward.

"Lunatic," Luka replied as she did the same.

"God, I've missed you." Misha ripped off the mask and embraced Luka. "It's been too damn long."

They hugged for several long moments, Luka the first to reluctantly pull away from their embrace. It was true. Fifteen months had passed since she and Hayley had visited Misha and Kris in Venice. Misha's dark brown hair was a little longer than usual, well below her collarbones. And though she was only thirty-six, the first tiny signs of crow's feet had begun to appear, marring the smooth skin of her face. "Every time we try to make it to Europe, I either get an art-restoration gig or an assignment."

"I know what you mean," Misha said. "I hate that it takes a friggin' pandemic to see you. I gotta tell you, retirement is looking better all the time."

"Maybe, but I'd prefer some personal time while I'm still young enough to enjoy it."

"Speak for yourself. I intend to keep going strong until I'm at least ninety."

The statistics weren't with them. They'd both seen too many of their fellow ops cut down in their prime. "I hope you're right."

"I'm always right," Misha joked.

Luka gave her a lopsided smile.

Misha, apparently disappointed not to get the usual sarcastic retort from her, sat in a high-backed armchair by the window. She pointed to its twin. "Take a load off, and pull up a memory or two. Dilbert won't be here for another thirty."

Luka didn't get the reference. It wasn't their contact's name, and her expression must have relayed her cluelessness.

"I can't help it if the guy looks like a cartoon," Misha explained.

It took her several seconds to connect the dots, and she was only able to because the syndicated strip appeared in Hayley's paper. She wasn't a big follower of popular culture. But Misha was right—their guy had the same flat-top, round glasses, and geeky ambience as his comic-strip counterpart. She smiled. "Come to think of it."

Misha laughed. "So? Come on. Sit."

Luka sat with a sigh.

"So what's eating you?" Misha asked, studying her intently. "I mean, except the lung-eating virus."

Most of the time, she envied Misha's ability to keep a positive attitude no matter what. But considering the current circumstances, Luka found her demeanor mystifying. "Isn't that enough? Aren't you worried?"

"Sure. Who isn't?"

"You don't sound it."

Misha rose and walked to the mini-bar. "Water, over-priced nuts, or wine? Go crazy, Monty's paying."

"Water's fine."

Misha threw her a bottle of Evian from across the room, then paced as she took a long swig from one of her own. She finally stopped. "In fact, I'm terrified." She wiped a drop of water from her chin. "I don't know what I'd do if anything happened to Kris, or you, or Hayley. But I don't want to think about it too much. It's pointless and…depressing."

"How can you not think about it?"

"That's the difference between you and me, Luka. I'm a half-full kinda gal," Misha replied seriously. "I will not allow this virus or whatever else comes after this to stand in the way of my happiness. Not after I waited so long to find it. I intend to do whatever I can to stop whomever or whatever is behind this. That's my focus. That's what's keeping me from screaming out my fear. You, on the other hand…" She seemed to be reconsidering what she'd been about to say. But the implication was clear.

"I what, Misha? I'm here, aren't I?"

"But you wish you weren't. You wish you could run and hide and keep Hayley safe by closing the two of you off from the world."

"So what? Now you're calling me a coward?" Luka fought to contain her growing annoyance over Misha's assessment. "Just because I'm aware of this screwed-up situation? I'm a coward because I want to protect the woman I love?"

"There are more ways to protect her. Do it by ending this."

Luka stood and faced her. "And that's another difference between us. I'm realistic and you're overinflated." Misha's flippancy was increasingly irritating her. Normally she found it charming or funny, but right now, too many things were at stake.

Misha approached her slowly from across the room. Luka expected her to be irritated as well, but instead, Misha stopped in front of her and put her hand on Luka's shoulder.

"Yeah, I'm cocky. But you know what? It works for me. Being here, right now, knowing we could possibly make a difference and, more important, keep the ones we love safe, simply…works for me," she repeated.

Each op had their own way of dealing with the life-and-death situations they faced, and Misha's tactic had always been to face things head-on, with humor and a touch of arrogance. Luka couldn't fault her for that, because it had helped Misha succeed, and survive.

"And the best part," Misha said, "is that I get a shot at it with my best friend. My wing woman. A very resourceful and competent individual I have always been able to count on."

Luka's irritation departed as quickly as it had flamed. "Same here."

"Hayley is the luckiest woman on the planet to have you." Misha wrapped an arm around Luka's shoulder and squeezed. "You could never disappoint her. The two of you will be fine."

Luka looked away as tears burned her eyes.

"There's more, isn't there?" Misha said softly.

Luka didn't see any point in denying it. She needed someone to talk to, someone she could trust, and that had always been Misha. "There could be three of us," she said.

Misha chuckled and released her, clearly not getting the message. "Well, I didn't know you guys swung that way but—"

"Hayley could be pregnant." It was the first time she'd said the words to anyone, and they came out barely above a whisper.

Misha laughed. "Sorry?" She'd turned away and was headed toward the duffel bag of equipment. "I thought you said Hayley was pregnant."

"I did."

Misha froze and turned to her, wide-eyed and mute.

"If you keep staring like that, your eyes will pop out," Luka said when long seconds passed with no change.

Misha plopped on the bed. "How?"

"Obviously not the traditional way."

"Donor?"

"Yes."

"Sperm bank?"

"No."

Misha frowned. "Are you gonna tell, or are we going to play twenty questions?"

"Are you upset?"

"I'm not sure." Misha looked a bit bewildered.

"The donor's her brother." Luka sat beside her on the bed.

Misha shook her head and stared down at the floor. "That's dangerous, not to mention…incestuous."

"Neither. The—"

Misha's head shot up and she turned to Luka, wide-eyed again. "Oh, my God. The baby is yours."

"Technically, yes."

"She's carrying your child."

"Our child."

"Huh?" Misha's eyes were glazed. "Oh, sure. Yeah."

"Hayley insisted it be my child. She wanted to give me the ultimate gift. Her way of telling me that although I was adopted and don't even know my family, my roots are just as important. That I count."

Misha didn't respond, and Luka couldn't read her expression. "Are you okay?"

Misha got up and walked over to look out the window to the dark beyond. "Do they know?" she asked without turning around.

Luka knew she was referring to the governing trio. "Not yet."

Misha went silent again as she continued to stare out the window.

Luka finally broke the quiet and got to her feet. "Say something." Misha was the last person to ever judge her, and would keep her secrets. But she didn't know what to make of the quiet storm that was clearly brewing in Misha. "Look, I know it's against the organization's policy but I…we both want this so much. I've always wanted to belong to a family, a real family." She put her hands on Misha's shoulders from behind, but Misha still didn't turn around or say anything.

"Hayley is the woman of my dreams, like Kris is yours," Luka said. "She keeps me sane. And you…" she added, shaking her. "You're my sister, my confidant, and my savior in many cases. But…"

"You want to give a child the life you never had," Misha said quietly.

"Yes."

Misha finally turned and looked at her. Her eyes were red, and a single tear made its way down her cheek. "I'm so happy for you, Luka. For both of you. I'll make sure nothing happens to the runt or its mothers."

Luka wrapped her in her arms, and Misha embraced her tight. A knock at the door interrupted the moment.

Luka looked at her watch. "It's Dilbert."

"Hold on," Misha shouted. "We're in bed…naked."

Luka rolled her eyes. She was about to walk to the door when Misha grabbed her wrist.

"You have to promise me two things."

"Name them." Luka grinned.

"One, that I'm present when you tell Monty about Luka Junior." Misha smiled back, that familiar mischief in her eyes.

"Why?"

"Because it'll make this month's traffic violations pale in comparison, and I'll look good for once." She grinned. "And two, I get to be the godmother."

"We don't even know if the embryo implantation has taken."

"That's irrelevant. You'll keep trying if it hasn't, so it's just a matter of time. That's why I'm calling dibs."

Luka laughed. "As long as you don't get to teach the kid how to drive."

"That's inevitable." Misha waved one hand absently as though the matter wasn't up for discussion. "She or he will have to learn from the best. Deal?"

"Deal."

Misha crossed to the door just as Dilbert knocked again. "We're coming," she shouted again. "Real hard."

Both of them laughed as she opened the door, but then it was down to business. Their mission had begun.

❖

"The first cases were reported here on October ninth, with the first deaths a day later. That would mean the patient zero was infected sometime around October third, give or take forty-eight hours. Beijing time frame was about the same," their contact said. "The Kinshasa, Cali, and Dallas outbreaks all followed by a day or more, so Munich may have been the first location targeted." Dilbert sat on the couch, with Luka and Domino flanking him. Before them on the coffee table lay various documents the contact had brought.

"The outbreak probably started on the University of Munich campus, because the bulk of the first cases were either students or teachers admitted to the medical center there. The hospital's the second largest of its kind in Germany, with nine thousand staff members and twenty-three hundred beds." Dilbert extracted several sheets of paper from the pile: a campus map and computer printouts with staffing lists and other relevant information.

"This university do research with viruses?" Domino asked.

"Yes. The Max von Pettenkofer Institute houses the Departments of Virology and Bacteriology. Both do research and lab diagnostics of infectious diseases, and work in close conjunction with the medical school and university hospital."

"Seems like a long shot someone there would be behind this," Domino mused aloud. "They wouldn't risk choosing a patient zero in their own backyard, unless it was an accident. But we have to rule out that possibility."

"The government and WHO officials have been trying to access the medical records of the initial cases," Dilbert said, "but the requests are still tied up with the hospital's lawyers. So that's the obvious place to start." He pointed to a duffel bag he'd left by the door. "That has everything you might need. Netbook, navigator with blueprints, clothing changes, several different IDs, and so on."

"It's a lot faster for us to retrieve the hospital and school records than to have Reno try to crack those databases," Allegro said. "He can cross-reference whatever we feed him. If we can track the commonality of the initial cases, we should be able to isolate where they were infected."

"What's the situation regarding security around the university buildings?" Domino asked. "Surveillance cams?"

"Pretty good coverage there," Dilbert replied. "They've got cams inside and outside most classroom buildings, faculty offices, within the hospital, and in many parking areas." He indicated the relevant documents. "They keep their digital video records for a year."

Reaching into his pocket, he withdrew a pair of white security cards with magnetic strips and two keys on a ring. "Some of the more sensitive areas of the university—including the research labs and much of the hospital—require passcards. These are masters and will get you in everywhere. The keys are to a white van parked in the lot downstairs."

He got to his feet. "Your boss knows how to reach me if you need anything else. Good luck. You'll need it."

CHAPTER FIFTEEN

Guaviare Jungle, Colombia
October 19

Zoe's willingness to work hard without complaint was rewarded. After several backbreaking hours the day before gathering load after load of firewood, she'd been allowed to move freely about the camp and eat with the other hostages. And a candle stub and box of matches were waiting in her hut that night. She used the feeble light to search the area around the hammock for spiders before she retired, so weak and sore from her labor she had trouble getting comfortable enough to sleep. Then a thunderstorm had blown in a few hours before dawn, making further sleep impossible.

Everything in this environment was reduced to animalistic basics, she thought. The hostages' main objectives were centered on their primal needs for food, water, warmth, shelter, health, and sanity. The rebels treated them as dogs to be trained, doling out an immediate reward for mindless obedience and punishment for misbehavior.

Her feet throbbed. They were badly swollen, and every muscle in her body ached as it never had before. She couldn't endure much more without collapsing. She'd made it through the day before only through sheer determination.

But as awful as her situation was, it was nowhere near as bad as that of the other hostages. They had endured this hell for as long as two years, and Kylee looked to be in danger of losing her life as well as her mind. In the late afternoon, Zoe had been able to spend some time with her, the one hostage she hadn't really talked to yet.

Kylee had been sitting on the ground outside her hut, rocking back and forth with a glazed expression, seemingly unaware of her surroundings. She was so painfully frail and thin it was clear she couldn't survive much longer; her foot was so badly infected the rebels had to carry her everywhere. Zoe sat beside the Aussie for an hour, trying to communicate with her, but Kylee had failed to even acknowledge her presence. Once again, Zoe had wondered where the rebel doctor had gone and whether she'd be back.

Now as she lay in her hammock, Zoe listened to the sounds of the jungle and the camp coming awake, delaying the necessity of putting her weight on her tortured feet. The buzz of insects seemed ever-present, punctuated by the howls of animals and laughter from the rebels. She was beginning to get some sense of the routine and the pecking order of the guerrillas and filed away every detail of everything she saw and heard. Something might be useful if an opportunity arose for escape.

Guards were posted along the perimeter of the camp around the clock, some of them within sight and some not. In the evenings, after the hostages were locked up, off-duty rebels usually gathered around the fire pits for a couple of hours to socialize. Most of them staggered off drunk to their cots. The river where they all bathed was likely close to the camp—Zoe had seen rebels carrying water make a round trip with their buckets in less than ten minutes. Perhaps the waterway could lead her to a village.

A full bladder finally pushed her out of the hammock. After relieving herself in the bucket, she went to peer out toward the kitchen tent. Her stomach was growling, but the cook was only now building up her fire, so breakfast was at least an hour away.

Zoe hated everything about this place, but perhaps most of all she hated her total loss of control. Because she was now totally dependent on someone else's whim, she'd gained a new appreciation for the pampered life she'd led.

Breakfast was a mushy mass of oatmeal, brown sugar, and some unrecognizable, half-rotten fruit. She was hungry, but pushed the bowl away after only a few bites when she found a bug in one of the lumps of fruit.

Marcella joined her, frowning at the uneaten food, and patted Zoe's hand sympathetically. "They are taking us to the water later, to bathe and wash our clothes. It will lift your spirits. You'll see."

Zoe looked down at herself. The pantsuit she had lived in since her kidnapping was so caked with dried mud she could detect only small patches of its original navy color. The arms and legs were badly shredded from the long march here through the thorny underbrush, as was her once-beige silk blouse. She couldn't imagine how foul she must smell after so many days of marching and hard labor without a shower or deodorant. Somehow she'd gotten used to it, except for rare moments when she caught a whiff of herself.

She almost laughed, remembering how she'd once complained when her father's secretary had mistakenly booked her into a three-and-a-half-star hotel during a business trip. How outraged she'd been because the room had no bath salts or down pillows. The bed was too firm, the décor too cheap, the room service inferior.

Amazing how, in only a week, the prospect of being allowed to bathe in a cold jungle stream could suddenly sound like heaven.

Though Fetch hadn't slept for well over sixty hours, she was able to push aside her fatigue and insistent, splitting headache for the long hike back to the camp that held the Western hostages. Her mission demanded her there, so she returned at her first opportunity, trekking alone through the jungle. The noonday sun shot brilliant beams of light through the rare open spaces of the canopy overhead.

In two seconds, she'd gone from fast asleep to alert on her feet, rifle at the ready, when Barriga and another rebel had entered her tent without warning three nights earlier.

The rebel chief told her that a hostage from the neighboring camp had taken ill and she was to leave right away. The FARC didn't give a damn about the well-being of hostages and tended their injuries only because they weren't worth a cent to them dead. It was all about protecting their merchandise.

Fetch had made her cot with military precision, prepared her medical kit, and grabbed a duffel with a change of clothes. She didn't want to leave the hostages she was assigned to, but it would be impossible if not dangerously suspicious to refuse. She also didn't mind a few days away from Zoe Anderson-Howe.

Ever since the Brit had arrived, she'd managed to irritate, infuriate, and disturb Fetch. She wasn't sure why Zoe got under her skin. The woman certainly wasn't the first hostage to fight against her predicament, but she was the first to so bluntly confront the trigger-happy soldiers and play Russian roulette with her own life. Did Zoe not care what happened to her? Or was she really naïve enough to think that her father's money was all the leverage she needed to stay alive? Either way, she'd picked a dangerous course.

She couldn't relate to Zoe's reaction at all. She was used to following orders even if she didn't agree with them, even if the outcome made her miserable. She was a soldier, trained to obey and serve. A soldier was to show initiative in dire situations only, never in regard to her own safety or sanity. Granted, plenty of times since she entered the FARC she'd felt like taking them all out, one at a time. But she had to endure these megalomaniacs and focus only on the hostages.

The only time she'd ever gone against protocol, and while on assignment no less, she had ended up losing all that had ever mattered to her. As much as she hated to admit it, the organization was right. She couldn't even dream of sharing a future with someone.

That said, she couldn't help but wonder how Zoe would cope in her absence. So far she'd managed to keep the Brit alive long enough to get in and out of trouble every few hours. But how long would Zoe survive on her own? She was nothing like Sam, a competent woman and soldier trained to deal with dangerous situations.

Zoe thrived on flirting with adversity. How could she possibly keep Zoe safe without becoming too obvious, especially since it would take a task force to keep her out of trouble? The difference between Sam and Zoe was almost comical. Sam, the cute, blond, girl-next-door type, and Zoe, the bombshell playgirl. Never anyone's girl next door, because rich people don't have neighbors.

But why was she even comparing them? Fetch couldn't put her finger on it, but it had something to do with the way Zoe made her feel when she looked at her. She rubbed her face to force away the memories. She didn't want them and she didn't need them, but mainly they were irrelevant.

Generally, her life was a blank canvas, and she'd learned to find comfort in that fact. Fetch didn't want to ever feel homesick or even miss the comfort of a well-worn pair of jeans. She didn't want to glance at anything animate or inanimate before she shut the door for an assignment. Detachment had helped her stay alive.

Her assignments lasted longer and were more uncertain than those of other ops. As long as she didn't have anything or anyone to miss, or miss her, she could bear these long absences and uncertainties. She especially didn't want anyone worrying about her when she was gone, because someday she wouldn't return. It was only a matter of time, and she didn't want to put anyone through that kind of pain. Especially not someone she loved. Now, more than ever, after Sam's death, she knew what it was like to be left behind to mourn, to have to live with the resulting hollowness.

Fetch was attached only to memories, because she didn't have any power over them. She couldn't walk away from those like she could from everything else. She had tried to, in the months that followed Sam's death, but eventually gave up and was partly relieved. She wanted to hold on to the one person that made her feel more than just a soldier, a trained machine, more than one of the guys. That's all she had been considered most of her life, just one of the guys in the barracks.

Initially, she had fought for her place in a world comprised of and defined by men. She had to prove that she was just as good by being ten times better. She had to accept and silently deal with the sexual and sexist remarks and self-serving compliments, until she became deaf to them. But when Sam looked at her, she'd made her feel what whole platoons of men never had. When Sam had said she was beautiful, Fetch believed her. For the first time, she didn't feel uncomfortable or lied to, that those words were yet another prelude to, "I've had a hard-on for a month so let's fuck."

Sam had made her feel like a woman. Not a lust object, or a soldier, or a buddy, but a desirable woman. God, how she missed that feeling.

Fetch shook off the memories as she neared the camp with Zoe and the other Western hostages. She was ready to collapse. She'd stayed at her patient's bedside the whole time she was at the other encampment. The FARC expected her to save the hostage no matter what, or her own life was on the line. The sleepless nights had taken their toll. Her headache had reached new limits and her heart was booming from exhaustion. She was desperate for a few hours of solitude and rest.

Her spirits lifted slightly when she rounded a bend in the trail and recognized where she was. The river that ran near the camp was just ahead, which meant she was only minutes now from the chance to finally sleep.

As she closed the distance, she heard voices coming from the river. A woman was yelling in English, something about wanting clean clothes. It was Zoe. Fetch suppressed the urge to roll her eyes and picked up her pace.

When she reached the clearing, she spotted Zoe up to her waist in water, her back turned. She was naked, trying to wash her clothes, all the while complaining loudly to one of the female guards on the bank that she needed something new to wear. A handful of other female rebels were in the river as well, bathing and doing their own laundry. Most were ignoring Zoe.

"Just look," she said angrily as she held up her shredded pantsuit and ruined silk blouse. "How the hell do you expect me to get into these again? They're nothing but rags."

She had a point. Most of the time, hostages received a mismatched change of clothing when their own had become too worn out to wear. Most likely, Zoe's big mouth and even bigger attitude had prevented her from getting any favors.

Fetch approached one of the other women guarding Zoe. "What's going on?" she asked in Spanish. Zoe continued to rant to the rebel on the opposite bank, unaware of her presence.

"The British woman is upset about her clothes," the woman replied.

"Then give her something clean to wear."

"That's not my decision," the rebel said. "I want to, especially since she was good yesterday and today."

"Good?" Fetch couldn't believe what she was hearing, but the guard nodded.

"She gathered wood yesterday and helped the cook this morning clean the dishes."

Fetch knew her shock registered on her face. "She did?"

"*Sí*. But the others don't want her to have any special favors. They give her very little to eat, and today she not even eat that. Coming here, she had to sit to rest, she is so weak. If she does not eat more, she will get sick like the other soon."

Fetch walked to the edge of the river. Zoe still had her back turned. Her upper torso was covered with scratches and insect bites. A few looked infected, but more worrisome was the visible outline of her spine. She was losing weight too fast. *Not good.*

"I hear you've been demanding clothes," Fetch called, "and that you've been a lot more accommodating lately. Maybe you deserve them." She tried to sound condescending for the other soldiers' benefit. "I might even arrange something for you if you're extra nice at dinner," she added, hoping she could get Zoe to eat tonight.

Zoe froze when she heard the medic's voice. How long had she been there? She was glad the doc was back, since she was the only person who seemed to care about her well-being. But her ever-present superior tone had already gotten on her nerves. Who the hell was she to determine whether she deserved a damn clean anything?

Ordinarily, Zoe wasn't shy about her body. Most people found her attractive, not that their opinion usually mattered. She was comfortable in her own skin and not the slightest bit prudish. But for some reason, the medic made her all too aware of her nakedness.

She held her ratty blouse to her chest and thought about the best way to respond. Every reaction here had repercussions, both good and bad.

She could swallow her pride and make sure she got new garments, or she could go with her anger, which would get her absolutely nowhere. If she'd learned one thing so far in this hell, it was that, unlike in the real world, playing the obedient zombie got you places.

Zoe slowly turned around, with the biggest smile she could muster. "Yes, I have been a rather good girl today, Doc," she said brightly. "I think I've definitely earned some clean…well, whatever passes here as clothing."

She waded toward the woman, her eyes on the river as she negotiated the rocky bottom, her sore feet protesting every step. A wisp of breeze chilled her wet skin as she emerged, and she shuddered. When she got to the shore, she glanced up and stumbled when she saw the medic's expression.

The doctor was openly staring at the uncovered half of her body. She'd seen that look before, from men and women alike, and had rarely been affected. But this was different.

It was entirely unexpected and inappropriate, especially considering her current situation, but Zoe felt a rush of unexpected warmth at the appreciative ogling. And the sudden realization that the doctor found her attractive made her involuntarily re-examine the medic, knowing she was lesbian. She studied the woman beneath the fatigues, seeing more than just a soldier for the first time.

The doc certainly had a fabulous body, that was apparent, especially since she wore only a pale green tank top and slim-fitting camo pants. The day was warm, and sweat had made the shirt cling to her upper torso, outlining her breasts, the dark areolas of her nipples faintly visible through the thin fabric.

When Zoe's own nipples hardened in response, she forced her gaze upward to the doctor's face. The medic was really beautiful, Zoe realized with a start. Her long, dark lashes framed eyes the color of coffee beans. Smooth, olive skin, high cheekbones, even features. Her short hair was nicely cut and suited her oval face and long neck.

How had she not noticed all this before? Had she been too self-absorbed?

Get a grip. What was she doing? She was in the jungle fighting for her life, and now she was preoccupied with how attractive one of her guards was? Stockholm Syndrome, maybe. She'd read about it—when hostages began to have irrational, positive feelings about their kidnappers.

She forced those thoughts from her mind, determined instead to utilize this new knowledge. The doctor's expression had shifted from confident and in control to uncomfortable in a matter of seconds. She could use that.

If the doc and the other rebels made Zoe's life miserable, then she could try to profit from the doc's weakness. She dropped the shirt from her chest as she walked the rest of the way out of the water, standing naked before the medic. The doctor didn't even try to look away; her eyes were now fixed on Zoe's breasts.

"How nice do you want me to be at dinner?" Zoe asked provocatively. "In other words, what'll it take to get a clean shirt?" She drew closer, practically pushing herself up against the medic. "Well?" Zoe added when the woman didn't reply.

The doctor's gaze traveled upward, to her mouth. "I...uh... food...eat."

"I don't know what you're trying to say, but that came out very 'special needs.'" Zoe smiled and put her hand on the medic's chest, between her breasts.

The doctor finally looked away. "I meant, if you promise to eat tonight, I'll try to get you some clothes." She said it just above a whisper, as though she didn't want the others to hear. "Cover yourself. Now." When she gestured toward a stack of towels on the bank beside them, Zoe could see that the doctor's hand was shaking.

"Or what?" Zoe teased, keeping her hand on the medic's chest. "We won't be able to contain ourselves? We'll finally give in to that undeniable attraction and have a go at it right here? Is that what you want? Will that get me a pair of clean underwear?"

"Don't flatter yourself," the rebel doctor replied, tiredly rubbing her temples. "I realize you're used to getting what you want and who you want, but I am not interested in you."

"I can tell you're a dyke."

"So? You're not my type. And I'm certain I'm not yours. You don't have to screw me to get a pair of panties."

Zoe pulled her hand away. How dare she talk to her like that? She didn't know whether she was hurt, disappointed, or both. But either way, she was angry. "Screw you? I'd rather peel off my skin and jump in a tub of salt."

"I know," the doc said, taking two steps backward. "So what exactly are you trying to accomplish?"

It was one of those rare moments when Zoe didn't know what to say. "I was just..." Just what? What was all this getting her? She was pissing off the one rebel who'd shown any real caring for the hostages. "Nothing."

CHAPTER SIXTEEN

Fetch's headache was blaring so furiously she found it hard to think. This unexpected and confusing interaction with Zoe had disoriented her. She had to end this exchange and get some rest, sort it all out later.

One thing was clear. She certainly couldn't encourage this inexplicable change in Zoe's behavior, whatever the motivation behind it. If she tried this sexual come-on with any of the other rebels, it would have disastrous consequences. She picked up one of the towels from the stack and tossed it to Zoe. "Cover yourself," she repeated, as she feigned an expression of distaste.

Zoe caught the towel and wrapped it around her torso. "Happy?" she snapped.

"Do you care?"

"No. Now do you think you can take your disdain somewhere else?" Zoe stood there dripping, her head held high, her expression one of challenge.

"There's nothing I'd like more, but you need clothes. Wait here while I get you something to wear."

Surprise registered on Zoe's face. "What did I do to deserve such generosity?" she asked sarcastically.

"Just wait here." Fetch was no longer in the mood for conversation. She needed to lie down for a while.

"I'll wait in my hut."

"You can't enter the camp looking like that." Fetch forced herself to remain aloof, but she was having a hard time keeping her eyes off Zoe's chest. The towel was so small it barely covered Zoe's ample breasts, exposing far too much cleavage, and ended just below the dark triangle of hair she'd glimpsed at the apex of her thighs.

"You should have thought about that before you allowed me to wash my rags. How did you think I would walk about without a change?"

"Like the rest. With your clothes wet."

Zoe looked shocked. "You're all animals," she shouted.

The female guerrilla standing nearby turned in their direction, as did some of the women bathing in the river.

"Keep your voice down," Fetch said between her teeth.

"Don't tell me what to do." Zoe's hands, at her sides, became fists. "You've all been ordering me around and treating me like a friggin' criminal. How much more humiliation will I have to endure in this hell? Why hasn't anyone sent for me?" Tears sprang to her eyes.

"I told you, it takes time." Fetch knew she should appear cold and indifferent, but how could she blame this woman for wanting to get the hell out of here?

"How much bloody more time? Days, weeks, months? What? Some of these people have been here for years."

Fetch couldn't lie. "Probably later than sooner."

Zoe just stood there, her face expressionless but for the tears now streaming down her face. Fetch wanted to put her arm around her to comfort her but couldn't.

"I told myself this morning that if I complied, if I played nice, I would manage to make the best of this hellish situation," Zoe said. "Maybe even…I don't know, convince you to let me go for good behavior. But then I remembered the other hostages. They've been here so long most don't even know what month it is. Some look like they don't even care anymore. And that one, the Aussie… Kylee? I think she's simply gone mad. She was plucking out her hair and eyebrows this morning. I tried to talk to her and get her to stop, but she was completely out of it. Finally she just collapsed, and they dragged her back to her hut like a lamb being taken away for slaughter. Nothing I do will matter, will it?" She stared off mournfully into the distance.

"Nobody gets out of here for good behavior," Fetch said softly. "I'm sorry."

"Sorry?" Zoe looked at her, a sudden storm brewing in her deep blue eyes.

"I realize this is a horrible situation for you but it's not—"

"Sorry?" Zoe repeated, louder. "Are you kidding me? Sorry is what you say to someone for accidentally stepping on their toe, not deliberately ripping away their life."

"It can't be any other way."

Zoe took a deep breath. "Look, I'll do whatever it takes. Get me out of here and I'll pay you whatever you want. I won't even go to the police," she pleaded.

Fetch had heard all this before. Desperate hostages would promise virtually anything.

"Not that I could lead them back to this place anyway," Zoe mumbled almost to herself as she scanned the dense jungle around them.

"It's not about personal gain," Fetch said. "I have no need for money." That was one of the few truths she'd spoken so far. Fetch did her job because she believed in her cause. She wanted to help and save people. Sure, the EOO paid well, like most private organizations, but she kept only a fraction to support herself. Her lifestyle was very low-maintenance, and she didn't see the point of wasting her money on ridiculous luxuries when she could use it to help others instead. The bulk of her earnings went to charities and research institutions. Foundations, like Doctors Without Borders and War Child.

"Of course. The money is for your noble cause," Zoe shot back. "Tell me again how drug trafficking fits in that righteous…"

Fetch watched a transformation take place. Zoe closed her eyes and took a deep breath, as though she was calming her anger and reconsidering what she was saying.

When she opened them again she smiled, and her tone changed from sarcastic to seductive. "None of my business, is it?" She stepped forward and ran a finger slowly down Fetch's chest. "My judging you will not make things better for me."

"No, it w…won't," Fetch stuttered as Zoe slowly traced a path down her stomach.

"But I can offer something your precious cause can't," she added provocatively. "Don't push me away again, Doc. I know you want me." Zoe cupped Fetch's face tenderly with one hand. "You're a beautiful woman."

Fetch grabbed her wrist. There it was again. Those same words, said all too often. "Don't say that," she snapped as she pushed Zoe's hand away. "We've already been through this." She wanted to feel indifferent, or used, like all those other countless times when men and women had tried to seduce her just to get something from her. That was clearly Zoe's motivation as well.

Why, then, did her heart want to believe Zoe was being sincere? And why did Zoe make her feel as Sam had, looking at her that way, like she *was* a beautiful, desirable woman? She wanted to look away, but Zoe's gaze held her fast. Her stomach was full of butterflies; she had to stop where this was going. "If I wanted to have you I would. I don't need your permission."

"But that would be rape," Zoe said. "And you don't look like the type."

"You don't know my type."

"I know you're not like the rest," Zoe stated with conviction. "You wouldn't be a doctor otherwise. You help and heal people. I can see your compassion when you're around the other hostages. I felt it when you tended to my wounds. Frankly, I don't understand why you're here."

Fetch shrugged. "Just doing my job."

"Maybe, but there's more." Zoe studied her, head tilted to one side, gaze unflinching. "You're not as detached as you think. Not when you're around us. Seeing the Aussie woman like this pains you. I've seen you sneak food into her hut. You care, though you almost seem to hate that you do. In fact, you seem remote only when you're around your own."

Fetch didn't know how to respond. No one had ever seen her as anything but detached, not even she herself, because she considered it a weakness. The only other person who had ever thought otherwise was Sam. This conversation was taking a turn she didn't care for. "I have to get back to camp. I'll have one of the women bring you clothes."

"Think about my offer, Doc. Get me out of here and I could make it worth your while." Zoe started to reach for her once more, but Fetch caught her wrist again and kept her at a distance.

The prospect of Zoe touching her wasn't repugnant. In fact, she was apparently so starved for the gentle contact of another woman her body was involuntarily reacting to every glancing caress. But she absolutely could not let this happen, and she had to make it clear to Zoe that this new tactic could only lead to disaster. "I don't doubt that. Seems like you've had plenty of practice."

Zoe scowled. "Don't believe everything you read."

"For the record, be careful who else you make that offer to. It could get you raped or killed, or both—and not necessarily in that order." Fetch said it flippantly but felt anything but as she walked away.

She was in the dense patch of jungle between the camp and the river when Zoe marched rapidly past her. Fetch was so self-absorbed, replaying their conversation in her mind, she didn't react right away. Picking up her pace to catch up, she said, "What are you doing?"

"Going to my God damn hut," Zoe called over her shoulder, never slowing.

"You can't be seen like this." Fetch grabbed her from behind, wrapping her arms around Zoe's, pinning her against her body.

Zoe struggled to break free. "Let go of me!"

Fetch held on tight as her mind and body involuntarily memorized their forced spoon-like embrace. Where she had clamped her hands together at the base of Zoe's breasts, she could feel the curve of them with every one of Zoe's rapid exhalations. Zoe's ass was firmly pressed against her groin. Fetch involuntarily thrust her hips forward, and when Zoe groaned, Fetch moved her hands down the towel, stopping low on Zoe's abdomen. Fetch inhaled the clean scent of her hair, and as her face brushed against Zoe's exposed upper back and shoulder, she shuddered at the sensation of warm, soft skin against her cheek and bunched the towel in her fist, wanting nothing more than to pull the fabric away to touch that warm body.

"If the men see you like this, there won't be any stopping them," she whispered, her lips beside Zoe's ear.

"What's the difference between you and them?" Zoe began to breathe even more heavily, and Fetch wondered if she was doing the same. "You want to fuck me as much as they do."

"Don't be ridiculous," Fetch snapped, and turned her around, but still held her by the arms. "You're playing with your life."

"You're the one playing with my life," Zoe yelled. "Now let me go."

Zoe tried to pull away again, but Fetch only tightened her grip. "What are you trying to prove?" she asked, forcing Zoe to look her in the eyes.

"That I still have some God damn say in my life!" Zoe shouted. Without warning, she managed to knee Fetch, hard, in the crotch.

Fetch was so taken aback she released Zoe and bent over, wincing.

Zoe took off like a rabbit.

It was almost half a minute before Fetch recovered enough to go after her. She'd just broken into a run when Zoe screamed. Picking up speed, she found her in a small clearing. A guerrilla she didn't recognize had evidently tackled Zoe and now had her pinned under him on the hard dirt. The towel had been stripped off and tossed to the side; Zoe was naked, and the rebel's hand was between her legs. With the other, he had one of her hands pinned over her head. She was fighting hard, kicking and scratching with her free hand, trying to get out from under him, but he easily overpowered her.

Instinctively, Fetch leapt toward them, grabbed the rebel's groping hand, and pulled his arm behind his back. Keeping it straight, she brought her elbow down on his outstretched arm and heard the bone break. The man fell to the side, squealing in pain and cradling his arm.

"Who are you? Fetch demanded, relieved to confirm he was a stranger. She'd have a lot of explaining to do if he was one of Barriga's men, but she would've stopped him just the same.

The guerrilla screamed obscenities at her in Spanish, before he calmed enough to explain he was from a neighboring camp and had been sent to borrow supplies.

"Next time stick to your own hostages. This one is mine." Fetch was angrier than she'd been in a very long time, and it wasn't just the headache or the aggression due to lack of meds. She glanced over at Zoe, on her knees several feet away. She was clutching the towel to herself and shaking uncontrollably, terror in her eyes.

How dare this bastard touch Zoe. She looked down at the rebel again and, with blind rage, kicked him in the head. The man passed out. "Don't ever touch her again," she whispered in English.

She slowly approached Zoe. "Did he hurt you?"

"I'm okay." Her voice shook, but Zoe had composed herself enough to wrap the towel back in place.

"Let's go back to the river." She offered her hand, and Zoe took it and got to her feet. "I'll bring you some clothes myself." Fetch sensed that the last thing Zoe needed right now was another soldier from the camp, even a woman, to be around her.

When they reached the water, Fetch sat her down on the grass. A few of the female rebels were still bathing. "I'll be right back."

"Aren't you going to say 'I told you so'?" Zoe asked softly, her eyes on the river. She seemed almost in a trance.

Fetch knelt in front of her so she could see Zoe's face. "Just please be careful from now on."

Zoe nodded slowly. "Thank you."

After she'd given Zoe some of her clothes and gotten her settled into her hammock, Fetch lay down on her own cot. She still seethed with rage, but exhaustion finally overtook her and she nodded off. After only a couple of hours rest, however, loud sounds just outside roused her. Some of the male rebels were whistling and hooting at one of the female guerrillas about something.

She wanted to go back to sleep, but she was too concerned about how Zoe was faring to allow it.

CHAPTER SEVENTEEN

Zoe sat in the corner of her hut, back against the wall, numbly watching the spiders and roaches climb over obstacles and up the rough boards of her prison. She was too distraught to think clearly.

What had happened at the lake with the soldier and the doctor had left her afraid and disoriented. One rebel had almost raped her and another had saved her. Except for her mother's death, Zoe had led a fairly charmed life. No one had ever violated or even threatened her predictable and protected existence. She'd always called the shots and either won or lost the game, but no one had ever directed her future. Now, in the space of a week, she'd become nothing but a pawn in someone's brutal game.

She wanted just to shut her eyes and find the only escape she could, in a dream. She even tried humming her mother's song to find some peace, but sleep, just like the prospect of a future, eluded her. She finally gave up and sat on the floor, watching the spiders for a long while, then staring out between the boards. They'd taken her watch when she was kidnapped, so she had no idea what time it was. Late afternoon, probably, but she really didn't care. It was almost funny, she thought, that when you hurt, time was measured in suffering: in its lessening and its ending, and not in minutes, hours, or days.

Marcella and her daughter were standing by the kitchen tent. They'd understand what she was going through. But as much as she needed someone to talk to, she couldn't find the strength. She liked these strangers, but being around them also reminded her of how long she could be here. Listening to their stories only increased her despair.

The one person she did want to talk to, or at least felt she could be around, was the doctor. It wasn't like the medic had given her hope, but at least she'd made her feel safe. And she'd shown her the first bit of kindness she'd experienced since her kidnapping. Zoe recognized the sweatpants, socks, and T-shirt the doctor had given her as the medic's own—they'd been among the laundry on her cot that first day in camp. And when the doc had brought her back to her hut, she'd left without chaining that damn restraint around her ankle.

She watched the doctor's tent for a long time, hoping she'd return and maybe spend some time with her. It was hot in the hut and she was so thirsty her throat hurt when she swallowed. When she no longer had the strength to sit up, Zoe curled up on the floor and cried. She hated feeling so weak after she'd just promised herself she'd do anything to survive, but she couldn't find the energy to fight.

Spent from her crying jag, she leaned her head back and shut her eyes. She'd almost finally nodded off when a sharp rap on her door broke the quiet. She ignored it. Probably someone to tell her it was time for dinner or that she needed to help with hell knew what. She wasn't interested in either, even if that meant losing the few privileges she had.

"Zoe, you in there?" She recognized the concerned voice of the medic and was relieved to hear it, but too tired for confrontation. She didn't reply.

After a few seconds, the doc announced, "I'm coming in."

She heard the door open and close, but remained where she was, eyes still closed, too bone weary to move. "Since when do any of you announce your entrance?" she mumbled.

"Zoe, what's wrong?"

"Absolutely nothing," Zoe whispered, mostly to herself. "Never been better."

"Are you hurt?" The doc's voice was closer, just above her now.

Zoe just shrugged. A few seconds later, a cool hand pressed against her cheek, startling her so much she flinched and opened her eyes.

The medic had crouched down in front of her. She was frowning and her eyebrows were knitted. She slowly removed her hand, her eyes never leaving Zoe's. "It's almost time for dinner. You need to eat."

She shook her head. "Not hungry."

"You have to," the doc said. "You've had very little the last several days. It's important you keep up your strength."

"Are we going to go through this again?" Zoe plopped back against the wall again and shut her eyes. "I don't care. Food is the last thing on my mind."

"I know what happened earlier today was awful," the medic said gently. "Along with everything else you're going through. Stress and fear take a toll on the body. You have to—"

"I told you I don't care."

"I do."

Zoe opened her eyes and looked at her quizzically. "You care about what I'm *worth*. Don't bloody patronize me."

"I do care, damn it." The medic's face blurred. Zoe tried to concentrate, to bring her back into focus, but the effort was too exhausting. "I couldn't sleep, thinking about what might've happened," the doc said.

Zoe barely registered the words. All she knew was how alone she felt. "I needed someone to talk to after the attack, but you just left me here and went away. I know you're one of them but…it's crazy."

"I'm not the enemy here," the doctor said. "There's a lot going on I can't talk about right now, but—"

Zoe could hear the doctor's voice but her mind was so hazy it was hard to fully absorb what she was saying, and at the moment it felt irrelevant. "It's crazy, but I feel safe with you around."

The doctor cupped her face again. "Focus for a moment, Zoe."

She wanted to comply, but she was just too weak.

"Look at me," the medic said, louder, as she moved closer.

Zoe did her best to focus, but she felt like a camera with a broken lens. It took several seconds to bring clarity to the medic's face, now only inches from hers.

Her gaze fixed on the doctor's mouth. Her lips were lovely. So full and moist and inviting they transported her, at least momentarily, from her living nightmare. "I meant it, you know," Zoe murmured hazily. "You really are beautiful." She reached up and traced her thumb over the lush bottom lip. "And kind, and—"

The doctor gasped at the touch. "You need to drink and eat something, before you pass out," she said softly.

"What I need is to kiss you." Zoe bent forward and softly brushed the doctor's lips with her own. Once, twice. Slow, barely connecting. The third time, she lingered, pressing their lips together with infinite gentleness. Then she opened her mouth enough to trace the edge of the doctor's mouth with her tongue.

The doctor pulled away. "Stop," she said breathlessly.

"Please kiss me back," Zoe pleaded. "Make me feel… something, anything."

"I can't." The doctor groaned and stood.

"Don't go." For a brief moment, she'd been able to push aside the hell she was in, and she was desperate to reclaim that escape.

"You're coming with me." The medic held her hand out to help Zoe up. "You're going to eat, and I'm going to sit with you until you do."

Zoe tried to get up. "Will you kiss me if I do?" she asked, and dropped back, dizzy and exhausted.

The doc's eyes were sad, almost like she pitied her. "That can't happen again."

Fetch reached for Zoe to help her up, but before they touched hands, one of Barriga's deputies opened the door of the hut, startling them both.

"There you are, Medica," he said in Spanish. "The commander wants you. Now."

His words and the man's demeanor told Fetch that something was up, something important. He stood there waiting; he wouldn't leave without her.

"I'm coming." She headed toward the door but turned back to Zoe before she got there. "Please go out and eat something."

Zoe didn't respond, and she couldn't wait. Fetch hustled over to the rebel chief's tent. The deputy leading her pulled back the entrance flap to admit her.

Diego Barriga was alone, hunched over his laptop computer. He looked worried, and he didn't try to hide it when he glanced up and motioned for her to sit on the bench in front of his makeshift desk. "We are facing a grave problem, Medica, one that threatens the very existence of The People's Army." He spoke in Spanish in hushed tones, clearly to ensure that the man standing watch outside would not overhear them.

"A plague is sweeping through the world," he told her. "A fatal virus with no cure."

Shocked, Fetch gripped the edge of the bench until her knuckles went white.

"It is very bad here in Colombia," Barriga said gravely. "Thousands are dead already in San José del Guaviare, Bogota, and Cali. And now I hear that soldiers at two camps are showing some of the symptoms." He looked down at his computer. "This is what to look for: a bloody cough, diarrhea, vomiting, chest pain, high fevers, headaches, sore muscles, weakness. They say people die very quickly after the symptoms appear, usually within only a couple of days."

He looked up at her. "The Central Command has ordered we not tell our people about this danger. We cannot have panic or defections because soldiers are worried about their families. They are safer here, away from the cities. But we must do what we can to keep this at bay. We have stopped all leaves and transfers. No one will be allowed out of their current camp. We must make do with the supplies we have."

Barriga stood and came around his desk to stand over her. He placed a hand on her shoulder. "We are lucky to have you here. You are a good medica, one of the best we have had. You will do what you can to keep us safe," he said, "but you will not tell anyone what I have told you."

Fetch's mind raced as she absorbed the news. A global pandemic? With no cure? Was it in the United States? Had it reached the EOO campus? It was imperative that she contact headquarters immediately, both to find out the situation there and to reassess her mission. She had good intel to pass on now about the location of the hostages and the security around the encampment. If they could get the hostages out—and if it was still a priority in light of what was happening elsewhere—then they had to launch a rescue very soon, before the plague reached their camp.

"I'll need all the information you can give me about this," she told Barriga. "What is known about the progression of the disease, how it's transmitted, a full list of possible symptoms. What medicines and treatments have been tried, and so forth."

"I will have it for you soon."

She stood and faced him. "As I'm certain you're aware, sir, there is no way to ensure this is not already in our camp. A few of our people have been to San José del Guaviare in the last week. They may be infected, but not yet showing symptoms. We need to quarantine them in their huts immediately. We must also order everyone in camp to cover their mouths and noses with scarves, or whatever they have. They should avoid close contact with each other. Stay in their tents and huts. Post only minimal guards on the perimeter, spaced well apart. No congregating at meal times. Perhaps the cook can take the food around, or we can have them get their plates one at a time. We can tell everyone a bad flu is going around."

He nodded thoughtfully.

"I know that you said all travel is banned for the time being, Commander," Fetch said. "But you must make an exception for me, if we are to have any chance of keeping this contained. We need medical supplies, especially surgical masks and gloves. They provide much more protection than scarves."

She could see in Barriga's eyes that he was about to object, so she continued. "I know what precautions to take, Commander, rest assured. I do not wish to further endanger our people. I have a mask to wear and will be very careful. If the Jeep is waiting for me at the end of the trail, I can be to town and back by tomorrow morning."

He considered her request for a full minute before replying. "Very well. Give me a list of what you'll need. I'll make sure everything is waiting for you at our supplier. And I'll radio ahead to the outpost to let you through."

Fetch used the notepad on his desk to jot down what she required. "I'll be ready to leave in ten minutes. Have the information I asked for waiting for me when I get back."

She turned to go, but paused at the door and looked back at him. "Do you wish for me to make the announcement before I go?"

"No. I'll take care of that," he told her. "Go. And be fast. We need you here, Medica."

Fetch ran to her tent and emptied her backpack, taking nothing with her but her cell phone and charger, mask, latex gloves, flashlight, and water. She stopped at the kitchen tent for a block of panela, a rebel staple for long, fast marches because it provided a quick, potent energy boost. Made by boiling down the juice from sugar cane, it tasted like a blend of brown sugar and molasses.

Once she had negotiated her way past the booby-trapped perimeter, she broke into a run, her eye on the trail to avoid letting the myriad of vines and roots that encroached along the pathway trip her. She tried to stay focused on the task at hand, but her mind was churning as she wondered what was happening in the world beyond the jungle. She feared the worst: that the EOO itself might already have been irreparably compromised. They had all received vaccinations against every conceivable disease they might encounter, including shots of not-yet-approved drugs. But was it enough to protect them from this pandemic? Could this new virus already have wiped out all on campus, the governing trio, her fellow ETFs?

What if no one answered when she reported in? Should she return to the camp? Her sense of responsibility dictated she complete her mission and ensure the safe return of the hostages, even if it meant she had to try to do it on her own.

Perhaps the new restrictions she had suggested to Barriga would give her an opportunity. With only minimal guards about, she might be able to get most of the hostages out. But not Kylee.

She was too weak, and couldn't possibly travel on her infected foot. Fetch couldn't bear to leave her behind, but would have to.

She thought of Zoe. Zoe had gotten under her skin, especially recently, and she refused to consider anything happening to her.

Thank God at least no one in camp had exhibited any symptoms. At least, not yet. No one but her. If she'd told anyone about her headache this morning, Barriga might never have let her leave. She was certain it had nothing to do with the virus. It was a side effect she had experienced on several occasions, especially when she'd had too little sleep. With a nap and some ibuprofen, it had faded to a manageable level.

By the time she reached the trailhead, dark had long fallen and she was soaked with sweat, but she'd covered the distance in record time. She put on her surgical mask and latex gloves. The small rebel outpost there was usually manned by three or four guerrillas. They were the lookouts for the main camp, charged with radioing an alert to Barriga at the first sign of any Colombian military or nearby aircraft.

Since Barriga had radioed ahead, the sentries let her pass, and a driver in a Jeep was waiting a short distance farther on to take her to San José del Guaviare, the provincial capital and nearest town.

She turned on the Jeep's radio to listen to the news as they drove and got a much clearer picture of the extent of the pandemic. It was mostly a recap of the situation in Colombia but included updates on the global situation.

They reached the city a little after midnight. The streets of San José del Guaviare were empty of people and vehicles, and despite the mild evening, windows everywhere were closed. When they pulled up in front of the medical warehouse, Fetch told the driver she might be there a while, getting the supplies. He was happy to crawl into the backseat for a nap.

Fetch stole down the alley along the side of the building to the back, where she found a quiet place to call headquarters.

Engaging her scrambler, she dialed the number and held her breath until Montgomery Pierce picked up. "Fetch."

"Are you all right?" he asked her. She'd never been so relieved to hear his voice.

"Yes, sir. I just heard about the virus. It hasn't reached us, at least not yet," she replied. "I think we're still good. And there?" The question was entirely beyond protocol, but Pierce's quiet response told her it was neither unexpected nor out of line. These were unusual circumstances.

"The situation is horrible but all ops are safe so far."

"Are we protected?" she asked, referring to the score of vaccinations the EOO gave their operatives.

"Probably not."

"I see. I have the intel required. Are we a go?"

"No," he replied. "All necessary resources are unavailable, indefinitely."

She wasn't surprised to learn that the elite U.S. forces they'd planned to use for the rescue were tied up with higher priorities, and that the EOO itself had no way to assist on its own.

"You're to abort," he added. "And return ASAP."

"That would compromise the whole operation," she said.

"That's correct."

"They'd never let me back in and it would take months for someone else to infiltrate. These hostages have been here too long, sir. We need to get them out."

"The organization's priority is your safety."

"I understand, but I can't abandon these people. If the virus doesn't kill them, the guerrillas will if they fall ill and are worth nothing to them."

"It's a sad situation, Fetch." Pierce's voice was uncharacteristically gentle. "But maybe the jungle is their best bet right now. It'll take longer for the virus to spread there than in the cities."

"Some are doing very poorly. I need to get them out."

"Be here in twenty-four hours."

Was she being recalled purely for her own safety, or did the EOO need every available op concentrating on the pandemic? "Are we working this one?" she asked.

"Some of our own are in the field."

Fetch's heart sank. She couldn't leave the hostages to die in the jungle. But she'd never disobeyed any direct EOO order. "That's a negative, sir. I'd like a few more days. This crisis may allow me to pull this off on my own."

Pierce didn't reply immediately. He had great faith in the judgment of his ETFs and gave such unusual requests weighty consideration.

"I can't allow that. It's dangerous and there's nowhere safe to take them."

"I'm not leaving without them, sir."

Another long pause on the other end. "I expect you back in five days. That's all you get. I'll try to find a way to get a helicopter to pick you up. Give us the coordinates and an ETA when you know them."

"Affirmative. Thank you, sir."

"And Fetch?"

"Sir?"

"Take every precaution and make it back here in one piece. We need you."

"Yes, sir," she replied, but Pierce had already disconnected.

Fetch jogged two blocks to the bus terminal, where she kept a locker. The place was deserted but for a lone clerk behind the counter who wore a scarf over his face. She picked up her duffel bag, which contained her GPS, Glock, silencer, and ammunition, binoculars, maps, and other gear provided by the EOO. She'd need it all if she was to have any chance of getting the hostages out of there on her own. As she trotted back to the medical-supply warehouse, she replayed the phone call in her mind. Things had to be very bad for Montgomery Pierce to express such personal concern. It wasn't like him at all. Had he told her the whole truth about how much the EOO had been impacted by the crisis?

Her knock on the side entrance was answered by the owner, a man she was well familiar with from other resupply visits. A FARC sympathizer for nearly two decades, he was also wearing a mask. "Follow me," he told her in Spanish as they headed into the warehouse.

It was a large building, usually packed with row after row of boxes on pallets. But the extent of the pandemic in Colombia was clear when she saw that more than half the stock of the building had been depleted.

She'd worried that he would have long ago run out of masks and gloves, but he'd apparently set aside an ample supply for the guerrillas. Everything she'd requested was waiting for her in a neat pile. She thanked him and quickly stowed the supplies in her backpack. Five minutes later, she woke her driver and they headed out of the city in the Jeep.

As they drove, she worked on a plan to get the hostages out. She couldn't take them to San José del Guaviare. The guerrillas would stop them long before they could reach it on foot. She'd just made the trip from the camp to the trailhead in less than six hours, but that had been at a run by a well-conditioned soldier used to the terrain.

It would take the hostages at least ten hours or more to walk that distance in their condition, and this time of year, the sun rose early, before six a.m. Even if they left at midnight, probably the earliest they could get away, the camp would awaken long before they reached the trailhead. Barriga would have alerted the outpost and the sentries would be waiting for them, likely reinforced with guerrillas sent by vehicle from town, while rebels from the camp would be close behind. She and the hostages would be trapped between them with nowhere to go.

And Fetch didn't dare an alternate route through the jungle. That was too slow, and easily tracked, and Barriga would have men stationed on the way to town anticipating she might do that.

There were no other roads or settlements near the camp, so their only chance of escape lay in heading in the opposite direction, farther into the jungle interior. Barriga probably wouldn't suspect she'd try that, at least not initially. But it would make for slower going. They'd all have to be loaded down with supplies because they might be on their own for several days until extraction was possible.

When the Jeep neared the trailhead, Fetch downed eight hundred milligrams of ibuprofen and chewed the remainder of her panela in preparation for the long trek back to camp. As she ran, she thought more about the best way to get the hostages out: the when, the how, what supplies she'd need, and, most important, where she would lead them. She couldn't take them to anywhere the guerrillas were well familiar with. And it should have a clearing close by big enough to land a helicopter.

She'd been transferred between several mountain encampments during her six months undercover. Each time, she'd used her FARC-supplied compass to roughly ascertain their locations. And whenever she traveled between them, she'd thoroughly scanned her surroundings, especially when on the high ridges where she had an unobstructed view for miles. She noted where every major clearing was, every abandoned coca farm and distant settlement, every sign of civilization at all, so she could give the best intel possible for any rescue attempt.

One of the high camps she'd visited was a two- or three-day march away. No, probably four, she reconsidered, given the slower rate the hostages could maintain. She remembered pausing on an overlook not far from there for water and seeing a brief flash of light in the dense valley below. Sunlight reflecting off a tin roof, she'd surmised. Impossible to see unless conditions were exactly right, so doubtful many guerrillas, if any, knew it was there. It was her best bet, especially because there'd been a small clearing not far away.

Fetch was exhausted by the time she arrived back at the hostage camp, just as the cook was serving lunch. Though the painkillers had helped, she needed a few hours' sleep before she collapsed. Her medical training was needed here now more than ever before, and she had many sleepless nights ahead if the virus reached them. She'd be useless to the rest if she were wasted.

But she stopped at the commander's tent first to update him and deliver a handful of surgical masks for him and his guards. She had donned hers as she entered the camp. Barriga had obviously already imposed the restrictions she'd recommended. Only four guards were positioned at the perimeter this morning, and most of the guerrillas and hostages were apparently eating in their tents. The few gathered near the cooking fire all had their mouths and noses covered, and were standing well apart from each other. Zoe was not among them.

The commander's eyes were grave when she entered. He had a scarf wrapped over the lower portion of his face. Before she even had a chance to speak, he relayed the bad news. "Two of our soldiers have this virus, I think. After you left, I asked whether anyone felt sick, and Alejandro and Mateo said they both had been throwing up since last night. Alejandro went to town last week to post the Howe woman's proof of life. They are quarantined in a hut at the edge of camp."

The knowledge that the virus had reached them only added to the urgency of Fetch's mission. Who knew how many more in camp might already be infected and not showing symptoms? Pierce had only given her five more days anyway, but even that was too long. She had to get the hostages out of there very soon. "This is bad, Commander," she replied. "I will check on them immediately."

Fetch slid the backpack from her shoulders and removed a handful of masks and gloves. As she set them on his desk, she said, "I advise we tighten the restrictions even further. Everyone should remain in their huts except the cook, who can deliver food and leave it outside. And me, of course. I advise even you, Commander, to remain isolated. Those soldiers who are currently sharing huts should be split up. Have we enough extra tarps and tents for all?"

He nodded thoughtfully.

"No one from other camps should be allowed in," she added, thinking of the rebel who'd assaulted Zoe, "and we should pull all the guards." Fetch hoped Barriga would bite.

For the first time, Barriga visibly bristled at her recommendation. Before he could object, she said, "I heard on the Jeep's radio that all planes and helicopters have been grounded, except for emergencies. And the military right now is too busy keeping public order to think about us. Many have been killed by this virus as well. We've nothing to fear from them. But any or all of the guards may already be infected. Until we know how this spreads, we need to strictly limit who moves about the camp."

Barriga considered her suggestion only briefly before shaking his head. "I don't want our people mixing with the hostages. Because they will have to fend for themselves, we will leave them unchained.

So I must keep some guards posted to make sure they don't escape." He got up, took off his scarf, and replaced it with one of the masks Fetch had given him. "I will tell them not to get close to each other."

The chief had one final message, which was chilling. "If any of the hostages become ill, shoot them. We can't risk them making our own sick, and I won't waste our food on soon-to-be-dead people."

Fetch spent the next hour going around the camp with her backpack, distributing the masks and latex gloves. She was happy that no one seemed to be panicking or unusually concerned about the precautions. They all believed it was just a bad flu. Some of the rebels even expressed delight at having the unexpected free time to lounge in their tents.

She found the Aussie hostage Kylee curled into a ball, asleep on her cot. She mumbled something when Fetch called her name but didn't awaken, so she placed her latex-gloved hand on the woman's forehead. Kylee felt feverish, but that was nothing new. She'd been running a temperature for several days from the infection in her foot. There was no evidence she'd been vomiting or had other symptoms of the virus. Fetch made a mental note to check on her again later.

The tent of the two infected rebel teenagers was at the edge of camp. Both had a high fever and complained of headaches and nausea. Alejandro was weak from vomiting, and Mateo had a bad cough. She gave them aspirin and Tamiflu, and encouraged them to drink as much water as possible to stay hydrated. After she left, she instructed the cook to make sure the boys were delivered food. It was all she could do.

She saved Zoe's hut for last.

Chapter Eighteen

October 20

Zoe hadn't moved from her hammock in hours and lacked motivation to change the status quo. She wasn't hungry, though she should be after missing three meals. And she didn't need to use the waste bucket, because she'd had only a few sips of water in the last twenty hours. She was thirsty now, desperately thirsty, but hauling herself outside to get something to drink seemed too much effort in her weakened condition.

She wasn't on a hunger strike, some protest against her treatment by the FARC. She was just too tired of losing battles, this one included.

During her long time alone since the doctor had left her the day before, she'd run through the gamut of human emotions, at least all the negative ones. Fear and panic, when she recalled the attack by the rebel. Despair and despondency over her uncertain future. Anger and frustration at herself, at the realization she was rapidly letting go of her determination to survive. Now she mostly felt nothing, her mind hazy.

She'd had only a brief moment of feeling anything remotely good, when she'd kissed the doctor. Or at least she thought she'd kissed her. The more time that passed, the more Zoe wondered whether it had all been a dream or hallucination. She had been momentarily transported from her endless prison. But perhaps she'd just wanted so desperately to feel alive again that she'd imagined it.

One of Barriga's men had come to her hut not long after the doctor departed, to announce a flu was going around. He ordered her to stay there except for meals, and said everyone was to cover their noses and mouths and keep away from each other when they went outside. She couldn't have imagined that—she could see through the boards in her hut that no one was out there right now but the cook, and she had a scarf over her face.

And her two visitors this morning had been dressed the same. When she hadn't gone out for breakfast, Marcella and Willy had come to her hut. Willy gave her some water, and Marcella pleaded with her to eat and asked her what was wrong. But she told them to go away and leave her alone. The one person Zoe wanted to see was the doctor. It was only with her that she didn't feel so alone. But the medic hadn't stopped by even once to check on her.

Why should she fight it anymore? What was the use? She closed her eyes and drifted off.

Now someone was calling her name. When she opened her eyes, she saw the doctor standing over her, wearing a surgical mask.

"You've missed some more meals," the doc said.

So the medic cared enough to keep tabs on her. Why, then, hadn't she come by to check on her? "You did, too," she replied. "You don't see me complaining."

"Are you sick?" The doctor moved closer, her face just above her now. "Do you have a headache? Any nausea?" She placed her hand on Zoe's forehead.

"No."

"No fever," the doc said, mostly to herself. The surgical mask covered much of her face, so it was hard to read her expression, but the medic's eyebrows were knitted. She slowly removed her hand, her eyes never leaving Zoe's.

"I must be pretty sick, or else you couldn't find a toothbrush," Zoe said.

"The mask is for precaution. You need to eat, Zoe."

"Precaution?"

"A virus is going around. We can't afford to have the camp get sick."

"I remember someone coming by last night about it," Zoe said. "The flu, right?"

The doctor looked away. "Sure." The tone of her voice and the avoidance of eye contact was a dead giveaway.

"You're lying," Zoe said wearily. "But I don't care. Whatever it is, it can't be worse than this hell." You could get all sorts of weird tropical diseases in South America. As he always did before she went abroad, her father had insisted she see her uncle to make sure she was up to date on all her inoculations, and Eddie had given her a couple of new shots for South America. Thinking of her father and uncle only added to her depression. Would she ever see them again?

The medic reached into a backpack she'd set next to the hammock and pulled out another surgical mask. She held it out for Zoe to take. "Would you wear this at all times? And please eat. Your immune system will need all the boost it can get to stay healthy."

She didn't reach for the mask. "I told you I don't care."

"And as I told you yesterday, I *do*." The doctor's forehead creased. Was she frowning?

"Then why did you stay away last night?"

"What?"

"Forget it. None of my business."

"I had to go into to—"

"No." She must have imagined the kiss. It couldn't have happened. "Never mind. Like I said, it's none of my business."

"We'll talk about that later," the medic replied. "Right now, we're getting you out of here and you're going to eat, whether you like it or not." She bent over the hammock and pulled her mask briefly aside so Zoe could see she was smiling encouragingly. Her voice was gentle. "Don't make me hurt you."

Fetch replaced her own mask and placed another over Zoe's face before they left the hut. Barriga had ordered that everyone stay indoors, but Zoe needed to get out of that oven. She was rapidly dehydrating. Only once outside did Fetch notice how bad Zoe looked. She was pale, and black circles marred her beautiful yet unfocused eyes.

"I can't eat with this on," Zoe said, squinting against the bright sunlight.

"You can remove it after I fix you a plate and move you to the edge of the jungle."

Zoe was so weak she could barely stand on her own. Fetch had to put one of Zoe's arms over her shoulders to support her weight while she propelled them forward toward the makeshift picnic table by the kitchen tent. Fortunately, everyone else had finished, and the place was deserted except for the cook.

She left Zoe slumped on the bench while she grabbed a flask of water and scooped a triple portion of stew onto a plate. Balancing the plate in one hand, she handed the flask to Zoe. "Can you carry this?"

Zoe shrugged. "I guess."

Fetch got Zoe's arm over her shoulder again and hoisted her back on her feet. "Lean up against me, we're going over there." She tilted her head to the shade at the edge of the camp.

Once she had Zoe seated at the base of a large tree, propped against its trunk, she pulled Zoe's mask off.

Zoe was so out of it she started off gradually, scooping the food into her mouth and chewing slowly, almost in a trance. But as the stew started to hit her stomach she perked up and began to shovel it in like a starved animal, stopping only long enough for the occasional pull from the flask to wash it down. Before long, the color started to return to her face, and her eyes looked focused and alert. When the plate was clean and the flask empty, she looked up at Fetch. "So, how dire is this epidemic?"

The question took Fetch so completely by surprise she knew it registered on her face. "What makes you think it's serious?"

"Pure deduction." Zoe wiped a smear of gravy from her chin. "I saw two sick soldiers being moved to the far edge of camp yesterday after you left, most everyone is staying in their tents, and everyone has their faces covered. The chief over there…" She pointed to the commander's tent. Barriga was outside, talking to two of his men.

"He seems pensive. He hasn't stopped pacing and is looking at everyone suspiciously. And the first thing out of your mouth when you walked into my hut was to ask if I was sick."

"You're very perceptive." There was certainly more to Zoe than met the eye. The woman had keen intuition and exceptional observational skills.

"Human calculus, if you have a knack for it, is the easiest math of all."

"I'm impressed." Zoe was continuously surprising her with accurate insights and poignant remarks.

"You wouldn't be, if you put aside your preconceived notions." Zoe got to her feet. "There's more to me than parties and casual sex."

"Clearly." Fetch grinned.

"Maybe I should take advantage of the current situation." Zoe glanced around.

Fetch took a step backward. Did she intend to try to kiss her again? God, she hoped not. They were out in the open, but, primarily, what had happened earlier had turned her very organized world on its axis. She hadn't expected to feel like that with a woman again. Although the kiss was brief and Zoe confused, it tied Fetch's stomach in knots and put her libido in overdrive. It was ridiculous, considering the circumstances, but disturbingly true.

But that was apparently not what Zoe had in mind. "I could make a run for it," she said in a low voice. "With everyone hiding and avoiding each other, I don't think they'd notice."

"Why are you telling *me* this?"

"I don't really know. But I doubt you'd shoot me if I tried."

"I would never allow you to enter the jungle on your own. You'd never make it."

"But you wouldn't kill me."

Fetch took a long time to answer. "No."

"Then let me go. I'll take my chances." Zoe's eyes bored into hers, beseeching her to agree.

She shook her head. "I can't do that." Fetch understood the sentiment all too well. She too would rather die a free person or in pursuit of freedom than stay imprisoned. She had known enough soldiers and civilians taken prisoner to know what detention did to the human condition. But Zoe had no chance of surviving on her own, and she intended to get her out of here anyhow.

"I won't make it in here anyway, and I prefer to die out there. Can you understand that?" Zoe pleaded.

Fetch didn't answer.

"You think I'm weak," Zoe said.

"On the contrary." Fetch reached down and picked up a rock and threw it into the jungle. "I think you're a fighter."

"Is that your way of telling me that I should hold on to my sanity until I'm free to go?"

"What I'm saying is that I agree with you. No one can truly live unless they're prepared to die."

"I've never thought about it like that." Zoe looked at her curiously. "You obviously have."

"Yeah."

Zoe went quiet for several seconds as her gaze moved past Fetch to take in their surroundings. "Is this the kind of life you'd always dreamed of, Doc? This camp, taking hostages, riots, bombings?"

When Fetch didn't answer, Zoe said, "Do you plan to live and die like a soldier of misfortune?"

"I don't have a choice."

Zoe snorted derisively. "Life is all about choices."

For most people, maybe. "Sometimes it's about duty."

Zoe seemed to think about this, too, for a while, and Fetch wanted to know where her mind had wandered off to.

"Yes, I guess you're right." Zoe finally answered.

"What about your choices?" Fetch asked. "Are you happy with…" The more she got to know Zoe, the more curious she was to know how much of what she'd read about her was accurate. But she stopped herself when Zoe scowled.

"Say it," Zoe snapped. "Everyone else does."

"I'm not judging you."

"Bull. You've done nothing but, since I was dragged here."

"Are they all lies?"

"Yes. No." Zoe looked down and ran her hands through her hair as though exasperated. "Either way, my life doesn't hurt others."

"So your father is happy about his daughter being constantly criticized and publicly judged for her promiscuity?" Fetch asked. "How do you think your mother would feel about your choices?"

Zoe's head shot up and Fetch instinctively pulled back. She recognized in Zoe's face the kind of hurt anger she'd seen only on the battlefield.

"I'm sorry," Fetch said.

"Don't ever bring up my mother. You have no right." Zoe stressed each word dangerously slow through a clenched jaw. "That woman was my world."

"I didn't mean to offend you," Fetch said sincerely. It was public knowledge that her mother had passed at least a decade ago. Fetch had no idea Zoe was still so sensitive about it.

Zoe turned her back to Fetch and sat crossed-legged, facing the jungle. She stared out toward the trees, not speaking, clearly lost in memories of her mother.

After a minute or two, Fetch sat beside her. Zoe's anger had dissipated. The firm set of her jaw had relaxed, and the fire in her eyes had been replaced by tears.

Fetch picked up a stick and began to lazily draw shapes in the dirt. A circle gained rays and became a sun. A cylinder, a trash can. She wasn't really thinking about what she was doing. So it came as a surprise when she realized her square had become a house that clearly resembled the one Sam had died in. "I lost someone, too," she said, staring down at the image in the dirt. "They die, but the pain never does. Even long after they become like those faded Polaroid pictures. So blurry you can't quite remember their face or smell."

"Family?" Zoe asked.

"As good as."

"A soldier, then."

"You really are very good at this," she told Zoe.

"Was she killed?"

Fetch nodded. "She was too busy covering my back to save herself. She never saw it coming."

"Maybe she did," Zoe suggested. "Maybe she stayed to cover your back so you could live."

"She's crazy if she did." Soldiers risked their life to save another soldier, but they did not become a human sacrifice, because that's what it came down to. Fetch leaned back on her elbows and looked up at the sky. The thought that Sam might have given her life for her was infuriating. Sam had so much to live for. A family, friends. Fetch had nothing and no one to go home to. No one to miss her except Sam.

"Was she?" Zoe asked. "Wouldn't you have done the same for her?"

"That's different."

"It always is," Zoe replied softly. "But it never is."

Fetch considered her words for a long while. Zoe was less and less what she'd imagined her to be. She sat upright again and shifted position so they were facing each other. Before she spoke, she scanned the camp to make sure no one was within earshot. The place looked deserted, and even Barriga had retreated inside.

"Zoe, I'm going to tell you something and I want you to listen like your life depended on it," Fetch said in a low voice. "Because it does."

"Okay," Zoe said cautiously.

"This virus is very dangerous. You've been cut off from the world in here, but in the past week, more than a million have died worldwide and the death toll is skyrocketing daily. Bogota alone has started to resemble a ghost town. Air traffic has stopped in most countries, and people have been instructed to stay indoors."

"My God. My father! I have to reach my father." Zoe tried to get up, but Fetch pulled her back down.

"Zoe, listen. The virus has reached the camp. We can't stay here much longer."

"So you're going to move us to yet another camp? I can't do that. I need to see my father."

"No. There is no other camp. None are safe."

"So we're going to sit here and watch each other die?"

Fetch shook her head. "I intend to get you and the other hostages out."

"What?" Zoe's brow furrowed, as though she couldn't believe what she was hearing. "How?"

"I have a plan," Fetch said, "but I need you to cooperate and be ready to move when I tell you."

"Where will we go?" The words were barely out when Zoe raised her hand to stop Fetch from answering. "Never mind. I don't care where we go. Just get me the hell out of here and back to my father."

"Make sure you keep eating and drinking as much as possible. You'll need all your strength to get through the jungle."

"I will," Zoe said with conviction. "How about Kylee?"

"I'm afraid she's too sick to be moved. She'd never survive the trek."

Zoe frowned, but nodded in understanding.

"You cannot tell any of the other hostages," Fetch said. "Leave that to me."

"I promise."

Fetch saw two of Barriga's deputies come out of the commander's tent. They began to tour the camp, checking in on everyone, calling each rebel and hostage to their doorway to inspect them while keeping their distance.

"Go back to your hut and stay inside," Fetch told Zoe. "Keep away from everyone. We don't know who might be infected."

"How long does it take for the symptoms to—"

"Five to seven days, roughly." Fetch picked up Zoe's plate and got to her feet.

"How do we know that we or the others haven't already been infected?" Zoe asked as she stood as well.

"We don't."

Zoe froze, and Fetch saw realization dawn. "I kissed you."

"I know."

"Why did you let me?"

"We didn't know about this, then. You were out of it and needed someone," Fetch lied. She couldn't have stopped herself even if she'd wanted to, and she hadn't.

"You felt sorry for me."

She shook her head. "I wanted to help you."

"You should've stopped me. I was…" Zoe studied Fetch's face, likely seeking some sort of response. But Fetch remained silent, thankful that her mask helped conceal the turmoil of emotions within her. Zoe said softly, "I was confused. I didn't mean to force myself on you and certainly not have you kiss me out of pity." Fetch could've sworn she looked hurt. "It won't happen again."

"I know." Fetch had to agree, but was disappointed. It was crazy, especially considering the danger of infection, but it stung that Zoe so readily vowed to never kiss her again.

They walked slowly back toward Zoe's hut and spotted one of Barriga's deputies working his way in their direction. "Put your mask on," she told Zoe.

Zoe quickly complied. "Doc?"

"In a day or two at the most," Fetch said, assuming Zoe wanted to know when she expected to move them.

"I was going to ask your name."

Fetch considered how to answer. She could give Zoe the Spanish cover name she'd used to enlist in the FARC, but decided against it. Instead she said simply, "We are all more complicated than our name."

"Or what others write about us. But that doesn't answer my question."

"I'll tell you some other time," she said as she opened the door to Zoe's hut. "Remember what we talked—"

Both of them froze at the sound of shouting. Barriga had come out of his tent with his rifle and was yelling at his deputies to bring the sick forward. He stomped over to each hostage's hut and pounded on the door. "Come out now," he ordered in English. His tirade brought all the rebels out of their tents as well.

Four soldiers came from the right, dragging Mateo and Alejandro, the two sick guerrillas, boys barely old enough to shave.

Fetch realized Kylee had not emerged from her hut. Fearing Barriga's repercussions, she headed toward it, intending to carry her out if she had to.

"Where are you going, Medica?" Barriga shouted at her.

"To get the Australian," Fetch replied. "She's not able to walk with—"

"Fuck the crazy woman," Barriga said. He motioned with his rifle for Fetch to join the others, who were gathering around the sick boys in a wide circle. Mateo and Alejandro clung to each other, fear on their faces. Mateo fought back tears.

As Fetch went to stand beside Zoe, Barriga took center stage, standing inside the circle but well away from the boys.

"The next person I see with no mask," he said in Spanish as he took turns pointing his rifle at every hostage and rebel in the circle, "or the next one to get sick," he shouted furiously, "will die because of me, not this sickness."

He walked up to Zoe and stuck his rifle to her cheek. "You eat in your hut like others," he said in heavily accented English, "or next time you eat through the hole I put in your stomach."

Fetch fought the urge to grab Barriga by the throat. If she moved right now, he would shoot her. Of that she was certain. His fear of the virus had clearly panicked him. Not because he was losing his soldiers, they could be replaced, but because he feared losing his collateral. If the hostages died, all his work and hopes for financing his war would vanish. He'd have to start over, which was no easy feat. Kidnapping and negotiating hostages was risky and time-consuming, a business that was facing a temporary setback, but would continue long after this virus was gone.

Zoe didn't flinch, and though her coolness partially impressed Fetch, she wished Zoe would express her certain fear. For men like Barriga, fear was a synonym for respect.

"Understand?" the chief yelled when Zoe didn't react.

"Yes," Zoe replied calmly.

Barriga smacked her so hard across the face, blood seeped from both her nostrils. "I didn't hear you, *puta*."

He wanted to see fear and wouldn't stop going after Zoe until he did.

"I said yes," Zoe said louder, but Fetch knew it still wasn't loud enough for Barriga. She could practically hear Zoe clenching her jaw. She wouldn't concede, and Barriga wouldn't, either. He'd keep hitting and humiliating her until he was satisfied. Fetch had seen rebel commanders do that, and a lot worse.

The chief raised his hand to strike Zoe again, but Fetch caught his wrist. "Enough," she said, disregarding her own safety.

Barriga took a step to the right to stand in front of Fetch, his eyes blazing with rage. "Like I said, Medica, we need you, but don't think you can't be replaced." He slammed the butt of his gun in her stomach. "No one," he shouted, "interferes when I'm dealing with hostages."

Fetch doubled over in pain, the wind knocked out of her. Barriga kicked her feet out from under her and she crumpled, gasping for breath. Before she could recover, he began kicking her repeatedly, in her back, thighs, stomach, her sides. She tried to curl into a ball and protect her head; the pain was excruciating.

"I understand!" Zoe shouted at the top of her lungs. "I said I understand!" She yelled it repeatedly until Barriga stopped. "Please! I'll do anything you want."

Fetch had almost lost consciousness. She clutched her middle and looked up at the commander.

"Next time you waste my time…" Barriga smiled at Zoe, then pointed his rifle at Fetch's head. "I kill her." He turned on his heel and returned to the center of the circle.

Fetch couldn't get up. The pain in her stomach and sides was too immense, and she was still fighting to breathe.

Zoe crouched and touched her shoulder. "I'm so sorry."

Fetch coughed. "Don't," she whispered. "Get up." She wheezed; every word was an effort.

Zoe stood reluctantly, never taking her eyes off Fetch.

Only two things stopped Fetch from shooting Barriga right then and running for her life: the hostages she needed to rescue and the shortage of oxygen in her lungs, not enough to run. If the bastard wasn't so well guarded at night, she'd pay him a deadly visit before she left.

"So," Barriga said, walking in a small circle to ensure he had everyone's attention.

Fetch was still curled in a fetal position, on her side, clutching her middle in pain, too weak and winded to stand. But she forced her focus away from Zoe and shifted her body until she faced the chief. She let her head rest on the ground but made eye contact with Barriga and held it, so he would know she was watching him as intently as the others.

"Anyone who gets sick," the commander said in Spanish as he signaled his four deputies with his rifle, "will be executed."

The guerrillas pushed the boys to the ground and stepped back. Mateo and Alejandro were both crying now, begging for their lives, their dark eyes full of terror.

Calmly, and without the slightest hesitation, Barriga raised his rifle and shot Mateo in the head, point-blank, then Alejandro a second later. Fetch flinched with each shot. The impact splattered bone and brain matter onto the ground even before their bodies fell.

"Burn them," the commander told his deputies, who immediately dragged the bodies away, leaving a dark trail of blood.

Barriga stared around the circle at each of them, a look of satisfaction on his face. "Let's see who's next," he said, before returning to his tent.

"I'm going to be sick," Zoe murmured as she dropped onto all fours and vomited.

Fetch struggled to her knees and held her while Zoe's body continued to convulse.

When she finally stopped, Zoe wiped her mouth with the back of her hand. "I can't do this. I can't do this."

Fetch pushed the hair away from Zoe's face. "It won't be long. Just hold on, okay? I'm getting you out of here."

Tears fell from Zoe's eyes in a steady stream. "I'm going to die in here."

"No, you won't," she whispered. "I promise." Fetch managed to struggle to her feet, though her sides were still killing her. "Come on," she said, extending her hand to Zoe. "You need to get inside, and I need to get things ready."

Zoe raised her head to look up at Fetch, her skin greenish-white. "You're in no condition to help me up." She got to her feet without assistance. "Much less, prepare anything."

"I'll be fine." Fetch managed only a few steps, mostly upright, before she doubled over.

Zoe grabbed her shoulders. "Let me help you."

"I'm okay." She gritted her teeth, the burn in her stomach unbearable. "Just go inside before he sees you."

"Let me help you to your tent, first." Zoe put her arm around Fetch's waist.

Fetch, still bent over, turned her head to look at Zoe. "That's... not...necessary," she managed. "Please go."

Zoe released her. "I'm sorry this happened to you because of me." She ran her hands through her hair and raised her mask briefly to wipe at her nose, which had nearly stopped bleeding. "God, I never meant to get you in trouble."

"You didn't. These people, they're ruthless. It's not your fault."

Zoe looked off in the direction Barriga's deputies had taken the bodies of Mateo and Alejandro. "He shot those boys like...like they didn't matter. They were just kids."

"Not in this world." She straightened a little as the pain ebbed, at least temporarily. Zoe turned to look at her. "When you put a gun in a child's hands, you take away his future," Fetch said. "Take away a child's future and he grows up real fast." She'd seen it too often in the eyes of a child. "War kills more souls than it does bodies."

She left Zoe and slowly walked toward her tent, still clutching her sides. "More souls than bodies," she repeated softly to herself.

CHAPTER NINETEEN

October 20

Domino pulled her long brown hair into a ponytail and flipped on the interior light long enough to check herself in the rearview mirror of the van, which they'd parked outside the University of Munich Medical Center. Though she tried to stay focused on the mission, the fact they were about to mix among hospital staff only made her think of Hayley. Had the lab tests come back yet, confirming the implantation had taken?

"This is the first time I've played doctor," Allegro said from the back, as she slipped the long white lab coat over a light blue button-down shirt and black pants.

"Doubt it." Domino smiled and joined her. She'd already donned the white nurse's tunic and matching trousers Dilbert had provided.

"You know me too well." Allegro laughed. "By the way, black panties under white trousers?"

"Not exactly like I counted on this. Why can't they just wear scrubs? And why do I have to be the nurse?"

"It's killing you, isn't it? That I called it first."

"At least I don't have to wear that name tag." Domino chuckled as she slid open the side door and got out. "Remind me again why I like working with you?"

"Because I'm the only one who can make your soon-to-be-bourgeois life exciting," Allegro replied, following her.

Domino rolled her eyes. "I should have never told you about the baby."

"Too late." Allegro grinned.

After they adjusted their tiny earpiece microphone-receivers, Domino walked ahead while Allegro remained by the van.

She was a few feet from the main entrance when she heard Allegro in her ear.

"Can you hear me?"

"Loud and obnoxious," Domino replied. Allegro caught up and they both put their surgical masks on as the hospital doors slid open.

They walked in silence, scanning their environment. It was just after midnight, past visiting hours, so the large lounge/reception area was deserted. The woman behind the information desk glanced up when they passed by, but, when she saw they were wearing whites, returned to the book in her lap. Like them, she was wearing a mask.

They rode the elevator up two floors to the first massive patient wing, where the situation couldn't have been more different. Code alarms blared as monitors registered a sudden change in a patient's status, patients hit their chiming call buttons nonstop, pagers pealed, intercom announcements erupted, and quick consultations among staff buzzed intermittently. Doctors and orderlies were dashing around, and the central nurse's station was crowded with men and women scanning charts and typing into computers. The hallways in both directions were filled with bedridden patients, most of them in their twenties. Everyone was wearing a mask. No one even glanced their way.

"Packed," Allegro said.

"Yeah, you'd think a pandemic was on the loose," Domino mumbled.

"Well, aren't you carnival-clown funny tonight."

They walked down various corridors searching for an appropriate location.

"Hey, Helga, at ten o'clock, check it out," Allegro whispered.

"I'm on it, Doctor Assmann." Allegro groaned as they split up, Domino headed for the small auxiliary nurse's station, and Allegro down one of the main patient hallways.

Only two nurses were behind the counter. The tall one was young, her obese companion much older, probably in her sixties. Both looked harried and overworked. "Hi, I'm Helga," Domino said in fluent German. "Neuperlach Hospital sent a few of us for reinforcement."

"It's about time," the heavyset nurse said, sounding irritated.

Domino rested an elbow on the counter. "You both look exhausted. Why don't you get yourselves some dinner and coffee? I'll take over for a while. I was lucky to get a whole eight hours of sleep."

The nurses looked at each other and the younger one glanced at her watch. "We can be back in fifteen minutes," she said to her colleague. "It's been quiet."

"I don't know," the other replied.

Allegro casually approached the desk. Domino knew she'd heard the entire conversation in her earpiece.

"Good evening, ladies. What's going on?" Allegro asked, her German as fluent as Domino's.

"Evening, Doctor Assmann," Domino replied. "I was just telling them they should grab a bite. I can take over."

"Go," Allegro said with authority. "Be back in twenty minutes."

Both nurses ran off without further hesitation.

Domino went to the station's computer and, with two clicks of the mouse, had accessed the hospital's patient records.

"Be fast, Helga," Allegro said as she turned to walk away.

"Go look important," Domino replied, her eyes fixed on the computer screen. "I know how much you love that."

The database was straightforward. She isolated the first fifty victims admitted with H1N6. Their birth dates verified that all but three were young, in their late teens and twenties. Further inspection revealed that, as expected, they'd been students of the University of Munich. The three older victims were all professors or assistant professors there. She needed their dates of admission, state of health when admitted, and dates of death. Hopefully Reno would find some pattern in cross-referencing this data with information from the university's student records.

So far, the Munich victims were the only ones with this kind of casualty concentration, but neither the government nor WHO officials could establish any solid conclusions without legal access to the confidential files.

Domino pulled the memory stick from her pocket and had just inserted it in the computer USB port when Allegro spoke in her ear. A man, apparently a doctor, was asking her who she was.

"Sent from Neuperlach hospital to assist," Allegro told him.

"Good." He sounded relieved. "Most of the cardiology crew is in the ER helping with the H1N6 patients. I'm glad they sent help."

"We all need to pull together at times like this," Allegro said. "I'm here to do what I can."

"How is Mister Gottlieb?"

"Who?" Allegro asked.

"You just came out of his room," the doctor replied, confusion in his tone. "He was operated on this morning."

"Oh, right," Allegro said.

Domino quickly typed in the name and looked up the patient's chart, then relayed the relevant information into Allegro's earpiece.

"Ah, yes, cardiopulmonary bypass," Allegro said with just the right amount of casual authority. "Aside from a minor infection that's being treated with cefazolin, he's doing fine."

"Good. Does he have—"

"Oops, my pager vibrated," Allegro said. "Looks like they need me in the ER." Domino heard the sound of her rapid footsteps as she hurried away.

"Good save," Allegro said in her ear.

"Do pagers vibrate?" Domino asked as she studied the progress of her file transfer.

"Who the hell knows?"

"You owe me. What were you doing in a patient's room, anyway?"

"Dodging," Allegro said. "Are you done?"

"Almost. Just another three minutes. Where are you now?"

"Visiting a patient in Room 241."

"Will you at least read his chart this ti—" Domino heard voices coming down the hall toward her and glanced up over the counter. "Damn."

"What's up?" Allegro asked.

"The nurses are coming back. I can't pull the stick yet." Domino covered the file-transfer window with the patient file she'd called up for Allegro as the two women neared the desk. The senior, heavyset nurse came to stand behind her.

"What are you doing?" she asked.

Just then one of the patient lights in the large console beside them began blinking red, and an alarm blared. The heavyset nurse frowned as she noted the number beneath the light. "Room 241," she said, hurrying off down the hallway with her younger colleague at her heels.

"And before you ask," Allegro said in Domino's ear, "no, I didn't kill him."

"How big of you." Domino closed the patient file and the file-transfer screen reappeared. "Another few seconds and we're done. Come get me."

"By the way, I think we're even." Allegro joined her just as Domino pulled the stick.

"Let's get out of here before you burn the place down," Domino said.

"Yeah. Hospitals make me sick."

As Allegro drove to the second location, Domino got the small laptop out of the duffel and sent the records to Reno for analysis. The netbook was brand-new; the only thing added to the standard equipment it came with was hi-speed Internet access.

The information their contact had given them indicated that the University of Munich had eighteen separate faculties, most of which had their own admissions office, so student personnel records were scattered among several different buildings. From what Dilbert had been able to determine, there seemed to be only one possible place where they might find a single database that covered the entire student/teacher population—in the chancellor's office at the central university administration building.

"Ah, yes, breaking and entering. Finally something I like." Allegro pulled the van up close to the large brick structure. They'd stripped off their hospital garb and were both wearing black turtlenecks and pants.

"About time you got useful," Domino replied. "Cam to the right, hidden behind the tree. I can see the red light." She pulled away from the window back to the dark interior of the van.

Allegro looked up through the front window of the vehicle. "Once burned, twice shy?"

"Let's say cameras and I have a past."

"I can't see if it's a CCTV." A closed-circuit monitor would likely have the campus security center constantly viewing it. Allegro glanced down at her handheld navigator. "According to the blueprints, we need the office in the middle." She pointed to the window.

"We have to go in through the front," Domino said.

"Looks like I have some climbing to do." Allegro smiled. "Wait here until I give you the signal." She handed the navigator and her set of picks to Domino before going to the back to extract two ski masks from the duffel. Tossing one to Domino, she slipped the other over her head. Another rummage through the bag yielded a pair of pliers, which she slipped into her pocket, and a long nylon rope with a four-pronged grapnel hook attached to the end. "In a few."

Allegro got out of the van. Keeping to the dark shadows, she approached the enormous oak from behind the camera's view. She could see a large, sturdy branch just below and well behind the camera, mounted twelve feet off the ground. She aimed the grapnel and threw, and it wrapped around the limb. After a quick tug, she scaled the tree and straddled the branch. Carefully releasing the grapnel in a clear spot where it wouldn't get hung up on its way back down, she then shimmied forward toward the security cam. "I'm there."

"If someone's observing the monitors—" Domino said in her ear.

"We should have a few seconds to get in."

"It'll take you longer than that to climb back down."

"Amateur." Allegro checked the wire leading from the camera to the building. "I won't climb down anything." She removed the pliers from her pocket. "Three, two, one." She counted down and cut the power. "Now."

A millisecond later, she dropped from the branch to the ground, wincing when she hit the grass. Twelve feet normally wouldn't have been a problem, but her ankle had just healed from a similar stunt in Turkey. "Ouch."

"Good going, monkey girl." Domino joined her and stowed the grapnel behind the tree, for pickup on the way out.

"Come on, let's go."

"Right behind you." Domino handed Allegro the set of picks as they raced to the entrance.

It took Allegro a few seconds to get them in. They entered the women's restroom, the one place that wouldn't be monitored. Allegro used the navigator to call up the blueprint. "Not too bad. Just one floor up and down the hall to the right."

Staying close to walls and in the darker recesses, they made it to the office apparently undetected. There were no alarms, and a glance outside showed all was quiet in the parking lot. "Guess no one monitors the cams," Domino said.

They accessed the chancellor's computer, and Domino copied the student records of the early victims onto the flash drive. The files included their admissions forms, majors and minors, class schedules, grades, extracurricular activities, and emergency-contact information.

Allegro watched the progress over Domino's shoulder. "I see a pattern here," she noted, as Domino called up one of the last of the records.

"That's right. Biology." Domino next accessed the three records of the teachers who'd died, and they took a few moments to study their files.

"All professors or assistant professors within the Biology Department." Allegro stood and glanced out the window again to ensure no one was responding to the break-in. "Reno should be able to cross-reference all this fast."

They left the way they'd come in, and when they were back in the van, headed away, Allegro got Reno, the EOO's best computer op, on her cell phone.

"I'm sending you the student/teacher records of the first fifty victims, as we speak," she told him. "Already noticed a strong link to the Biology Department with most if not all of them. I need you to confirm that and narrow down commonalities. And see if you can use the hospital data to give us the best idea of exactly when the first infections occurred."

"No problem," Reno answered. "I can have that in a few minutes. Running it now."

While they waited for the results, Domino consulted the campus map and located the Biology Department. It had been recently moved into new facilities within the HighTech campus, a few miles away in the Martinsried-Großhadern district. Allegro headed that way.

As she drove, she glanced over at Domino, who had gone quiet and was staring out the passenger window. "You could just call her, you know."

"What are you talking about?"

"Give me a break. I can hear you thinking way over here."

Domino smiled ruefully. "You know I can't."

"Screw that," Allegro said. "You need to hear her voice and she yours. You could be on your way to dirty diapers. Don't you think she wants to share that with you?"

"Of course she does."

"Then call her, for Christ sake."

Domino chewed at her lip with uncertainty. "I don't know."

"We're stopping at a pay phone later. Monty will never know." As she pulled into the lot of the new biocenter, Reno called back.

"All the students were Biology Department majors," he confirmed. "They shared a lot of the same classes, four in particular, all prerequisites. Three of those classes were taught by the professors who died. The teacher of the fourth class—an advanced botany course—isn't on the list. His name is Gunther Zimmerman."

"Have you cross-checked his name against the government's official list of all the H1N6 victims to date? Maybe he got sick later than the others," Domino said.

"Uh…not yet."

"Come on, man, do I have to spell it out?" Allegro said. "I know you gotta be tired, but find out everything you can on this guy."

"I'm on it. Get right back to you." Reno disconnected.

Allegro parked in front and turned off the ignition. "See if Dilbert's included any info on where Zimmerman's office is, and his home address," she told Domino.

While Domino examined the printouts, Allegro studied the massive building. It was brand-new, all steel and glass, and had several exterior lights. A security camera was mounted high over the main entrance and another over a side door, accessed by an alley running alongside the building. All the windows were dark. She glanced at her watch. It was a few minutes before two a.m.

"His office is on the third floor, botany wing," Domino reported. "And his apartment is within walking distance. A mile or so."

"There." Allegro pointed to the side entrance when Domino looked up. Headlights were coming toward them up the alley beside the building. When the vehicle reached the exterior lights, they could see it was a van of some sort. It stopped beside the side entrance and five people got out, four women and a man. Their matching drab uniforms and buckets pegged them as the overnight cleaning crew.

Allegro's cell phone vibrated against her thigh. She answered and activated the loud speaker. "Go ahead."

"Zimmerman is dead," Reno reported. "But he's not on the German list of official H1N6 victims. The death certificate was signed by the coroner. It lists his COD as heart failure, complications of swine flu."

"Swine flu?" Domino repeated. "H1N1?"

"Roger that," Reno said. "And here's the really interesting part. His date of death is October eighth. That's at least two days ahead of any of the official victims on the list you gave me."

"Could he be our ground zero?" Allegro mused out loud.

"It says here swine flu. Nothing to indicate it was the N6 strain," Reno said. "But if they didn't know about the N6 yet…anyway, it's worth looking into."

"Good work," Allegro replied. "I take back everything I said."

"One more thing. I was able to narrow down the time of the initial infection, based on the hospital records and known data on progression of the disease," Reno told them. "We're looking at sometime around October first, most likely."

"You got what hospital he was admitted to, and who signed the death certificate?" Domino asked.

"One sec." After a short pause, Reno said, "A neighbor found him dead in his apartment. Coroner signed the certificate on October ninth. Hard to read his damn writing, first name Arne, I think. Last name starts with an S, maybe Schmidt?"

"So Zimmerman gets sick first, dies in his apartment, and is taken directly to the morgue," Allegro said. "And the coroner lists him as swine flu because the flood of cases hasn't started yet. It took them a while to recognize what was going on and even come up with this H1N6 designation."

"Makes sense," Domino replied. "A few days, this Schmidt guy was probably swamped with bodies and Zimmerman was in the ground. No way to verify he'd had it, too, if he even thought about it. All he probably had at most was blood work that confirmed some variation of H1N1. Unless he did an autopsy."

"Good work, Reno. Later." Allegro disconnected, then started the van and handed the navigator to Domino. "Next stop, the morgue."

"I get to be the doctor this time." Domino reached into their duffel for their hospital whites.

"Only because I'll let you."

They put their masks and gloves back on and fished a new set of fake IDs out of the bag before going inside. Signs led them down two hallways to the morgue. The big double doors were closed, but the large round windows in each enabled them to see inside. Men and women were working among row after row of bodies on steel tables.

Most of the dead were in sealed body bags, and all the doctors were wearing hi-tech ventilator masks with their own oxygen supplies for maximum protection.

"All of a sudden I'm feeling a little underdressed," Allegro told Domino in a low voice.

"Ya think?" Domino replied, and knocked on her window. When a few doctors turned in their direction she chose one and motioned him over. "We're looking for Arne Schmidt?" she said in German.

The man studied her name tag. "I'll get him, doctor. Wait here."

Allegro watched him negotiate his way through the tables toward a baldheaded man. After a brief exchange, the latter joined them.

"What can I do for you?" he asked.

"Just need a moment. We're working with the World Health Organization," Domino said.

Once she told him they were part of a WHO task force to track the virus, Schmidt agreed to their request to look at the Gunther Zimmerman file. They went to his office, where he called up the record on his computer. He studied it for several seconds, as though trying to distinguish the deceased among the hundreds he'd seen in recent days.

His forehead creased in confusion. "Yes, I remember him. His neighbor found him dead in his apartment. Rigor mortis had already set in. Zimmerman had a history of aortic stenosis, and I listed his COD as heart failure, complicated by swine flu, not this virus. We didn't start getting those cases until a bit later, as I recall." Schmidt glanced up at Allegro. "You think he had H1N6 as well?"

"That's what we want to know. Did you do an autopsy? Allegro asked.

Checking the computer again, the coroner replied, "Only a partial, because of his history and the condition of the body. Blood work, examination of the heart, lungs, and other major organs. My notes indicate vascular hemorrhage and alveolar edema in the lungs." He looked up. "It's entirely possible I missed it if he was an H1N6. He died before we knew there was another possibility, and we had no reason to look further. We still can't isolate this virus in the lab."

Allegro thanked him and they returned to the van.

"This guy could have been infected anywhere. And that's if he was deliberately infected. We can't exclude the possibility he was in on this and infected accidentally, or singled out because he knew something and was silenced," Allegro said.

"Agreed. But because he was a botany guy and not a virologist, we start with the theory that he was a random target. And that he probably was infected in a one-on-one situation, or we'd have other victims with the same date of death," Domino said. "Which means it's unlikely he was out in public. More probably, they got him at his home or office. Spent the most time there, and easier to get him alone."

"Since the feds are convinced this is a big conspiracy with random victims, he probably didn't know his attacker," Allegro said. "We need to talk to his coworkers, friends, especially the neighbor who found his body. See if someone remembers something unusual, seeing anyone with him they didn't recognize around that time."

"They might also be able to tell us when he started getting sick, so we can further narrow the period when he was infected." Domino checked her watch. "Nothing we can do about that for at least another six or seven hours."

Allegro nodded. "If, and this may be a long shot, he was infected at the school, we might get something off the security cams. His apartment building might have some, too. That's something we can do now." She headed back to the HighTech campus.

"I really hate the prospect of having to sit through the hours and hours it'll take to screen several days of video," Domino groused. "We'll need to get a week's worth or so. At least a few days on either side of Reno's estimate."

"Yup, if we want to be safe," Allegro said. "Hope it's good-enough quality, too, that Reno can quickly match up any faces we send him."

The cleaning-crew van was still sitting at the side entrance, and lights were on in several windows on the fifth and sixth floors. Allegro parked their vehicle on the street and grabbed the master passcards Dilbert had given them, while Domino searched the contact's printouts to find any indication of where the camera recording equipment for the building was located.

"Any luck?" Allegro asked.

"Nothing specific. Basement, probably. All the utilities are there—electrical transformers, computer servers, boiler room. Everything else is marked as offices, classrooms, and labs. Nothing marked security."

They grabbed the laptop and their earpieces, donned their ski masks, and used one of the master passcards to get in the side door. Keeping alert for more cameras inside, they took a stairwell leading down, then split up to search for the digital video recorder. Allegro found it in the room with the university's massive computer servers. "Got it. West-end hallway, second to the last room," she told Domino.

Within twenty minutes, they'd transferred a week's worth of video from all the cameras in the building to the laptop and were back in the van and en route to Zimmerman's apartment complex. The whole place was dark, with no security cameras, so they headed back to the hotel to start screening the tapes. They'd wait until morning to visit Zimmerman's building and start knocking on doors.

Three blocks from the Regent, Allegro pulled the van over and parked next to a pay phone. Domino would never agree to make a personal call from her room, because the hotel kept records. Allegro fished in her pocket for change. "Tell her I can't wait to be an aunt." She grabbed Domino's hand and placed several Euro coins in it.

Domino hesitated only briefly before getting out of the van. She was back within a few minutes.

"So?" Allegro asked.

Domino shook her head. "Still waiting for the results."

"What else did she say?"

"That you shouldn't be near the child during its formative years."

"She did not say that." Allegro started the van and headed toward the hotel.

"No, I did."

"Then it's a good thing I've learned to ignore you."

CHAPTER TWENTY

Geneva, Switzerland
October 20

The director-general of the World Health Organization had assigned two people full-time to feed information about the H1N6 virus into WHOSIS. The Statistical Information System, an interactive database, was their best way to keep up with the growing spread of cases in many of the organization's one hundred ninety-three member countries.

Ten days into the pandemic, the statistics were staggering. Sixty-three countries were now reporting cases of the mysterious virus, and more than two million fatalities had been recorded. The WHO's estimated death toll nearly doubled overnight, when they added the names of victims who had only been suspected of dying of the virus. Most of these reports were trickling in from third-world countries and isolated areas, where overwhelmed clinics and hospitals had neither the time nor the resources for accurate diagnostics. Even in the developed countries, it was still impossible to confirm the H1N6 infections through lab tests. Their record-keeping was imperfect because it was based on symptoms, location, and the known rate of the progression of the disease.

She hoped that was about to change. Several of the world's best labs were trying to isolate the stealth component of the virus through blood tests on people who were at the highest risk of having the disease but had not yet developed symptoms. They were the family, friends, neighbors, and coworkers of the dead and dying.

Though she tried valiantly to keep her focus on the myriad of tasks demanding her attention, she checked the latest reports from China every half hour or so. The explosive outbreak there was particularly worrisome, with a quarter of a million cases reported, and the spread was marching rapidly southward toward her home village.

Martial law had been declared in twenty-two nations, many acting because of widespread riots, looting, and hoarding. Borders throughout Europe, Asia, Africa, and North and South America were being closed to help contain the outbreak. Public gatherings were banned in many regions, and quarantines were springing up everywhere. Several major airlines had cancelled flights to the most severely affected countries, and some were considering a temporary shutdown of business altogether. People were afraid to travel, causing so many cancellations that planes were often flying with only a handful of passengers, and major airports like Amsterdam's Schiphol, London's Heathrow, and Kennedy in New York were virtually empty. Media Web sites crashed regularly because of the flood of panicked people seeking information on the virus.

The transportation of goods and services had stopped nearly everywhere. Surgical masks and over-the-counter flu medications had sold out globally in the first couple days of the crisis, and grocery shelves in the stores that remained open were virtually bare. Tens of millions were heeding the WHO's advice to remain in their homes and avoid all contact with other people.

It was only a matter of days, the director-general thought, before panic ensued in a way that hadn't been seen since the Spanish-flu outbreak of 1918, when a third of the world's population had been affected and as many as one hundred million people had died. People had killed their pets when it was rumored dogs carried the virus. Relatives had withheld food from affected loved ones. The normal conventions of society had broken down, and the economic, political, and other repercussions had been felt for many years after the threat passed. And this new virus could spread so much faster and farther today with air travel. The potential effect was unimaginable.

Already several people had committed suicide. Most had been infected; they couldn't deal with the agony of the final days. But also some took their lives because their families had been decimated, or because the growing economic impact of the virus had wiped them out financially. There would be many more of those, she knew, in the weeks and months ahead. *God help us all.*

❖

London, England
October 20

Derrick Anderson-Howe was on the phone in his den, asking yet another of his well-heeled business contacts for money for Zoe's ransom, when the cell phone in his suit jacket vibrated against his chest. The caller ID read Chez Maurice.

"Let me ring you right back," he said abruptly into the landline before flipping open his cell. "Collier, please say you have something good to tell me."

"On the contrary, I'm afraid," his friend with British intelligence replied. "I've just learned some very disheartening news, Derrick. I'd received information that the contacts I told you about—the ones who apparently have someone in place in Colombia—were planning to stage a rescue mission of Western hostages. I'd hoped they might be able to locate Zoe and include her. A slim chance, probably, which is why I didn't tell you. I didn't want you to get your hopes up."

"And?" Derrick loosened his tie.

"I've gotten word through the grapevine that they've recalled all their people from the field, to help with this pandemic," Morris reported. "And the latest intel indicates that all the resources they might have called on for any rescue are being reassigned as well. Helicopters and planes have been grounded in Colombia, except for extreme emergencies. To put it bluntly, my friend, this virus has altered everyone's priorities. Nearly every able-bodied man and woman in military, intelligence, covert, and even private organizations worldwide are now being utilized to stop this thing from spreading and prevent chaos."

"I understand, Collier," Derrick said. "I know you've done everything you can. I appreciate your efforts."

"Don't be too discouraged. Zoe is valuable to these people. And at least she's probably being held in an isolated location, which may be the best thing for her right now."

"I'd thought of that."

"Stay positive," Morris said. "I'll keep an eye on the situation and let you know if I hear anything more."

The words of encouragement made no difference. With each passing day, Derrick grew more certain he'd never see his daughter again.

❖

Budapest, Hungary
October 20

Doctor Andor Rózsa was reading the latest report from the World Health Organization when the head of Pharmamediq, Incorporated tapped on his half-open office door. "Yes, sir?"

"Any progress?" the man asked.

Andor suppressed a smile. He'd received the same question every day since Pharmamediq had joined the dozens of other labs worldwide who'd suspended all other research to help search for an antivirus. Everyone was racing to isolate the stealth component of the virus, the first step in finding a cure. But he would never claim credit for that—it would raise suspicions later when he announced to the world he'd found the cure. "Not yet, I'm afraid."

His boss, as usual, frowned in disappointment, not because he was deeply concerned about the dying and the dead, but because he was well aware that the company that came up with the antivirus would make billions from the formula. "Keep at it. If you need to hire more lab technicians or whatever to speed this up, let me know."

"Will do, sir."

Unlike his superior, Andor was a patient man. He'd waited this long, so he didn't mind waiting a few more weeks or months. The world was overpopulated, anyway. Someone would eventually isolate the stealth component. But even when that happened, it would still take a very long time for anyone to discover the cure. It had taken him eight months, after all, and he'd created Charon.

The antivirus grew exponentially more valuable daily. He planned to wait at least three months after the stealth component had been isolated before he announced the cure. By that time, the pandemic would have spread far and wide. Every nation would want the antivirus, and every laboratory in the world would be needed to produce it to meet the global demand.

CHAPTER TWENTY-ONE

Guaviare Jungle, Colombia
October 21

Fetch groaned as she gingerly extricated herself from her cot and stood to dress. Every muscle in her body ached and she hadn't had nearly enough sleep. She'd managed a few hours the previous afternoon, thanks to a heavy dose of painkillers and the fact that the camp had been deathly quiet after Barriga's execution of the two sick boys. But she'd spent most of the night preparing for the escape. And she still had much to do.

Barriga had four guards posted overnight, and they were taking their duties extra seriously because of his unpredictable behavior. Fetch didn't blame them, but their vigilance had made it difficult to surreptitiously obtain the supplies they needed. She'd had to watch them for hours, waiting for an opportunity to slip from her tent to the kitchen area unnoticed. The right moment came at two a.m., when the guards chanced congregating for a smoke, and probably the opportunity to discuss what had happened.

She had stashed water, rice, beans, and other staples under her cot, in and behind her duffel. Her backpack was stuffed with medical supplies, clothes, a blanket, and the personal items she'd brought from her locker. Fetch was grateful the kitchen had ample supplies. The cook wasn't likely to immediately notice that a handful of crates at the bottom of several stacks were half empty.

Tonight, she had to get the rest of what they needed from the supply tent. Rucksacks for the hostages and assorted other essentials, including insect repellant, water-purification tablets, a machete, and tarps.

Downing another pair of painkillers before she put on her mask, she left her tent and surveyed the camp. The guards from the night before had been replaced with four new ones. The cook was making breakfast, and a handful of rebels waited for their food or headed into the jungle to relieve themselves. All wore masks and gloves, and no one dared get within fifteen feet of each other.

She slowly walked toward the nearest tent, trying to ignore the persistent ache in her abdomen and the pain that radiated through every muscle and joint when she took a step. "Back away from the entrance," she called out loudly to the rebel inside, then paused before opening the entrance flap. "How are you feeling?" she asked in Spanish.

"I'm fine. No problems," the man replied quickly. "I'm not sick."

She repeated the process at each tent and hut and got the same answers. Even so, she looked carefully at each man and woman for signs of sweating or other symptoms, and spent an equal amount of time visually examining their waste buckets, cots, bedding, and floor for evidence of blood, vomit, or diarrhea.

At the sixth tent, she immediately noticed the lingering and distinctive scent of vomit when she pulled back the flap. She saw no sign of it inside, so the young female rebel had evidently cleaned up her mess and disposed of the evidence. But she was sick, though she denied it vehemently. Her forehead had a sheen of perspiration, and though the morning was cool, she wore only a single layer of clothes.

When she reached the hut that housed the three Italian hostages, Fetch glanced around before she went inside to make sure no one was within earshot.

The parents were huddled together on the floor in one corner, and the daughter sat alone at the far end. "How are you all feeling?" Fetch asked, looking at them one at a time. She never removed her mask anymore in the presence of others. No one could be trusted, especially since they most likely wouldn't even know if they'd been infected.

"We are all fine," the father, Tino, answered immediately. "But getting a bit crazy in here."

"It's for your own protection. So none of you feel sick?" Fetch asked again.

"How much longer we have to remain indoors?" Tino asked.

"That's what I came to talk to you about." In a low voice, Fetch explained what she had planned and that she would come get them that night for the escape. "You cannot say a word to anyone, not even the other hostages. If they find out, they'll kill us all. Do you understand?"

"Why are you doing this, Doctor?" Marcella asked.

"Because if we stay here, we'll die."

Marcella looked at her daughter, then back to Fetch. "But why do you care about us?"

"Is this a trap?" the husband asked.

"The guerrillas don't need to trap you to kill you," Fetch replied. "If they want you dead, they just shoot. And if you stay here long enough to get sick, you'll be worthless to them. This virus can kill within a few days. They will not let you live and put their own lives in danger."

"Kills in days?" Marcella repeated with alarm.

Fetch nodded. "Let's hope they find a cure fast."

The father was clearly still wary. "Why do you want to help us?"

"Because...I just want to," Fetch said, for lack of a better explanation.

"You are not like them, are you?" Marcella asked.

"No, but we can talk about that after we get out of here."

Marcella put her hand on her husband's arm reassuringly. "We will be ready tonight, Medica."

Continuing her rounds, Fetch found that two more guerrillas among the next dozen she visited also had signs of infection, though like the other rebel they had tried to conceal it and adamantly denied being sick. No one wanted a repeat of the previous day's events.

Fetch came to Willy's hut and knocked. The Aussie hostage didn't answer. Steeling herself, she opened the door and stuck her head inside. Willy was on his hammock, covered in blankets. He appeared asleep but was shaking, his brow sweaty. *Damn it.* She shut the door without going inside. Willy would never find out about her plans.

The next twenty-two rebel tents yielded three more obvious sick. All denied it, and she didn't let on she knew they were lying.

At Kylee's hut she had no answer to her knock there, either, but she really didn't expect one after her last visit. The Aussie woman had been deteriorating for weeks, both physically and mentally. Fetch stuck her head inside. Kylee was curled up in a corner.

Although she didn't intend to include this hostage, she needed to say good-bye in her own way. "Kylee," she whispered loudly, not wanting to startle the already emotionally fragile woman. When she didn't get an answer or sign of movement, Fetch approached and bent over to get a better look. Kylee was facing away, and it was hard to see much of anything in the dark hut.

With her gloved hand, Fetch touched the woman's arm. It felt cold and stiff. Fetch turned her over and only then saw dried blood around her mouth, and on her cheek and hair. Fetch turned her back over to face the wall.

"I'm so sorry this happened to you, Kylee." Fetch fought back tears. How unfair and cruel to have to die like this. To have to spend the last year of life in this prison and go crazier by the day. Had the rescue mission gone through, it would've been too late for this woman to fully recover anyway, even if she had made it back to her previous life.

In war there was no such thing as an unwounded soldier. Only one thing was worse than being killed: being caught and held in captivity. Most hostages and POWs could pull through with the help of family and psychiatrists, and return to at least an imitation of their former selves. But some were too damaged to ever make the mental journey. "You can't save them all," Montgomery Pierce had said when she'd returned from a disastrous SAR mission in Gaza. "All you can do is try." Why was that never any consolation?

She left Kylee, and instead of going to the next tent in order, she detoured to Zoe's hut. Without knocking this time, she stormed in. "When was the last time you saw Kylee?"

Zoe was in her hammock. She sat up in alarm. "What's wrong?"

"Just answer."

"I don't know…" Zoe paused, as though trying to remember. "Two days ago."

"Was she sick?"

"She's always seemed…unwell."

"I don't mean that. Did she show any symptoms of the virus?"

"I don't know," Zoe replied, getting out of the hammock. "Why?"

"She's dead. Has been, for a few hours. Willy's sick, too."

Zoe was wearing her mask, but Fetch could see the shock in her eyes. "Oh, my God."

"Don't tell anyone about this."

"Fine," Zoe said defensively. "Look, I'm sorry about—"

"I've talked to the Italians. Be ready to move tonight." She had no time for discussions and apologies. Things were escalating too fast. "I'll knock on your door when the time comes," she said, and strode from the hut. She'd been abrupt, but the thought that she might lose someone else, especially Zoe, was too much. She had to get her out of there immediately.

❖

Munich, Germany
October 21

By the time Domino and Allegro returned to their hotel with the digital video from the biocenter security cameras, it was nearly three-thirty in the morning. They still had five or so hours to kill before they could head back to Zimmerman's apartment complex to begin interviewing his neighbors, so they took turns screening the tapes, allowing the other to catch some sleep.

The task was mind-numbing because they had to go through tape from several cameras: two at the entrances, one mounted down the hallway from Zimmerman's office, others near the labs and classrooms he went to, and additional ones near the cafeteria and elsewhere that might have picked him up interacting with someone.

Domino took the first shift. She started with the eight a.m. to eight p.m. loop shot by the main entrance camera on October first, the date that Reno had determined was the likeliest period Zimmerman had been infected. Using photos that Reno had sent them from Zimmerman's driver's license and passport, she found the professor entering the building at eight twenty a.m., according to the time stamp. He was alone. Consulting her blueprint of the building, she called up the next nearest camera's tape from the same time period and tracked him heading toward a lab. Using this method, she was able to follow Zimmerman fairly effectively as he went about his day, but it was a time-consuming process. And there weren't cameras everywhere, so she lost sight of him several times.

In the two-and-a-half hours she had before Allegro relieved her, she was able to find only one occasion when he might have been infected—alone with a student in his office at ten twenty a.m. She captured a still photo of the student and sent it to Reno, to match against the university records for identification.

"Anything?" Allegro asked, as she entered Domino's suite through their connecting door.

"This'll take forever," Domino groused. "I've only gotten through the first four hours of the first day." She got up to stretch. "I sent one possible off to Reno, but I think it's just one of his students."

Allegro took the seat she'd just vacated and stared at the laptop. Domino had paused the tape she was watching. It showed an empty hallway, and the time stamp read: 1/10/11 12:10PM "What am I looking at?"

"Last time I had him he was heading back toward his office from the cafeteria. He'll pass by here en route, I think. Good luck." She crawled into bed.

Allegro woke her two-and-a-half hours later. "Time to head to the complex."

"Did you turn up anything?" Domino asked sleepily as she pulled on her boots. She was feeling much more jet-lagged than usual on a mission. No doubt, she thought, because she hadn't slept well before she'd left, worrying about Hayley and anxious about getting their results back.

"Isolated four more photos and sent them to Reno," Allegro said. "But I think they're all just faculty members."

Forty minutes later, they arrived at Zimmerman's apartment building.

"We split up, we can do this faster." Allegro pulled on her mask and gloves as they mounted the front steps.

"I'll start with Zimmerman's floor," Domino said, reaching into the back pocket of her trousers for hers. "Call me if you get anything useful."

Domino began to knock on doors, asking those who answered whether they had seen anything or anyone unusual during the time period they thought Zimmerman had been infected, and she asked whether they'd noticed if he'd been ill. Some of his neighbors refused to open their doors, and at others she got no response at all—meaning the residents were away, ill, or dead. She made notes on them all.

When she stopped at one door at the end of his hallway, a middle-aged man finally answered after she knocked repeatedly. She stepped back automatically when she got a good look at him. He had blood on the front of his pajamas and sweat on his forehead, and he seemed so weak he could barely stand.

Domino quickly ran through her questions, then advised the man to go immediately to the hospital, though they could do nothing for him. Likely he already knew that, which was why he was still at home.

"Anything?" Allegro asked in her ear an hour later.

"Covered his floor, and the floor above," Domino replied. "Nothing useful."

"I'm through the first two," Allegro said. "A lot of not-at-homes. Bag it for now and come back tonight?"

"Meet you downstairs," Domino said.

Allegro was waiting for her at the entrance, staring out at the empty streets. When she heard Domino approach from behind, she turned to face her. "Hey, I'm starving. How—"

"What is it?"

"Was anybody you talked to infected?" Allegro was uncharacteristically somber, and Domino knew something was up.

"Yes," she said. "Why?"

"You have a rip in your mask."

Domino pulled it off and saw a two-inch tear in one side. She'd snagged it on something and hadn't noticed when she'd put it on. Her heart sank. She headed toward the van, thinking of Hayley and the baby they hoped was on the way. Allegro trailed her.

When she got inside, she pulled a new mask out of the duffel bag and put it on.

"Damn, Luka," Allegro said when she shut the car door.

Domino stared out the windshield. "Yeah."

"What if—"

"Keep your mask on around me from now on," Domino said. "Fuck."

❖

October 22
Guaviare Jungle, Colombia

At midnight, the camp was quiet and virtually deserted, except for four guards Fetch could see stationed at the perimeter who stayed far apart from each other. Most of the rebels and hostages had stayed inside their tents and huts all day, emerging only to retrieve their meals, not willing to risk Barriga's wrath.

After completing her rounds that afternoon, she'd stopped off at the commander's tent to report the situation unchanged. She refused to tell him she had found one hostage dead and another sick, and a total of fourteen guerrillas showing symptoms. Fortunately, he was apparently too afraid of getting sick to check to see whether she was telling the truth.

Once it had gotten dark, Fetch had used her binoculars to note the positions of the guards and their routine. They were stationary for the most part, but every hour or so, two of them would patrol the camp perimeter. The sky was partially overcast, occasionally obscuring the nearly full moon, so it'd been relatively easy to get what she needed from the supply tent undetected. Now it was time to put her plan into action. Dressed in black fatigues, she snuck again from her tent and slipped past the perimeter between two of the guards.

She carried three rucksacks packed with food, supplies, ammo, and whatever else they might need. After she stashed them in the jungle, she returned for her backpack and a fourth rucksack and hid them with the others.

Carrying her FARC-issued M14 rifle, she approached the guard positioned nearest to the Italians' hut. "Time for my shift," she told him.

He mumbled something and took off, looking tired. The other closest guard was to her right, some distance away. She walked over slowly, trying to keep a friendly expression in her eyes since her mouth was covered. After glancing about conspiratorially, she asked, "Have anything to drink?"

"Mine is finished, Medica. How about you?"

"Back there," she said, pointing to the edge of the jungle.

Although the rebels weren't allowed to drink when on duty, most did, but some were always more than willing to snitch. And considering recent events, this guard seemed especially leery of having any infractions reported to the commander. "Get it," he said.

"Not here," she replied in a low voice. She tilted her head to the right. Another guard had just lit a cigarette, giving away his position fifty feet from where they stood. "Come with me." She led him away from the other guard, back to her old position, and stepped into the thick jungle.

Fetch picked up her flask and poured some liquid into a cup and handed it to him. When the soldier turned away from her to look at his post while he drank, Fetch smashed the back of his head with her rifle butt and he crumpled to the ground. The constant buzz of insects effectively covered the sound. He was out cold, but she had to make sure he couldn't come to and sound the alarm. She still had to get the hostages and move them away from the camp.

She brought her heavy army boot down on his head a few times until she was sure he was dead, then dragged his body farther into the jungle into a dense thicket of undergrowth.

Keeping track of the other guards' positions, Fetch quietly made her way to the Italians' hut and knocked softly. When the door opened, she motioned for them to be quiet and follow her. After leading them to the beginning of their escape route in the jungle, well out of sight of the guards, she went to Zoe's hut. Zoe opened when Fetch knocked. She hushed Zoe as well and led her to the others. In silence, she gave each hostage a rucksack and shouldered her backpack.

She pointed in the direction they were headed and led them to one of the faint trails out of camp that was free of booby traps. They'd barely reached it when Fetch detected movement in the leaves several feet in front of her and to the left. She turned and motioned to the hostages to stop and get down. They all immediately complied. She crouched as well and whispered, "Wait here."

They were crowded close together, and in the faint light penetrating the canopy above, she could make out the fear in their eyes. "I'll be right back," she whispered as she set down her rifle and removed a knife from her belt.

Zoe watched the doctor creep cautiously away, the knife at her side shining in the moonlight. They were so close to escaping that the thought of being caught made her want to lose her dinner. She knew all too well what that would mean.

The medic disappeared into the blackness of the undergrowth on one side of the path and Zoe tensed, listening intently, but all she could hear were insects and the distant cry of a bird or animal of some sort. After only a minute or two, the doc reemerged, retrieved her rifle, and motioned them to move on.

The path was wide enough here that Zoe could walk beside the doctor while the others stuck close in a tight group just behind them. But they'd gone only a few more yards when the medic grabbed her arm. "Stay behind me," she said quietly.

Zoe looked down at the woman's hand. It was too dark to see well, but the once-pale surgical gloves now appeared black. "Is that blood?" she whispered.

"Not now."

"Are you all right?" Zoe asked

"It's not mine," the doctor answered coldly. "Stay behind me."

Zoe fell back a step, knowing it had to belong to a guard about to discover them. Had the doc killed him? After the incident with the two boys, Zoe knew all too well these guerrillas killed, and mercilessly. And now the doctor had killed one of her tormentors. Things like this only happened in movies. Seeing someone's blood on the hands of another was not reality, not *her* reality.

Could someone live with the fact that they'd killed? Zoe had a hard time believing *she* could forget, and she'd only witnessed it. What turned a healthy person into one capable of taking a life? It was self-preservation, Zoe thought. If she had to, she'd have probably done the same. Yeah, that was it. The doc wasn't a killer, per se.

But something in the medic's eyes just now—the detachment, the emptiness—told her that this woman was no stranger to taking lives. The ease and calculated proficiency with which she drew her knife told Zoe the doctor was as dangerous as all the others. And right now, Zoe was happy to have her on her side.

After a couple of hours of walking, the path narrowed and became almost indiscernible, the brush on either side grazing their rucksacks and slowing their progress. All the hostages, Zoe included, were gasping for air from the exertion in the high altitude.

The medic allowed them five minutes' rest while she quietly briefed them on how to move most efficiently in the thickets—turning their bodies sideways to slide through the gaps, varying their stride to avoid tangling themselves in the roots beneath. She warned them not to try to use vines or brush to help them up the steeper slopes they would soon face, because much of the vegetation had thorns or sharp spines.

Too soon, they set off again, the doctor allowing them no further rests except brief stops to relieve themselves. More time passed in a blur. They'd been marching for what felt like all night. It was hard for Zoe to tell. All she knew was that the fear and freedom that had pushed them all forward when they started was slowly turning into exhaustion. She didn't understand how the doc found the energy to keep going, especially after the beating she'd taken the day before.

"What time is it?" Zoe asked the medic.

"Time to keep moving," she answered without stopping.

Zoe caught up and grabbed her wrist. "We've been walking for hours."

"We can't stop yet." The doc shook her off and continued forward, glancing at her watch. "The camp will be up in another forty minutes. It won't take long for them to realize we're gone."

"Please," Tino pleaded from behind them. "My daughter needs to rest for a little. "She is going to...*sprofondare.*"

Zoe turned around. Octavia was lagging several feet back from the rest, and she was stumbling rather than walking. In the moonlight Zoe could see how pale she was. "Just a few minutes," she begged the medic. "You heard Tino. I don't know what sprofowhatsit means, but she's about to drop."

"Collapse," the doctor replied dryly. "It means collapse." She stopped so abruptly Zoe crashed face-first into her back. She turned and looked down at her. "You okay?"

Zoe rubbed her already aching nose through her mask. The metallic tang of blood hit her lips. "I think it's bleeding again."

The doctor looked past her to the others, who had stopped well back and stood gasping for breath. "Ten minutes," she said. "Drink, but not too much, and do not share your flask."

Then she turned her attention to Zoe and looked closely at her face. "Yeah, it's bleeding."

Zoe pulled her mask away enough to wipe her nose with her sleeve.

"Wait," the doc said, letting her backpack drop from her shoulders. She pulled out a fresh pair of surgical gloves and put them on, stashing the bloody ones in a side pocket. She reached into the pack again and withdrew a roll of toilet paper.

Zoe reached to take it but the doctor brushed her hand away. "Let me," she said, and gently lifted Zoe's chin.

"I can do it."

"I know you can. I want to make sure nothing's fractured." The medic pulled down Zoe's bloodstained mask to get a better look. "He got you good." She was standing so close their bodies were almost touching.

"It was stupid," Zoe mumbled. "My display of pride with that primate."

"I won't argue that. You should be more careful when picking your weapons for survival. Pride is rarely the best option. In the worst case it'll ruin you. In the best, you always feel ashamed when you fall."

"I'm sorry I got you hurt."

"Stop talking and let me see the damage." The doctor dabbed at her nose and mouth with the softest touch Zoe had ever felt. The unexpected tenderness almost put her in a trance and she couldn't look away from the medic's eyes. Her surgical mask covered her beautiful mouth.

"I take it that's a no," the doctor said.

Zoe had been so enthralled she'd obviously missed something. "Excuse me, what?"

The doc had put away the toilet paper and was gazing at her with a hint of a smile in her eyes, her hand now cupping Zoe's face. "I asked if I was hurting you," she said, stroking Zoe's cheek with her thumb.

Zoe was aware she was staring. Although she could hear the doctor speak, it took a moment to register the words. "I…um…no, not at all. I must look like a wreck." She ran her hand over her hair, suddenly self-conscious.

The medic gently placed a new mask over Zoe's mouth and nose. She was done, but she didn't move away. "Your nose and upper lip are swollen," she said. "But otherwise…beautiful." For a long moment both stood silent, staring at each other.

The doctor stepped back first. "Drink some water. We have to move again." She sounded almost agitated.

The sky was beginning to lighten. Dawn was fast approaching, and Zoe had never dreaded daylight more. The camp would soon come awake, and it probably would only be a matter of minutes before Barriga knew of their absence. The hunt would start.

Could they pull this off? Zoe couldn't let herself think otherwise. Not only would they drag her back and hurt her and the other hostages in brutal ways, they would most likely kill the medic on the spot. She watched the doctor's back as she led them to God knew where. Why was this woman helping them? If she was afraid of getting sick, all she had to do was save herself. Why was she taking the risk of rescuing a bunch of strangers? It didn't make sense, not that much in her life did at the moment. But this soldier's actions were far beyond her understanding. She couldn't imagine watching the doctor die before her eyes.

Zoe looked up as the sun pierced the horizon through the trees ahead. She wasn't the only one. For a moment, all of them stopped to stare. She turned and looked back at the Italians. Fear was plain in everyone's eyes.

"Keep moving." The doctor pushed on again, but veered off the faint trail they'd been following and into the jungle.

"How far are we from where you take us?" Marcella asked from behind Zoe.

"Three or four days' walk, if we don't waste too much time with stops," the medic said over her shoulder.

"Are we going to a town?" Tino asked.

"There's only one town anywhere close, and it's days away on foot. We'd never make it," the doctor replied. "When Barriga finds out we're missing, he'll radio every camp in the region, and he'll be expecting us to go that way. We'd be surrounded and caught within hours."

"Where, then?" Marcella asked loudly, clearly tired and agitated by the uncertainty of the situation.

"Please keep your voice down," the doc snapped, half turning to glare at the Italians but never slowing her stride. "We're going to a safe house. It's an abandoned shack in a valley, on the other side of the next big mountain. We'll trick them by moving farther into the jungle."

"They will not find us there?" Marcella asked.

"Of course not." Tino said something in Italian that calmed her down.

The daughter, Octavia, hadn't said a word the entire journey until now. "Do you think they are after us?" she called out from her position at the end of the line.

The barrage of questions was driving Zoe crazy and only increasing her anxiety. Now was not the time to panic or develop second thoughts. She was determined to make it out of this jungle and she refused to allow the Italians' loud voices and hysteria to stand in her way.

She stopped walking and turned to face them. "Listen, I realize you're hungry and tired and scared out of your skulls, but you have to keep it together." She tried to speak softly. "Let the doctor do her job. Distracting her with questions won't keep us alive. We need her alert."

Zoe turned back around, ready to start off again. The medic stood with her arms crossed a few feet ahead, staring at her, eyebrows raised in surprise.

"Why are you angry with us?" Tino's voice was as petulant as that of a scolded child. "You do not feel afraid?"

Zoe turned her head to glare at the man. "No, I feel like I caught a rainbow and put it in my pocket," she shot back, and heard the doctor snicker. "Of course I am. I'm terrified. But I will not allow fear to stand in the way of my freedom. If we're to stay alive, we have to fight. Now save the third degree for the next stop."

She pivoted and forged ahead, passing the doc, who'd paused to watch the interaction. Zoe could tell by the medic's eyes she was smiling. "Wipe that grin off your face and lead the way."

CHAPTER TWENTY-TWO

Fetch was pushing the hostages to their breaking point, but they had to continue moving on quickly, with few pauses. They would have only a six- to eight-hour head start at most after Barriga discovered their escape, and she couldn't guarantee he'd single-mindedly pursue the obvious route toward town.

He had at least seventy guerrillas who weren't showing symptoms the day before, men and women who could navigate through the jungle blindfolded and cover ground much more quickly and efficiently than her own crew. Many more rebels had probably become ill since she'd last checked on them, given the escalation in the number of victims from the night before. But Barriga might still have enough left healthy to dispatch search teams in all directions, especially since they had no valuable hostages left at camp to guard. And he could easily radio the news to other nearby encampments, asking for assistance.

They'd been traveling forward steadily, but slower than she'd have liked. Zoe had kept up with her from the beginning, but the Italians, the daughter in particular, had not been able to match the pace she wanted after the first hour or so, and kept lagging far behind. Adrenaline had sustained the hostages initially, but it was short-lived. They'd pushed on when exhaustion set in, and again when the hunger pangs first started. She knew they desperately needed calories, but she hadn't dared stop to eat.

Now, an hour after dawn, they were on a steep, uphill climb and even she was struggling. The thin air was making it difficult to breathe even though she was acclimated to it. Her sides had started to hurt again, and her thigh, where Barriga had kicked her, was throbbing. She paused on an even piece of ground and turned to see how the rest were faring.

The Italians were far back, but Zoe, as always, was close behind her. She still wasn't used to seeing Zoe wear her clothes. The sweatpants fit all right around the waist, but Fetch was three or four inches taller than Zoe so they really bagged around her ankles in an almost comical way. And Zoe's breasts were bigger than hers, so the black long-sleeved T-shirt she'd given her was stretched tight across her chest.

Still, they fit her better and were in much better shape than the clothes the rebels had given the Italians. They were all wearing torn, faded peasant clothes that FARC enlistees had been glad to trade in for fatigues. Tino looked like a farmer in black cotton trousers and oversized gray shirt; Marcella wore brown men's trousers, a too-tight beige T-shirt, and a traditional fringed shawl; and Octavia was in faded navy sweatpants and a round-necked pink blouse that once had lace around the edges.

"Tired?"

"Seriously?" Zoe managed to say, between big gulps for air. Her surgical mask dented in and out sharply with each gasp. "You have to ask?" she practically barked back.

Yup, the natives were getting restless. "Hungry?" Fetch dared inquire.

Zoe bent over to clutch her knees. "I could even eat you right now," she replied as she fought to catch her breath.

Fetch tried to keep a straight face. Surely Zoe hadn't meant that the way it came out, but it was funny, and a disturbingly exciting image nevertheless.

"And, yes, I realize what I just said." Zoe wheezed. "But I'm too tired and hungry to rephrase." She looked up at Fetch. "We must be in China by now. God, can we eat yet?"

Fetch laughed. "Most call me God, but you can call me Gianna."

Zoe stood. "That's your name?"

Fetch nodded.

"It sounds very…" Zoe gestured with her hand, while she tried to place it. "Italian."

"I guess."

"At least it's the only other place I've heard it." Zoe looked at her curiously. "But you're not Italian."

"Yes and no."

"I knew you looked different."

The Italian family neared, and Tino called out, "Medica, we need to eat. My daughter is weak."

"Take off your gear," Fetch said, shedding her backpack. She set her rifle against a tree. "Time to eat."

"Thank God. Or, rather, Gianna." Zoe exhaled loudly as she slid her rucksack off her shoulders and sat down beside it. "Are we ordering in, and where's the menu?"

"Don't get too comfortable." Fetch fished into her backpack and withdrew a tin of beans, spoon, and can opener. "We have to eat on the way." She peeled back the lid of her can and handed the opener to Zoe.

Zoe took it and reached into her rucksack for her own can. "Great. By the time we're done eating, we'll be starving again."

"We can't stop." Fetch stretched to remove the ache from her shoulders while the can opener was passed to the Italian family. From this height, she could see a good distance back in the direction they'd come. So far, she could find no sign anyone was pursuing them. Yet.

Once everyone had their cans open, she reshouldered her backpack and looped the sling of her rifle over her shoulder. She was about to get them moving again when Tino crouched and pulled the mask off his daughter. The family had stopped several feet away from her and Zoe.

"You have to eat," he said in Italian.

Octavia was sitting on a large rock half-buried in the slope, her face pointed downward as though she was staring at the ground. When Tino put his hand beneath her chin to raise her head, Octavia coughed weakly.

Fetch froze when blood trickled down one side of the girl's mouth. Looking closer, she could see that Octavia was soaked in sweat, with black circles under her eyes. She looked listlessly at her father, as though having trouble focusing.

"I never thought I'd enjoy eating this crap," Zoe said from behind her.

When Fetch didn't respond Zoe asked, "What are you... bollocks, is she sick?"

"Damn," Fetch said under her breath. She stood in silence while Tino and Marcella quietly fussed over their daughter, speaking Italian. Marcella said they had to move on, not let the others find out. "For at least a day or two, from the looks of it," she told Zoe quietly.

Zoe had risen and was standing beside her. "Why didn't they say something?"

"Denial at first."

"Then they were afraid they'd get left behind."

"I knew some of you might be..." Fetch took a deep breath. "How didn't I see this?" she said to herself, rubbing her face.

"Because it was dark when we left, and they've been keeping her far behind us the whole time."

"God damn it."

"They're just trying to survive."

Fetch turned to look at her. "By putting us all in danger."

"Can you blame them?" Zoe still held her half-eaten can of beans. She set it down and picked up her mask to put it back on.

"No, I can't," Fetch finally replied. The two of them stood watching the family in silence for another minute. Now and then, Marcella glanced their way, but quickly returned her attention to Octavia.

"I would probably have done the same," Zoe said quietly.

Fetch studied her for a long while, looking for any hint she was infected. Zoe seemed healthy, aside from a few scratches she'd gotten on her face and neck from the dense jungle undergrowth.

"Don't look at me like that," Zoe said. "I'm fine."

But Fetch continued to scrutinize her, panic slowly rising to the surface.

"I swear, I'm *fine*." Zoe glared daggers at her. "Never better, picture of health, etcetera, etcetera."

Fetch looked back to the Italians. The daughter was weakly trying to refuse the beans her mother was forcing through her lips with a spoon. Some ended up in her mouth, some on the ground, and some on the front of her shirt.

"What do we do now?" Zoe asked.

"If the girl's this progressed, it's only a matter of time before the parents start showing symptoms, and before they infect us." Fetch faced away from them all to clear her head. "It takes about a week to begin showing symptoms. Which means she was infected before we knew about this and began to take precautions."

She felt Zoe's hand on her shoulder. "What are our chances of having it, too?"

The chances were high, but Fetch couldn't let herself believe that, much less take away Zoe's hope. "Can't say for sure. These three have been bunking together, and they've been here a lot longer and have weaker immune systems. Malnutrition and untended infections make them a lot more vulnerable. You haven't been here long, and we're both in a much better physical state."

"I hope you're right," Zoe said.

That makes two of us, Fetch thought.

Zoe looked back at the Italians. "Even if they're going to…die, we can't leave them behind."

"Every minute we waste, the guerrillas gain," Fetch replied. Zoe was right. She couldn't walk away, but she also couldn't do anything to change their destiny. Octavia wouldn't be able to travel much farther. And her parents would likely be in the same state soon.

Fetch turned back toward the Italian family. Tino looked up and saw her staring. "She's just tired," he said, wiping at his forehead with his sleeve.

They'd all been hiking with heavy rucksacks, but it was still early and cool, with a light breeze. Neither she nor Zoe was visibly sweating, especially after a few minutes' rest, but Tino sure was.

"We will be ready in a minute. A few minutes," he begged, looking from Fetch to Zoe.

"We're not going anywhere without you," Zoe assured him and turned to Fetch.

"Zoe, we can't wait for a miracle," she said quietly.

"Please don't do this. They've made it this far."

"It'll be another three days at least before we reach the safe house," Fetch told her. "None of them will survive it."

"I can't leave them behind," Zoe said resolutely. "I have to—"

"To what, Zoe? Let them slow us down until Barriga's men catch us? Octavia has maybe only hours left."

"Then we'll go at their pace until she does."

"And do the same with the parents until they die, too?"

"Yes, if we have to."

"You're playing with your life."

"Maybe, but I can't live with myself knowing that I walked away from three dying people," Zoe said. "Look, I don't have the right to ask you to do this for me, for them, especially since you'd be risking your own life. But both of us know we don't stand a chance without you, so I'm begging you, Gianna."

Fetch paced, her mind racing. She couldn't leave Zoe behind; that was out of the question. But Zoe was also in danger if they stayed with the Italians. And so was she. If *she* got sick, then Zoe would be on her own anyway.

"They're not bloody roadkill," Zoe said. "These are human beings who've managed to escape one nightmare only to find themselves in another."

"Don't you think I know that? They're the reason I'm here in the first place," Fetch said. She'd risked her life to enter the FARC and had put up with their cruelty and injustices only so she could save lives.

She lived to save; she existed to serve. She knew victory only when she saw elation in the hostages and soldiers she had freed, and felt happiness only when she delivered them to their families. Maybe most of her best moments were borrowed, and even vicarious, but that's all she'd known, except for a brief moment in her life.

Leaving a wounded soldier behind was never an option. And when it was clear they'd never survive, you stayed to whisper false reassurances, listen to their last gasp, and shut their eyes when they were gone. She never walked away until the last man standing was she. But a soldier also calculated the risks to their own self-preservation. Because even when the face of death became as familiar as that of an old friend, it never made the prospect of dying any easier. On the contrary, it only made the hunger for life stronger. Why had Sam disregarded her own safety and desire to live, and why did Zoe have to be just as stubborn?

"What does that mean…that they're the reason you're here in the first place?" Zoe asked.

"It means we'll keep them with us and push on as long as Octavia is able to travel. And reevaluate the situation then. But I want you and me to keep a distance from them always."

She allowed the Italians another few minutes' rest, watching Octavia closely. The girl's mother made her drink some water, while Tino took almost everything from her rucksack and stuffed it into his and Marcella's. Together, they got her to her feet, with one on each side, supporting her weight.

"We're ready now, Medica," Tino said. "She's just very tired, but we'll help her."

And so they pushed on, but at a much slower pace, with Fetch constantly looking over her shoulder.

Zoe exhaled her relief when they began moving together again, with the doc keeping a pace the Italians could manage. She was putting herself and the medic in danger, but how could she desert the only people who'd been kind to her? She hoped Gianna's decision to take a less obvious, more obscure escape route would help delay the rebels' pursuit.

For a while they went on as before, but pausing more frequently to rest, about once every hour or two. At the first stop, she noticed blood on Octavia's mask, but no one, not even the doctor, said a word about it. Not long after, Tino started coughing behind her, though he tried to suppress it. At a later stop, he coughed more, and both he and his wife were visibly sweating. Octavia was talking to herself, clearly hallucinating, but still no one dared speak of what was happening.

Zoe was alarmed at the speed with which all three were deteriorating. Soon, she could hear both Octavia and Tino coughing frequently. But she was also impressed by the parents' determination to keep going at whatever cost. In the early afternoon, she glanced back to check on them and realized the Italians had shed two of their rucksacks in order to be able to stay upright. Tino and Marcella were nearly dragging Octavia now, struggling to support her weight and keep her going.

Dusk was fast approaching when Tino yelled that they needed to stop, and she looked back to find Octavia on her knees by the side of the trail, vomiting, her mother beside her, holding her.

Zoe approached the family, aware that Octavia was not wearing her mask. When the girl stopped vomiting, Marcella laid her down and cradled her daughter's head in her lap. Octavia's eyes closed.

Gianna had followed Zoe and stood a few feet behind her.

"She'll be better soon," Tino said to both of them.

"No, she won't, Tino." The doctor sounded tired as she rubbed her eyes. "She has the virus."

Though it had been painfully obvious all day, the mother wasn't ready to hear her worst fears confirmed. She started to sob, and Zoe went to her.

"I'm sorry, Marcella." She put her hand on the woman's shoulder.

"She cannot go on. What will we do now?" Marcella asked.

"We're not leaving without you," Zoe said again. She dug in her rucksack for her toilet roll and water. After she soaked a large wad of the tissue, she sat by the sick girl and placed it on her forehead.

"Please let me," Marcella said. "No need for you to be close to us."

"I have my mask on," Zoe replied.

Marcella grabbed the wet paper. "No. It's not safe with us." Octavia was shaking, and she was mumbling something in Italian, apparently delirious.

Zoe moved away to let Marcella treat her.

"You cannot stay here. They will find you," Tino said.

Zoe looked at the doctor, pleading with her eyes.

The doc gave her an almost imperceptible nod. "Probably, but we're staying together."

Tino picked up his daughter's hand and whispered some endearment. Tears were in his eyes when he looked back to the doctor. "So we can die together?"

"We'll hide," Zoe replied.

"You cannot hide from these people," he told Zoe. "They follow your smell like dogs." He gave the doc an apologetic look. "I'm sorry, Medica, but it's true. You are not like them, but your people…they are evil."

"I know," Gianna replied.

Marcella stroked her daughter's hair, and Octavia went quiet and lay unmoving in her lap. "How long does she have?"

"I'm not sure," the doctor replied. "Hours. Maybe until tomorrow morning."

Tino's tears turned into sobs. "And then it's our turn."

"Don't say that," Zoe said. "You don't know that."

"Yes, I do, Zoe. Look at us. Marcella and I, we already have it." He took off his mask and Zoe saw dried blood around his mouth and on his beard. "I'm sorry we lied. But we did not want to believe that we would die in that prison. We want so much to go home."

"You don't have to apologize. What you did was human. You wanted to save your family," Gianna said.

"Yes, and now look," Tino said. "We are all dying anyway, and we put you in danger, too."

"We'll be fine." Zoe stooped and took the man's hands to console him. "We're fine."

"But for how long?" he asked.

"I don't know," Zoe replied.

"Maybe we already gave it to you," Tino said, his voice breaking. "You have been close to us many times since they brought you here. Ate with us, drank from our water."

Zoe couldn't meet Gianna's eyes. She knew she'd find compassion and affirmation of what Tino had said, and she wasn't prepared for that struggle yet. If death was coming for her, she'd face it when the time came and not a second before. She couldn't let fear consume her.

"Maybe," the doctor replied. "But we'll deal with that later." It was like Gianna had read her mind.

Shocked at her response, Zoe looked up at Gianna. Not because of what she had said, but how she delivered it—stone cold, almost indifferent.

"How long do we have?" Tino asked the doctor.

"It's hard to say. I can't be—"

"How long?" he repeated.

"Maybe a day."

Tino got up and paced, scratching his beard. After a while, he faced the doctor. "Can I talk to you alone?"

The two of them walked several feet away and began talking in low voices. Zoe felt left out, but she understood the sentiment of a private conversation with a doctor.

"I can't do that," Gianna said, loud enough for her to hear.

"You have to. Do it for her," Tino replied.

Gianna looked in Zoe's direction. For an instant, Zoe saw concern in her eyes, immediately replaced by a cold, empty stare. Almost like she was seeing through her. What was going on? Was Tino asking her to leave them behind?

"Then tell her yourself," Gianna said.

Tino came to stand over her. "Zoe," he said hesitantly, "I have asked the doctor to take you and leave."

"No!"

"Please. You cannot stay here. We will stay with our daughter until she is gone and then…" Marcella met his eyes.

"Wait here until you die?" Zoe asked.

"We will die anyway, the geography does not matter. But you are still well and we want you to go home to your father." He wiped a stray tear from his eye. "I know how much you miss him. Do not give up on home, Zoe. If you stay, we will make you sick, and if we don't, the guerrillas will find you. Either way you die because of us." He shook his head and looked lovingly at his wife and daughter. "I am not a murderer. I want to die knowing that at least one of us beat these devils and got out of this hell alive."

Zoe turned to the doctor. Gianna gazed at her, and this time, her stare was not distant. Caring and concerned, it also contained something stronger and more intimate. Gianna finally nodded.

Zoe got to her feet and turned to Tino, tears streaming down her face. "All right. We'll go." She wanted to hug him good-bye and hold Marcella, the woman who had helped her from their very first meeting, but she couldn't. They wouldn't let her close, afraid they might infect her. She wept as she walked away and Gianna approached the family for a few final words.

The doctor joined her not long after, and they headed away from the family in silence. When Zoe couldn't fight the need any longer, she turned for a last look at them. Tino and Marcella held their daughter between them as they cried.

CHAPTER TWENTY-THREE

More than four hours of nonstop walking had passed since they'd left the Italians, Fetch noted, glancing at her watch, and Zoe still hadn't said a word. She never complained about exhaustion or hunger, and took a few sips of water only after Fetch insisted. Zoe never even slowed; she just quietly complied by pulling out her water bottle, drinking as she walked.

Fetch wasn't sure what drove Zoe on since they'd left the family, but she functioned as if on autopilot. Devoid of any emotion, she marched on. Her gaze focused in the far distance, but the expression in her eyes seemed blind to anything beyond the thoughts in her head. People had different mechanisms to deal with sorrow, and silence was evidently Zoe's medicine of choice. Fetch understood and gave her the space, but she was leery of the volcano that might erupt.

They strode on for another ninety minutes, until Fetch spotted a level clearing at the bottom of the slope they were descending. It was nearly midnight, and her head was ready to explode; another headache had been building all evening. She halted at the grassy spot and took off her backpack and rifle. Zoe had been keeping pace with her, but staying sixty to eighty feet behind. When she caught up, Fetch said, "We need to stop for a while and rest."

"Not on my account," Zoe replied coldly.

"We've been walking for almost twenty-four hours. We're far enough now to take advantage of the dark and get a couple hours' sleep."

Zoe shook her head. "I'm not tired."

"It's the adrenaline. After you sit down, you'll realize how tired you are."

"Jesus, I *am* talking out loud, aren't I?" Zoe snapped. "I said I'm fine."

Fetch tried to keep an even temper. She, too, was exhausted, hungry, and sore. Although Zoe had every reason to be angry and upset, Fetch was too tired for discussions. And her headache made it difficult to think. "It's not a request, Zoe. I'm calling a time-out." She sat down and stretched her legs out in front of her.

Zoe remained standing, her arms folded across her chest defiantly. "Of course," she said, her voice dripping sarcasm. "Don't let what I want sway you from your decision."

Fetch leaned against her backpack and sighed, wishing the pain behind her eyes would subside. "Fine. Do it for me. Do it because I'm too exhausted to move, and my head and every other body part Barriga kicked is killing me."

"Let's get one thing straight." Zoe flung off her rucksack and sat down opposite her. "Just because you developed a conscience, or decided on a bloody career change," Zoe pointed at her, "I don't owe you any favors."

"I never said you did." The volcano had started to rumble and Fetch didn't have enough energy to quiet it. "But unless you're prepared to carry me, I need to rest."

"Whatever," Zoe said, with a dismissive gesture.

Fetch casually pulled off her mask and tossed it beside her. At Zoe's sharp intake of breath, she explained, "Since there's only two of us now, I guess we can take turns. I'll ditch mine when we rest. You can take yours off when we hike, since you're less acclimated to the altitude. It'll help you breathe."

"Whatever you say. You call the shots."

"That's right."

"I can see how democracy is a foreign concept for you people."

Fetch ignored her and when Zoe didn't talk again she finally closed her eyes. She didn't know how much time had passed when Zoe broke the blissful silence.

"I don't know how you can live with yourself. You walked away from those people like they didn't matter. Like they were an inconvenience."

"Not true," Fetch said, without opening her eyes. "I was willing to wait. And walking away was just as difficult for me."

"Really?" Zoe said. "Because I had to convince you to stay, and you jumped at the first opportunity to get out of there."

Fetch looked at her. "Only because you agreed to."

"Don't you *dare* put this on me."

"We'd still be there if you hadn't—"

Zoe cut her off, spewing rage, her voice louder with every word. "You are cold, selfish, and cowardly for trying to blame me."

"I'm not blaming you. You made the right—"

Zoe laughed inanely. "I mean, seriously, I must be an idiot for putting my life in your hands. Trusting one of the barbarians that got me here. A self-serving, kidnapping murderer."

Fetch forced herself to remain calm in the face of her own rising anger. "I know you're upset and need someone to take it out on. So if this…" she gestured from herself to Zoe, "makes you feel better, then by all means. But can you resume in an hour?" Fetch laid her head back against her pack. She needed a few more moments of silence as much as Zoe needed someone to blame for the decision to leave the others behind.

But Zoe continued to rant. "Nothing I can say will make me feel better because you don't give a shite about what I think anyway. I know I can't hurt you because you don't have a conscience. They ask you to steal, hurt, and kill, and you do it. Only a sociopath can do that without emotion." Zoe shifted closer to Fetch until they were a foot away from each other. "Tell me, soldier, what's it like to kill? I know what you did to that guard last night with your knife. How did that make you feel?"

"Enough, Zoe." Fetch's hands were shaking. She'd relied on pills too long to know how to deal with emotions without them, and right now she was fighting the urge to scream against the sting of Zoe's accusations, even if some were true. She rubbed her temples, trying to will away the pain, and strove to keep her voice steady. "I think it's time you stopped talking."

Zoe got up on her knees and leaned over Fetch until her mouth was next to Fetch's ear. "Don't *think*. You're not a thinker, soldier," she hissed with enough venom to kill an elephant. "You're a machine that jumps to orders and kills on command." She pulled away to glare at Fetch. "You disgust me, soldier."

Truths clashed with lies, and right now, Fetch didn't know what was real. Without thinking, she grabbed Zoe by the waist and threw her down. Fetch pinned her to the ground with her body and roughly restrained Zoe's hands above her head.

"You're hurting me," Zoe cried, struggling to free herself.

Over her, blind with fury, Fetch kept her voice low and menacing. "Don't *ever* assume to know what I've done." Zoe stilled and stopped struggling. "Or what I've seen or endured. Don't ever assume to know who I am. Do you understand?"

When Zoe didn't answer, Fetch pressed even closer, until her face was nearly touching Zoe's mask. "Do you?" she demanded between gritted teeth.

"Yes," Zoe replied with a quivering voice.

"Because of people like *me*, people like *you* get to see another day." Fetch pushed herself up and away from Zoe. "I intend to get twenty minutes' rest and I don't want to hear another word." She reached into her backpack for the bottle of ibuprofen and downed four pills with a bit of water, ignoring Zoe as she settled back again against the pack. She shut her eyes to ease the pain in her head, as Zoe's words, "Y*ou disgust me, soldier*," created an ache in another part of her body.

Munich, Germany
October 22

It took two full days for Domino and Allegro to catch up with and interview all Gunther Zimmerman's neighbors, friends, coworkers, and students. Those who were still walking around without symptoms, anyway. Several people who'd encountered the botany professor were either dead or dying in the university medical center.

The neighbor who had found his body, a widow who often brought him meals and had a key to his apartment, was among the deceased. But on their second visit to the complex, they had found her daughter packing up her mother's things. She told them her mom was already feeling ill when she discovered the body and passed away less than forty-eight hours later.

A thorough search of Zimmerman's apartment yielded no clues about how he'd been infected or evidence he knew anything about the virus or was in a plot to spread it. They took his address book with them and called every friend and business contact listed, with no success.

And they struck out as well at the university. None of the professor's surviving students, or the faculty who had offices near his, remembered anything helpful. They were dependent on the security-camera video for any leads.

They sent the photos of everyone who interacted with Zimmerman to Reno to match with university records and drivers' license photos. After striking out with all the tapes from October first, they went back a day to September thirtieth and did the same, drawing another blank. They'd spent most of today combing through video from the following day, October second. They traced all the professor's interactions that day during business hours first; Reno was currently identifying those individuals.

Allegro sat at the desk in her hotel suite, staring at the laptop screen, while Domino ate the pizza she'd ordered from room service in the room next door. Since they'd discovered the rip in Domino's mask, each had always worn her mask when they were together, and Domino took her meals in the other room so she could remove hers to eat. Allegro had tried to talk to her about it several times, but Domino always told her to get her mind back on the job.

Allegro hit Pause and rubbed her eyes. She was getting bleary-eyed after watching hours of boring hallways. When she hit Play again, images flashed by that the hallway cam outside the professor's office had caught during the late night and early morning between October second and third.

Zimmerman was evidently working late that evening. He'd still been in his office when the eight a.m. to eight p.m. loop from the camera ended, so she was looking for his departure, along with any abnormal activity. The eight p.m. to eight a.m. tape started where the previous one left off; two people were in the hallway—a professor whom they'd previously identified and a student. They chatted briefly, the student left, and the professor disappeared into his office, three doors down from Zimmerman's. The man reemerged a few minutes later with his briefcase and departed.

Allegro fast-forwarded until the next flash of movement caught her eye. At eight forty on the time stamp, another known faculty member emerged from an office at the far end of the hall, this one a woman, dressed in her coat and carrying her purse and a stack of papers. She paused briefly at Zimmerman's open door, apparently to exchange a few words with him, but didn't go in. After she departed, nothing changed until the hallway darkened at ten p.m.

This was routine. The building's main entrance was locked at nine-thirty, after the last of the evening classes there had let out, and lights were dimmed in the classroom and office wings a half hour later, probably to save energy. Light still spilled from Zimmerman's office, but he looked to be the only one still working late in the hallway she was watching.

At ten fifteen on the time stamp, another flash of movement made Allegro stop the fast-forward and rewind.

"Hey, come look at this." Allegro replayed the image at normal speed. "She's way early."

"And not one of the regulars," Domino said, looking over her shoulder.

A woman was pushing a cleaning cart down the long hallway toward Zimmerman's office, her back to the camera the entire journey. But even in the diminished light, Allegro could see she wasn't wearing the right drab uniform that was standard for the company that serviced the building. It was a uniform, all right, but with a different style and lighter color.

They knew the crew always started work around two a.m. and didn't hit this hallway until an hour later. They'd also memorized the faces of the five regulars, one man and four women, and none of them had the long dark hair this one did.

The two ops watched the cleaning woman bypass the closed office doors and go directly to Zimmerman's. She paused outside briefly, then pushed the cart inside. After six minutes, she reemerged, keeping her head down at an unnatural angle.

"Someone's obviously camera shy," Allegro muttered. All of a sudden, the woman's head turned abruptly, back toward Zimmerman's open door. She went back inside the office for only a few seconds, and when she came back out, she pushed the cart back down the hallway and out of sight, keeping her face obscured.

"Go back," Domino said excitedly.

"I saw it, too." Allegro backed up the tape at slow speed and froze the image at the moment the woman had lifted and turned her head toward the door. "Gotcha." There were three frames of her face or a portion of it, each a slightly different angle. They were dark, but hopefully, with some enhancements, they'd be enough for Reno to identify her.

She called Reno as she sent the images and told him to give them top priority. While they waited for his callback, they checked the video of several other cameras in the building to see if they could get a clearer shot of the woman. They found her going into the main entrance at nine p.m. and picked her up again going in and out of a janitorial closet, where she'd picked up the cleaning cart. Her face was never visible in either instance. She was clearly avoiding the security cameras.

Reno called Allegro's cell four hours after he received the images, and she put him on speakerphone. After he revealed the woman's name and address in Frankfurt, he reported, "Lengthy criminal record, including three years in prison for assault. Arrested twice in connection with murder-for-hire schemes, but not enough evidence to convict her either time. I checked the name against an international-flight database from the last month, without luck. Then I did a broad search of news reports and found her in the *Frankfurter*

Allgemeine online. She was killed in a single-vehicle auto accident a week ago, on the fifteenth, not far from her home."

"Damn. Send me everything you have on her, and check for aliases." Allegro disconnected and turned to Domino. "Whoever's behind this hired professionals to make sure they didn't leave tracks. I say we head to Frankfurt, see what we can pick up there?"

"Sounds like a plan," Domino replied. "I'll update Monty while you get our gear together."

CHAPTER TWENTY-FOUR

Guaviare Jungle, Colombia
October 23

Zoe had been too restless to sleep when she'd had the opportunity, and now she was paying the price. Undone by her confrontation with the doctor and the day's events, she'd paced last night, her mind churning, as Gianna rested. The medic had seemed to fall asleep the moment she'd reclined against her backpack, but not long after, when Zoe glanced in her direction, the doctor opened her eyes as though she sensed she was being watched. And every time she seemed to drift off into the next superficial slumber, she'd almost immediately awaken again, groaning and rubbing her temples. Gianna was clearly in pain, and Zoe had started to feel guilty about attacking her.

She knew the doctor was trying to save her and keep her safe. But the anger and hate she felt right now for all FARC guerrillas was stronger than reason, because they'd forced her to make a decision that would haunt her the rest of her life. She'd never forgive herself for leaving the Italians behind.

After fifteen or twenty minutes of unsettled repose, the doctor had gotten to her feet and announced it was time to move. She put her mask back on and told Zoe she could take hers off. Without another word, she'd shouldered her backpack and, with rifle in hand, started off again through the black jungle. It was so dark Zoe had to stick very close to her to keep from getting lost.

With nothing to chronologically orient her, Zoe had looked up hours later to greet another dawn, thankful that its presence brought with it another day of freedom and another day without symptoms. They still might make it. Tino had told her not to give up on home. For Zoe, her father was home, and as long as she could breathe she'd never give up on him. With renewed optimism she marched forward behind the medic, who had been practically power-walking after their brief pause.

But now, as the noonday sun beat down on them as they crossed a high ridge above the tree line, she was regretting she hadn't rested. They'd paused only twice since then, just to relieve themselves, before marching steadily onward. The doctor had given her some panela to munch on for energy, but Zoe was still having a hard time keeping up, stumbling more frequently. Thank God, at least she'd been able to shed her mask. They were so high now she was struggling as it was to take in enough oxygen. The view all around them of the high Andes was awesome, but Zoe refused to acknowledge any beauty in this place. They'd been walking for what seemed like decades, and her T-shirt and even the waistband of her sweat pants were drenched with sweat.

The doctor showed no sign of slowing down. Occasionally she'd reach for her flask, or take a bite of panela, but she never faltered. She hadn't spoken since the night before and had barely looked at Zoe.

Let her sulk. Zoe didn't give a damn if the woman was angry or if she never spoke to her again, as long as she got her out of this overgrown botanical freak show to somewhere safe. Too proud to ask Gianna to slow down, she gritted her teeth and picked up her pace.

Another couple of hours passed before she finally got a chance to get off her feet, and only then because they'd reached a place where the jungle foliage was so dense it was impossible to get through it with their packs on.

"Wait here," Gianna said, as she took off her backpack and set her rifle against it. She withdrew a machete from the pack and began hacking through the undergrowth with short, efficient strokes.

Zoe stretched out on the ground and closed her eyes, lulled to sleep at once by the metallic singing cadence of the machete. But, too soon, the doctor's voice awakened her, telling her they were leaving. The sun had barely moved. She doubted she'd been asleep for more than a half hour.

The next stretch took them higher into the mountains. Even without her mask, Zoe was gasping for air with every step. Huffing, she reached for her flask, but only a mouthful of water remained. The other two bottles she'd set off with were gone, too. *Bloody brilliant.* She'd used much of her water to make the wet cloth for Octavia, who was now probably dead. Would her parents cover the body or sit beside her until they could join her in eternity? Zoe tried to push the thoughts away by moving faster.

Fetch shut her eyes and sniffed as she walked. The jungle was so dense where they were it was impossible to even glimpse the darkening sky. But the scent of coming rain was unmistakable.

Zoe hadn't complained about the long trek. In fact, she hadn't spoken to Fetch all day. The only indication she was still following were the muted sounds of her footfalls, usually close behind, changing in cadence every so often. Fetch didn't know if Zoe's usual misplaced pride or her anger drove her along, but she was glad they were making up lost time and relieved Zoe wasn't blaming her for her misery.

Fetch had spent the whole day trying to forget Zoe's words. Even though her hurtful accusations were based on misinformation, it still stung that Zoe thought her disgusting. Maybe she wasn't a guerrilla soldier, but she was a soldier, nonetheless, and both had much in common. The cause might be different, but both fought for ideals and pledged to live and die for them.

Fetch made no excuses for what she did, and if Zoe had a problem with her, then too bad. It was ironic, though, that during the short period she'd known her, Zoe had displayed courage and strength and even compassion for her team. Her will to fight for her freedom, even if it meant losing her life, was a trademark of a brave soldier.

Zoe was breathing heavily behind her, but she seemed otherwise all right, drinking and snacking as they walked. Clearly, she was getting the message that if she ignored her body's needs she'd collapse and they'd lose time again. They were making good progress, even though the terrain today had been some of the worst they'd faced. When they weren't battling through the thickets, they were baking in the open spaces of the exposed plateaus. And it was rarely level this high in the mountains; the constant slip-sliding up and down one steep slope after another was murderous on the feet. Zoe's had healed quite well from her previous long trek, but they had to be hurting, though she never complained. Still, at this pace, they should reach their destination in another day, two at most.

They were moving along a rocky ridge, headed toward another stretch of jungle, when Fetch heard a thud behind her and Zoe groaned, "Ungh."

She pivoted and found Zoe on the ground, wincing and clutching her knee.

"I'm fine," she said, without looking up. "It's nothing."

"Will you let me look at it, or should we spend thirty minutes arguing about why I'm not worthy?"

When Zoe didn't respond, Fetch looked closer at her knee. The sweat pants were torn, and blood was seeping into the material. Zoe sat rocking while she held her leg.

"Zoe?"

"It hurts."

Fetch pushed Zoe's hands away and gently rolled up the leg of her sweatpants. A gash, about four inches long, at the base of her kneecap was bleeding and needed immediate attention to keep from getting infected. But she was relieved it wasn't deep enough to require stitches. "I'll clean this up and you'll be good as new."

"I doubt that." Zoe leaned back on her elbows. "Good and new are two words I can't fathom at the moment."

Fetch cleaned and disinfected the wound with Betadine before she wrapped gauze around the knee. Zoe didn't recoil or complain. As she pulled the leg of the sweatpants down over the bandage, she felt the first few drops of rain. Within seconds, the trickle turned into a steady stream.

Zoe lay on her back and stretched out her arms. "That feels so good," she said as the rain poured down. "It's been so bloody hot."

"We need to settle until it passes. Let's get under the trees. It won't be as bad there."

"I don't want to move." Zoe opened her mouth wide to catch the drops.

Fetch found it difficult not to stare at the way Zoe's T-shirt was conforming to her breasts as the rain soaked it. She was beginning to see the outline of her nipples, which dangerously distracted her. "It feels good now, but you'll regret it once the sun goes down and you cool off." She extended her hand and, surprisingly, Zoe took it and allowed herself to be hoisted to her feet.

Fetch led her under the trees, but it was starting to pour and even the jungle's dense canopy felt inadequate. Shrugging off her backpack, she quickly dug through it for a tarp. "Get under here." She shouted to be heard over the loud drumming of the rain as she unfurled the canvas.

Zoe ducked under with her, and together they held the tarp over themselves while they ran to a fallen log nearby, Fetch carrying her backpack with her free hand. She tied the corners of the tarp to trees with quick-release knots, so it formed a canopy over them while allowing her to see in all directions. Zoe shed her rucksack and they sat side by side on the log.

"Get comfortable," Fetch said, keeping her gaze forward so she wasn't further tempted to ogle Zoe. "We could be here for a while."

"Can we collect some of this?" Zoe asked, looking longingly at the deluge all around them. "I ran out of water hours ago, and I'm thirsty as hell."

"You should've said something. Get your flask and bottles." Fetch dug into the backpack for hers as well. She angled one corner of the tarp so the water hitting it streamed into the containers, filling them all within minutes. Zoe drank greedily from her flask, then handed it back to Fetch to top off again. "We should eat something, too, as long as we're stopped anyway."

"Cold beans again, I presume?" Zoe asked as they opened their packs.

"I didn't have much choice." I had to take what wouldn't be missed right away."

They took turns eating because they were sitting so close together. Zoe put her mask back on while Fetch ate, then Fetch donned hers so Zoe could. When they were finished, they stared out at the clearing they'd just come from. Neither spoke. The sky was the color of dark charcoal and it was dumping so much rain now there was a virtual wall of water in the open spaces. Huddling with Zoe under the tarp felt intimate to Fetch, but even their touching shoulders and thighs didn't seem to help bridge the awkward distance between them.

When the deluge subsided, Fetch finally spoke. "We should be at the safe house in two days."

"Thank you for taking care of my knee," Zoe said at the same time.

"Welcome," Fetch replied. "We've made good time today."

"I'm not surprised. We've practically jogged our way here."

"I know, but it was necessary."

Thunder boomed close by and Zoe jumped. "If I ever see a rainforest again it'll be too soon."

"It may be more refined, but the jungle you're going back to is just as merciless."

"But it's one I can navigate." Zoe sighed. "And take a long hot bath." She didn't speak for so long Fetch had started to think she'd dozed off.

"I don't know what scares me more," Zoe finally said. "Getting caught by the guerrillas or getting sick." She went silent again for several seconds. "What are the odds we escape both?"

"We have so far."

"I keep waiting for that first cough."

"Sounds to me like you've answered your own question," Fetch replied. Zoe was clearly terrified about the possibility—no, the probability—she had the virus. She was, too, but it was pointless to worry about it.

"Aren't you afraid you'll be next?"

"Sure, but I deal with fear differently." Fetch tried to sound optimistic. "I let it serve me and not the other way around. If I let fear take the upper hand, I let it distract me from fighting the dangers ahead."

"But fear is necessary for survival. Natural selection and all that."

"Very. But the trick is to take it from an instinctive to an intellectual level. Instead of letting it freeze you, listen to what it's telling you and calculate your next move." She'd learned that lesson early at the EOO, and it had saved her ass on more occasions than she could count.

"All that sounds untenable when you're running for your life."

"Maybe you shouldn't be running. Sometimes your best odds are to fight."

"I can see how that would apply to a bunch of trigger-happy Neanderthals," Zoe said. "But how do I fight this disease?"

"You can't. But don't let the eventuality of it distract you with fear. We'll worry about that if and when it happens. Right now, we have another battle to win, and nothing's uncertain about that one."

Zoe went quiet, as if contemplating their conversation. "It doesn't make sense," she said after a long while. "I should be sick. It just doesn't make any sense."

"Maybe you got lucky."

"How?" Zoe asked. "Tino was right. I drank from their water, ate from their food. I spent a lot of time with Octavia, and I was with Kylee the day before she died. I didn't know she had the virus, but she was apparently ill."

Fetch didn't know how to reply. Realistically, Zoe *should* be dead, or dying at the very least.

"Why am I still alive?" Zoe turned and looked at her, her deep blue eyes beseeching Fetch for an impossible reassurance.

"I don't know, Zoe," Fetch replied quietly. "The incubation time is five to six days before the first symptoms."

"So I should have—"

"But you don't." Zoe was right. She shouldn't still be asymptomatic. *Unless*...The thought almost made her smile from relief. "Maybe some people are naturally immune. It happens."

Zoe shook her head as though the idea was impossibly far-fetched. She broke a stick from the log they sat on and poked at the ground absentmindedly. "My luck has sucked so far," she said. "Why would I be spared this disaster?"

"Luck has nothing to do with it." The more Fetch thought about it, the more convinced she became she'd stumbled upon the truth about why Zoe wasn't almost dead, despite all evidence she should be. Her spirits lifted. "Zoe, if you *are* immune, you could possibly help stop this virus."

"We don't even know that for sure." Zoe still sounded discouraged, but Fetch could tell by her face that her enthusiasm was at least getting Zoe to consider the possibility she might be on to something.

"It makes sense. It's the only thing that *does* make sense." Fetch was exhilarated. "You could be the cure."

"Even if you're wrong about this," Zoe said, tossing the stick away, "I feel much better knowing I may live to get out of this bloody zoo."

Fetch wanted to believe she was right, and at the moment, she had every reason to. Not only might Zoe survive, but she could be the key to saving millions of others. Fetch glanced over at her, and, for the first time, saw hope on her face. Zoe was grinning as she stared out at the rain, and Fetch realized she'd never seen her smile so genuinely and spontaneously before. The result was breathtaking.

They sat and watched the rain pour down. Almost by tacit agreement, they simultaneously relaxed against each other—a wordless acknowledgement of a shared, new optimism for the future.

CHAPTER TWENTY-FIVE

Zoe was startled awake by a sharp boom of thunder. She'd fallen asleep, without really meaning to, and found herself snuggled up against Gianna, with her head on the soldier's shoulder. "Sorry about that," she mumbled, and pulled away.

"You needed it," Gianna said.

"How long was I out?"

"About ten minutes." Gianna reached for her water and took a sip, lifting her mask just enough to drink.

"Why can't we both get rid of these things?" Zoe pointed to Gianna's mask. "I mean, if you were sick, you would've shown symptoms by now."

"I was in San José del Guaviare right before we left," Gianna said. "Although I was careful, I can't be sure."

"But if I'm immune, it doesn't matter."

"True, but for now it's a theory. A good one, but—"

"Still a theory."

"Let's wait another day, okay? Just to be safe."

Zoe reluctantly nodded and dug into her rucksack for her mask. "Only fair, then, that you get a turn to get rid of yours for a while. I've had mine off all day." She put hers back in place and got up to stretch. The rain had slowed some within the protection of the jungle canopy, but it was still pelting down in the clearing.

Twin bolts of lightning lit up the dark sky as she watched, followed by the distant rumble of thunder seconds later.

"Beautiful, isn't it?" Gianna asked.

"Humbling, more like." After a minute or two more of watching the sky, she returned to her place on the log.

Gianna had removed her mask and looked lost in thought.

"What are your plans after we get out of here?" Zoe asked. With every passing day, she grew more curious about the doctor, who remained so much an enigma.

Gianna shrugged. "I don't know yet."

"Do you have an actual home? Or have you always lived out here?" She nodded toward the vast Colombian landscape beyond the clearing. "I mean, I don't know how you people actually live."

"It's different for everyone. I have a place I go to."

"But it's not home?"

"No."

"Is...*was*, this place, the jungle...home?" Zoe corrected herself. She found it sad to think that the doctor had given up the only life or home she'd known to rescue her and the others. Something about this whole story didn't make sense.

"No."

Gianna obviously wasn't comfortable talking about herself, since all she was getting were one-word answers. Still, Zoe wanted to know more about the woman who was risking so much to save her. Understand why she was doing all this. "Do you have anyone waiting for you...somewhere?"

"Not anymore."

Zoe remembered their earlier conversation about Gianna's partner being killed. "How long has it been since she died?"

"Sam. Her name was Sam," Gianna said quietly. "Three years ago."

The tone in her voice told Zoe it was still a very painful topic. "There hasn't been anyone since?"

"No one worth mentioning."

"How long were you together?"

"Not long enough." Gianna ran her hand though her short dark hair. "A few months."

"Love at first sight, huh?"

Gianna smiled wistfully. "It would appear so." She stood up and sighed. "My turn to stretch."

Zoe watched as she moved away a few steps and limbered up, methodically stretching her arms, legs, shoulders, and torso in much the same way a marathon runner did before a race. The rain had let up, at least for the moment. But Gianna's still-damp clothes clung to her body, outlining every curve and muscle and accentuating her small but well-proportioned breasts. When the medic turned her back and bent over to touch her toes, Zoe couldn't help admiring the toned ass beneath the thin camo pants.

Gianna's expression was distant and almost melancholic the entire time. She was evidently far away from this place in her mind, consumed by memories.

"I asked her to marry me," the doctor said when she'd returned to her seat on the log.

"So soon?"

"Yup."

"Pretty intense." Zoe had almost said a little too fast, and corrected herself. "I mean…that's wonderful."

"Why delay, when you can't wait to start forever with someone?"

Zoe didn't know what to say. She couldn't identify with that kind of fierce chemistry. She fidgeted with the end of the tarp uncomfortably.

Gianna turned to her. "How about you? Anyone you can't wait to be with?"

"Aside from my father?"

Gianna nodded.

"No. I…uh…I've never had anyone like that."

Gianna's eyebrows rose in surprise. "You've never been in love?"

"Other than a crush on my high-school art teacher, no." She'd never felt more than a passing interest for another person, but her life was full without a better half. "I've never felt it necessary, and the U-Haul scenario isn't for me. I'm not the type to fall in love with someone new every full moon either."

"Neither am I," Gianna said defensively. "I didn't even know I was capable of love until I met Sam. I guess that's why I knew it had to be right."

"Then you're fortunate," Zoe said.

"Somehow her death doesn't make me feel very lucky."

"I'm sorry...that came out wrong." She paused to find the right words. "What I meant is, even if it was for just a very small moment, you got to feel what it's like to love someone so...passionately. At least you know you can. I can't even begin to fathom what that must be like, never mind recognize it should it happen."

"You'll know when it does," Gianna said with conviction.

"How?"

This time it was apparently Gianna's turn to consider her answer carefully. A full minute went by before she replied. "Because you'll know you're willing to give your life to save theirs. Or die if it meant bringing them back."

Zoe didn't respond. She had nothing to say. Did love like that really exist? And if it did, was she willing to experience it? Did she have the emotional capacity for such a commitment?

She glanced at Gianna, whose face held a bittersweet serenity as she remembered her lost partner. Did anyone exist who could make Zoe feel that way, and would anyone ever feel like that for her? More important, would she ever get the chance to find out?

A long silence followed as both of them remained absorbed in their own reflections. The rain had started again, pouring sheets in the clearing. The sky was still so dark it was difficult to tell what time it was, but Zoe thought sunset had to be only a couple of hours away at most. She finally shook off the questions raging in her head and asked, "What happens when we reach the safe house?" She turned toward the medic. "We obviously can't stay there forever. They'll find us eventually."

Gianna looked away, as though deliberately avoiding eye contact. "No, we can't. And, yes, they will."

Zoe tried to suppress the renewed sense of panic that hit her at the doctor's seeming certainty the rebels would eventually catch them. Surely she had some idea of how to get them out of this. "But you have a plan, right?"

The doctor didn't answer for a very long time, which only added to Zoe's escalating anxiety. Gianna took a long swig of water before she finally spoke. "I'll call in with our location. The extraction shouldn't take long after that."

"Call who for what?" Zoe almost choked. "You can't seriously trust any of them. They'll kill us and...well, you betrayed them."

"I don't mean the guerrillas."

"I'm sorry? You lost me."

"I need to tell you something," Gianna said, but didn't elaborate or explain for another minute or two. She seemed uncomfortable and it was driving Zoe crazy.

"How long is the dramatic pause going to last?" she asked. "What the hell is going on?"

"Six months ago," Gianna said, "I was sent on an SAR mission. I had to locate hostages, and the fastest way was to infiltrate the FARC."

Gianna had her complete attention, but Zoe was having a hard time absorbing what she was saying, in part because her voice had suddenly changed, quite dramatically. "On a *what* mission?"

"Search and rescue," Gianna explained, speaking very slowly and deliberately.

There. She was certain of it now. Gianna's fairly thick Spanish dialect had completely disappeared. Now she sounded like she was from the States. "What happened to your accent?"

"Let me get through this before I answer your questions," Gianna said, as a hint of a smile lifted the edge of her mouth. "After the hostages were located, I was to call in the coordinates for a rescue. Inform them of the number of soldiers present and eliminate as many obstacles as possible. Neutralize traps, poison the water buckets to make guerrillas sick, and, at the last moment, blow up their ammo. In a few words, weaken them and prepare the hostages for extraction."

Zoe was still a bit fixated on the change in Gianna's voice, but she was listening intently to every word.

"It took me six months to locate my targets," Gianna said. "Kylee, Willy, and the Italians. I had to go through a dozen other camps before I was sent to the one I was looking for. All that fell apart when the pandemic broke out. The military and everyone else originally involved in the mission were…*are* needed elsewhere, so the rescue took a backseat."

Zoe didn't know what to say. Her mind was whirling as she tried to process everything. She opened her mouth a few times but nothing came out.

"I know it's a lot to take in at once."

"So you're not a guerrilla?" That was the only question she could manage.

"No."

"And you're American, obviously."

"I have an American passport, but that's a whole other irrelevant and somewhat complicated story."

"I don't know what to say." Zoe stood up, feeling restless and edgy and she didn't know what else. It was all too much, suddenly finding out that everything she thought she knew about someone wasn't at all close to reality.

Gianna laughed. "That's a first."

"Really, Doc?" Zoe faced her. "You picked this moment to develop a sense of humor?" She left the protection of the tarp and paced in the rain. "What am I saying, you're not a doctor. You're a…what are you, exactly?"

"I work for a private organization."

"Military?"

"Not exclusively. Although I specialize in hostage SAR missions. Mostly in the Middle East."

"So that makes you a private contractor."

"Of sorts, yes."

"Like Blackwater?"

"They're called Xe nowadays. And no, nothing like those goons." Gianna looked at Zoe curiously. "You seem to know a lot about the topic."

"My father has contacts in British intelligence. MI5 and what not. I hear things."

Gianna raised an eyebrow.

"Don't look at me like I'm some bizarre aberration. There's more to me than sexual intrigue and Manolo Blahniks."

"What's a Manloblanik?"

Zoe rolled her eyes. What self-respecting modern woman didn't know about the finest fashion footwear ever made? She looked down at Gianna's well-worn combat boots. "Never mind."

"You're soaked. Get back under here."

Zoe had been too absorbed with the mind-boggling revelations of the last few minutes to realize she was getting drenched. She returned to her seat under the tarp to dry off. "When will this rain ever stop?"

"Soon, I hope."

Zoe stared at Gianna's profile. It still hadn't really sunk in that she wasn't a guerrilla, but some of the things she'd said in recent days now made sense. "Why didn't you tell me all this before?"

"I couldn't jeopardize the mission or my cover. I didn't know if I could trust you. If they suspected anything, they would've tortured us both until they got what they wanted. And killed us anyway."

"Why did you tell me now? We're not exactly tucked safely in our beds yet. We have another two days, you said, before your people come get us."

"Because I trust you. And, frankly," Gianna shrugged, "at this point it doesn't matter. If they find us, the guerillas won't be interested in the whos or whys. They'll shoot me first, then you. If you're lucky. If not, they'll take you back and make hell seem like a pretty good place." The brief, tortured look in Gianna's eyes told Zoe she was speaking from firsthand experience. "Even if you told them about me, they still wouldn't know who I work for, and it would only alert them to any potential mission to get you out."

The words "make hell seem like a pretty good place" reverberated in Zoe's mind. What the rebels might do to her terrified her. "I can't go back there."

"You won't. I refuse to let that happen."

Zoe found the resolve in Gianna's voice reassuring. She needed to believe it was true. If she was caught, no matter how much she was determined to get out of this situation alive, she wouldn't be able to endure the kind of cruelty the rebels were capable of. She'd had only a taste of it during the twelve days the FARC had held her, and it had already been worse than any nightmare she'd ever had or could have imagined. Though she'd never considered taking her own life, right now it felt like the only alternative.

She had to control her fears. Like Gianna had said earlier, they would only distract her. She had to master them and use them to her advantage. She was with a specialist now, and the knowledge that this woman had done this many times before gave her newfound strength. "They're the reason I'm here," she'd said about the Italians. Now it made sense. And last night, she'd told Zoe, "Don't ever assume to know who I am."

Zoe also replayed the hurtful and malicious accusations she'd thrown back at Gianna. *Christ.* "I feel really stupid now about the things I said to you last night."

"You didn't know."

"That doesn't matter. I've been meaning to bring it up all day but…" Heat rose to her cheeks from her shame and embarrassment. "Apologies are not my strongest suit."

Gianna smiled. "I can see that."

"Funny," Zoe said, and laughed. "Guerrilla or not, you risked your life to save me, and I had no right to hurt you."

"You didn't." Gianna looked away.

"You're not that good an actor," Zoe said quietly. "You were quite angry when you threw me down. I must have hit a nerve."

Gianna sighed and looked at the ground. "You said I disgusted you."

"I didn't mean it. I…I needed someone to blame for my decision to go along with leaving the others behind."

"I know that, rationally. But I wasn't feeling great, and it all got to be too much."

"You were in pain. I noticed you rubbing your head."

"I take different meds for various reasons when I'm on the job. I had enough for four months, but recovering the hostages took longer than expected. They ran out two months ago and headaches are one of the side effects."

"How do you feel now?"

"It's been better today. But I can feel one coming on."

"I'm sorry."

Gianna dug into her backpack for a bottle of ibuprofen, then returned to her seat on the log. "These help some," she said, and took a few with a long swig of water. She closed her eyes and bent forward, resting her elbows on her knees, and began to rub her temples.

Zoe watched her, wishing she could make Gianna feel better, then suddenly remembered a technique her mother used on her when she complained of a headache. It had always seemed to work. She got up and stood in front of Gianna. "I might be able to help."

Gianna looked up at her. "Don't worry about it."

"Let me try something." Zoe moved closer, nudging Gianna's legs apart so she could stand between them. "Just relax," she said softly, as she cradled the sides of Gianna's face in her hands, her thumbs over the other woman's temples. It was hard to see her expression under the dark canvas, but Gianna complied with a nod.

Zoe rubbed her temples with slow circular motions, starting gently, then with a bit more pressure. After a while, she inched her movements slowly across Gianna's scalp toward the back of her head, exerting pressure with her fingertips first along the base of her neck, then moving upward. Zoe heard her groan. "Am I hurting you?"

"No," Gianna said. "I never knew it felt so good," she drawled lazily.

"What?"

"Massage," Gianna mumbled

"You've never been massaged?"

"Huh? By specialists, for…injuries, but…not otherwise." Her voice was barely audible. "No one's ever offered."

How strange. Zoe kept on massaging Gianna's scalp, moving over her entire head with slow, circular strokes. *Surely, Sam must have…* When that question entered her mind, she pushed it away. Right now, she didn't want to think about Gianna with any other woman.

Her mother's remedy was apparently having the desired effect, because Gianna groaned again and relaxed so much her head started to fall back. Zoe caught it and pulled it gently forward until Gianna's face was resting between her breasts, then continued her massage, moving down to work on Gianna's shoulders and biceps.

After a few more moans of pleasure, Gianna fell silent. As she worked, Zoe tried to ignore the feel of Gianna's warm breath between her breasts, but it was becoming increasingly difficult. She looked down at the dark head as Gianna turned her face a bit; her mouth was now practically on Zoe's nipple.

As her breath caught at the warm sensation, Gianna placed her hands on Zoe's hips.

Without realizing it, she'd stopped massaging and was now stroking Gianna's hair, gently pushing her head closer to the desired target. Zoe was so starved for contact she thought she might come if Gianna put her mouth on her nipple. She gasped when Gianna's hands moved higher up her sides, until her thumbs were just beneath the curves of her breasts. Zoe was so aroused her heart was pounding, and she was panting for air. A moan escaped her.

"This is wrong." Gianna was breathing hard, too, and her hands gripped Zoe's sides tighter.

"Is it?"

In response, Gianna abruptly pushed her back a step and released her, then shot to her feet. "It's stopped raining," she said hoarsely, before turning to face Zoe, her chest heaving, hands making fists at her sides. Her eyes were almost black, and her lids only half-open. "Time to move again."

"Do you feel better?" Zoe asked, staring at Gianna's lips and wanting so much to rip off her mask to kiss her.

"Painfully so," Gianna replied, turning away to take down the tarp.

CHAPTER TWENTY-SIX

Fetch rolled up the tarp and stashed it in her backpack as she fought to bring her body under control. "You can take your mask off," she told Zoe as she reached for her own and set it back in place, almost grateful for the opportunity to hide her expression from the other woman while she worked through in her mind what had just happened between them.

Ten minutes later, after reapplying mosquito repellent and breaking off more panela to munch on, they were marching through the jungle again, neither speaking.

As she walked, Fetch tried to push away the unfamiliar sensations that Zoe had sparked. Sure, Zoe was an attractive woman; that was a fact no one could deny. But what Fetch had felt back there was beyond physical need. It had been years since she'd felt comfortable in a woman's embrace, or even allowed it.

Before Sam, her sexual encounters had been brief, anonymous, and inconsequential. She didn't even give them her name. Fetch never took women back to her hotel room, nor had she ever seen the inside of their homes. It was always done in clubs in some dark corner, or occasionally a room in a nearby motel.

And it was perpetually about giving and never taking. Not because she didn't *need* to be touched, but she didn't *want* to because it would be like allowing someone to take part of her. Like giving away pieces of a puzzle she had struggled to put together. The puzzle that was her life—her goals and who she had ultimately become. To lose that self-image was to lose control of her life. Giving someone that power, even a piece of it, was out of the question.

Years of training and years in the field had taught her that unless she was the sole owner of her life, she'd never be able to completely focus on what needed to be done. Instead, her focus became those she left behind and the promises made to them, because that's what happened when she left pieces of herself behind.

Sam had been the only woman she'd allowed in, and Fetch had given and taken not because Sam asked her to, but because she hadn't. Sam had never demanded a promise or a touch. She, like Fetch, knew the score. All Sam had asked for was *today*, and it wasn't until that moment that Fetch realized she wanted to give her a tomorrow.

For two years after Sam's death, she had no need for the hunt or another woman's body or the small talk that preceded superficial sex. Her libido had fallen into a coma.

And even when her body did reawaken, the thought of having to put effort into satisfying her needs exhausted her. The solution came in the form of a business card given to her by another op, Landis Coolidge. Landis, like Fetch, liked to keep it simple. The card was for a girl-only escort service. The sex was satisfying, varied, and impersonal, and that suited Fetch fine. She'd immediately chosen and settled on a woman going by the name Mira. Mira had never asked her name, and Fetch hadn't cared to ask for her real one, either. Her own world was comprised of aliases anyway.

But what Zoe made her feel was a sensation she'd long forgotten and considered forever lost. The need to be close to someone and not care about the consequences. Fetch had lost herself in Zoe's touch and had felt comfortable to let Zoe see it. So comfortable, in fact, she'd compromised their safety. She hadn't immediately realized it'd stopped raining, and if she'd missed that, she could have missed the sight or sound of approaching guerrillas.

That temporary loss of control had shocked and angered her. She couldn't afford to give that power to anyone, let alone a woman notorious for her promiscuity. Although Zoe had surprised and impressed her with her compassion, strength, and insight, Fetch would never fit or feel comfortable in a world of spotlights and gossip. She cherished her privacy and largely depended on it.

Zoe would tire of Fetch's subdued and secretive life too soon, anyway, and move on to the glam gals she was used to. Fetch couldn't blame Zoe; she was well aware of the patience someone would have to possess to be with her. Her absences were long and her future uncertain, not to mention the moodiness that came after her return from a mission. She often cocooned in a remote part of her mind no one could access.

"Isn't it gorgeous?" Zoe said from behind her, breaking Fetch's reverie.

She stopped and turned to see what had captured Zoe's attention, but it was nearly dark and Fetch couldn't immediately make out what Zoe was pointing to in a thicket beside the path. "What are you looking at?"

Fetch gasped when she finally saw it. She couldn't be sure how long it was because it was curled around branches, but the black and yellow serpent was one of the biggest snakes she'd ever seen. Instinctively, she bent over to release the Glock with its silencer that was strapped to her calf.

"What are you doing?" Zoe stared at the gun with a horrified expression. "It's harmless." She started toward the snake.

"Stay away from that thing," Fetch whispered.

"Put that down. It's only a yellowtail cribo."

"I don't care what it is."

"I've never come across one of these. But snakes are a hobby of mine. I used to keep one as a child, and I've read tons of books on them. These babies can get to be ten feet long, but they're not venomous, and generally docile."

Fetch's expression must have given away how terrified she was of the slithery damn things because Zoe laughed.

"Look at you," Zoe said, clearly enjoying her discomfort far too much. "All weak-kneed about a snake."

"Don't like 'em."

Zoe got even closer to the serpent and it turned its head in her direction.

Fetch stepped back, ready to use the 9mm if necessary.

"What kind of a soldier are you?" Zoe asked bemusedly.

"Can we move on now?" Fetch broke out in a sweat.

"Give me a second. Just when you need a camera," Zoe mumbled as she stopped in front of the snake to study it more closely. Her face was mere inches away from the thing. "See, I told you. It's just a cribo. They're a member of the Drymarchon genus, which kill their prey by grabbing it and swinging it around until they immobilize it and swallow it whole."

Fetch almost passed out when the snake suddenly unfurled from the branch and crawled onto Zoe's shoulder. "Aw, isn't that cute?" Zoe turned to smile at her as the serpent made its way down over her breast and wrapped around her waist. "It likes—" Zoe stopped when her eyes met Fetch's. "Gianna, get a grip, you've completely blanched."

"Don't like 'em," she said again. Fetch pivoted and started off in the direction they'd been headed. "If you don't come with me now, you're on your own," she called back over her shoulder.

"You wouldn't," Zoe said.

"Catch you later." Fetch continued walking, but hid behind a large tree nearby. She wasn't about to let Zoe out of her sight. A few seconds later, Zoe frantically ran past her, whispering her name.

Fetch caught up from behind, moving quietly. "Looking for me?"

Zoe spun around. "Thank God. Don't ever do that again. It's not funny. I thought something had happened to you."

"You didn't really think I'd leave you. I was just a few feet away." Fetch smiled.

"I also never thought someone like you would be afraid of a little snake."

"I'll never hear the end of this," Fetch muttered to herself as they set off again.

"If it wasn't for snakes, the world would be overrun by rodents, you know."

"I don't care if they hold the key to the universe."

"They're very necessary for the balance of—"

"What will it take to unsubscribe from this conversation?" Fetch sighed. "I think they're freak shows."

Zoe laughed and Fetch stopped to looked at her.

"I just think it's funny."

Fetch had to laugh, too. "Like you don't have any phobias," she said.

"No," Zoe replied, a little too quickly.

"Nothing?"

"Not a thing."

"Yeah, right."

"I'm just different." Zoe smiled. "And by different, I mean better."

"So the panic attack over that little spider in your hut was a show of endearment," Fetch replied, and smiled back.

"What? Can't hear you," Zoe said, and covered her mouth to muffle her voice. "I'm in a tunnel."

They both laughed again, and Fetch realized how much she'd missed that simple act. It'd been so long since she'd had any reason to.

As darkness fell, Fetch veered even farther from the faint path between Barriga's camp and the next one. They were getting close to the other rebel encampment she'd been to, near the safe house, and Barriga might have radioed that camp to send men out after them. Fetch cleared a way through the dense foliage, pushing leaves and branches aside but careful not to break them. She didn't want to leave a trace of their passage should the guerrillas come that way. Zoe followed close behind.

"I guess I was surprised with your reaction to the snake because you always seem to have everything under control," Zoe said. "Even when Barriga hit you, I felt like you let him do it. Like you could've killed him if it wasn't for me."

Fetch wasn't sure how to answer. "It would've been a bad move since I was highly outnumbered."

"How can someone kill the way you did that guard and be afraid of a snake?"

"I'm sorry if I gave you the impression that killing is something I do casually."

"You didn't," Zoe quickly replied, her voice apologetic. "I don't know why I said that. It came out all wrong. Please forget I said it."

Fetch didn't reply right away. It bothered her that Zoe thought of her that way. "It's never easy," she finally said.

"Then how do you do it? How can anyone kill, for that matter? Can something like that be taught?"

"Yes. But the reasons and consequences are different for everyone."

"How?"

"Some hate it in the beginning, but eventually become immune. They don't realize half the time it's a human being they killed. It's merely a target they eliminated." Fetch paused. She'd seen many soldiers lose themselves in that spiral. "Thankfully, only a very few see it as a hunting game and get pleasure from it. I think in many of those cases, they're taking out all their anger from the life they left behind. That's the cruelest kind of war."

"How about you?" Zoe asked.

"I'm like most. It's a matter of survival. But every life I take haunts me."

"Even the guard back there?"

"Even him. Just like any other soldier, he was following orders."

"The orders of a drug-smuggling, kidnapping megalomaniac," Zoe mumbled.

Fetch paused and turned to look at Zoe. It was so dark she couldn't really see her face, but she needed to set her straight. "Because the megalomaniac told him the profits would help the poor of his country and give his family the life and choices he never had. He was just a pawn." She kept pushing her way carefully through the thick brush.

"Why do you do it if it haunts you?" Zoe asked next. "Your job, I mean. Does it make you happy?"

"It's not about making me happy. I want to help save lives and keep people safe. I have to believe that for every life I've taken, I've saved hundreds in return."

"But it doesn't make you happy."

"It makes me necessary."

They trudged on in silence for several more minutes before Zoe spoke again. "Do you think it's your responsibility to save others?"

"In a way. I can't imagine turning a blind eye. What would happen if we all did?"

"Why can't people just get along? Or at least ignore each other if they can't?" Zoe pondered aloud.

"Because there's one element behind every war. One reason that obliterates any reasoning. One motive that makes people disregard everything that really matters, and that's money."

"And power."

"Which is impossible without the first. Sadly money *can* buy you everything. From respect, to health, to sex, and even love."

"Love?" Zoe repeated skeptically.

"When you have cash, people can't wait to love you."

"But then it's not real."

"The buyer doesn't care, as long as it's convincing, or as long as they have what they want. Strange, isn't it, how we have everything we want and very little of what we need?" Fetch mused. "Our instincts tell us what we should be doing with our lives—giving back instead of constantly taking, enriching what's on the inside. But we treat those instincts like annoyances, ignoring them to focus instead on the things that line our pockets."

"I know. I see it every day. It's ludicrous, the extent to how much we're worth defines our significance."

"It's the world we live in."

"And we're all guilty of it."

Fetch paused again to glance back at her. "Some more than others," she couldn't resist pointing out before moving on. Why, she wondered, was she telling all this to a woman who lived the kind of life she didn't understand? Even if it wasn't Zoe's fault, she lived in a shallow world, where war and pain existed only as long as the news networks allowed.

Zoe caught the deliberate hesitation before Gianna's remark, but couldn't believe the words were directed at her personally. "I hope you're not implying that I'm in the *some* category."

"That's not for me to say. I don't know you well enough to—"

"You don't know me at all. I may live a privileged life, but I'm not oblivious to what goes on around me."

"I'm sure you're not."

Zoe bristled at the patronizing undercurrent. "I am well aware of how rough life is for many, and I do not think less of those who—"

"What are you doing about it?"

"What I can. I give donations. I support Amnesty International, The Global Hunger Project, CARE."

"That's very noble of you."

"Are you being sarcastic?"

"Not at all," Gianna replied, in that irritatingly placating tone. "It's all you're prepared to do, and that's better than nothing."

"Would I be a better person if I grabbed a gun and joined the army?"

"No. Like I said, you're doing what you can. Considering your life, I don't see how you could fit more in."

"I have an actual job, you know. It's not like I sit around waiting for the next party."

"Do you enjoy your work? Is it satisfying?"

"It's a job. One that, should I survive this," Zoe gestured to the jungle, "and the virus, I will no longer have."

"You quit?"

"I was fired. And cut off financially."

"By your father?"

"Yes."

"Why?"

"Because he got tired of picking up my mess. The nasty exposure I keep getting in the stupid tabloids is hurting his rep, I suppose."

"Not yours?"

"I used to care about that, but not anymore. They'll write anything to fill those rags. They don't care if it's true or who it hurts."

"None of it has any merit?"

"Most are lies."

"And the Greek tycoon's wife was also a lie?"

How the hell had she found out about that?

"They sell those rags here, too, you know."

"I would've never considered you the type to read that trash."

"I don't. Just happened to see the cover."

She was glad it was so dark Gianna couldn't see her face clearly if she decided to turn around again right then. The anger that had been building for the last several minutes gave way to shame. In retrospect, she'd deserved much of the criticism. She didn't know why Gianna's opinion of her seemed to matter so much, but it did, and Zoe wished she wasn't as familiar as she apparently was with her history. "Yes, I have been promiscuous," she said. "I have gotten drunk in public. And I have been seen without my makeup, five pounds overweight, and in sweats. Yes, it's all true. Happy?"

"How you choose to live is up to you, and you're right, I don't know you but…" she paused to clear the way again. "The Zoe I have seen here is a woman so full of potential."

"Please don't sound like my father."

"If I am, then he's a smart guy. You are compassionate, driven, and a fighter. I've seen you stand as tall and as strong as any soldier, and you do it from instinct, from the heart. Not because you were taught or told to. You don't realize it, Zoe, but you are built not of stereotypes but of stone. And I know you could be doing so much more with those qualities."

"Like what?" Zoe was exasperated, not because of Gianna, but because she knew and had known for a long time that what she was saying was true. Yet she'd never found the motivation to change the status quo.

"I think you know the answer."

"What if I don't?"

"Then you're not listening to your intuition. Choose the life you were meant to live, not the one you've settled for. People like you and me need to be challenged or we become numb. And I think numb is exactly what you are."

Zoe couldn't have put it better herself. "Is it that obvious?"

"When you become indifferent about hurting those who love you, then, yes."

Until this moment, she hadn't really spent much time thinking about how her father must have anguished over some of her poor choices. "I don't like hurting my father. I don't mean to. We've been each other's best friend since my mother died," Zoe said. "He means the world to me."

"I bet he knows that."

"Because?"

"He fired you."

Gianna had been painfully on target with her insights so far, but Zoe thought she was wrong about this one. "He said I needed to grow up. But I think he wanted to distance himself from the disappointment I've become."

"To the contrary. I suspect he knows you're disappointing yourself more than you could ever disappoint him, and he let you go so you can find what *matters*. He knows it's not the company or your job. I wouldn't be surprised if *he* knew what *you* still haven't figured out."

"Maybe—" She froze when Gianna abruptly pivoted and covered her mouth with her hand.

"Get down," Gianna whispered in her ear, as she wrapped her arm around Zoe's shoulder and guided her quickly but quietly to the ground.

Zoe's breathing accelerated instantly and her heart pounded. She remained completely still. Seconds later, she heard it, too. Voices, heading toward them.

CHAPTER TWENTY-SEVEN

D on't move," Gianna whispered.
Zoe nodded, not knowing if Gianna could see her in the dark. When Gianna pulled her down, she'd put Zoe on her side. Their packs rubbed against each other as Gianna settled and lay still, facing in the opposite direction, toward where the voices were coming from. Zoe had to be alert to anything coming at them from her side, the side Gianna couldn't see. Not that she could see anything. It was pitch black, and they were lying in a thicket as tall as they were. Control the fear, she told herself, repeating it like a mantra.

The voices were getting closer. Listening intently, she began to discern the sound of their boots crushing the undergrowth. Soon, she could hear them clearly, and if she had known Spanish she could have followed what they were saying. She tried to make out how many of them there were by the different tones. Two—no, three.

One of them said something that sounded very loud—he had to be almost on top of them. Then Zoe heard his footsteps pushing through the grass; his boots snapped a branch so close she thought he would trip over them any second. The footfalls abruptly ceased, and Zoe thought her heart would stop. Had he seen them?

Then she heard the distinctive sound of a steady stream of liquid beating against leaves. He was peeing. A few moments later, the footsteps resumed, but headed away. She'd been holding her breath.

The three men congregated nearby, talking with each other for a few more minutes, then apparently walked away, their voices fading. Zoe still didn't dare move because Gianna hadn't. They stayed as they were for another fifteen minutes, until Gianna grabbed her wrist.

Zoe turned her head to look at her, still too scared to speak.

"We're lying low for a while," Gianna whispered. "I'll find us a place to rest. Stay here, and don't move. I'll be back before you know it."

Zoe squeezed Gianna's hand to stop her. She'd kept it together so far, but the thought of being left alone, with the rebels so close, terrified her. "I'm coming with you."

"I'll move faster alone. I'll be nearby, I promise." Gianna quietly removed her backpack and set it next to Zoe.

"Don't leave me."

"Never," Gianna replied. "I'll be back in a few minutes." She slipped a cool metal object into Zoe's hand. "Take this."

It was the handgun she'd seen Gianna pull earlier with the snake. She tightened her fingers around the grip.

"It's ready to use," Gianna whispered. "Point, shoot, and don't hesitate."

"God, what if I shoot you by mistake?"

"I'll signal you. A bird call, okay?"

"Just a few minutes, right?"

"Right." Gianna moved away in a crawl with her rifle, disappearing instantly into the high grass.

Zoe hefted the hard, heavy metal in her palm, feeling its weight. She'd never held a weapon before, much less used one. How could she aim properly, not knowing what to do, and with her hand shaking like it was? She didn't even dare put her finger on the trigger, terrified she'd fire it by mistake and bring the guerrillas running back.

She'd never felt so afraid, and every noise increased her panic. Though she'd come to recognize many of the normal sounds of the rainforest—the hum of insects, the screech of monkeys in the treetops, the screams of parrots—now she interpreted everything as the possible return of the guerrillas. She contemplated running in the direction Gianna had gone. Go after her instead of waiting. "Control the fear," she remembered. "Use it to tell you what you need to do." She listened to her instincts. They were telling her to wait.

The rain started again and Zoe was glad to have it wash away the sweat pouring into her eyes. The drops tickled her nose, but she didn't dare move. Her stomach rumbled loudly and she clenched her abdomen, hoping that would stop the noise. *Please, not now.*

Each second that passed seemed eternal. It felt like Gianna had been away for months. What if they'd found her? What if she was dead? The mere thought of someone harming Gianna added anger to her fear. No. Surely she would have heard something.

Finally, a bird call sounded from close behind, and Zoe would have sighed in relief if she'd dared. She felt the hand on her shoulder before she heard the words.

"Follow me," Gianna whispered in her ear. "Stay very close."

"All right." She gave the handgun back to Gianna and they started to move deeper into the jungle, keeping low and moving quickly but quietly. It was so dark she could barely see a few feet; she kept running into fronds and brush and who knew what else, so she grabbed Gianna's waistband and held on. Not long after, they stopped at a massive tree several feet in diameter, negotiating their way over the enormous roots that snaked out from it in all directions.

When they reached the other side of it, Gianna got down on her knees and Zoe followed. They crawled under what must have been roots and into a deep depression that felt very cave-like, with damp earth surrounding them except for the opening they'd come through. It was so dark she couldn't see her hand in front of her face.

Beside her, Gianna was rummaging in her pack.

"This should keep us dry and the crawlies at bay," Gianna said, keeping her voice just above a whisper.

Zoe felt the familiar material of the tarp against her hand. She helped Gianna spread it out, lining their little cave beneath and behind them. "Where are we?" she asked, in the same hushed tone.

"Under the tree's roots."

"I feel safe here," Zoe said. "Can't see anything, but I don't care."

"Good, because we'll be here at least a few hours."

Zoe felt around her surroundings. There was enough room for both of them to lie down, she gauged, if they put their packs at their feet by the entrance. "I was so afraid. I'm still shaking."

"Yeah."

"You?" She was surprised. So far, she hadn't witnessed Gianna showing fear at anything. Well, okay, except the snake.

"I'm okay now," Gianna said.

"I don't know how you can do this for a living."

"Do what?"

"Live in constant fear."

"It's not always this bad."

"Once is enough for me."

Silence fell between them, and Zoe tried to relax and get a nap. But she was too charged up with adrenaline, and she couldn't stop thinking about what might have happened if the guerrillas had discovered them. She was desperate for a distraction. Any distraction. So she said the first thing that popped into her head. "What do you do for fun?" she asked Gianna.

"What?"

"When you're not off in some country saving lives."

"I don't know. Whatever normal people do. I read a lot."

"How often do you get to go home?"

"It depends. I'm not permanently stationed anywhere. I get assigned to a job every few months. They last anywhere from a week to a couple of months. This is the longest I've been away."

"Do you hang out with friends back home?" Zoe knew she was babbling, but she didn't really care. It was keeping her mind off her panic.

"Not really. I don't know many people. I hang with Landis. We work for the same organization. She's ten years older but I feel comfortable with her. We talk about work and...all kinds of stuff."

"Is she a soldier too?"

"No. She gets different jobs."

"What's your company called?"

"I can't talk about that."

"Sorry. I didn't mean to pry."

"Don't be. It's a natural question."

This Landis was the first person other than Sam that Gianna had mentioned, and Zoe was curious about their relationship. "Do you party with her?"

"I used to. But then I stopped going to bars and clubs."

"They do get tedious after a while."

"Yup."

"Do you date?"

"Why the third degree?"

Gianna didn't seem to mind her other questions, but her tone changed when she brought up women. Was she still mourning Sam? "You don't have to answer. It's just...well, I need to talk to keep from panicking. I've always done that."

Gianna didn't say anything for a long while. "Sam was the first woman I ever dated, if you can call it that. I never had the chance to take her out on a proper date. We met in Afghanistan where she was serving and I was sent there to extract hostages. We kept very quiet about our affair."

"You never got to be together outside of that?"

"No."

"So she died there."

"She died making sure I wouldn't get hit."

Zoe could hear in Gianna's voice how painful it still was for her to talk about Sam. "I'm truly sorry for your loss."

"So that was the first and last time I...dated." Gianna said it in such a way that it sounded like she had resolved not to let herself experience that kind of pain again.

"You don't think you ever will?" Zoe asked.

"I don't think about it. After Sam, I didn't want to be anywhere near another woman. Besides, my life isn't conducive to a permanent relationship. It's easier to keep things simple."

"By doing what?"

"Keeping things superficial."

"With women, you mean."

"That's what you were asking, right?"

Something wasn't quite adding up. Gianna wasn't dating anyone regularly, Zoe got that. But she'd also said she didn't know many people, and that she'd stopped going to bars and clubs. "How do you meet anyone if you never go out?"

"A little while ago, I found another way to get a few hours of… company."

Zoe didn't know what Gianna was alluding to. She couldn't possibly mean… "You pay for it?"

"Yeah."

"Why? I mean, you're gorgeous. You could have your pick of women."

"I don't need or want to spend the energy on getting to know someone I don't plan to invest in. And it's not fair to them, either."

"It is if they know the situation."

"They always *say* they do, but it's seldom the case. Often enough they walk away feeling bitter, upset, or used when I refuse to give them my number or don't ask for theirs."

"Do you enjoy it with…" Zoe tried to find a politically correct term. She didn't want to offend Gianna.

"Call girls?" Gianna supplied. "It's…satisfying, I suppose."

"Don't you miss the emotional connection?"

"Don't you?"

"I honestly don't know. I don't have anything to compare it to. It's always been about the act, never the person."

"I miss it occasionally," Gianna finally said.

The conversation was helping Zoe's nerves, and Gianna was becoming more interesting with every revelation. Zoe had never met anyone like her. How, *if* she got back home, would she ever be able to revert to empty conversations with the circle of people she regarded as friends? Except for her best friend, who was now a mother and devoted wife, the rest were only interested in parties, clothes, and expensive gadgets. After all she was going through, and after getting to know Gianna, the prospect of returning to her gratuitous life now seemed unbearably devoid of significance.

"Once I thought I knew what I wanted. But after my mother passed away, the will to carry out that vision died with her."

"What was it?"

"She was a true philanthropist and humanitarian. She spent every spare minute campaigning and raising funds for Doctors Without Borders. I envied and admired her persistence. So much, I almost became obsessed with studying medicine so I could join. I'd just started my first year at Oxford when she died. My goal reminded me too much of her, and I eventually dropped it. Instead, I signed up for economics and business management. I never liked it, and between partying and recreational drugs, I barely finished."

"It's not too late."

"I guess. But I wonder if anything I have to offer will make a difference. So much pain and war, hunger," Zoe said. How could she possibly change lives? "Sometimes I feel only an act of God could make any difference. And I'm far removed from any divinity."

"It depends on how you look at it. God can exist in a much more tangible form. For the hungry, God is a plate of food. For the dying, someone who comforts them. And for the orphaned child, God is a woman's warm embrace."

Again Zoe was struck by how different Gianna was from anyone else she'd ever spent time with. She'd obviously seen and done more in her life than Zoe could even imagine, and Gianna viewed the world with an unusual depth of understanding and compassion. "And for the soldier?"

"The enemy who shows mercy."

"That happened to you?"

"To me, to others. I'm alive because someone once decided to spare me. That makes him a God in my eyes."

"Yes, it does," Zoe said softly. "And I'm glad they did."

She still couldn't see anything in their dark hole, but she heard movement beside her. Gianna was evidently changing positions to get more comfortable.

"Try to get some rest," Gianna told her. "We'll have to move again soon."

"Okay. By the way, it's your turn to ditch your mask. I'll put mine back on."

"Deal."

Zoe fumbled in her pack for her mask and pulled it on, then stretched out on her side and put her hands between her legs, trying to warm them. She'd felt a bit chilly since the sun went down, and now she was cold. The tarp didn't protect them against the cool earth of their little cave, and her clothes were still damp from the rain. The stress of the last hour probably wasn't helping either. She was shaking, so she rocked herself trying to get warm.

Moments later, Gianna's warm body spooned up against her from behind. Gianna's arm encircled her waist. "Better?" Gianna asked.

"Much." She relaxed into the sweetest embrace she'd felt in years and was soon asleep.

Chapter Twenty-eight

October 24

Fetch lay awake long after Zoe's trembling stopped and her breathing slowed. She heard her mumble in her sleep a few times, restless, and held her tighter to reassure her. When Zoe sighed and snuggled back against her, Fetch realized how much, under other circumstances, she would be content to lie for long hours in such an embrace. She was protective by nature—of hostages, other ops, the innocent. It was why she was so good at her specialty in the EOO. But with Zoe, her guardian instinct was much more profound and deeply personal. She didn't just want to keep Zoe safe from the rebels, but from any pain, now or in the future.

She was alert to all the sounds around them, making sure the guerrillas hadn't returned. After a couple of hours, she allowed herself to drift off, thinking she'd better get an hour of sleep or so. Then they had to get moving again.

She woke up to rays of light coming in through the roots. Cursing under her breath, she checked her watch and found it was nearly six. She was lying on her back, and Zoe was curled up around her, her head on Fetch's shoulder. She nudged Zoe's arm lightly. "Zoe, wake up."

Zoe immediately sat up, fear in her eyes. "What's wrong?"

"Nothing. We overslept."

"That all?"

She nodded. "Get your gear ready. We have to leave ASAP. We've lost too much time." She reached to put her mask back on, but Zoe stopped her.

"I'm okay with mine on. Let's just get out of here."

Not long after they emerged from the hole, they reached an open ridge with a clear view for miles. Fetch dug her HUD contact lenses and cell phone with its portable hand charger from her pack. After cranking it for a couple of minutes to ramp up the phone's battery, she put in her contacts, turned on the phone, and activated the GPS. Their coordinates immediately lit up in front of her on the optical head-up display on the lenses. Then she oriented her direction, removed the lenses, and soon they were slogging through the jungle again. "No talking today," Fetch told Zoe in a low voice. "They may still be around and I don't want any more surprises."

"I've had enough excitement, trust me."

"Take this." Fetch handed her the Glock. "Always keep it pointing down unless you mean to use it. And try not to shoot your foot."

"I can't promise." Zoe looked bewildered.

"You'll do fine." Fetch smiled at her. "Stay close."

She led Zoe in the direction of the safe house, constantly alert for any sign of movement and listening intently for any voices or other man-made noises amid the constant din of the jungle's inhabitants. Trying to quickly cover as much ground as possible, she zigzagged through the sparse undergrowth under the thick canopy. She had her M14 ready in her hands, and when they reached places where high, dense plant life blocked their way, she used the rifle's barrel to part the way, careful not to leave a trail. Zoe stayed right on her heels, and Fetch was proud of how quietly she was moving.

They drank water and munched panela as they went, stopping only once during the next six hours. A little after noon, they skirted an exposed ridge Fetch recognized. She'd seen it from a distance while walking between Barriga's camp and the rebel encampment nearest the safe house. She relaxed a little. They were making good time and were now a good distance from any known guerrilla camp or trail. And if she was right, the slope they were about to descend should lead to one of the many small tributaries of the Guaviare River that ran through the area.

"Water," Zoe said when they glimpsed a stream through the trees.

"Yup. I knew it was around here." It was a very picturesque spot. A waterfall fed a clear pool, about twenty feet across and surrounded by emerald green fronds. The pool fed the wide stream they'd first spotted.

"Can we stop for a little?" Zoe asked.

"Enough to fill our flasks and bottles."

"Ten minutes, *please*."

"Why?"

"It won't take me longer than that to wash. I can't stand my own smell any longer. In and out, I promise."

Fetch thought about it. "It's been quiet so far. No sign of them having been this way."

"In and out."

Fetch looked over at the waterfall. The force of the water had carved a wide, deep depression in the cliff face behind it. "Should be safe behind the fall," she said. "Follow me."

"Thank you, thank you, thank you."

She threaded her way through the fronds until they reached the cliff face. From there, she could see a wide rock ledge behind the waterfall, a couple of feet above the surface of the pool. It was perfect. She hugged the rock face and climbed over to it, with Zoe right behind her. The ledge was dry, about five feet wide. The water between the ledge and the thick wall of water cascading down from above them was deep but clear. The bottom was mostly sand, with scattered clumps of large rocks.

"You can take a break from the mask," Fetch said. "I know you can't wait to dive under." She pulled her own mask back on as Zoe removed hers.

"How about you?"

"I'll wait my turn. And stay on the lookout."

As Zoe started to undress, Fetch averted her eyes. Not because she wanted to, but because it was the decent thing to do. Also, she'd seen that lovely body before and did not need that kind of distraction after yesterday. She positioned herself under one edge of the waterfall, where no one could see her if they approached the pool, but where she could occasionally step out to check the area.

A big splash behind her told her Zoe had jumped in, so Fetch turned to watch her.

"It's wonderful." Zoe smiled broadly as she slowly treaded water. "First, a good night's sleep, and now this." She ducked her head under to wet her hair. "A bar of soap and conditioner and this could be heaven."

As much as Fetch hated to admit it, the sight of the clear water was mouthwatering. She couldn't remember the last time she'd bathed, and it took all her restraint not to dive in. "You almost done?"

Zoe laughed. "Jealous?"

"Yeah."

Zoe swam to the ledge where Fetch waited. "Give me a hand?"

Fetch averted her eyes while she pulled Zoe out.

"Your turn," Zoe said as she slipped past Fetch and headed to where she'd left her things.

Fetch set her rifle against the cliff and practically tore off her mask and clothes. She dove in and came up close to the waterfall, then climbed onto a large flat rock that allowed her to stand directly beneath the spray. Closing her eyes, she let the water beat on her body. It might be harsh out here, but at times like this it was exhilarating. After a couple of minutes, she slipped off the rock into the pool outside the waterfall to survey the area. It was shallow here, the water only waist-deep. Satisfied they were still alone, she stayed in the shallows and ducked back under the stream of water, crashing into Zoe on the other side.

Zoe grabbed Fetch by the waist to steady herself. She had nothing but her mask on. "I couldn't resist," she said, looking into Fetch's eyes.

"Incredible, isn't it?"

"Yes, it is." Zoe pulled Fetch close. "And so are you."

Fetch's breath caught as Zoe's breasts touched her own. She looked down at the most beautiful breasts she'd ever seen. "You're amazing," she whispered, as she encircled Zoe's waist.

Zoe's gaze drifted down Fetch's body, too, taking everything in for several seconds. Then, looking back up at her with an appreciative expression, Zoe brought her hand up to Fetch's face. She slowly traced the contours of her features as if memorizing them—jaw, to cheek, to forehead and eyebrows, down her nose—and paused briefly when she reached Fetch's lips.

As she gently outlined them with the tips of her fingers, her eyes fixed on Fetch's mouth, Zoe said, "I want so much to kiss you."

"You are," Fetch replied, and threaded her fingers through Zoe's hair. She nudged her thigh between Zoe's.

Zoe gasped, and her head fell forward to rest on Fetch's shoulder.

Their breathing was so fast and loud it blocked out the sounds of the jungle. All Fetch could see, hear, and feel was the woman in her arms.

Zoe slowly moved against her leg as she traced Fetch's arm and the side of her breast with her fingertips.

Fetch wanted to rip that damn mask off Zoe's face and devour her. She pulled Zoe's head back, and the desire she saw in Zoe's eyes undid her. She cupped Zoe's full breast as she kissed, then sucked her neck. Zoe moaned, and Fetch grabbed her ass and lifted her until Zoe was riding her thigh.

Zoe dug her nails into Fetch's shoulders. "So good," she whispered hoarsely in Fetch's ear.

"This is crazy," Fetch murmured between bites and kisses.

Zoe lifted her head to look at her and their eyes met. "Please don't stop yet," Zoe pleaded, and moved her hand between them to Fetch's stomach.

Fetch was finding it hard to breathe; her heart was pounding so loud it was ringing in her ears. "We could be dying," she managed to say.

"Impossible." Zoe moved her hand lower on Fetch's abdomen. "I've never felt more alive."

The piercing screech of a nearby parrot startled them and snapped Fetch back to reality. Reluctantly, she set Zoe down. "We should go."

They dressed quickly, neither speaking of what had just happened, but every time Fetch glanced at Zoe, Zoe was looking at her, her eyes full of regret and longing. After they'd reapplied their mosquito repellent, filled their flasks, and shouldered their packs, Fetch pulled out her mask and put it on. Zoe merely nodded and put hers away.

As they headed toward the safe house, Fetch forced herself to focus on the dangers ahead, remaining alert to any sign or sound the rebels were nearby. But although her head was in the right place, her body rebelled against her decision to pull away from Zoe. She was still humming with arousal.

Because of the terrain, they would soon have to pass relatively close to the path that led between the two guerrilla camps. It was the only way they could get to the safe house by the deadline Montgomery Pierce had given Fetch, so from now on, conversation was out of the question. Zoe remained quietly behind, and both, as if by silent agreement, avoided eye contact.

As they marched on through the rest of the afternoon, Fetch replayed the recent change in the dynamics between them, focusing primarily on how she was different now. In the past days, she'd confided in Zoe not only her name, but parts of her life she hadn't shared with anyone. She had even *proposed* to Sam before she'd revealed her real name, and had definitely never talked about her past encounters with women.

Why did she trust Zoe? Because the possibility of imminent death loomed over them? Or, somewhere deep inside, did she know Zoe would never judge her? And she hadn't, even when Fetch had confided she paid for sex.

But the most dynamic shift in her world was that, for the first time, she felt safe around another person. Safe to be who she was, to express what she believed and explain how she lived. Although Zoe's world didn't resemble her own, Zoe hadn't once expressed distaste or lack of understanding. Instead, she'd listened and respected Fetch's ideals.

The real Zoe Anderson-Howe was nothing like the woman Fetch had imagined from the tabloid stories; she'd gotten under her skin in a way she'd never have thought possible after Sam's death. They were now only a day or so away from rescue, and she should be celebrating the fact that Zoe would soon be home with her father again.

But Fetch felt sad about their inevitable parting and the fact she'd likely never see Zoe again.

CHAPTER TWENTY-NINE

Zoe couldn't ignore the cramping in her gut any longer. Every time it rumbled, Gianna turned to look at her, puzzlement in her dark brown eyes. Like she expected a scene from *Alien* to unfold before her. When she could bear the persistent pain no longer, she finally tapped Gianna's shoulder. "I have to go," she whispered. How embarrassing, not only having to submit to bodily functions out in the open, but to have the woman she'd just shared the hottest ever make-out session witness it.

Another extraterrestrial sound rumbled from her abdomen, so loud it was audible several feet away. Her digestive tract had been giving her fits most of the time she'd been captive. Not surprising, given the stress, the marching, the lack of sleep, and the diet, especially recently with all the canned beans they'd consumed. But this was by far the worst she'd experienced. She had to have relief, and it wouldn't be pretty. "This is so embarrassing," she murmured, doubling over as another cramp tore through her.

"Sounds bad." Gianna looked around, her forehead furrowing.

They were in dangerous territory, but this would happen very fast. "I'm desperate."

Gianna retrieved the toilet roll from her backpack. "See those bushes?" she pointed to a dense thicket.

"That's too close." Zoe wheezed as another wave of cramps consumed her and she broke out in a sweat.

"It's not. I need to be close enough…just in case."

"Okay," Zoe muttered. "I can't believe I'm doing this." She grabbed the toilet paper and started away.

"Zoe," Gianna called after her in a low voice, "You have a gun. Use it if you have to."

Once she'd ducked behind the thicket, Zoe peeked over the top and saw that Gianna was only a few feet away. This was so not right. She'd never be able to function like this, and if she didn't, she'd explode or pass out. She glanced quickly around for another option. The area had lots of foliage and tall trees, but most of it wasn't thick enough to conceal her well. Finally she glimpsed a suitable place forty feet or more farther away and took off toward it.

Zoe set the gun on some moss in front of her and quickly pulled her sweats down. As she'd expected, it wasn't pretty, and even this far from Gianna she was glad for the ambient noise of the jungle. She finished and had just tied her sweatpants when someone poked her from behind. "Not funny, Gianna. This is a private moment."

"*Hola, chica.*" A man's voice, the words just above a whisper.

She froze for a second or two, startled, then went for the gun.

But he must have seen it, because he kicked it away before she could reach it. When she slowly turned around he was watching her with bemused brown eyes. Tall and lean, with a scruffy beard, he held a rifle. He spoke a few words in Spanish that she didn't understand, then another soldier in camo emerged from behind him, also carrying a rifle. He was stockier, and shorter—about Gianna's height. Both men were wearing masks. "You are difficult to find, Brit," he said, keeping his voice low. "But we always get them, heh?" he said to his friend.

"*Sí, siempre,*" the first man replied as he picked up Zoe's gun. "Nice," he said. "*Mina.*" He tucked it in his waistband.

"Take us to the others," the English-speaking soldier demanded, dragging her by the hair.

No way would Zoe lead them to Gianna. She jerked away from him. "There are no others."

The second rebel smacked her across the face. "Talk, puta. Where?"

"I don't know what you're—" The man hit her again, even harder, and she lost her balance and fell.

He pointed his rifle at her head. "Where?" He was scowling.

Zoe rubbed her face but refused to answer. They would kill her anyway. She wouldn't get Gianna killed, too.

When she didn't reply, he yanked her up by her hair. It hurt like hell, but Zoe didn't cry or show any pain. If she was going to die, she would do it with pride and not kneel to these fuckers. He held her in front of him like a shield and shouted, "We have your friend."

The other soldier stood ready with his rifle, scanning the brush in every direction. Every time he heard the slightest sound, he quickly pivoted in that direction. Left, then right, but it was always some bird or other creature.

"Come out, Medica, or I kill her," the man holding her yelled when there was no response. After more silence, he shouted, "Maybe me and Miguel fuck her first." He put his face beside Zoe's ear. "You want that, puta?" he asked, his foul breath escaping his mask.

Fetch froze for an instant, all her senses snapping to high alert, when she heard the male voice. She crept over to the bush where she'd sent Zoe, keeping low. From there, she glimpsed the guerrillas through the underbrush. Two of them.

She had a clear shot of the one with the gun, but the other rebel was hidden behind Zoe. If she took out the first, the other would kill Zoe on the spot, before she could reach them. As much as he needed to take her back to his chief, he wouldn't risk his own life.

Fetch moved closer from a different angle to get a better aim at them both.

Just then, the soldier holding Zoe pulled down her sweatpants and Zoe screamed. "Maybe your friend left you for us. Like a gift, right, Miguel?"

She tightened her grip on the rifle as she fought to suppress her rage. All she could think about was snapping his neck for touching Zoe. "Motherfucker," Fetch said out loud. "Leave her alone," she shouted in Spanish. "I'm coming out."

"You try anything and I kill her, Medica." He turned in the direction of her voice, keeping Zoe in front of him. The second man, the one he'd called Miguel, had turned as well and had his rifle pointed her way.

When she got fifteen feet from them, they both smiled. Zoe's eyes were panicked, and the mask on her face dented in and out with her rapid breathing.

"Drop the rifle," Miguel said in Spanish.

Fetch stopped in front of them and threw the rifle at their feet.

"Where are the other hostages?" Miguel asked.

"Somewhere safe," Fetch replied calmly. If she told them the virus had killed them, she'd have nothing to buy time or bargain with. She hoped Zoe would catch on.

"Where?"

"Fuck you."

As he approached, glowering at her, Miguel took her own Glock out of his waistband and shoved the end of it against her mouth. "I shoot you in your dirty mouth."

"I die, and you never find the others."

"We will. We found you."

"Maybe," Fetch said. "But you could be looking for a long time."

His face went red. "Tell me! They must be near. You would not leave them."

"Fuck you." Fetch hoped she could convince him she wouldn't reveal where the others were.

Miguel backhanded her with the butt of the gun in his fist. Fetch stumbled, but rapidly resumed her position in front of him. She spat blood at him, and it splattered across his mask. He was about to hit her again when the other rebel, the one holding Zoe, stopped him with a grunt.

"Who do you work for, Medica?" Miguel demanded. "Santos?" he asked. "You betray us for that pig?"

Fetch didn't answer. Let him think she worked for the Colombian president.

The soldier took that as a yes and kicked her leg. Fetch collapsed to her knees.

"Where are the others?"

"Somewhere in the jungle."

Miguel looked to the one holding Zoe, who was clearly his superior. The other nodded, and Miguel pulled Fetch up by the front of her shirt. He stuck the Glock in his waistband and, without warning, punched her in the face.

If she fought back, they'd kill her instantly and take Zoe back to camp. So she took the blows, as Miguel punched her until the pain dulled. She stayed on her feet only because Miguel still held her shirt, but soon she couldn't support her head, and it lolled to one side. Somewhere in the darkness of her mind, she could hear Zoe screaming.

"Do whatever you want to me, I don't care," Zoe shouted. "Just leave her alone!"

"Look away, Zoe," was all Fetch managed before Miguel punched her again.

If she talked now, told them what had happened to the others, the men would take them both back to camp and continue a long, slow torture until they died. She could not, and would not, put Zoe through that. She'd promised Zoe she'd get her out of there, and she would. Somehow. Fetch sank more with every punch.

Finally, Miguel let go of her shirt and she fell to the ground, choking on her own blood. She could hardly see from the swelling around her eyes.

"Gianna, please," Zoe screamed. "They'll kill you. My God, your face."

"I'm okay." Her mouth ached, every word an effort.

"If you don't care about your own life, Medica, maybe you care about hers," the senior rebel said. "Get up."

Fetch slowly made it to her knees and struggled to stand.

"Bring her here," the second rebel said to Miguel.

Miguel shoved Fetch forward, until she and Zoe stood side by side.

"So," the soldier in charge said, "here are the options." He spoke casually, as if about to announce the day's menu. "One." He stuck his index finger in front of her face. "You tell us where the others are. Or, two…" He stuck up another finger, "you watch me kill the Brit and then shoot you in your lying mouth. It's your decision." He shrugged and walked to stand behind them.

Fetch assessed their predicament and how she might get them out of it in seconds. She instantly analyzed how she might use her martial arts and combat skills to take advantage of their proximity, body positions, the terrain, and even the particular weapons used against them. The EOO had prepared her well, and she'd learned much for herself as a soldier.

Zoe was to her left, three feet away.

Miguel now stood ten feet in front of them. He held his old Chinese 308, a semiautomatic copied from the M14, at chest level, pointed in their direction, his hand on the trigger. But he had the cocky, relaxed posture of one certain his captives wouldn't try or be capable of doing anything to escape. Fetch's rifle was on the ground at his feet, and her Glock was in his waistband.

The one in command, covering them from the rear with a Russian AK-47 assault rifle, was left-handed, and he'd set the selector lever on the weapon to the full-automatic position.

"So?" the one in charge said in Spanish. "Where are they?"

The cold end of the rifle jabbed the back of Fetch's neck, but she didn't respond.

"Pity to kill her, no?" the man said next. Fetch turned her head slightly, so she could see in her peripheral vision the same action repeated against Zoe's neck. "But I..." he went on, poking Fetch again, "will be glad..." Zoe's turn, "to kill you both..." Fetch again. Both men laughed.

The men were only toying with them; they would follow Barriga's orders. Zoe was still very valuable to them, especially since she was the only hostage they had found, so they probably wouldn't kill her. The chief would reward them for showing up with her. But they, and others, would most likely rape Zoe or punish her in various ways for escaping.

As to Fetch's future, Barriga might have ordered them to shoot her immediately, or he might want them to bring her back to him alive so he could torture her for information about her alliance with the president before he killed her himself. One thing was certain.

The guerrillas would not go all the way back to camp if they thought the other hostages were nearby.

"Perhaps," the rebel behind her said, moving closer to caress the right side of her face with the barrel of the AK-47, "we fuck you both before we kill you." His breath was rancid.

"Or after," Miguel said, and they both laughed again.

During this moment of relaxed laughter Fetch sprang into action, targeting the guerrilla behind them first. In one fluid motion, she brought her right elbow back hard, dislodging the man's grip from his trigger hand as she grabbed the barrel resting on her shoulder with her left hand. Within a split second, she had pulled the rifle forward and held it. She shot Miguel in the face before he could get a shot off, then slammed the butt end of the rifle against the shocked face of the rebel behind. He reeled backward, stunned but still a threat.

Fetch pointed the AK-47 at him and said, "You forgot option number three," wiping the blood from her mouth with her left shoulder. "The option where we go home and you rot in hell."

The guerrilla smiled up at her. "Shoot, puta. What are you waiting for?"

"Get up." Fetch handed the rifle to Zoe.

The man didn't waste any time getting to his feet.

"What are you doing?" Zoe asked.

Fetch walked up to the guerrilla. "Don't get me wrong. You're going to die today, but on my terms." She punched him in the face, and when he tried to fight back, she furiously deflected every blow with her hands and forearms and kept punching until he was exhausted. One more blow in the stomach, and he bent over, wheezing. She kicked him in the face and he fell on his back.

"Get up. I'm not done." The man didn't move. "Come on, you couldn't wait to stick your dick in me a few minutes ago. What happened?"

The guerrilla slowly rolled over onto his stomach to get up. "I'm going to kill you, puta," he grumbled.

Fetch stood over him and stomped his spine hard with her boot. Then she kneeled, a leg on either side of his back. Bending forward until her face was close to his, she said, "No. I'm going to kill you." She grabbed his hair and yanked his head back. "Did you really think you would fuck her? No one touches her." With one swift twist, she broke his neck.

She got up and retrieved her M14 and her Glock from Miguel's body. "Let's go," she said to Zoe without looking at her. "If more are out there, they heard the shot."

CHAPTER THIRTY

Zoe watched from behind, still trembling, as Gianna cleared the way ahead. She limped, but Zoe didn't know how the woman was still standing after that beating, let alone how she'd managed to overcome both rebels and be able to keep going, her injuries not seeming to hamper her. Zoe wanted to ask if she was all right, if she was in pain, but Gianna wouldn't even look at her. She knew soldiers were trained to fight, but she'd never realized women were capable of such brutal strength and bravery. If she wasn't still half in shock, she'd be even more impressed by Gianna's pure power and controlled rage. But why, when Gianna could have shot the second guerrilla, hadn't she? Why did she have to fight and kill him with her bare hands?

"We should stop and take care of your face," Zoe dared suggest in a low voice.

"No need," Gianna replied curtly. "No time for that."

"This is all my fault. If I'd stayed where you told me, this would have never happened."

"They were already following us. Just waiting for the right opportunity."

"How do you know?"

"Because it's my job to know," Gianna shot back. "No more talking."

They walked without pause until the sun was about to set, not even stopping to remove food from their packs. Both reacted to every sound and shadow, and the constant alertness, nonstop marching, and lack of nourishment was quickly draining Zoe's reserves. Gianna was slowing down, too.

Finally, in an area of dense vegetation, Gianna stopped in a spot with a level patch of moss wide enough to accommodate them and their gear. "We should eat and rest for a while," she said. Still avoiding eye contact, she dropped her backpack and rifle and sat on the ground.

Zoe opted for a fallen tree trunk.

"Not there," Gianna said. "Stay low."

Zoe complied and sat next to her. Gianna's face was badly bruised and swollen. Her bottom lip was split in two places, and both her eyes were nearly shut. "Does it hurt?"

"Not too bad." Gianna dug in her bag, opened a can of beans, and poured some into her mouth. Her hands were swollen and bruised as well, the knuckles bloodied and raw.

Zoe got a can from her bag and started to eat, lifting the edge of her mask just enough to do so. "Why didn't you just shoot him?" she finally asked.

"I'm sorry you had to see that."

"I don't care. The arsehole deserved it."

Gianna looked at her, surprise on her face. "Sometimes," she said, "shooting someone isn't enough."

"Why not?"

"Because they deserve worse. They deserve to hurt as much as they hurt another."

"But why him?" Zoe asked. "The other guy hurt you."

"I know." Gianna looked away. "But he was the one who... who touched you."

"You broke his neck because he smacked me? That's nothing compared to what happened to you." She raked her hand through her hair. "Christ, Gianna. He hardly touched me and you risked your life for that?"

"I didn't risk anything. He didn't stand a chance."

"No, he didn't. I've never met a woman like you. Even a man wouldn't have survived that beating, let alone beat the crap out of another man like that. You seemed to black out for a while."

Gianna shrugged. "He didn't have the right to touch you."

"The last time I saw that look in your eyes was when the guerrilla attacked me by the river."

Gianna poured some more beans into her mouth and chewed slowly. "I'm sorry if I scare you," she finally said.

"You don't. I know you'd never hurt me. But you don't have to get yourself beat up just because someone—"

"He touched your body."

Zoe didn't know what to say. Yes, it had been horrible, and she'd also thought the two soldiers intended to rape her but…they hadn't.

"That bastard pulled your sweats off. He had no right." The muscles in Gianna's bruised jaw tightened. "No one touches you like that, Zoe. No one, ever again."

Zoe hunched in front of Gianna and looked into her eyes. "Thank you," she said. "But I don't want you getting hurt…or *worse*, just to defend my honor. If it meant keeping us both alive I would've let him—" she couldn't bring herself to use the word *rape*—"have me."

"I'll kill anyone who tries." Gianna's mouth twitched, and the muscles in her jaw bunched again. "You have no idea what that does to a woman. I've seen it enough to know. In war, horrible things go on. I can't let that happen to you."

Zoe pressed her lips to Gianna's forehead. "You're a remarkable woman," she whispered.

Gianna tried to pull away, but Zoe stopped her by putting her palm very gently against her bruised cheek. "Let me reward your chivalry by cleaning you up."

Gianna relaxed into her touch and nodded her consent.

Once she'd tended to Gianna with medical supplies from her backpack, they finished their food and were soon pushing their way through the jungle again toward the safe house.

❖

Frankfurt, Germany
October 25

Luka wiped the blood from her chin and remained frozen in front of the bathroom mirror. How could she tell Hayley, and how could she die now that they were starting a new family? Was it meant to be? Had some higher power made her decide to create a child, to leave a part of her behind before she left this life? If true, it was life's pathetic attempt at consolation. She exited the bathroom and sat on the bed, vacant of emotions and filled with a million thoughts.

She'd tried to ignore how feverish and headachy she'd felt that morning, though she'd been even more careful to keep a distance from Misha and ensure they both always had their masks on. Earlier that day, they'd been to the wrecker company that had hauled away the suspect's car and discovered two pinholes in the brake lines. It confirmed what they suspected—that the pseudo cleaning woman had been silenced for her part in the virus conspiracy—but they had no clues to who might have done it.

They planned to conduct another search of the woman's apartment after they had some dinner, but not long after Misha left for the deli down the street, Luka began to cough up blood. She'd undeniably come down with the virus.

She had to call Monty, tell him she could no longer work this mission. Not with Misha this close. She couldn't take the risk of infecting a stranger, never mind someone she loved. But where would she go? Was there a place to wait for death that didn't include loved ones? Hospitals were full and could do nothing for her anyway. Maybe Monty had a place for her at the EOO.

Misha would be back soon. Luka had to make that phone call while she was still alone. She dialed the EOO number and was put through to Joanne Grant.

"Domino?"

"I'm sick. And I can't go home. I need a place to stay until…"

Joanne was silent for a long time and when she spoke her voice was hoarse. "I'll make arrangements and call you back with details." Luka heard her sniffling. "Is Allegro…"

"She's fine as far as I know."

"Have you told Hayley?"

"Not yet."

"We'll work that out when you get here. Be at the Frankfurt Air Base as soon as possible. I'll have transport waiting."

She'd just disconnected when Misha walked in carrying two plastic bags of Chinese takeaway. "The deli was clo—What's wrong?"

Luka rubbed her face. "I'm, uh…I'm sick, Misha."

Misha dropped the bags and started toward her, but Luka raised her hand to keep her at a distance. "Don't. Stay away from me."

"Screw that," Misha said. "I have the God damn mask on." She sat on the bed next to Luka. Neither spoke for a long time. "Are you sure?" Misha asked finally.

"Coughing blood, fever, headache. I'm sure."

Misha bent over, with her elbows on her knees, and ran her fingers manically through her hair. "Fuck."

"I'm leaving for the air base soon. Talked to Joanne. She said they'll make arrangements for me to stay somewhere until—"

Misha shot up. "Don't you dare. Don't you dare say it."

Luka stood and walked to the window. Rain was beating against it and Luka traced the drops as they glided down the glass. "Maybe I was meant to leave a child behind."

"Stop it!" Misha shouted. "You're not going to… It won't happen."

"Chances are it will, Misha." Luka jumped and turned around when she heard a crash. Misha had thrown the bedside lamp across the room.

"Fuck." Misha slumped onto the floor, her back against the bed. She dropped her head and sat crying silently, her shoulders shaking as she tried to muffle the sound with her hand.

Luka sat on the floor across from her. She wanted to put her arm around her friend, her confidant. The woman who for years had been her only family. They had laughed and cried, fallen and risen, and survived bullets and free falls because they had each other. And, most of all, Misha had always managed to make her laugh when her life had made her cry. She put her hand on Misha's knee.

"I don't want to hear it," Misha said, her attention focused on the carpet between her legs.

"Misha…"

"No."

Luka squeezed her knee. "Okay, then let's work with probabilities and scenarios."

When Misha didn't fight her, she said, "If anything happens to me, I want you to take good care of yourself." Luka laughed softly. "I want you to be a bit less…reckless."

Misha didn't answer.

"For Kris's sake as well. I don't know why she puts up with you, lunatic, but she loves you to death." Luka kidded to lighten the atmosphere. "Will you do that for me?"

"Whatever," Misha mumbled, picking at the seam of her jeans.

"Is that a yes?"

"I guess."

"And I need you to do one more thing."

"Should it be necessary, right?"

"Right." Luka took a deep breath to brace herself. These were the hardest words to speak. "I want you to take care of Hayley and the baby, if there is one."

"Does she know?"

"No. Not yet."

Misha finally looked up at her, the tears running freely down her face. "I'll take care of them. I promise," she managed between sobs, her whole body shaking. She threw herself into Luka's arms, and Luka held her tight.

"I love you, lunatic," Luka said, as she cried on her shoulder.

"I love you too, freak," Misha replied as she kissed Luka on the temple.

❖

Colorado
October 25

Cassady Monroe woke from her post-sex dozing and rolled over to find Jack still asleep on the other side of her queen-sized bed. She was lying on her back, her face serene. She hadn't had any nightmares for the last few weeks. A good sign, she hoped, that Jack was making peace with her past and finding reasons to look forward to the future, despite the recent crisis.

The world pandemic had turned their lives upside down. Jack was forced to leave her job when the virus reached New York. Countless there had died, including many of the troubled children she was working with. She and Jack had retreated to Cassady's house outside Colorado Springs, where the death toll was still low, but rising. They avoided going out unless absolutely necessary, and Cassady kept up to date on the crisis through frequent calls to headquarters.

Cassady shifted to nestle against Jack, resting her head in the crook of Jack's shoulder. Jack stirred, embracing her closer. They lay silent in bed, each apparently lost in thought. When they made love today they had done more than express their feelings for each other. They had attempted to forget all that was going wrong in the world. They wanted to feel alive, thankful they hadn't been infected by the virus that was spiraling out of control.

"Any news from Fetch?" Jack's thoughts had obviously strayed in the same direction.

"She's alive, somewhere in the Colombian jungle. That's all we know."

"Is anyone closer to finding the antivirus?"

"They're working on it. Monty said they may have a lead."

"How did things go to hell this fast?" Jack rubbed her face with one hand. "So much death, so little hope."

"Don't say that, Jack. There's still hope." Cassady had to believe that. Silence fell between them again for several minutes.

"I can't imagine what I'd do if anything ever happened to you, Cass."

"Nothing will. We're both taking all precautions." Cassady's cell rang and she checked the display. "It's work." Jack's body stiffened, as it always did when the organization contacted her. Jack knew Cassady would never hurt her, but she still didn't trust the EOO. Even though Montgomery Pierce had made no move against her, she was wary of his intentions. Cassady sat up in bed. "Lynx 121668."

"Be at Peterson Air Force Base in four hours." It was Pierce. "You'll be briefed en route."

"Is Fetch—"

"As far as we know, alive. We're sending you to chase down that lead. You're going in with Allegro." Pierce disconnected.

Cassady stood up and turned to Jack. "I have to leave."

Jack threw the sheets off and stood up. "What? Why?"

"The lead panned out. I leave in four hours."

Jack grabbed her clothes off the floor and walked to her. "I'm coming with you."

"No, you're not. Even if you could, I don't want you there. It was only a matter of time before I got my next assignment."

"Not this, Cass. You know what's going on there."

"It's my job. I don't have a choice, and even if I did—"

"Yeah, I know," Jack said resignedly. "You'd do it anyway."

"Yes."

"I can't let you go. I can't risk anything happening to you." Jack cupped her face gently between her hands, and Cassady wrapped her arms around Jack's waist.

"I'll be fine." She gave Jack a sweet, brief kiss, meant as encouragement. "Besides, we have a house to build." The home Jack had always dreamed of building on Saint Lucia was on hold until the crisis passed.

"We have a life to build," Jack replied, and Cassady could see her struggling with the thought of letting go. "I love you so much it—"

"Hurts," Cassady whispered.

Jack nodded and kissed her, long and deep and full of passion. "Promise me you'll come back."

Cassady had never made that promise before. Not only because it was impossible to know what the outcome of any assignment might be, but because no one had ever asked her to. But right now, she knew she would do whatever it took to be with Jack again. Making her happy was one mission Cassady would never fail. She tightened her hold around Jack. "I promise. I'll come back to you."

CHAPTER THIRTY-ONE

Guaviare Jungle, Colombia
October 25

Fetch was glad Zoe had refused her offer to take her turn wearing a mask, once she'd cleaned her up. Her eyes were mere slits; she could barely see out of one of them, and she had to breathe through her mouth because her nose was so swollen. Zoe had put salve on her lips, which helped a lot—before that, they'd stung every time she sucked in the humid air. The mask would've made it still tougher to breathe, and even the slight pressure against her bruised face would've made her even more miserable. To top it off, her headache had returned, and the ibuprofen she'd taken hadn't touched it.

They'd walked through the night, stopping only long enough to catch their breath and fuel up with panela and water, and now, as dawn broke, they were only half a day or so away from the safe house. They hadn't seen any further sign of rebels pursuing them so far, which could only mean that the two soldiers Fetch had killed were either alone on a long-shot journey to find them, or they were far from the other soldiers.

Fetch stopped and turned to Zoe. "We should be at our target by dusk."

"I can't believe we're almost there." Zoe bent over, huffing to catch her breath.

Fetch set her pack down and dug out her HUD lenses and cell phone. They were in a clear spot on a ridge, so hopefully she'd get a signal here. After making sure the phone's battery was still charged, she put in her lenses. It wasn't easy with her eyes so swollen, but she managed after a couple of tries. She turned on the phone and activated the GPS, and their coordinates lit up in front of her on the lenses. Without looking down, she punched them into the cell phone while reading them off the optical heads-up display and added their ETA. All she needed was enough reach in the dense jungle to send the message. She checked the phone and read *Sent* on the display.

"What are you doing?" Zoe asked.

"Giving my people the approximate position of extraction and TOA."

"Do you think I can use your cell to call my father once they pick us up?"

"No problem. A few more hours and you can talk to your heart's content." Fetch looked down when the phone vibrated. The reply from Montgomery Pierce read *Roger*.

They walked on, closing in rapidly on their destination with the help of the HUD display. It couldn't be too soon for Fetch. Every step she took was an effort, and breathing through her mouth all day had wrecked her throat. She kept drinking water, but it wasn't helping much. Coughing, she reached for a small chunk of panela and sucked on it, hoping it would ease the irritation.

Finally, just before sunset, they reached the overlook where she'd first spotted the clearing. "Down there," she said to Zoe. "See it?"

"We're here?" Zoe was so excited she jumped.

"Just a short way down the slope and we're there."

"I'm so happy I could cry," Zoe said, and Fetch put her arm around Zoe's shoulder. "What am I saying?" Zoe sniffed. "I *am* crying."

Fetch squeezed her tighter. "We're going home."

Zoe wrapped her arms around Fetch and hugged her close, her mask crushing against Fetch's chest as she sighed loudly. But suddenly she pulled back, staring at Fetch's shirt. "Gianna," she said, her voice strained.

"Yeah?"

"You're burning up."

"It's from walking."

Zoe looked up at her and jumped back. "You're bleeding."

"What?"

"Your mouth."

Fetch wiped her mouth with her forearm. Blood.

"No!" Zoe said. "This can't be happening."

"Let's keep going." Fetch turned away from her. "They should be here soon."

Ten minutes later they arrived at the safe house—a small, dilapidated shack with crudely made furniture—and went inside to wait for the helicopter.

Fetch pulled a stool to the door where she could look out at the clearing and removed the optical HUD lenses. Darkness was coming fast.

Zoe brought another stool over and sat beside her. "This isn't true," she said. "You can't be sick. I won't allow it."

"I'll be fine, okay?"

"You will *not* die on me. Not after all this." Zoe's voice was full of emotion and she started to cry.

Fetch took her hand. "You're going home, Zoe."

"*We're* going home." Zoe's crying turned to sobs so intense her whole body shook. "I can't lose you."

"Hey," Fetch said. "Zoe, listen to me." She wanted to embrace her, hug her close and reassure her, but she didn't dare. "Who knows, maybe they've already found a cure."

"Wouldn't your people have told you?"

She shook her head. "I've had my phone turned off the whole time."

"And what if they haven't, Gianna? What if there is no cure?"

Fetch didn't know how to answer. She'd shut the door to her hotel room so many times, not knowing if she'd ever be back, and she'd learned to live with that. She had tamed the fear of death because she believed in what she did.

But here, in this savage world, surrounded by death, a remarkable woman had somehow taught her to live.

The sound of the approaching helicopter made them both look out. Fetch put a mask on and waited until the bird was close enough to see them. "Time to go home," she said to Zoe. They stepped into the searchlight that illuminated the clearing and Fetch waved her arms to signal the crew.

Zoe squinted against the dirt and debris stirred up as the helicopter descended and felt Fetch's hand on her head, urging her to keep low. When the skids touched the earth, a man in U.S. military fatigues in the open doorway hoisted her into the chopper. Both he and the two pilots wore oxygen masks, with tanks strapped to their backs.

When Gianna got into the cabin, she sat next to Zoe and tried unsuccessfully to suppress a cough. Zoe reached for her and brushed Gianna's hand away when she tried to stop her.

Zoe glanced toward the front, wondering why they weren't going up. Both pilots and the other guy were watching them. They must have seen Gianna cough and the stain of blood on her mask from it, because they all looked at each other.

"She'll be all right," Zoe said in annoyance, loud enough to be heard over the propeller.

As soon as they were in the air, the man who'd helped them into the helicopter came over to them and explained they were taking them to the air base near San José del Guaviare, where a plane would take them to their final destination.

Gianna pulled out her cell and wiped the mouthpiece, then wrapped a clean mask over it. "Call your father," she said as she handed the phone to Zoe.

Zoe glanced at Gianna's watch as she punched in the numbers with trembling hands. It was nearly midnight in London, but her father picked up right away and sounded wide awake. She had to cup her hand around her ear to be able to hear him above the noise of the chopper.

"Daddy, it's me."

"Zoe?"

"Who else calls you Daddy?" Zoe broke down at the sound of his voice.

"Where are you?"

"On my way home, Daddy," she said through her tears. "We were just rescued. U.S. forces picked us up ten minutes ago."

"My God, honey." Her father was crying now, too. "I tried to get you out, and then they told me they couldn't help because of this blasted virus." He stopped to clear his throat. "I kept trying, though, with my contacts."

"I know, Daddy."

"How did you—"

"This amazing woman, Gianna, she saved me."

"Who?" Derrick asked.

"I'll tell you all about it when I get home."

"Where are they taking you? I can have someone pick you up."

"We're going to the United States. To a hospital."

"Oh, my God, you're not..." Zoe heard the panic in his voice. "You don't have the virus, do you?"

"No, Daddy. I think I'm the only one who doesn't," she said, and looked at Gianna. "Everyone else got it. I don't understand. Maybe I'm immune, that's why I need to go to the hospital. I could be the cure. I have to be the cure."

"Could it be hereditary? Everyone around me is sick or dead, too," Derrick said. "All people that I've interacted with."

"Is it possible that we're both immune? Have you been checked?"

"I haven't had the time. I've been trying to find a way to get you out or come up with the ransom." He paused. "For a while, I thought Edward's vaccine might have something to do with it. You know, the one he gave you, too."

Zoe remembered the inoculations her uncle had given them a month before she'd left for Colombia. He'd been acting as their family doctor all her life, and he routinely gave them whatever they might need for their frequent travels. "It was just a flu shot."

"That's what I thought, too," Derrick said. "But maybe he finally hit the jackpot after all those years of research. He once talked about trying to come up with some kind of superflu vaccine that would be effective against more kinds."

"Did you talk to him?"

"I did. He's also fine, by the way, and said he'd look into it."

"And?"

"Haven't heard from him since, so I assumed it wasn't a miracle vaccine after all."

"Huh." Zoe thought it was extremely odd that all three of them weren't sick.

"Which hospital are they taking you to?"

"I don't know, Daddy, but I'll call you when I find out." Gianna was motioning to Zoe that she wanted to make a call herself, and to speed it up. "I should hang up now. My rescuer needs to use the cell."

"I love you, honey."

"Love you too, Daddy." Her voice choked with emotion. "I'll see you soon." She hung up and gave the phone back to Gianna. "How strange."

Gianna was looking at her intently. "What vaccine did you get, Zoe?"

Zoe explained about the shots she'd received weeks before she left, and what her uncle did for a living.

"I hate to say this, Zoe," Gianna said, "but it sounds fishy."

"I know."

"Who does your uncle work for?"

"He's a physician/virologist at Cambridge. He also consults a lot with labs all over. Government ones, private. He travels a lot."

Gianna called someone on her cell and informed them about their situation. Zoe heard her name mentioned. Then Gianna listened for a long while. "That's right, sir." A pause while the person on the other end said something. "No, I'm sick." Another pause. "I need you to check a name," Gianna said. "Edward Anderson-Howe, brother of Derrick." Pause. "I'm taking her with me, sir. I have reasons to believe she's either immune, but more likely has been injected against the H1N6." Pause. "I'm not sure." There was another long silence. This time, as Gianna listened, her eyes clouded with worry. "God damn it," she said as she hung up. She bent over and ran her hands through her hair.

"Radio ahead to the plane," Gianna yelled up to the pilots. "Let them know we're going to Andrews Air Force Base, then by chopper to the USAMRIID facility at Fort Detrick, Maryland."

Zoe smoothed Gianna's back with her hand. She didn't expect her to feel elated, but she could be the answer to saving Gianna's life. "This is good news, right?" she asked. "I could be the key."

"I sure hope so," Gianna replied. "One of our best ops and a hell of an incredible woman is dying."

CHAPTER THIRTY-TWO

USAMRIID
Fort Detrick, Maryland
7 p.m.

Montgomery Pierce left the BioLevel4 Patient Care Suite at the U.S. Army Medical Research Institute of Infectious Diseases and passed through the decontamination chambers, trading his Hazmat suit for a surgical mask and latex gloves.

He jogged to a nearby building where a colonel who owed him a favor had given him temporary office space and found Joanne Grant waiting with a carafe of coffee and a tray of sandwiches and fresh fruit. He'd had to pull a few of his considerable strings with the Department of Defense to secure beds for Domino and Fetch at the AMRIID Facility. The rest of the patients there were all senior-level officers and government officials who'd become infected with the virus.

"How is she?" Joanne asked as he pulled up a chair beside her at the small conference table and gratefully accepted the mug of coffee. Though they both wore masks all the time, they slid them down when taking meals alone together.

"No change. Do we have an ETA on Fetch?"

"Within seven hours."

"Have you reached Allegro and Lynx?"

Joanne nodded. "Allegro's en route from Frankfurt and should arrive here about the same time they do. Lynx was just landing at

Andrews when I caught her. I told her only that the plan had changed and she was to come here."

"Make sure the guard gate gets their names."

"Already done. I gave them Hayley's, too. She was rather insistent when I notified her. She's driving from Baltimore and should arrive any minute. I told them to direct her here."

Pierce fished out his cell phone and put on his reading glasses to find the number for his contact in British intelligence. He still hated having to wear the damned things in front of Joanne; they made him look ancient.

"Pierce," he told the man on the other end. "We've identified a person of interest and he's one of yours. Edward Anderson-Howe, a physician/virologist who teaches at Cambridge. Brother of Derrick Anderson-Howe." He relayed the information Fetch had given him about the so-called "flu shot" that Edward had given his brother and niece and asked to be kept informed about what they got when they questioned the man. Then he called Reno and asked him to find out everything possible about Edward Anderson-Howe.

"One of ours is on the team testing Fetch's theory," he told Joanne when he finished the calls. "He'll keep us apprised of their progress."

"If it's correct, I pray they're able to isolate and reproduce the cure in time for Luka." Joanne's expression was grave. "She's strong, but..." She choked, her green eyes filled with tears.

"I know, honey." He took her hand. "Try to stay optimistic." It was never easy to deal with the death of an ETF, though every mission was potentially deadly. He, Joanne, and David acted as pseudo parents to their operatives, and he knew Joanne was recalling, as he was, Luka growing up on the Colorado campus. She'd become one of the most successful, resourceful operatives in the organization's history, and her loss would hit them all hard, both professionally and personally.

❖

Hayley Ward parked her red Mustang next to the brick office structure and hurried inside. The fifty-mile drive from Baltimore to

Fort Detrick had taken an excruciating hour, including the fifteen minutes for the Maryland State Patrol cop to write her a speeding ticket.

Joanne Grant must have heard the rapid cadence of her footfalls on the long hallway; she appeared in one of the doorways at the end long before Hayley reached it. Her red-rimmed eyes, stark above her white mask, made Hayley panic. Was she too late? She clutched Joanne's arm to steady herself and fight the wave of nausea that hit her at the thought of Luka being dead.

"My God, is she—"

Joanne grabbed Hayley's shoulders. "No, she's not…" Hayley knew Luka had always had a special place in Joanne's heart, and the feeling was mutual, but even this strong woman, who must have lost operatives in the field many times before, apparently couldn't bring herself to say the words. "She's very sick but she's still holding on," Joanna finally said.

"Take me to her."

"I'm afraid that's not possible, Hayley, she's—"

Hayley held up a hand. "It's not up for debate, Joanne, so don't even try."

"Miss Ward." Montgomery Pierce appeared in the doorway. He seemed to have aged more than Joanne Grant since the last and only time Hayley had seen them. Nearly three years earlier, they'd all ended up in the same room with Terrence Burrows. Burrows, a screwed-up politician, had tried to blow them all up as part of a bid to bring down the EOO. But Luka had saved them.

"Where is she?" Hayley practically shouted, and looked from one to the other.

"In isolation," Joanne said. "I'm afraid no visitors are allowed and she's too weak to—"

"Listen to me." Hayley took a step closer until her face was inches away from Joanne's. "I don't give a good God damn if she's on another planet. If she's too weak to talk then I'll just hold her. Every time her phone rings is yet another time you take her away from me. I accepted long ago that a day could come when she'd never return. I have learned to live with the fact that Misha might call me to tell me that Luka is gone."

Hayley paused to take a deep breath. "That's why I make sure every day we spend together counts and that I save every moment in my memory for when I'll need it. I have even somehow convinced myself that I'll be able to cope with that loss, because she will have died in the name of duty. Died fighting for some noble cause. But," Hayley looked at Pierce, "the one thing that never ceases to terrify me is that she will have died alone. Suffered through those last moments without me. Do you have any idea how helpless…useless that makes me feel?" She looked from one to the other, and when neither replied, she shouted, "I will not let her die alone." Tears streamed down her face.

Pierce was silent for several seconds, his eyes moist. "Follow me."

Joanne grabbed his arm. "Monty, are you sure?"

"You'll need to get suited up first," he told Hayley.

Fifteen minutes later, the two of them stood outside Luka's room. The Hazmat suit made Hayley vaguely claustrophobic, but her discomfort disappeared when she read the words on the door. *Code-black isolation. No admittance by unauthorized personnel.*

"She tires easily, Miss Ward."

"I understand."

Pierce suddenly looked twice his age. "I'm glad you're here. Go be with her."

She was so afraid of what she would find on the other side that for the first several seconds after she opened the door, she looked everywhere but directly at Luka. The room was stark white, without decoration or warmth of any kind. Industrial tile in a vague green pattern covered the floor. Recessed fluorescent lights, dimmed to low, dotted the ceiling. The privacy curtains that surrounded the two beds were pulled back, and the bed on the left was empty.

Steeling herself, Hayley looked at the other and gasped.

Luka looked unbelievably small in the single bed and more frail than Hayley had ever seen her, a shadow of the strong, athletic woman who had captured her heart. Her skin was gray, except for a smear of red on her mouth and chin, and dried specks of blood dotted the front of her hospital gown. Surrounding her were numerous monitors, their digital displays keeping track of her pulse, blood pressure, and other vital functions. A nightstand held tissues and water.

Hayley approached the bed.

Luka's eyes were shut and her breathing shallow. Her nose and mouth were covered by an oxygen mask, attached to a respirator that whooshed softly every few seconds. Her eyes looked bruised from the red circles under them.

Hayley didn't fight the tears as she gently stroked Luka's hot forehead. "I'm here, honey," she whispered, "and I'm not leaving you."

Luka opened her eyes, squinting like she was trying to focus. "Hayley?" she mumbled.

"Expecting someone else?" Hayley joked in an attempt to cheer her.

Luka slowly lifted her hand to her mouth to pull the oxygen mask away.

"Is that a good idea?" Hayley asked.

"I'll put it back on if not," Luka said slowly, as though pronouncing each word took effort. Hayley held her hand. The gloves prevented her from feeling her lover's warm, soft skin. She wanted to rip them off, but under these circumstances it would be selfish. It wasn't just herself she needed to protect. "How did they let you in here?"

"I threatened Pierce with his life."

"Thatta girl." Luka attempted a smile. "Are you sure you're safe with me?"

"I've always been safe with you. I don't see how that could ever change."

"Yeah, but—"

"I'm safe, okay? Don't waste your strength on silly questions." Hayley wanted to ask Luka how she felt, but the question seemed so stupid, so pedestrian and unnecessary.

"I'm so tired, baby."

"I know." Hayley looked away. Tired was too mild a word for how Luka looked. She didn't know how anyone could deal with the death of a loved one. How would she cope with the pain of losing her when she was already failing at the mere thought of it? "Are you in pain?" She couldn't conceal the tremor in her voice.

"It's doable. I'd tell you not to worry but...I know it's pointless."

"Are they giving you anything?" Hayley asked, ignoring the comment.

"Yeah, don't know what. Don't care to ask as long as it helps. I think it's wearing off."

"Should I call for more?"

"No. I want to stay lucid a while longer. Don't want to sleep now that you're here."

Hayley caressed her cheek. "Will you tell me if it gets too much?"

"I promise."

"They could still find a cure." Hayley tried to sound positive. "They're working on it twenty-four seven."

"I don't think I can hold on much longer."

"Don't say that, honey."

"No one has survived this."

"Please stay positive, okay?"

"I'm being realis..." Luka sat up abruptly and started to cough. She brought her hand to her mouth, but not before a spray of blood covered the sheets. "Damn it," she said, when she could talk again.

"Just lay back." Hayley fixed the pillows for her. She plucked tissues from the box on the nightstand and wiped Luka's mouth and chin. She tried to keep her eyes away from Luka's because she knew she wouldn't be strong enough to handle what she saw. The woman she loved with all her might lay dying in this cold, white, windowless room, and she couldn't do a thing. She wanted to scream out her frustration and anger. Blame the whole damn world and whatever divine entities for wanting to take Luka away. Luka, the one person who had given her more love and happiness than she could even imagine was possible.

As Hayley wiped the blood from her cheek, Luka gently placed her fingers on the small window in her Hazmat helmet. "I can't even touch your beautiful face." Her voice was barely audible.

"Do you need the oxygen mask, honey?" Hayley tried to keep her voice and breathing steady. It was taking all her strength not to fall apart. Luka needed her to be strong and she needed to stay positive. Falling apart would mean admitting defeat, bowing to death, and accepting the inevitable. Hayley was not prepared to do any of the above.

"No. I'm…not done yet. I…want to tell you how much I love you."

Hayley pulled back and sat on the edge of the bed. She closed her eyes and let the tears flow freely for the first time. "You can't die. I can't do this without you. I don't know how to be without you."

"You'll find a way, honey," Luka said gently. "I know you will. You're the strongest, most persistent woman I've ever met."

"Christ, Luka, why now? Why now, when we…" Hayley wanted to pull her hair, wipe her eyes from the endless river of tears, but couldn't get to either because of the suit. A wave of nausea hit her again and she clutched her stomach as she bent over, struggling not to vomit.

Luka stroked her back. "Are you going to be sick?"

Hayley breathed deeply before answering. "I think it's over."

"You're not…sick, are you?" Luka asked, panic in her voice. "How long have you…"

Hayley gazed into her eyes. "Luka…I'm pregnant."

"No."

"I found out yesterday."

Luka dropped back on the pillows, crying. "We're…" She rubbed her eyes. "You're going to be a mother."

"We both are, sweetheart." Hayley grabbed Luka's shoulders. "This baby is so much of you. This beautiful child will be as brave and selfless as its amazing mother."

"Thank you for giving me so much." Luka's voice shook. "For giving me the gift of life and hope through this child. I know you'll do everything in your power to make sure it has the choices I never had."

"And I intend to spend the rest of my life," Hayley said between sobs, "telling our child about its mother. About…"

Luka started to cough again, violent expulsions that made her whole body convulse. The blood wouldn't stop coming, and when Luka started to choke, Hayley pressed the alarm button. Seconds later, two nurses and a doctor stormed through the door. One of the nurses pulled her aside while the other two tended to Luka. "You'd better wait outside."

"Will she be all right?" Hayley asked, trying to see past the nurse.

"We'll keep you informed. Please go to the waiting room. You can't be in here now." The nurse propelled her toward the door with an arm on her elbow.

Luka was still coughing and having some kind of seizure. Hayley thought she would lose her mind. "I love you," she screamed above the commotion as the nurse shut the door.

❖

October 26
2 a.m.

The helicopter that brought Fetch and Zoe landed on the hospital roof where three men waited for them, all in Hazmat suits. The three braced themselves against the downdraft from the chopper blades as it descended and were at the door as the skids touched pavement.

When Fetch jumped out she recognized Montgomery Pierce behind one of the trio of white helmets. She and Zoe were ushered into the hospital wing, where everything started to move in fast motion.

One doctor pulled her away, with Pierce following, and another one took Zoe. Fetch looked back and Zoe did, too, and said, "I'll see you soon."

They reached a sealed area and Pierce spoke to her for the first time, his voice muffled, as if it came from another room. "You look like hell, Truman."

"You should see the other guy."

"If I know you, he's already fertilizer."

Fetch smiled.

The doctor handed her a typical hospital-issued backless gown.

"When will we know?" she asked him, "if my friend is carrying the antivirus?"

"In a few hours."

Pierce turned to the doctor. "If that's the case, my people get it first. One of my own risked her life to get it to you."

"As agreed, sir," the doctor answered with a slight bow of respect.

"You can take the bed next to Luka when you're ready," Pierce told her, indicating the adjacent room.

"I don't need to lie down, sir. I'm still fine."

"Get your face cleaned up. That's an order."

"Yes, sir. How is she doing, sir? Luka?"

"Not well. Let's hope Miss Howe can change that." He left her to change.

Once she'd pulled on her gown, Fetch entered the isolation room where Luka lay. She looked pale, with dark circles under her eyes. And as she watched, Luka removed an oxygen mask that had been over her face and coughed blood into a bedpan. "You look like hell," Luka said when she spotted Fetch, and coughed again.

"I've seen you look better, too." Fetch smiled. She sat on the edge of the adjacent bed just as a nurse in a Hazmat suit came in.

Zoe was rushed to an empty room where five men wore the same white snowmen suits. If this were a dream, she'd think aliens had abducted her. She half expected someone to pull out an anal probe. They sat her down and took three vials of blood and left without saying a word. Seconds later, a woman wearing a similar suit entered and handed her a hospital gown. "How long will it take before you know?" she asked.

"A few hours. Get some rest, and I'll bring you some food soon."

"Can I shower?"

"In there." The woman pointed at a closed door and left without another word.

Not great conversationalists. Zoe hated that everything was so vague. She wanted to know how Gianna was faring and what they were doing to her.

Zoe took a long, hot shower and when she came out, a tray of food was waiting. She should've devoured it, she hadn't eaten in many hours, but she was too worried about Gianna. She kept waiting for someone to walk in, but exhaustion finally won and she dozed.

Her sleep was restless, comprised of vivid dreams. She was in the jungle running for her life again, and Gianna was comforting her, telling her they would be all right. Suddenly, they were transported to a house, a beautiful home, where she was safe in Gianna's arms. Somehow, she knew she was dreaming, and she wished she never had to wake up.

A knock on the door did exactly that. Zoe opened her eyes and a stern man who seemed familiar walked in, dressed in a navy suit and tie. She sat up on the side of the bed, immediately alert but unable to read the man's gaze.

"My name is Montgomery Pierce, Miss Howe," He extended his hand.

"And you are?"

"Gianna's employer."

"I think I remember," Zoe said. "You were wearing the snowman suit earlier. You left with Gianna."

"Correct."

"Why aren't you wearing a protective suit now? Why are you here?" She jumped up off the bed. "Is she all right?"

"Please sit down," he said calmly. "Miss Truman is going to be fine."

Truman. Funny how she'd never thought to ask Gianna's last name. "Does that mean we have the cure?"

He smiled. "Indeed we do."

Zoe sighed loudly. "Thank God. She'll be okay," she mumbled to herself. "Can I see her?"

"In a few moments. After I ask you some questions."

Zoe didn't want to wait, but the man's authoritarian demeanor made her sit back down. "What would you like to know?"

"We found certain components in your blood unlike anything we've seen before."

"So, I am immune after all."

"Yes, but not naturally. We found the exact components against the H1N6 virus. In other words, the antiserum."

"I don't understand."

"Truman…Gianna," Pierce said, "told me a family member inoculated you with some kind of antiflu serum."

"My Uncle Edward, yes. He works at Cambridge."

"And I understand he's done a lot of private consulting with labs all over the world?"

"That's right. Did he find the cure?"

"Miss Howe," his expression was serious, "we have good reasons to believe he is responsible for creating the virus."

"What? No, that's impossible. My uncle would never harm anyone."

"I know it's difficult to accept."

Edward? No. She couldn't accept this at all. "Why would he do this?"

"Money, Miss Howe."

"But he's not that kind of person. He's a good man."

"Millions have died so he could profit, but he was kind enough to spare you. At least he got that right."

"Are you certain? I mean, this is a strong accusation."

"We're quite sure."

The news was shocking, but apparently true. Gianna's boss wouldn't be saying this if compelling reasons didn't point to Edward's involvement. "I'm so sorry. I feel like it's partly my fault. He's my family."

"You had nothing to do with this, Miss Howe."

"Gianna could have died."

"Because of you, Miss Howe, she and billions of others get to live."

He was right, but she couldn't help feeling guilty. Her uncle—her sweet, harmless Uncle Eddie—had created this monstrosity. "I feel I should apologize for him, but no amount of apologies can bring all the lost lives back."

"No, they won't. But you shouldn't feel you have to apologize for another's actions."

"Does Gianna know about this?"

"Yes."

"Do you think she'll want to see me?"

He nodded. "She's been asking about you since they took you away."

Numb, Zoe stood and walked to the door. "Can I go to her now?"

❖

12 p.m.

Fetch looked over at Luka, dozing in the next bed. They'd been injected with the antivirus hours ago. It had worked in the Petri dish, but they were the first human subjects. Neither objected to being guinea pigs. What did they have to lose?

They'd spoken little as they waited for the serum to either take effect or…not. Like her, Luka was probably too worried or too exhausted to feel either hopeful or defeated. Besides, ops never talked about death or near misses; they didn't ponder such inevitabilities too much until they lost someone. This unspoken, unwritten law kept them sane.

Luka eventually fell asleep, and Fetch lay staring at the ceiling as she tried to make sense of Zoe's uncle and his decision to kill millions. What did this say about Zoe's family, her background, and the environment she grew up in? How would she take the news, and how would it affect her life? Fetch had been through enough with

Zoe to know that she would never hurt anyone. How did any family deal with a bad seed?

Although she had no blood ties to any of the ops, she felt a certain camaraderie, a special kind of kinship. She was closer to some than others, but they all shared a common past and goal. From the youngest to the oldest ETF's, all were soldiers trained to go to war, to give their life to save her, and others, if necessary.

They lived to battle with and for each other. Not for reward, because it didn't matter how much you earned when you had to pay by the minute. But because saving the life or having the back of another soldier was life's greatest reward. That's what soldiers did, and, to Fetch, family did too.

Someone knocked on the door, then said, "Pierce."

Luka, immediately awake, tried to sit up. Fetch met her eyes as Pierce came in, cleared his throat, and stopped between the two beds. Fetch didn't dare look at him, unwilling to face the truth. But, finally, Luka did. Was it because Luka had had more time to accept and make peace with death?

But a smile broke across Luka's face and she said, "We're going to be fine."

Fetch looked up at Pierce. The Hazmat suit was gone, and he was smiling, too. "She's right."

"I'm not burning up any more!" Luka said as she looked from one to the other. "I don't…I feel better."

Fetch fell back onto the bed. "We're going to live," she said, as she stared up again at the ceiling. The relief pouring through her was like a shot of adrenaline.

"Yes, you are," Pierce said. "Thanks to Miss Howe."

Zoe. "Does she know about her uncle?"

"I informed her."

"How did she take it?"

"She wants to see you."

Fetch sat up abruptly and smoothed the bedding. "I'd like that, sir."

"Hayley," Luka said. "I need to tell Hayley."

Pierce continued to smile as he walked to the door and held it open. "That's being arranged."

Zoe stood at the entrance to the room, feeling horribly uncomfortable. She glanced at Gianna, then at the other bed. Its occupant, a woman, had fared much worse than Gianna. Dark shadows marred her intense blue eyes; her lips were cracked and her complexion sallow. Her uncle had reduced an otherwise beautiful woman to a zombie.

"Hello," Zoe said to the woman. "I'm Zoe."

"Hi, there. Come on in. I'm Luka."

Zoe stepped forward, terribly afraid of facing Gianna. So far, she'd avoided eye contact, but it was inevitable. Gianna got up and went to the other bed. "Can we have a minute?" she asked Luka.

"As many as you want."

Gianna pulled the separating curtain around Luka's cot. Of course privacy was an illusion at this point, but the action forced Zoe to look at Gianna.

"I don't know what to say," Zoe muttered.

"Come sit with me." Zoe didn't hear any anger and couldn't detect any contempt, only compassion and kindness.

Zoe sat on the far edge of the bed, facing away from the curtain. "I'm so sorry."

Gianna sat close to her. "It's not your fault, Zoe. You're not responsible for this mess."

"But my family is."

"I won't pretend to know how you feel, though having someone you love and respect betray you is the worst kind of infidelity," Gianna said gently. "Make no mistake, Zoe, you're just as much a victim here as the rest of us."

"I'm not the one who almost died. I'm not one of all those people he killed…" Zoe wiped away a tear.

Gianna put her arm around her. "When you physically kill someone, their pain is over, but when you kill someone's trust, the pain lingers. Maybe forever. You have to deal with that pain, not guilt."

Zoe felt horrible that Gianna was having to comfort her. It should be the other way around. But because she felt partly responsible, she would be a hypocrite to think she could make anyone feel better.

She pulled away from Gianna and stood. "Is she the friend you told me about?"

"Yeah."

"She looks rather bad," Zoe whispered.

Gianna smiled. "She'll be fine. We all will, thanks to you."

Zoe turned away from her, unable to look into those sincere, understanding eyes. "I don't want gratitude. So please don't."

"Stop it, Zoe."

"You almost *died*," Zoe shouted, not caring if the other woman could hear. "And I can't stop feeling responsible. So stop trying to make me feel better."

Gianna didn't say anything.

"I don't know what I would've done if you'd died. I can't stand to think about it." Zoe wiped her eyes and turned to Gianna, then, inexplicably, she laughed. She felt almost manic from the mere thought of losing Gianna. "It's crazy. I mean I hardly know you, but I can't imagine existing in a world without you in it."

"I'm here, Zoe."

"And I can't look at you without hurting."

"You don't have to. I'm here…for you, and I'd do it all again if it meant saving you."

How could this woman show so much understanding and look at her with so much… Zoe wasn't sure how to describe that unfamiliar-to-her look, but it melted her heart and made her marvel at this woman's greatness.

Zoe walked over to Gianna, but before she got a chance to say anything more, a woman with strawberry blond hair and a brunette burst into the room. The shorter one, with the reddish hair, pulled away the curtain that enclosed the other bed.

Allegro paced in the sealed-off waiting room, feeling confined and edgy in the cumbersome Hazmat suit. Though she wasn't allowed to move past that one room, everyone in the AMRIID patient facility had to wear the protective gear anyway.

"Feel better?" she asked Hayley as she emerged from the attached restroom. She'd left a few minutes earlier, feeling nauseous.

"Yes. It's nerves. Don't worry about me," Hayley said as she took a seat on the couch.

Allegro had arrived more than nine hours earlier, recalled suddenly and without explanation by Joanne Grant. Hayley had arrived the night before and was permitted to see Luka briefly. Her grave assessment of Luka's condition was disheartening. Time was not on their side.

Allegro tried to see her, too, but was denied access, despite numerous loud threats to all hospital personnel within earshot. Her tirade did bring Monty to the waiting room. He'd told them about Fetch, and that the woman she'd rescued—Zoe Anderson-Howe—could be carrying the cure.

Fetch had been put in the other bed in Luka's room, and Monty said that for the moment, because of the battery of tests being conducted, not even he was allowed to see them.

So she and Hayley had passed the intervening hours in the waiting room together, leaving only to eat some tasteless cafeteria sandwiches on the roof, the one place they were allowed to remove their helmets.

"I wish they could do this blood test faster," Allegro said.

"Why won't they tell us anything?" Hayley frowned. "She can't die, Misha. Not now, not ever."

"I know."

Hayley looked up at her. "When will they know if that woman they brought in has the cure? It's been hours. I can't take this anymore."

"Just a while longer."

"What if she doesn't…" Hayley broke down, crying.

"Hayley, please don't do this to yourself, or me." Allegro knelt before her. "She's my best friend. My only friend. The thought of losing her makes me…" She pounded her fist on the empty seat next to Hayley, trying to purge her rage at the unfairness of it all.

"It can't happen," she said, and dropped on the floor in front of Hayley, lowering her eyes so Hayley wouldn't see her tears. She needed to be strong for her.

"I love her so much," Hayley said, sobbing.

"I know." Allegro was crying as well. "Me, too."

A man entered the room—one of Luka's doctors—and Allegro shot to her feet. He'd removed his helmet and was smiling.

"For real?" Allegro managed to choke out.

"Your friend will be fine," he said.

Hayley got up and they hugged, then Allegro turned to the doctor. "Let me see her," she said as she took off her helmet.

Hayley did the same and drew a deep breath. "And not later. Now."

"You'll have to wait a while. She's still too weak to—"

Allegro grabbed Hayley's hand and pushed the man aside. "Run!" she told Hayley, and they took off down the hall.

The doctor ran after them, shouting, "You're not allowed in there."

Allegro paused and turned as he caught up. "Stop me, and I swear I'll shoot you."

The man stepped back and raised his arms in defeat. Allegro grasped Hayley's hand again and they continued through a set of double doors past a nurses' station. The nurses and everyone around them had either removed their Hazmat helmets or taken off the suits altogether. Three doctors down the hallway were congratulating each other and smiling.

Hayley led the way to Luka's room and hurried inside ahead of Allegro. She pulled back the curtain around Luka and rushed to her, kissing her forehead and taking her hand. Luka, looking pale and tired, smiled up at her.

Allegro approached the bed. "Thanks for taking care of my girl," Luka said, holding Hayley's hand.

"Yeah, well, you know me. I live to serve you."

"And it only took a near-death experience for you to admit it." Luka grinned at her.

"Don't ever pull this shit on me again," Allegro said gruffly.

"Crying is bad for her rep," Hayley said.

Luka pretended to be shocked. "She even cried over me?"

Allegro felt herself blush. "Yeah, whatever." She quickly looked over to the other bed. "Hey, is that you, Gianna?" Gianna was facing away, talking to an attractive brunette. When she turned, Allegro said, "Whoa. What ran you over?" and walked over for a closer look.

Gianna merely smiled.

Allegro offered her hand to the attractive stranger. "Misha Taylor."

"Zoe Anderson-Howe," the woman replied in a British accent.

"As in the cure," Allegro said.

When the woman didn't answer, Gianna jumped in. "Looks like."

"Thank you for saving her life," Hayley said from behind them. She, too, walked over to Zoe and embraced her. "For saving so many lives."

"Please, it's the least I could do." Zoe replied and hugged her back. "Especially since—"

"No, Zoe," Gianna said. "None of this is your fault."

Hayley released Zoe and stepped back with a puzzled expression.

"What's going on?" Allegro asked.

"Guys, not now," Luka said, and they turned to her.

"It's a simple question," Allegro replied. "What's not her fault?"

"Let it go, Taylor." Montgomery Pierce had materialized in the doorway. "We'll talk about this later."

A doctor shoved past Pierce and entered the room with a cart, breaking the tension. He was the one she'd threatened to shoot if he stopped her and Hayley. "Everyone who hasn't been vaccinated needs to get a shot now."

Allegro walked over to the glaring doctor and rolled up her sleeve. "You had to go and interrupt the unfolding drama," she told him as he injected her. Then she stepped aside for Hayley. "You're up."

She took a few hesitant steps, then stopped. "I don't know if I should...if it's safe."

"Of course it is. They're not using us as guinea pigs." Allegro looked at Pierce. "Right?"

"Stop being your usual irritating self," Pierce replied.

"It's not that. What I mean is…" Hayley faced Luka. When Luka smiled and nodded, Hayley turned to the others. "I'm pregnant."

"What?" everyone except the British woman and the doctor said in unison.

"I'm six weeks pregnant." Hayley took Luka's hand. "We're going to have a baby."

Luka was grinning. She looked over at Allegro. "I can't believe I'm about to make this lunatic a godmother."

Allegro grinned. "That's right, folks, you heard it here first. I'm the chosen one."

Montgomery Pierce walked briskly from the patient center to the temporary office space they'd been given and found Joanne watching CNN's latest update on the pandemic. He'd already called her with the news that the antivirus had worked and Domino and Fetch were out of danger, but he wanted to deliver the latest update in person.

"What it is?" Joanne asked.

"Hayley's pregnant."

Joanne hugged him. "Oh, that's wonderful!"

"Yes. A day for good news," he said, embracing her back. "Now, I want you over there to get inoculated. I'll call Cassady at the hotel and get her over here, too."

"And the rest?"

"They're putting together a shipment of the antivaccine right now. We'll expedite it to the campus and have Arthur send everyone to the infirmary."

Joanne put a hand on his cheek. "And Jaclyn?"

How did Joanne sense what he was thinking? "I'll leave that to Cassady. She'll make sure it gets to her."

CHAPTER THIRTY-THREE

Hampton Inn
Frederick, Maryland
7 p.m.

Fetch stared out the window of her hotel room at the empty streets. Soon life would get back to normal here and elsewhere. The end to the pandemic was in sight, thanks to Zoe, who was in a suite down the hall. Allegro and Lynx had been booked into rooms on either side of her, and Hayley was one floor below, resting until Luka's condition improved enough for her release. Because of a shortage of beds at the AMRIID patient facility, they'd discharged Fetch as soon as they confirmed the effectiveness of the antivirus.

She felt worlds better. Her fever was gone, her coughing had stopped, and she was regaining her strength. The aches and bruises from her beating remained, but she was beginning to feel like her old self. Allegro had lent her some clothes, so after a long, hot shower, she'd put on clean jeans and a royal blue, long-sleeved T-shirt.

For the moment, they were all in limbo. All commercial flights had been suspended while they were in the jungle, so Zoe had been unable to book a flight to London. And Pierce was having trouble finding a military jet to get the EOO people back to Colorado.

When she answered the knock at her door, Zoe stood on the other side, a bag in one hand and a tray with two coffees in the other.

She had been wearing a pair of hospital scrubs when they were dropped off at the hotel, but had apparently accepted Hayley's offer to let her borrow a few things. She now wore a pale pink button-down shirt and blue jeans. She'd even, apparently, used a little of Hayley's makeup, just some blush and lip gloss. But she looked stunning, though she still wore Fetch's combat boots.

"May I come in? I have dinner." Zoe studied Fetch's face intently.

Fetch moved back a step and Zoe set the tray on a small table. Then she glanced at Fetch's tightly made bed and asked, "You haven't slept?"

Fetch shut the door. "I got up thirty minutes ago."

"I had no idea the chamber maids came this late."

"They don't. I made it." She shrugged. "Occupational hazard."

Zoe looked around the room. "If I didn't know better, I'd think no one had ever occupied this room."

"I like order."

"Is your house like this?"

"I don't have a house. Never have. I stay at a hotel." Fetch stood with her arms tightly at her sides and her chin up. When she thought she might have to explain herself, she always stood at attention.

"Why?"

"It's easier."

"What is?" Zoe asked.

"To shut the door when—"

"When you have nothing to look back at before you leave."

Fetch nodded.

"Nothing to remind you to be safe, and no one to promise to return to."

Fetch nodded again.

"Where does that leave you when you get too old to fight wars?"

"Wars never cease, and people always need to be saved. I'll continue with a different kind of war."

"Until when?"

"Until my body can't keep up with my needs."

"And then?"

"By then hopefully I'll have fought enough wars and won enough battles to find peace with no longer being able to help."

"And you'll have lived a perfectly detached life. Is that what you really want?"

"I don't have a choice. I cannot form emotional attachments."

"And Sam?"

"Sam was a soldier. She understood that one day she'd get a phone call."

"But she didn't."

"No. She never got the chance."

"Because life is wonderfully screwed up that way."

"What do you mean?" Did Zoe find Sam's death a wonderful screw-up?

"That you've lived your life according to your own rules and fears and decided what's best for you without ever considering life."

"Explain."

Zoe sat at the table. "You assume that the other will lose by being with you so you haven't considered the opposite. No one knows what the future holds, but you've convinced yourself you can control it if you deny yourself a life."

"That way no one gets hurt."

"If you don't want to take that risk again it's up to you, but is it fair to decide for another? Isn't that selfish?"

"I don't want anyone to hurt over me."

"But maybe they're not willing to forego love and happiness, contentment and companionship because of what might happen."

"But it's pointless when—"

"Love is worth the pain, Gianna."

"Why are you telling me this?"

Zoe held her gaze. "Because I'd die if it meant saving you."

Fetch stared at her, silent.

"That's how much you mean to me," Zoe said. "You said I'd know when it happened. I know now."

"You can't, Zoe." Fetch retreated a few steps and propped herself against a wall. "You can't."

"I can," Zoe said adamantly. "I do."

"You're still in shock. You think I'm some kind of hero because I got you out of the jungle."

"I know damn well what I feel," Zoe said, "and it's not shock. Yes, you'll always be a hero to me. And not just because you got me out of the jungle, but because you got me out of my previous life. I can't go back to that empty place. Not after knowing you." She stood in front of Fetch. "Aside from my parents, I've never needed and I've never missed not having anyone in my life, but after knowing you I can't exist in a world without you."

Fetch ran her fingers through her hair, trying to absorb what Zoe was saying. She felt helpless and exhilarated. She wanted to run to and from Zoe all at the same time. This was crazy. Zoe needed a constant in her life, someone to give her a steady, stable relationship. Not someone who showed up every few months and left again with a million uncertainties about her next return.

Zoe reached out to touch her arm, but Fetch pulled back. "This can't happen. You and…me…it's impossible."

"Why?"

"Our lives are so different. Yours is full of—"

"Cheap thrills and frills. Nothing meaningful." Zoe sighed. "Can't you see that I can't…I *won't* go back to that. Not after everything that's happened. Not after knowing you."

"Eventually, you'll get tired of waiting for me to come back to you. You'll hate not knowing where I am, what I'm doing, and how long it'll be before I return."

"I know how much your job means to you. I'll learn to accept and live with it. What you do…it's…who you are, and I want all of you. Not just the parts that are convenient and uncomplicated."

"I won't be there when you need someone to talk to. When you need someone to hold you."

"So we'll take advantage of every moment we can share."

"Zoe, I can't give you what you need."

"You can. But you don't know how."

"I don't want to hurt you."

Zoe placed her hand around Fetch's neck. "You will if you walk away." She pulled Fetch's head to her until their foreheads touched.

"Don't you get it? That's what I do. I walk away. Every few months, I walk away and I don't know if I'll be coming back."

"You'll *go* away, Gianna." Zoe kissed her cheek. "Big difference." Her lips felt so warm, so soft. Zoe moved into her until their bodies were tight together. Fetch practically jerked at the contact. How often she'd dreamed of those lips, and now they were so close, so inviting. She could look at nothing else. Her hands started to shake. The emotions were too strong, too powerful to command, and she didn't know how to cope with them without meds.

"You won't *walk* away, because that means running from me." Zoe kissed the corner of her mouth. "I don't want you to run." She rubbed her lips against Fetch's neck, then put her warm, moist tongue there. Fetch's whole body started to shake.

"You're trembling," Zoe said breathlessly, and brushed her lips against hers.

"I know." Fetch murmured. The nearness of those lips intoxicated her. She placed her hands on Zoe's hips to stop the shaking.

Zoe kissed her softly. "Is that good or bad?"

"I need you." Fetch pulled her head back to look at her. "I need to touch you so much it hurts," she said, feeling as though she was coming apart at the seams.

Zoe looked at her through half-open lids. "God, I hope you will."

Fetch groaned and devoured her lips and tongue with the hunger of a starved predator, probing the inside of her warm mouth. Her lips were still split and bruised, but she didn't notice. Zoe kissed her back with equal ardor, making up for all the times their masks had separated them.

Fetch squeezed Zoe's ass so hard she might have bruised her. When Zoe moaned in her mouth, Fetch tore Zoe's shirt open, silently cursing when she felt a bra. She tore that off as well and soon her hands were on Zoe's breasts.

Still kissing her, Fetch backed her up against the wall and disengaged only long enough to pull off Zoe's jeans and panties. Then she was kissing her again and thrusting her thigh between Zoe's. Zoe moaned and writhed against her, demanding more.

With one hand, she raised one of Zoe's legs, holding it against her waist while she used her other hand to penetrate her. It was the kind of sex Fetch was familiar with, the type of encounters she'd had so often in bars. But after a while, it wasn't enough. She wanted better access and a better view, so she picked Zoe up and put her on the waist-high mirrored dresser. Spreading her legs, she continued to fuck her, both of them breathing so hard now it was difficult to sustain their passionate kisses.

Zoe tried to take her shirt off, but Fetch was in such a frenzy she pinned Zoe's wrists over her head with one hand, while she continued to penetrate her with the other.

When she pulled her head back for a moment to breathe, Fetch saw herself in the mirror and was struck by her almost detached expression. Suddenly, what they were doing was too similar to all the impersonal sex that had been the norm. She wanted more with Zoe. More contact, more intimacy, more of everything that was missing in her previous encounters. And for the first time since she'd been with Sam, she was as concerned, or more, with Zoe's pleasure as her own needs. Did Zoe want a rough, fierce fuckfest on a hard piece of furniture? She slowed her strokes and released Zoe's hands and hoarsely asked her just that.

"God, yes," Zoe moaned, her eyes closed and head thrown back in ecstasy. Blindly, she threaded her fingers through Fetch's hair and led her lower as she spread her legs farther apart. "I love what you do to me."

Fetch pulled Zoe to the edge of the dresser as she got down on her knees. She traced the tip of her tongue down Zoe's abdomen, moving lower, pausing to bite and nip at the soft skin, until she reached Zoe's center. Her hands on Zoe's thigh's, she spread her wide and inhaled the scent of her arousal. Fetch met Zoe's eyes. "You're amazing," she said, before claiming her clit with her mouth. Zoe shuddered at the first contact and moaned, gripping Fetch's scalp tighter.

Fetch took her time, lavishing attention on every sensitive area, alternating firm strokes of her tongue with light ones, sucking Zoe to swollen readiness, then backing off to prolong her pleasure. Zoe moaned and bucked, urging Fetch with her hands to deliver her, until finally she did, stroking her to climax with her tongue while she thrust quickly, deeply into Zoe.

Zoe cried out as she came, and the sound reverberated through Fetch, amplifying her arousal tenfold. She carried Zoe to the bed, throwing her down on the mattress to cover her with her own body. Kissing her again with fierce intensity, she edged her thigh between Zoe's legs as she fondled one of her ample, magnificent breasts. "Tell me what you want."

Zoe's hands, which were around her waist, pulled at the back of Fetch's T-shirt and the waistband of her jeans. "I want to feel you. Take your clothes off."

Fetch hesitated for several seconds. She wasn't used to being touched. But she rose to her knees, straddling Zoe's waist, and pulled off her T-shirt. As she did, she felt Zoe's hands on her breasts over her bra. By the time she'd shed the shirt and tossed it aside, Zoe had risen to a sitting position, pulled her bra aside, and had her mouth on Fetch's right nipple. The intense, unfamiliar sensation drove Fetch higher, until her heart was thumping hard against her chest and her hard, fast breathing was audible. In her haze of lust, she didn't immediately realize Zoe had unbuttoned her pants and lowered the zipper. Only when she felt the tug of denim against her thighs did she become aware Zoe was trying to remove her jeans.

She cradled Zoe's face in her hands and gently pulled her mouth away from her nipple. Zoe stopped tugging at her pants and looked up at her with a puzzled expression. Her pupils were dark, nearly obscuring the blue surrounding them, and she was breathing as heavily as Fetch.

Zoe was bewildered by Gianna's hesitation to undress or allow her the same free rein of touch she'd had. "What's wrong?"

Gianna gently stroked Zoe's cheeks with her thumbs. "I don't…I'm not used to this."

"To what?"

"Being touched."

Zoe tried to mask her shock. "Never?" She remembered what Gianna had volunteered about her sexual past. It was understandable that the strangers she'd picked up in bars hadn't touched her, or the call girls she'd said she'd used more recently. But she couldn't believe it possible with Sam, though she couldn't bring up that painful part of her past right now.

"Only with one other person," Gianna answered, confirming her suspicions but apparently just as reluctant to mention Sam.

Zoe tried to reconcile Gianna's hesitation with her obvious arousal. She had removed her shirt, and she hadn't stopped Zoe when she touched and sucked her breasts. So although Gianna seemed uneasy with the unfamiliar, she didn't necessarily want her to pull away. Perhaps she just needed gentle coaxing and some time to adjust.

She had her arms around Gianna's waist. Very slowly, Zoe began to caress Gianna's lower back, while she kissed her stomach. The kisses became small nips and licks. She slid her hands forward, up Gianna's sides, until she was caressing the bottom curves of Gianna's breasts with her thumbs. Gianna moaned.

"Do you want me to quit?" Zoe asked softly, then continued to lick Gianna's stomach, moving lower.

Gianna didn't respond, but her breathing accelerated, and she moved into Zoe's touch.

"Do you like this?" Zoe palmed Gianna's breasts, skimming over the erect nipples and licking her with long strokes of her tongue.

"Yeah." It sounded like a sigh.

"And how about this?" Zoe descended farther, nipping at Gianna's lower abdomen until she reached the V of flesh exposed by the open fly of her jeans. She darted her tongue over the delicate soft skin.

Gianna groaned.

"I take that as another yes," Zoe murmured. She smoothed her hands down Gianna's sides to the waistband of her jeans, and as she continued to move her mouth over Gianna's lower abdomen, she started edging down the jeans. As she tugged at them in small increments, she thoroughly enjoyed gradually viewing Gianna's body.

She glanced up as she gave the jeans another tug, bringing the waistband halfway down her ass and exposing her center. Gianna's eyes were closed, her expression one of rapture. Zoe squeezed Gianna's ass as she ran her tongue lightly over the neatly trimmed triangle of dark hair and heard another moan.

"You can stop me if you want," Zoe said, between more licks and nips of Gianna's newly exposed flesh. "Is that what you want?" she asked as she lightly raked her nails over Gianna's lower back and ass. Lick. Suck. Nip.

Gianna mumbled something incoherent.

"I didn't get that." Suck. Nip. Lick. "Was that a no?" She pulled the jeans down several more inches. "I sure hope that's a no," Zoe said, "because I really want to taste you."

Gianna cupped Zoe's face and gently raised her chin until Zoe was looking up at her. "Please don't stop." Her voice was low and hoarse, almost unrecognizable, and her eyes were glazed. Her breasts rose and fell with every rapid breath.

Zoe tugged the pants sharply until they were low on Gianna's thighs and buried her face in the triangle of hair, licking lower, flicking her tongue over the hood of Gianna's clit. The tight jeans prevented Zoe from complete access, but her strokes were having an undeniable effect. Gianna thrust her pelvis forward, seeking greater contact, and moaned again, a low rumble from the back of her throat.

"I think it's time you removed your pants." Zoe gripped Gianna's ass and pulled her down, on top of her, then rolled them until Gianna was beneath her. Rising, Zoe pulled off Gianna's jeans to find she was wearing nothing beneath. Going commando, she thought, and almost smiled, until she got a close view of Gianna fully naked. A number of long-healed scars marred the otherwise smooth, muscled flesh, including a three-inch one above her left knee.

And though most of the bruises inflicted by Barriga and the rebel who'd punched her had faded, several large purple-yellow reminders of the abuse she'd suffered to protect Zoe remained, especially on her thighs. She bent to softly kiss the worst of them. "Do they still hurt?"

"Not when I'm with you."

She crawled back on top of Gianna and their bodies made full contact for the first time since their brief encounter at the waterfall. Gianna pulled her close and kissed her, a passion-filled kiss of hunger and need, her tongue probing the warm interior of Zoe's mouth.

"You feel so good," Zoe murmured when they parted. She raised herself slightly and started to slide her hand between their bodies, but as soon as she did, Gianna rolled them again until she was on top.

Gianna attacked her neck with kisses and bites while she shifted her weight to one side, then urged Zoe's legs apart with her hand. Zoe gasped and shuddered when Gianna entered her, filling her, driving her wild. She clutched at Gianna's shoulders, pulling at her with every thrust.

"Please," she managed, as she neared climax again. "Let me touch you."

Gianna pulled out of her and reached for Zoe's hand, leading her to the apex of her thighs, giving her consent.

Her first feel of Gianna's warm, wet center made them both tremble. "Tell me what you need," Zoe said.

In response, Gianna gazed into her eyes and reached for her again, slowly stroking her, exploring her wetness, and Zoe mirrored what she was doing. They watched each other as their pleasure built, and the prolonged eye contact fueled Zoe's arousal even higher.

"You're so wet," Gianna whispered as she pushed inside Zoe. "So open."

"That's how much I want you," Zoe replied, as she penetrated Gianna for the first time.

Gianna arched her back, rocking into Zoe's thrusts. "Can you feel…" she said, panting for air, "what you're doing to me?"

A rush of wetness coated Zoe's hand. "It makes me want to taste you, feel you in my mouth. Will you let me?"

"I don't think I can stop you." Gianna gritted her teeth in pleasure.

The muscles of Gianna's jaw moved with each of Zoe's thrusts. "Tell me how you want it."

Gianna inhaled sharply and withdrew from her. She rose to her feet, took Zoe's hand, and pulled her up, too. Maintaining eye contact, but saying nothing, she sat on the edge of the bed, her feet on the floor, her legs spread apart. As Zoe went to stand in front of her, Gianna reclined on her elbows.

"I want to watch you when you make me come," Gianna said.

Zoe knelt in front of her, stroking Gianna's legs, then bent to lick her inner thigh. She took her time, exploring with her mouth, while she stroked Gianna's abdomen with her hand. Gianna's stomach clenched until the hard surface spasmed under her touch and her whole body shook. She glanced up to find Gianna watching, her eyes either meeting Zoe's or fixated on her tongue. Zoe stopped to look at the amazing woman who had so willingly surrendered to her touch. "Please believe me when I say you are so beautiful. In every way."

"I do." Gianna replied in a raspy voice, never taking her eyes from Zoe. "Please, Zoe, I need to come." Zoe moaned, working Gianna's clit in earnest, and Gianna thrust her pelvis forward. When she fisted the bedsheets and arched her back, nearing climax, Zoe entered her with deep strokes and sent her crashing over the precipice.

Gianna fell back on the mattress, breathing hard and fast, and Zoe crawled on the bed to lie on top of her. After only a minute or two, Gianna opened her eyes and looked up at her. "I'm not done."

"I can give you more," Zoe replied, stroking her arm. "Much more."

"I'm not done with *you*," Gianna said with a mischievous smile.

The look in her eyes sent a heat of anticipation through Zoe. "What do you want?"

As Gianna slipped from beneath her and got off the bed, Zoe lay on her side, watching her. Gianna flipped her onto her stomach, then lifted her hips and pulled her to the edge of the bed. Zoe, on all fours, looked back as Gianna spread her legs and went down on her from behind. Gianna's mouth on her sped her into another heightened state of arousal. When Gianna started raking her nails over Zoe's back and ass as she worked her with her tongue, a rush of moisture poured out of her.

Gianna climbed up onto the bed. As she kissed Zoe's back, and neck, licking and nipping at her skin with soft bites, she entered her and thrust into her with slow strokes.

"More," Zoe murmured, her body awash in sensation. "Harder."

Gianna quickened and deepened her thrusts, then brought her other hand around Zoe's front to work her clit, and within seconds, a powerful orgasm coursed through her and sent her crashing, spent and boneless, to the bed.

Zoe had never surrendered to anyone with such abandon, had never been so aware of someone's every move and sigh. And she'd certainly never been more aroused by a touch or mere gaze. Gianna had turned the embers of her life into flame.

Gianna lay beside her, embracing her while Zoe's heartbeat calmed. She breathed in the scent of their lovemaking, more content than she could ever remember. She never wanted this moment to end.

But just as she was about to doze off, Gianna's cell rang, shattering their bliss.

Fetch stiffened but didn't move from Zoe's embrace. The tremors in her hands had stilled. For the first time in memory, she felt safe enough to stay exactly where she was.

"I don't want you to move." Zoe traced Fetch's shoulder with her finger.

"That makes two of us. But I don't have a choice." Finally, after too many rings, Fetch grabbed the phone and checked the display. She kissed Zoe. "I have to take this." Naked, she went into the bathroom and shut the door before answering.

"The Brits haven't been able to get anything out of Miss Howe's uncle. His brother tried, too, but he's still not talking," Pierce told her as soon as she answered. "They've been in touch with authorities in every country he's been known to have done private consulting work in the last year, and teams have been dispatched to all those labs, but so far, they've found no evidence that any of them were involved in creating this virus or the antidote. They also struck out when they searched his residence and office at Cambridge. Have you spoken with Miss Howe since you checked in?"

"Yes, sir," Fetch replied. "She's here with me now."

"See if you can get anything further from her that might be helpful, and let me know."

"Roger, sir." She disconnected and returned to Zoe, who was watching her intently.

"Is something wrong?" Zoe asked.

"It was about your uncle."

"God, what's he done now? Drop an A-bomb?" Zoe sounded infuriated.

"He won't talk," Fetch said calmly so she wouldn't re-ignite Zoe's guilt. "He won't tell the authorities who he's working for... or with."

"Blundering idiot." Zoe sat up. "Why is he willing to protect whoever is in on this? I mean, it's over. He was caught. His whole plan of world domination has been shot to shit. What's he still trying to protect?"

"Himself, I think."

"But he's already destroyed."

"Someone's probably out there he fears even more than prison," Fetch said. "Fears enough to let a lighter sentence for cooperation slip through his fingers."

"Have they spoken to my father? He might be able to get Edward to talk."

"They've tried that. Can you think of anyone or anything that might help? Has he ever mentioned anyone to you or your father?"

"I'm not usually there when they talk about business. He just talks to me about his dreams of curing diseases and helping others. He's always appeared so noble. I find it hard to believe it was all a lie. He's always been so comfortable around me and has often said that I'm the only one who seems to be proud of him." Zoe bit her lip wistfully.

"But he's never mentioned—"

"Take me to him." Zoe stood up.

"I don't think I can do that."

"If he'll talk to anyone, it's me. If I can't reach him, no one can."

"I don't think they'll allow you."

"What do they have to lose? I can't guarantee anything, but I'm willing to try."

Fetch dialed Pierce's number. "It's Fetch, sir. Zoe thinks she can get her uncle to talk. How fast can you get us there?"

CHAPTER THIRTY-FOUR

Budapest, Hungary
October 26, 9 p.m.

Doctor Andor Rózsa poured himself a gin and tonic and settled into his favorite armchair as he waited for the top-of-the-hour news update from the BBC. He tuned in every morning before work and every evening when he returned from Pharmamediq, to get the latest figures on the spread of the pandemic and information on efforts to identify the stealth component of the mystery virus.

"As the death toll from the H1N6 pandemic tops eight million people in ninety-eight countries, we have breaking news from the World Health Organization," the newscaster reported. "WHO officials say a laboratory in the U.S. has successfully isolated the genetic makeup of the virus, which is apparently a chimera of the H1N1 virus and the pneumonic-plague bacteria."

Andor frowned and turned up the volume.

"It is not clear when the U.S. Army's AMRIID laboratory in Maryland achieved this breakthrough," the announcer said, "but it was apparently some time ago, since the WHO press release indicates the renowned facility has also come up with an experimental antiserum that appears, at this early stage, to effectively battle the disease's symptoms."

Andor absentmindedly set down his drink on the antique cherry table beside his chair, missing the coaster. It couldn't be true. It was incredible that any lab had even isolated the stealth component so soon. But the prospect of also coming up with any kind of effective antivirus? Impossible. It had to be wrong.

"WHO officials say that human trials of the experimental vaccine will begin immediately at the Fort Detrick facility, and, if all goes well, widespread production of the antiserum could be underway in a matter of days. So far, that's all we have on this breaking but encouraging news from the World Health Organization. We will be following this story closely and bring you updated information as we get it."

Andor turned down the sound and sat unmoving for several minutes, clenching the chair's padded armrests. Impossible, he repeated to himself. Perhaps this lab had discovered something that muted the symptoms temporarily, or delayed the rapid progression of the disease. That might be entirely possible, given AMRIID's considerable resources and track record. But surely these human trials would prove that their experimental vaccine was ineffective as an actual cure.

He would have to greatly accelerate the timetable for announcing his own antivirus. But he'd still make billions. Once AMRIID's failure was confirmed, disillusioning the public that a quick end to the nightmare was possible, he'd be even *more* acclaimed.

❖

Andrews Air Force Base, Maryland
October 26

Zoe had flown many times in her father's private business jet, so she wasn't as impressed with the Falcon 7X they were boarding as someone who'd never seen the luxury of such planes. She wondered, however, how Gianna's employer had managed to commandeer it as well as get clearance for their flight into Heathrow, since that airport was technically closed.

She and Gianna were the first to arrive. A steel-and-glass half-wall separated the nearly forty-foot-long cabin into two sections.

The forward compartment contained the galley and eight large swivel leather chairs with tables, while the rear held an executive console desk with computer, a long couch, and the restroom.

They took seats together on the couch. Gianna placed her hand on Zoe's thigh, and Zoe covered it with hers. "Is it wrong to want you again?" Zoe asked.

Gianna smiled but didn't reply.

"I must be crazy. I'm about to confront a man I thought I knew and ask him to confide in me, tell him with conviction that I care about him when all I want to do is shake some sense into him…" Zoe gazed into Gianna's dark eyes. "And I can't stop thinking about how you felt in me, how you taste, and how I can't wait to be alone with you."

Gianna kissed Zoe's palm. "You're not crazy. I feel the same."

The sound of boots on the metal staircase stopped them.

"Ready to kick some British ass, Fetch?" a female bellowed before anyone came into view. Misha appeared in the forward cabin a few seconds later with a broad smile on her face and a beautiful blonde on her heels. Her grin disappeared when she spotted Zoe. "I didn't know we had company, *Gianna*."

"Pierce didn't tell you?" Gianna asked.

"Nah. No time. Said we'd be briefed on the way."

"You know Zoe."

"Yeah." Misha glanced at her, then back to Gianna. "This is very unconventional."

Gianna finally broke the silence that followed. "She's our last chance to get Edward Anderson-Howe to talk."

Misha's face was expressionless. "You seem to be that a lot. Everyone's last chance, I mean."

"Hi, I'm Cassady," the blonde behind her said, scooting around Misha to offer her hand.

"Zoe Anders—"

"I know. Thanks for saving our butts." She gave Zoe a genuine, welcoming smile. "And don't mind my friend here." She motioned with her head to Misha. "She can't stand the thought of someone else saving the world."

The pilot's voice over the intercom told them to take their seats and buckle up for takeoff.

Misha and Cassady took the two seats nearest the front, facing each other, while Zoe and Gianna claimed side-by-side seats farther back, across the aisle. The jet took off and no one spoke for a long while. Zoe kept glancing at Misha, in the rear-facing seat. Misha kept staring out the window as though deliberately avoiding them, all the while exuding a sullen anger.

"Misha doesn't like me," Zoe whispered.

"She's cautious, that's all," Gianna replied in an equally low tone. "Luka is her best friend, sister practically."

"And she almost died."

"I think the shock of what could've been is what she's angry at."

"If you say so. I think she dislikes me. That was the second time I heard the name Fetch," she added, hoping Gianna would explain.

"It's my name when I'm on a job...mission."

"Like a code name?"

"We call it cover."

"You all have one?"

"Correct. And no, I can't disclose theirs." Gianna smiled.

Zoe studied Misha and Cassady for several seconds, wondering what their cover names were. Fetch suited Gianna well, she thought, since she'd said she often rescued hostages. "Your company has a lot of women," she said.

"Yes."

"Why?" This was traditionally a man's job. Was she really that conservative?

"Because women are just as able to fight, chase, track, and apprehend, but with an added benefit. No one sees them coming and no one suspects them. Briefly, women are more lethal because they're the perfect secret weapon. What they lack in muscle they more than compensate for with technique and invisibility."

"Invisibility?"

"Their sex makes them undetectable when you're expecting men. And only a woman can get a man of any stature, any background, no matter how secretive, to talk. The vaguest prospect of sex can make even the hardest crumble."

"That would explain why you're all attractive. But they…you, don't actually…"

Gianna laughed. "No."

"How did you all get involved in this work? How did you find them?"

"We didn't. They found us."

"I don't understand."

"I'll tell you what I can about that some other time. Right now, though, we should get some rest."

❖

London, England
October 27

After landing at Heathrow, the jet taxied to a private hangar where a black sedan was waiting for them. Zoe was sandwiched in the back between Gianna and Cassady, while Misha sat in front beside the driver, a taciturn man in a dark gray suit. Though it would have taken a commercial jet more than seven hours to cross the Atlantic, the Falcon had made the journey in five, so it was nine a.m. local time when they arrived.

Gianna squeezed her hand encouragingly as they headed into central London, but no one spoke. When they pulled up in front of the Paddington Green police station, the four of them got out, Gianna leading Zoe into the building.

"Are you certain you don't want me in there with you?" Gianna asked as they were escorted to the visitor's room where her uncle had been taken to meet with her.

"He'll talk more freely if I'm alone with him, I'm sure. But stick close."

"We'll be just outside."

Zoe took a deep breath as the guard outside admitted her.

Her uncle's appearance had changed radically since she'd seen him at the Loose Cannon party just three weeks ago. His casual, relaxed demeanor had given way to a gaunt, haunted appearance, and his usually crisp, button-down shirt and navy suit were disheveled, his tie gone, no doubt a result of the many hours of questioning he'd already undergone.

He brightened only slightly when he looked at her standing in the doorway, a downcast expression quickly replacing his half smile of recognition. "Hello, Zoe."

"Hello, Uncle." She forced herself to remain calm and friendly. Castigating him for what he'd done wouldn't get them the information they needed. She kissed him on the cheek before settling into a plastic chair opposite his. They were alone in a visitor/ attorney room, free of cameras and recording equipment.

"I…I'm so sorry you and your father have been dragged into this," Edward said. "It's all a big misunderstanding. I've no—"

"Uncle Eddie, I know you would never have intended that your work cause the deaths of so many. You're not that kind of man. But please don't deny your involvement in this." She met his eyes and didn't look away. "You've never lied to me before, and now isn't the time to start. You made sure father and I were protected against this, and I'm grateful. I know how much you love us both."

"I do, Zoe. I would never, ever—"

"But millions of innocent people are dying right now. Millions," she repeated. "And you're the only one who can stop this. Every minute you delay telling authorities everything you know, thousands die. Our friends, their families, people out there who might one day discover something that could change the world for the better. You have to help them."

"Zoe, I can't," he said, burying his face in his hands. "I just can't. I'm not worried about myself. I'll take whatever punishment they give me. I deserve it."

She went to him, stooping to put her arm over his shoulders. "Then why? Why won't you tell them what you know?"

"There's…" Edward's voice broke, and he paused. "The man behind all this…he's crazy. Brilliant crazy, and extremely ruthless," he told her in a low voice. "He's been very careful to make sure this plan of his goes off without a hitch. If he finds out I've led authorities to him, he'll make sure you and your father pay for my betrayal. I can't let anything happen to either of you, don't you understand that?"

"Uncle, even if that were true, our two lives are certainly worth saving millions of others. And I'm sure we can be well protected until he's caught and put away."

"You don't understand. You may find this man, but no one will be able to hold him for long. He's destroyed all evidence, except for some personal records, which I'm sure are well hidden. He may have to wait to come after you, but he will eventually if he learns I turned him in. You can't stay protected forever. And worse..." Edward's hands were shaking and his eyes kept scanning the room, as though he was paranoid the man he was talking about could somehow know what was going on

"Worse?" Zoe prompted him.

"This man has developed many other viruses, Zoe. Some maybe even more dangerous than this one. I don't know what he plans to do with them. Release them, sell them to a government or terrorist group somewhere. Who knows? I'm afraid if I tell authorities about him, he'll just disappear after he's released from questioning and immediately unleash some worse evil."

"Then you have to tell what you know. He probably already has plans for these viruses, and you may be the only one who can help stop him."

"I just can't, Zoe. I'm sorry." Edward slumped back in his chair. "I'm telling you, the police won't be able to find anything on him. I'll only put you and your father at risk."

Zoe could see he wouldn't reveal anything to her that she might tell authorities. "Don't leave, Uncle. I'll be right back." She knocked on the door and the guard opened it. Gianna, Cassady, and Misha were waiting just outside. She led them away from the guard, out of earshot, and briefed them on what her uncle had told her. "What should I do? He obviously knows a great deal, but he's not willing to tell me anything I might pass on to the police."

"We need to call in," Cassady said to Allegro and Gianna. "You thinking what I'm thinking?"

"Wait here, Zoe," Gianna told her.

Zoe watched as the women ducked into a vacant visitor room farther down the hall. While she waited for their return, she backtracked to the nearest desk and asked the officer if she could use his telephone. Her father answered on the first ring.

"Daddy?"

"Zoe? Is that you? Where are you?"

"I'm in London at the Paddington Green police station. I'm trying to get Uncle Eddie to talk to me."

"Have you had any luck?"

"I'll tell you when I see you. Can you come pick me up? I should be through soon."

"Of course, honey. I'll leave right now. I can't wait to see you."

"Me too, Daddy."

She returned to the visitor-room hallway just as Gianna came out of the room farther on with the other two women. As they walked toward her, Zoe noticed that all three had a no-nonsense, determined air. The benign women she'd witnessed before had turned into a rapacious, almost-dangerous force.

"We want to go back in with you," Gianna said. "We may be able to convince your uncle to tell us what he knows."

"All right," Zoe said. Once more, the guard opened the door, and she led the others into the room. Edward immediately sat up straight and looked wary.

"These are some friends of mine, Uncle. I trust them completely. Gianna," she indicated with a tilt of her head, "rescued me in Colombia."

"We work for a private organization," Allegro told Edward. "We work outside the realm of local law-enforcement restrictions. And we have an excellent track record of being able to find what others cannot," she said with a cocky smile. "No matter how well this man has hidden his records, these virus formulas…if anyone can find them, we can. And we will do it very quietly. He'll never find out you tipped us off. Once we have the evidence, we can lock him away for good, where he's no threat to anyone."

"You have to accept your responsibility for your part in this," Zoe told him. "Trust these women. Do it for me, if for no other reason. I've never asked you for anything. Now I'm literally asking for the world."

Edward buried his face in his hands again, apparently torn. Zoe stooped beside his chair, stroking his back but holding her tongue. She wanted to lash out, tell him how angry she was for his part in this madness, but her softer approach was apparently having results.

Finally, he looked up at them with a resigned expression. "The man you want is named Andor Rózsa. He's a virologist with Pharmamediq, Incorporated in Budapest, though you'll probably find no proof there of what he's done. We did all our research at a secret laboratory in the Carpathian Mountains."

"Where exactly is this lab?" Cassady asked.

Edward described the location and how to get there. "Rózsa shut down the lab just before the virus was unleashed and cleaned up the evidence of what went on there. He has to have his research records somewhere, but I'm sure he hid them well. He told me no one would ever be able to find any evidence against him. That he'd planned it too well."

The rest of the story spilled out of him, how he'd met Rózsa four years prior at a virology and bacteriology conference, where Edward was giving a seminar on biological weapons. Rózsa had later enlisted his help in creating the deadly chimera that he'd named Charon, but Edward denied knowing it would be used for a global pandemic. He claimed Rózsa told him that he learned that the Russians were perfecting a biological weapon that combined H1N1 and pneumonic plague, and he only wanted his company, Pharmamediq, to have an antidote ready when that weapon was released.

Zoe wanted to believe him, but at this point she didn't know what her uncle's real involvement or motivation was.

"I think we have what we need," Misha said when he finished.

Zoe knew that every minute counted. "We have to leave now, Uncle Eddie. Thank you for talking to them." She let him embrace her for several long seconds while he stammered further apologies, then said good-bye and followed them out the door.

Cassady stopped just outside the room and offered her hand. "Thank you for everything," she said. "We all owe you so much."

"I'm happy I could help."

"If you ever need anything, let me know." Cassady gave her a final smile and turned to go.

Misha stepped in front of her. Zoe knew Misha disliked her and, in some way, held her responsible for her friend's near-death. Misha looked her straight in the eyes. "You did good," she said. "Luka, Gianna, they're safe because of you. I…thank you."

"It was the least I could do." Zoe looked away. Rationally she knew none of this was her fault, but part of her still couldn't release the guilt and shame.

Misha's hand landed on her shoulder. "It's not your fault you're related to that crazy-ass scientist," Misha said. "Okay?"

Zoe nodded.

"Hey." Misha squeezed her arm and Zoe met her eyes. "You've survived FARC camps, guerrillas, the jungle, saved lives… and…" Misha looked to Gianna and back at her again. "Got this one to loosen up and smile. You're a good woman, Zoe."

Misha had just pointed out everything she'd come to hate, love, and accomplish in the past month. Having so much change happen in only a few weeks overwhelmed and frightened her. But it was true. She'd made it home, and somewhere along the way she'd found the answers to questions she'd never considered.

"Thank you," Zoe said. Then she did something that was alien to her; she hugged the virtual stranger. "You're a good woman, too, and Luka is lucky to have you as a friend."

Misha smiled. "Yes, she is, and I make sure to remind her every chance I get." She turned to Gianna. "See you in a few," she said, and headed toward the entrance.

Zoe turned to Gianna. "You're going with them."

"Yeah."

"Why?" Zoe's voice was louder than she intended. "How can your employer send you to work? You're still healing."

"Just a few bruises. The rest is gone. Zoe, I wasn't asked to go. I asked for permission to."

"But—"

"It's what I do," Gianna said gently. "We need to move on this quickly, before this Rózsa guy disappears. We bought a little time by telling the WHO and the media only that AMRIID had come up with an experimental antivaccine. But the news will get out that it's a real cure. Or that British police have a suspect in custody who knows something about the pandemic. And when that happens, who knows what Rózsa will do?" She put a hand on Zoe's shoulder. "The girls need all the help they can get. I want to be there for them. Make sure we all make it back." She paused and looked at her intently. "We look out for each other, Zoe. Like family."

Gianna had told her that she had avoided relationships of any sort for this exact reason. "How long will you be away?" she asked, trying to keep her voice steady. She had to show Gianna she could deal with her life.

"I'm not sure. A few days maybe."

"And then what happens?"

"After that, it's back to the U.S."

"Of course." Zoe bit her lip. "It's where you live, after all."

"How…how about you?" Gianna asked, staring awkwardly at her feet. "What will you do?"

"Hope you get back in one piece."

"Don't worry about me. I'll be fine."

"It's hard not to worry when…you care."

"I bet you can't wait to see your father."

Zoe tried to smile, but she knew it was only halfhearted. "He should be here soon to pick me up."

"Good." Gianna looked pensive, like she wanted to say or ask more. Zoe wished she'd say something about them, about coming back to her. She had tried to let Gianna know that she was prepared to endure her lifestyle, maybe even one day embrace the work she did, because it was something Gianna loved and needed. But had Gianna understood? Zoe had to know. She needed an answer before Gianna left, because she couldn't bear the limbo, but at the same time she was terrified of the answer.

"What…" Zoe stopped and took a deep breath. *Man yourself,* she thought. "Where does that leave us?"

"There you are!" someone shouted, and both of them turned. Zoe's father came running down the long hallway.

"Daddy!" Zoe fell into his outstretched arms. They embraced for several moments before Zoe pulled back for introductions. "Gianna, this is my father."

"Sir." Gianna stuck her hand out.

Zoe's father grabbed it and shook hard. "Thank you for what you've done for my daughter. For us."

"No need to thank me. She's a wonderful woman, sir, and I'm lucky to have known her." Gianna turned to Zoe. "I'd do anything for her," she said, never taking her eyes from Zoe's.

Then Cassady and Misha appeared from the other end of the hall. "Gotta go," Cassady said pointedly.

"Wrap it up, Gianna," Misha called.

"I have to go." Gianna shook Zoe's father's hand. "Take good care of her."

"I will." Derrick cradled Gianna's hand in both of his.

Gianna turned to Zoe. "I…" Gianna looked from her to her father. This was so not how Zoe wanted to end this. "I have to go," Gianna finally repeated, and walked away.

Zoe watched her go. The other ops waited at the far end.

Her father placed his arm around her shoulders. "Let's get you home, honey."

Zoe looked from him to Gianna's retreating back. *Please look back. Please don't walk away.*

And Gianna did. She stopped, turned, and stood looking at Zoe. Zoe left her father's embrace and ran after her, Gianna meeting her halfway. They came to a halt and stared at each other.

"I'd do anything for you, Zoe," Gianna said.

"Come back to me."

Gianna lifted her off the ground and kissed her soundly on the mouth before she put her back down. "As soon as I can," she said, and ran off.

CHAPTER THIRTY-FIVE

Budapest, Hungary
2:30 p.m.

En route to Budapest, Fetch, Allegro, and Lynx received an abundance of information on Andor Rózsa from Reno. He'd sent copies of Rózsa's passport and driver's license photos to the jet's computer, along with the addresses of his home and office at Pharmamediq, his work schedule, and the make and model of his car. He'd also enhanced a satellite photo of Rózsa's house, which told him there were exterior security cameras there, so he'd cracked several local security-company databases until he was able to obtain specifics about the type of system installed.

Montgomery Pierce would feel bound to contact Interpol with the information they'd gleaned on Rózsa from Edward Anderson-Howe. But they'd managed to persuade him to give them a six-hour head start. They hoped they could either find the documents they needed—his virus formulas and evidence he was involved in the current pandemic—or track Rózsa to them if he got tipped off the authorities were looking for him and tried to flee.

From what Edward had told them, they decided to concentrate on Rózsa's home and secret laboratory. It was less likely he would store anything at Pharmamediq, and it was the most difficult place for them to break into, anyway, especially during business hours. Interpol might get to Rózsa and arrest him there before he left work, but that would only be a minor impediment. Without any evidence against him, he'd eventually be released and they could track him then. In the interim, they'd be free to keep searching for his formulas.

Lynx rented a car and headed to the secret laboratory, while Allegro and Fetch got another and went to Rózsa's home, a two-story, red-brick structure in a northern suburb.

As Fetch parked curbside across the street, Allegro scanned for cameras. They were right where Reno had said they'd be. "He's got a rotating cam above the front door and another over the side entrance. The house is rigged with an alarm as well."

"That's not a problem, right?" Fetch checked her watch against Rózsa's work schedule.

"Cover me."

"You have eighty-six minutes."

"Gotcha." Allegro grabbed her tools, the first thing she packed for every mission, and put in her earpiece transmitter. After exiting the car, she approached the house from the side without the camera, carefully timing her final dash to the structure while the front cam was rotated away from her. Fortunately, no one seemed to be at the adjacent homes, and the street was empty of cars and pedestrians. "Read me?" she asked Fetch.

"Affirmative." Allegro thought back to Luka and that the last time she'd been breaking and entering was with her. They'd laughed so much together. But Fetch was a competent op and one she trusted as much as she did Luka.

Allegro crept to the back of the house. No wires or cams, just as Reno had indicated. She looked through the window for visible alarms or motion detectors. As she expected, a red light was blinking at the top of the window frame. If she tried to open it, she'd set the alarm off. She retrieved her glass cutter. "The electricity box is on the left side of the house," she told Fetch. "I need you to pull it until I get in to deactivate from inside."

"Is there a fallback?"

"I'm gonna go with yes," she replied as she pulled on a pair of latex gloves. "It'll take one minute to activate. Should be enough time."

"On my way," Fetch said. A few seconds later, she added, "Ready?"

"Go." Allegro attached the cutter to the window, then removed the glass piece and opened the latch from inside. Boosting herself in, she ran to the front door. After removing the cap from the home-alarm control panel, she attached the code-breaker wires to the motherboard. "Hit the lights," she said. "I have twenty seconds to punch the code before it goes off."

The moment the electricity was on the device started running cryptanalytical algorithms. In less than ten seconds it had the code. "We're good," Allegro said.

"Of course," Fetch replied. "Let me know if you need anything else."

Allegro did a fairly quick search of the ground floor—front room, kitchen, dining room—looking in all the usual places where people kept safes. When she didn't find anything promising, she ran upstairs. The doors to the two bedrooms, bathroom, and storage closet were open, but the one at the end of the hallway was locked. She opened it with a pin. "I'm in his office."

A laptop was sitting on Rózsa's desk. While she waited for it to boot up, she searched the rest of the room. In a closet full of clothes and boxes, she moved things around until she spotted a small cutout panel behind the clothes—a door of some kind. When she opened it, she found a Czech-made Buldok combination safe the size of a couple of shoeboxes. "Bingo."

She set her stethoscope in her left ear and twisted the dial, listening for the telltale clicks that would help her discover the contact points. In ten minutes she found all five numbers and opened the safe, which contained several files of documents. Most were the usual personal papers: insurance policies, passport, stock certificates, birth certificate. Nothing about virus formulas. But in one manila envelope was a safe-deposit-box key and account information from a Budapest bank.

"Contact headquarters and get Monty to inform Interpol to send their people to the FHB Bank on Üllői Street," she told Fetch. "Looks like Rózsa has an account there, and a safe-deposit box, under the name Artur Varga."

"Will do."

The last file in the safe contained more financial records. "I have a Cayman bank printout... Holy shit, the guy's got twenty mill in it."

"One guess where that money came from."

"I hope Reno can nail some names," Allegro said as she photographed the documents with her cell phone, including some transfer codes. They might reveal where Rózsa was getting his funding, perhaps some clients he'd sold formulas to.

"You've got fifteen minutes to get out of there," Fetch said.

"Gotcha." Allegro did a quick scan of Rózsa's laptop. Several files were heavily encrypted, so she pulled the hard drive to send to Reno for analysis. Finding nothing else of value, she hurried downstairs, reactivated the alarm, and ran to the window she'd come in. She was back outside within the minute before it armed.

Fetch already had Reno on speakerphone by the time she reached the vehicle. "Whatcha got, Allegro?" he asked.

"Rózsa's hard drive for you to analyze. But first, I need you to track his twenty-mill Cayman account."

"Not too shabby for a scientist," Reno said.

"Can you find out who put it there?" Allegro punched his e-mail into her phone and sent him the documents.

"You know that answer." Reno sounded almost offended. "But it'll take time. Maybe days."

"How long do you need to access his account?" Fetch asked.

"I can crack that pretty fast. Maybe fifteen minutes. Why?"

"Move the money," Fetch said.

"What?" Reno asked.

"They're about to grab him," Fetch said. "When they find out they've got nothing to keep him—"

"He'll take the cash and run," Allegro said.

"And start all over," Fetch added.

"Transfer it to the Organization's account," Allegro instructed Reno.

"Is that legal?"

"We're not keeping it, nerd."

"Besides, it's probably stolen and laundered. Nobody'll be in a hurry to claim it," Fetch said.

They settled in to wait for Rózsa to return home from work.

❖

3:55 pm

Doctor Andor Rózsa sat at his computer in his office at Pharmamediq, checking the latest news reports before he left for the day. He found nothing new about the experimental antivirus developed by the American lab in Maryland. The human trials they were conducting would surely prove the vaccine ineffective, and he'd still be able to cash in on his own formula. It took him eight months, with the help of the best virologists, to create an antivirus for Charon. The Americans couldn't possibly find a cure in a few days.

Just as he was about to shut down his laptop, a chime alarm alerted him that one of his security cameras at the secret laboratory had detected movement. The system was fine-tuned to eliminate things like mice or rats, so he immediately accessed the multidisplay that showed the current feeds from all twelve cameras.

On camera three, which was mounted above the entrance to the dormitory wing, he saw a blond-haired woman, dressed in black trousers and a black shirt, fiddling with the access panel beside the door. He brought the camera full screen and peered intently at the intruder, his heart racing. Who the hell was she, and how did she find out about his lab? Most important, what was she looking for? She was obviously no petty thief, because she'd already managed to get through the electronic gate. But she didn't look like the police, either.

He pulled up the multicam display again, checking to make sure she was alone. Were authorities somehow onto him? With shaking hands, he punched in the code to remotely access his home security system. The alarm was still on and active, but he picked up movement on the hidden wide-angle spy cam mounted by the basement window. A woman he didn't recognize was just getting into an unfamiliar car parked at the curb across the street from his house. Another figure was in the car behind the wheel, but even after her companion joined her, the car didn't move.

They were waiting for him.

Cursing, he went to the window of his office and peeked through the blinds at the parking lot below. No sign of any police cars, though he couldn't see into vehicles well enough to determine whether anyone was waiting down there as well.

Returning to his desk, he called up the lab cameras again. The woman intruder had gotten inside and was moving through the dormitory to the kitchen. Who the hell were these people, and why were they stalking him?

He stared at the multicam display and watched the woman break through the door to the wing with the labs. As he picked her up on the next camera, she reached for her cell phone. He remotely accessed the speakerphone system outside the patient cells and turned up the volume.

"I'm here, and inside," he heard her say. "All quiet. Howe was right, it looks like the place has been abandoned for a while. Found an operating room. Just now getting into the wing that probably has the labs and offices."

Howe. Edward Anderson-Howe had betrayed him and informed authorities about his involvement in the pandemic.

"I'll let you know if anything turns up," the woman said to whomever she was talking to, then ended the call.

They knew. He grasped the edge of the desk and stared at his white knuckles. They would come for him soon. He needed to retrieve his formulas, but he certainly couldn't go home. And he couldn't get to the duplicate set on the flash drive in his safe-deposit box. The bank had closed an hour ago, and authorities might be staking out the place. He had to get to the files in his computer at the lab. First, though, he had to distract his pursuers long enough to get away and decide what to do next. He slammed the laptop shut. "I've worked too fucking long and too fucking hard to let anyone stop me now," he said out loud.

Only one man could help him. He picked up his cell and called Patrik.

❖

3:55 p.m.

Lynx's specialty was swords and knives, not security systems, but every ETF in the Organization had learned how to override the most commonly used access panels. She found herself in a large dormitory of stripped beds and empty lockers.

The dorm led to a dining area and kitchen. The pantry contained some canned food, but clearly no one had been around for some time. No cooking odors lingered, and she spotted mouse droppings here and there.

The last area of the wing she was in was apparently an employee rec room, with a large television, chairs and couches, and game tables. At the V of the complex was a small hallway, with doors leading outside to the courtyard and one providing entry to the other wing. The latter also had a security access panel. She overrode it and stepped inside. To her left was a well-equipped surgical suite. On her right, a concrete room with an enormous furnace. Ahead, another door leading to the rest of the wing. As she stepped through it, her cell phone vibrated in her pocket. It was Allegro.

"How's it going?"

"I'm here, and inside," Lynx replied. "All quiet. Howe was right, looks like the place has been abandoned for a while. Found an operating room. Just now getting into the wing that probably has the labs and offices."

"I pulled the hard drive from his home laptop. It has encrypted files on it, but no way to know whether the formulas are in them. We're waiting for him now. Should be here any minute."

"I'll let you know if anything turns up," Lynx said, and disconnected.

She was in a long hallway with several rooms on either side. Each door had a window and a pair of heavy-duty bolt locks mounted outside. As she stepped toward the nearest room, she noted the self-contained meal slot below the window.

It looked like a prison cell. Vacant and immaculately scrubbed clean. The mattress on the cot had been removed. All the other rooms on either side were identical. Where the human trials had been conducted, Lynx surmised. She shuddered at the thought of the poor wretches who'd been part of Rózsa's experiments.

The next area contained the biolabs, four in all. Hazmat suits hung outside in a neat row. Each lab was accessed through a security panel far more sophisticated than the ones at the entrances. These required a palm print and retinal scan.

Lynx used her flashlight to illuminate each room through their massive windows adjoining the hallway. The labs all had refrigeration units, computer terminals, incubation chambers, centrifuges, glove-box chambers, and other high-tech equipment.

Continuing through a set of double doors, she reached a series of offices. Most had simple wooden doors and key locks, but one had a steel reinforced door accessed through another electronic security panel, this one requiring a passcard. Rózsa's office, she presumed. She set to work on gaining access.

❖

5 p.m.

"Where the hell is he?" Allegro asked, glancing at her watch. "It's fifteen minutes at most from Pharmamediq."

"Maybe running errands. Groceries or something," Fetch replied. "Or maybe Monty jumped the gun and he's in custody already."

Allegro pulled out her cell and dialed Pierce. "Have you contacted Interpol yet?"

"A little while ago," he replied. "They're putting together a team to send to Pharmamediq, and they'll cover his Budapest bank in the morning. Reno informed me about the Cayman account. Have you found anything else?"

"Lynx is at the lab, and we're staking out his house. But he should've been here by now. We thought maybe he'd been arrested at work."

"Not possible," Pierce said. "Only got off the phone with them a short while ago. It'll probably take them another hour to get everything together to start looking for him."

"No leaks about Edward being in custody or anything that might have tipped Rózsa off?"

"No. I've got someone monitoring the news feeds."

"Okay, we'll keep you posted," she told him, and disconnected.

"If he doesn't show in another half hour or so, maybe we should try Pharmamediq and see if his car is still in the lot," Fetch suggested. "Could be working late."

"Sure hope we haven't guessed wrong, and he's already in the wind with his formulas," Allegro said.

Another forty-five minutes passed. Twilight came and went, and activity in the neighborhood busied as Rózsa's neighbors returned home.

"Got another possible," Fetch said, as headlights turned onto the street from the direction of Pharmamediq. They both watched the vehicle in their side mirrors as it neared, then turned into Rózsa's dark driveway.

"That's it," Allegro said. "A Smart Roadster Coupe. Did you get a look at the driver?"

"Too dark," Fetch said, watching the figure emerge from the car through her binoculars. The dark silhouette hurried into the side entrance. "About the right height and build, can't see much more."

A light went on inside, then another, but the curtains had been drawn. Less than two minutes later, both lights went off again, in reverse sequence, and the silhouette reemerged and got back into the car.

The driver pulled out and sped away with a slight screech of tires. They still hadn't been able to get a clear look at the figure; the nearest street lamp was a long block away.

Fetch followed at a discreet distance as the Coupe wound through the streets of Budapest, heading north.

❖

5:50 p.m.

The access panel to Rózsa's office had been a challenge for Lynx, but after ten minutes, she finally got inside. Breaking into Rózsa's file cabinets had been much easier, but unproductive. They'd all been cleaned out. She hit another snag when she booted up his computer, and had to call Reno for help in quickly breaking through the password screen.

Of the dozens of files, many looked like patient charts, and others were lab-analysis reports. One folder, named Future Projects, was locked, and took another ten minutes to access.

Lynx was no scientist, but she knew enough chemistry and biology to realize she was looking at what she'd come for—Rózsa's virus formulas. Ten in all, including one named Charon. Glancing through some of the others, she saw that Rózsa had also developed deadly chimeras using the Ebola virus, smallpox, anthrax, and other lethal biological agents.

It took her several minutes to bluetooth all the files to her phone. Once that was done, she e-mailed them to headquarters. Then she pulled the hard drive from Rózsa's computer and smashed it against the desk until it was in pieces.

She got Allegro on the phone. "Mission accomplished. I've located the virus files and sent them to HQ. The originals have been destroyed."

"Great news. I got his bank info, and Reno's transferred Rózsa's funds into Monty's account. Twenty mill."

"Rózsa had twenty-million dollars and you put it in the EOO account?"

Allegro laughed. "And we're about to wrap this up. We're tailing Rózsa and he's headed your way. Should be there in another fifteen minutes or so."

"I'll be ready from this end," Lynx said, and disconnected as she headed toward the door. When she turned the handle an alarm blared, and overhead a rotating bulb like the one on cop cars bathed her in red light. She tried the handle again, and nothing happened. She was locked in with no security access panel on this side.

But she didn't begin to truly worry until an automated voice came over the loudspeakers. "Intruder alert. The detonation sequence has been activated. This building will self-destruct. You have ten minutes to override."

She searched the door as her heartbeat accelerated. It was steel, and the hinges were on the outside.

"Nine-and-a-half minutes to detonation," the mechanical voice stated.

She began to search for some kind of override button. Nothing around the walls. No large air vents she might escape through.

"Nine minutes to detonation."

"Fuck," she said, fumbling through the desk drawers. Her heart was racing now, and she had to fight to remain calm.

"Eight-and-a-half minutes to detonation."

In the final drawer, which she had to pry open, she discovered a large pile of paperwork. She scanned the documents. Nothing there to help her get out of the room.

"Eight minutes to detonation."

After exhausting the contents of the desk, she pulled volumes from the built-in bookcase, tossing them to the floor as she searched for some secret mechanism to override the alarm.

"Seven-and-a-half minutes to detonation."

She moved every piece of furniture, so she could examine each inch of the floor and wall space for an escape route.

"Seven minutes to detonation."

The ceiling was solid, except for a quartet of air registers, far too small to help. A security camera was installed high in one corner. She stood on a chair and thoroughly examined it for an override button. Nothing.

"Six-and-a-half minutes to detonation."

CHAPTER THIRTY-SIX

Andor Rózsa pounded on the desk in Patrik's office as he stared at the computer, watching the intruder trash his office as the detonation sequence counted down. In a single day, all his plans had gone to shit. All those months of hard work for nothing. He couldn't go home, because authorities were likely expecting him to do just that. And though he'd hoped to be able to use his lab again for further research once the pandemic was over, it would have to be destroyed now.

But the worst blow was the loss of his primary Grand Cayman fortune. He couldn't believe it when he heard the intruder say they'd transferred his millions to another account, but a quick check on Patrik's computer had confirmed they'd spoken the truth. The account had a zero balance. He didn't dare try to use an ATM to access his Bulgarian bank account, which had less than a million forints in it—the equivalent of about seven thousand U.S. dollars. It was likely already blocked, and any effort to use his card would only tip off authorities as to his location.

The automated voice announced five minutes to detonation. Rózsa turned up the volume on his office intercom when the intruder pulled out her cell phone.

❖

Lynx dialed the one person she couldn't leave this world without saying good-bye to. The only person that mattered, and the one who would have a long painful road to travel.

Jack picked up.

"Baby, it's me," Lynx said.

"Miss me?" Lynx knew from her tone that she was smiling. She loved that smile.

"Baby, listen." Lynx tried to keep her voice steady. "I'm in trouble."

"Where are you?" Jack immediately sounded concerned.

"Budapest."

"I'm coming over. I can be there—"

"Listen to me, Jack. There's no time."

"Time for what?" Jack's voice was abrupt and near-panicked. "What the hell's going on, Cass?"

Lynx took a deep breath, to keep her voice from betraying her own panic.

"Talk to me, damn it," Jack shouted.

Tears began to stream down her cheeks. "I want you to know you were the best part of my life," she finally said. "Please know I'll always be there."

"Cass, honey, tell me what's going on." Jack sounded manic.

"I won't be coming back, baby. I have a few minutes before this place blows." Just as the words left her lips, the mechanical voice announced four minutes to detonation.

"Cass, no!" Jack shouted.

"I love you, Jack." Lynx didn't want her to hear the moment her life ended—to witness her death through the sound of an explosion.

"No!" Jack yelled. "No, this isn't happening. No, baby. I love you, don't...No!"

"I love you so much, baby." Lynx hung up, Jack's screams still echoing in her head.

❖

The Coupe pulled into the open gate of the laboratory compound, which covered several acres, but instead of heading toward the main

V-shaped structure, it kept to the perimeter and headed toward some outbuildings tucked a good distance away in one corner, in a wooded area. Fetch, who'd been following at a distance with the lights off, parked the rental in the trees and cut the engine when the Coupe stopped and Rózsa emerged from behind the wheel.

She and Allegro got out and split up to follow him on foot. Fetch veered to his right, keeping in the shadow of the trees, while Allegro approached him from the front. Fetch trained her night-vision binoculars on him and got a good look at his face. "It's not Rózsa," she told Allegro through their earpiece mics.

"Then who the...cover me while I find out who the hell he is," Allegro replied.

Fetch trained her Glock on the figure as Allegro emerged from behind a tall boulder several feet in front of him, holding her gun as well. "Who the hell are you?" she asked the man.

The driver of the Coupe took a step back, seeming surprised, but recovered quickly. "You're trespassing," he said calmly. "I should be pointing a gun, not you."

"Still doesn't answer who you are."

"I work here."

"Doesn't look like anyone's worked here for months. This place is a ghost town."

"This matter is none of your business."

"Maybe not, but it's my problem."

Fetch kept her gun aimed at the man as she edged closer to them.

The man's cell phone rang and he looked at Allegro.

"Go ahead. Tell Rózsa I can't wait to meet him," Allegro said. "I want your movements nice and slow."

The man reached into his pocket and pulled out the phone. He spoke in Bulgarian, and Fetch could see through the binoculars that his eyes never left Allegro. He ended the call and lowered his hand back to his pocket. Fetch followed his movement and saw him replace the cell with a gun. Allegro couldn't have seen it from her angle in the dark. "He's got a gun," Fetch warned Allegro.

Allegro dove behind the boulder for cover as she shot at him at the same time he fired his weapon. Then he ran for cover as well, racing through the trees toward the outbuilding.

"I'm on him," Fetch told Allegro as she raced after him. He slipped behind the outbuilding—one that housed generators, from the sound of it. Fetch detoured silently through the trees to get behind him.

He was crouching behind the corner of the building, looking out the way he'd come. When he started firing blind in Allegro's direction, Fetch jumped him from behind. She got him in a headlock with one arm and grabbed his wrist with her other hand. Then she banged his gun hand against the wall until he dropped his weapon. "I have him," she said in her earpiece as he continued to struggle.

He reached into his pocket with his other hand and pulled something out, but she couldn't get a good look at it. "What's that?" she said, squeezing his throat with her arm as she grappled for it.

Finally she got it away from him and stared down at it. It was a remote detonator.

"Too late," the man rasped. "In a few seconds, only dust will remain." Fetch bashed his head with her gun butt and he went limp in her arms.

"The place is about to blow," Fetch shouted to Allegro.

"Lynx!" Allegro yelled back. "Lynx is still in there."

Fetch spotted her running toward the main structure and took off after her. Allegro would never make it; they were nearly a quarter mile from the labs. Fetch ran as fast as she could, and when she was close enough to Allegro she tackled her. They'd just touched the ground when the building exploded. Fetch kept Allegro covered with her body as debris rained down on and around them.

"We have to get her," Allegro shouted, and struggled to get away from under Fetch.

Fetch loosened her hold slightly and they both got to their knees. "You've been hit," she said. Blood was pouring from Allegro's head from a large gash in her scalp just above her forehead. Allegro kept wiping at her eyes because blood was pouring into them. "I'll go look for her," Fetch said. "Stay here."

But as soon as they got up, another explosion threw them both a few feet back. More debris hurtled at them, and it was several seconds before they could get to their hands and knees. Fetch struggled to breathe amid the widespread dust and looked up as Allegro did. The whole main building was now enveloped in flames, several walls were gone, and the structure was caving in on itself in pieces.

"She's gone," Allegro said. "She's gone."

Everything was moving in surreal slow motion. Without thinking, Fetch got up and started to walk toward the building.

Allegro grabbed her by the shoulder. "What are you doing?"

"I have to get her out," Fetch said. "Maybe she's still alive."

"She's not, Gianna, and I can't let you go in there. Look…" Allegro pointed at it. "Nothing's left, and it's still exploding."

Fetch stared at the flames as a pair of smaller blasts shook the ground under their feet. Allegro was right. Lynx could have never survived. "I didn't save her," Fetch said, looking up at the sky. She was telling Allegro and Sam and whatever else was out there listening that she had failed. Failed again to save another soldier.

"God damn it," Allegro said as tears mixed with the blood running down her cheeks.

Fetch dropped to her knees and watched in a trance as the building burned, the fire heating her face "We can't save everyone, right?" she asked bitterly, repeating Pierce's words. "All we can do is try."

Allegro dropped down next to her. "That's supposed to be a fucking comfort?"

"No. Just a fucked-up fact."

CHAPTER THIRTY-SEVEN

Southwestern Colorado
One week later, November 3

Fetch and the EOO had had to deal with endless questions from National Security and Interpol while the atmosphere amongst the ETFs and her bosses was unbearably glum. Lynx's death had devastated and shocked them all. The conciliatory words of ops and friends hadn't consoled her and Allegro. No one could have prevented what happened, just as they couldn't help thinking they'd failed. Failed to save Lynx and failed to catch Rózsa. The fact that they'd found the formulas and his bank account, basically what they were asked to do, didn't even begin to exorcise the desolation.

Worse, they couldn't give their fellow ETF and friend a proper funeral. The organization didn't salute any flag or support any religion. A memorial service commemorated the deceased before the body was incinerated. Although this ritual usually provided some closure and finality, Lynx's body had never been retrieved. Probably burned to ashes in the explosion. All they had left to eulogize was a picture.

Nearly every op was present during the ceremony in the Organization's speech room. Most had cried during Joanne's speech, but Montgomery Pierce had stood alone at the end of the room, expressionless. His eyes occasionally drifted to Joanne or to Lynx's picture, but he primarily stared outside.

Fetch, who'd stayed in the back as well, went to him when the speech was over and everyone had started to break into small groups. When Pierce turned to her, she recognized her own hurt in his eyes. Fetch nodded slightly in recognition of their mutual pain, and Pierce nodded back and returned to looking outside.

Fetch followed his gaze and saw a woman with short, dark hair, dressed in black, down on the playground outside the junior dormitory. She swung back and forth on one of the children's swings with a bottle in her hand, and despite the appropriately gloomy, overcast day, she was wearing sunglasses. Fetch didn't recognize the trespasser. Security was tight and few outsiders were allowed on EOO grounds, certainly never unescorted. She looked at Pierce. "Sir, do you know her?"

Pierce never took his eyes off the stranger. "Yes."

"Is she one of us?"

"Not anymore," he replied.

Strange. No op ever walked away, and this one wasn't old enough to have retired. Although Fetch wanted to ask more, this topic was clearly not up for discussion. "Is she here for Cassady?"

Pierce merely nodded.

"She didn't attend the ceremony."

"I let her know she was welcome. But she's not interested in this." Pierce motioned to the room behind him still looking outside. "For her, Cassady will always be by the swings." He turned his face away from her, but not before Fetch saw a tear escape the corner of his eye.

When someone below their window opened the door to go outside, the stranger immediately got up and left.

Fetch was too restless to return to the dormitory where she'd bunked while awaiting the memorial service, so she left the building to walk on one of the numerous trails that led off campus into the adjacent Weminuche Wilderness Area. A week had passed since she'd returned to the States from Hungary, but she'd lived it in a daze. Her only clear memory was of her brief conversation with Zoe her first day back.

She'd told Zoe where she was and that they'd lost Cassady. Fetch had wanted to confide more, or tell her nothing at all; it didn't really matter as long as Zoe was on the line and she could hear her breathe.

Zoe hadn't pressed for answers concerning her return or said anything other than she missed her. Even Lynx's loss hadn't suppressed the unfamiliar pleasure of being missed. Zoe had given her plenty of those new feelings. But the one that had rocked her thoroughly was the one she'd experienced back at the London police station, when, for the first time, she had needed to look back before heading off on an assignment. When she'd found Zoe looking right back at her, Fetch knew those were the eyes she wanted to see from now on before she shut any door. Before she left for all her uncertain returns.

But could Zoe live with those insecurities and fears? Zoe had said that love was worth the eventual pain, and Fetch now knew that was true. Had she known the outcome with Sam, she wouldn't have changed a thing. Sam had taught her she could love. And Zoe made her feel she was worthy to have someone love her.

❖

London, England
One week later, November 10

Zoe taped up another box and stacked it atop the others piling up in one corner of her London penthouse in Soho. Her bedroom and kitchen were done and she was making good progress in her living room. Her books were all packed, the bookcase shelves empty. She was determined to get through her desk tonight before she turned in; it would help exhaust her so she might actually be able to get more than a few hours' rest. But first she'd finish reviewing the materials she intended to mail to Oxford in the morning.

Reinventing her life and her preoccupation with what might be happening with Gianna had consumed her since she'd arrived home two weeks ago. Gianna had called two days after they'd parted in London and said she was back in the States but had to stay there indefinitely for the debriefing about the Rózsa case.

Although it had been wonderful to hear Gianna's voice again and know that she was safe and well, it broke Zoe's heart that she was in so much pain over losing Cassady. Zoe had met her only briefly, but recognized the kindness the beautiful woman exuded. How often did Gianna lose colleagues? The job these people did involved so many risks, that if she hadn't met Gianna she couldn't have comprehended the willingness to endure such a life.

Gianna had shown her a new world of people who lived to serve a greater purpose. Where what they gave, not what they had, defined them.

Gianna had been right. Zoe *had* become numb. She had become so comfortable in her empty life she'd never stopped to question it. Now she knew what she had settled for all those years was indifference. And nothing killed a person's willingness to change her life or make a difference more than apathy.

One way or another, with or without Gianna in her life, Zoe refused to return to that lethargic state. When her father had offered her job and anything else she needed to her, probably out of guilt for his brother, Zoe had turned him down. She was determined to live the life she was meant to.

Zoe was filling in the forms that would help begin her new life when the doorbell buzzed. Surprised, she walked to the intercom. Who'd be calling at midnight, unannounced? God knew she wasn't ready for another crisis. She pressed the button. "Who's there?"

"I know it's late, but can I come up?"

"Gianna?" Zoe asked in disbelief.

"Yeah."

Zoe buzzed her in. Her heart pounded as she waited for the private elevator doors to open into her penthouse. Glancing around, she frowned at the mess and scurried to clear the couch of her forms and brochures, stacking them haphazardly on the coffee table. She ran a couple of dirty glasses to the sink and threw the shoes and sweaters she'd taken off earlier into the bedroom. Then she stopped in the bathroom to run a brush through her hair. Could be worse. At least she hadn't put on her very comfortable but not at all sexy pajamas yet. She wore her favorite low-cut jeans and a knit, long-sleeved red shirt with a deep V-neck that displayed a little cleavage.

By the time she returned to the living room, the doors to the elevator were sliding open.

Gianna took her breath away. Zoe was so used to seeing her in camouflage or T-shirts, the transformation was a bit unsettling. In a very good way, like she was meeting her for the first time. Gianna wore a deep purple button-down shirt, tailored nicely to her slender build. She had one hand in the pocket of her black dress trousers, which gave her a cavalier stance that didn't quite mesh with the nervousness in her dark brown eyes.

Black leather dress boots, polished to a high gloss, had replaced the combat boots. Her short dark hair was stylishly askew and shone in the overhead light from the elevator. Some remnants of the bruises on her face remained, but they had faded significantly and didn't detract from Gianna's dazzling beauty.

Gianna stepped out and paused just over the threshold, taking in Zoe from top to bottom, as if memorizing every change and detail just as Zoe had done.

Zoe remained rooted beside the couch. It was ridiculous, considering everything they'd been through. She had dreamed and daydreamed of throwing herself in Gianna's arms when and if she saw her again, but instead, here she was, frozen and tongue-tied and almost shy. She hadn't felt like this since she was young.

Gianna cleared her throat and took in all the packed boxes piled in the room. "Is this a bad time?" she finally asked.

"No, of course not…please come farther," Zoe said. God, why was she acting like such an idiot?

Gianna slowly walked to the couch where Zoe was. She stopped a few feet away and stood like a soldier at rest.

"Can I get you something to drink?" Zoe asked.

"No, I'm good. I'm sorry I didn't call."

Great. Now Gianna thought she was angry with her.

"It's been hectic back home with all that's happened."

"I'm so sorry about Cassady."

"Yeah." Gianna looked over Zoe's head, concentrating on the wall behind her with an empty stare. "Thanks."

"Please, sit down," Zoe said, taking a seat on the couch. "I'm sorry about the mess."

"You're leaving?"

"I'm moving in with my father. I can't afford this place any longer and decided I'd rather sell it and make better use of the money."

Now Gianna was staring at something on the coffee table, this time with interest. Zoe followed her gaze. It was her Oxford enrollment forms. "I'm going back to university," she explained. "I've been looking at folders and filling in forms all week. That's what I plan to use the money for."

Gianna picked up a few pamphlets. "Medicine."

"It's what I've always wanted."

Gianna smiled. "I'm not surprised. You'll make a hell of a doctor."

"You really think so?"

"Yeah, I do." Gianna met her eyes and gazed at Zoe like she wanted to say more but couldn't, or wouldn't.

Zoe prayed for something—*anything*—to break this awkwardness. More than anything, she needed to feel Gianna's lips on hers. She *ached* to kiss her. But why was it so difficult? She wanted her so much, but she couldn't make her limbs move or her mouth verbalize that need.

As Gianna continued to look at her expectantly, Zoe realized how much she wanted her to stay. Not just for now, or for the week. She wanted Gianna in her life. But Gianna wasn't here to stay; she'd made it clear that she never stayed. The prospect of spending a few hours or days with her before she left again made Zoe hurt beyond comprehension. Why did it always feel like they were saying good-bye?

Suddenly, Zoe needed some space to breathe. "I'm going to get myself a glass of wine," she said as she got up and walked to the kitchen.

She stood at the counter, taking deep breaths as she poured Merlot in a glass. "Are you sure you don't want anything?" she called.

"I want you," Gianna said in her ear.

Zoe jumped and set the glass back down. She hadn't heard Gianna enter the kitchen. Gianna put her arms around her from behind, kissed her neck, and pulled her closer. Zoe felt Gianna's breasts against her back and moaned.

"I've missed you." Gianna nibbled her ear.

"I've...missed...you...too." Zoe gasped. Gianna's spicy cologne filled her nostrils, a heady scent that was entirely too irresistible. This felt so good, so right and so wrong. Zoe pulled away from Gianna's embrace and slipped past her.

Gianna looked confused.

"I'm sorry, I can't do this." Zoe grabbed her glass and headed back to the couch.

"Do what?" Gianna asked as she followed her to the living room.

Zoe set her glass on the table and faced Gianna. "Keep saying good-bye."

"I thought you understood," Gianna said, looking away. "I... my work, it's not easy but—"

"Gianna, I'm desperately in love with you."

Gianna's head slowly turned to her.

"From the moment you left, I've spent every waking moment thinking of you and every sleeping moment dreaming of you. I..." Zoe plopped down on the couch, feeling exposed. "I'm sorry for the drama." She hid her face in her hands. "I'm never like this, it's just...I've never felt like this and it terrifies me. Never mind that ever since you walked in, I feel like a bloody teenager wondering if the school stud will ask me to the big dance, yet knowing that unless a miracle transpires, she never will. And, great, now I'm babbling."

Gianna pried her fingers from her face and lifted Zoe's face to hers. "Zoe, you have no reason to be afraid." Gianna grinned. "Besides, I've never asked anyone to a prom. The educational system I was in didn't include those."

"Military school?"

"Something like that."

"Well, that's exactly why I'm terrified, Gianna." Zoe got up to pace. She needed to keep space between them or she'd never be able to focus. It would be so easy to jump in bed, or on the couch, counter, or every other surface she'd envisioned in the past weeks, and wake up tomorrow full of regrets and dreading Gianna's departure. "You're a born soldier. You get up and leave to go fight wars and rescue people."

"It's all I know. It's who I've become, or maybe always was." Gianna remained on the couch but watched Zoe as she paced. "Someday, when I get too old for this and start to get other kinds of assignments, life will slow down. And you know what? I'll miss it. Yes, what I do is dangerous, but when you've lived on adrenaline so long, you don't know how to be without it. When you survive…" Gianna ruffled her hair while she stared at the coffee table as if she'd find the words there. "When you fight and survive an attack, you've lived more in those minutes than is possible during a lifetime."

Gianna paused to look at her. "Going from that to worrying about laundry and dirty dishes while I wait for the next job won't be easy. You can take a soldier out of war, but you can't take the war out of them."

"In other words, you have no space in your life for anyone or anything else that doesn't include or present a constant rush," Zoe said. "All you ever offer anyone is moments. Fragments of your life."

"That's right."

"I want more. It's selfish, but I want all of you, not just a fast and furious encounter whenever you're in town."

"Zoe, I want more, too."

"Don't get me wrong, I'd love fast and furious, and anything else, for that matter, with you, but—" Zoe stopped pacing. What did Gianna just say?

Gianna got up and came to face her.

Zoe looked up into those deep brown eyes. "Did you just—"

"*You* give me that rush. Being with you makes me feel just as alive and appreciative of life as being out there. You terrify me as much as any firefight."

"I do?"

Gianna nodded. "Because you remind me of how much I stand to lose, and for the first time in my life I want to be reminded of that." Gianna touched Zoe's lips with her fingertips. "You completely consume me." Gianna brushed her lips with hers. "Head over heels, crazy in love with you."

Zoe finally did what she'd wanted to do since Gianna appeared at her door. She wrapped her arms around her and held tight. "How will we ever make this work?" she mumbled in Gianna's neck.

"Well, that's another thing I wanted to talk to you about."

Zoe pulled back and looked up at her. "I'm listening."

"I didn't know you'd be going back to school, so I meant to ask you to come back with me. To the States. We could find a place and…" Gianna stuttered and turned red.

Zoe smiled. "God, I'm crazy about you. Are you asking me to move in with you?"

"Yeah."

Zoe hugged her again. "I'd love to."

"And your studies?" Gianna embraced her, too.

"I haven't enrolled yet. I could study there. It's just four years. Then I could be away at the same time you're gone. If that's possible."

"Be away?" Gianna repeated.

"I plan to join Doctors without Borders when I'm done."

Gianna lifted her until Zoe's feet no longer touched the floor. "I'm so proud of you. You really are an amazing woman."

"I don't know about that. But thank you for showing me I have potential."

Gianna put her back down and kissed her, a slow, sensual kiss. It was a promise, a sealing of their future together, embodied with all their depth of emotion for each other.

"Where do we start?" Zoe asked when they finally parted to breathe. "I mean, what do we do now?"

"Live," Gianna replied, and kissed her again.

EPILOGUE

New York City
Five days later, November 15

Montgomery Pierce took a deep breath and paused in front of the door. Although he was about to bring her news, he wasn't looking forward to the anger—or worse, indifference—he was sure the woman behind this door would receive him with. He felt Joanne's hand smooth over the back of his suit jacket, a quick stroke of encouragement.

A familiar voice from within answered his two sharp knocks. "Who the hell is it? It's open."

He entered the apartment with Joanne Grant and David Arthur flanking him. Although it was dark, one quick look around the small space was enough to see that it hadn't been cleaned for weeks. And by the smell of it, hadn't been aired for at least as long. Comic books, soiled clothes, and empty Jack Daniel's bottles covered every surface. Jaclyn must have been drinking nonstop since the explosion in the lab nearly three weeks earlier.

Joanne pointed to the couch, and he and David turned to see the dark figure lying there. Jaclyn looked barely conscious. Her head was resting on the armrest, and she was struggling to open her eyes. She looked so disoriented Monty wasn't sure whether Jaclyn had even noticed the three of them. He was about to approach her when Jaclyn spoke.

"What do you want?" Jaclyn slurred, seemingly unimpressed by their presence.

"You're a mess," he said quietly, with more observation than accusation.

"You've always been a glass-half-empty kinda bastard," she replied. "I'm simply going through a nihilistic phase."

"You're coming with us, Jaclyn," Monty said, ignoring her remark. The news he came to announce would have to wait. Jaclyn was in no position to handle any discussion, and he feared an irrational reaction. He needed to get her cleaned up and sober, and that wouldn't happen unless he took charge. He hadn't intended to take her back with him, but he hadn't expected her to be this far down a self-destructive path.

"The hell I am." Jaclyn pulled a Sig Sauer from between the cushions faster than he thought possible in her present state.

Arthur pulled his piece from his holster just as fast.

Never abandoning her horizontal position, Jaclyn merely turned her head to aim from one to the other. "It's like I told Cass. The only reason you hadn't come after me was because of her. Did you make her plead to let me live, you son of a bitch? Did you enjoy it when she begged?"

"That's not what happened," Joanna said.

"The hell it's not." Jaclyn lifted her head. "Thanks for the fucking invite, by the way," she said, clearly referring to the memorial ceremony. Monty had left voice-mail messages for her on both her cell phone and the landline at Cassady's Colorado home. "You could've just taken me out right there, you know."

"That's right," Monty said. "And we didn't. Why do you think that is?"

"Because you'd have too much explaining to do to all the others there. Besides, you know I would've taken you down first." She pointed the gun at him. "I'm faster than you, old man." Jaclyn was obviously wasted.

Monty said, "We can talk about—"

"Listen, if you've come to finish what you should have years ago, you're too late. I'm already well on my way, you son of a bitch." Jaclyn precariously waved the gun from him to Arthur. Monty was unarmed, as was Joanne. He was incapable of harming Jaclyn, and Joanne shared his sentiment, either because she cared for their former op or because she knew what Jaclyn meant to him. Knowing Joanne, it was probably both. She treated all ops like they were her own children.

"Take it easy, Jack. You're drunk," Arthur said, backing up a bit and keeping his gun trained on her.

Jaclyn pointed her P226 at him. "In a world in flux, Arthur, it's good to know that some things are stable. You still have a talent for pointing out the ridiculously obvious."

Arthur said, "If you'd just shut up and put the gun down, we're here to—" but Monty put a hand to his arm.

"Not now," he whispered. Jaclyn was too drunk and unpredictable. His mere movement had prompted her to shift her aim from Arthur back to him.

"Don't do anything stupid, Jaclyn," Joanne said. "We're not here to hurt you."

"Screw you, Joanne."

"That's enough, Jaclyn," Monty said austerely, disregarding her unpredictable state. "Don't talk to her like that."

Jaclyn glanced from him to Joanne, although it looked like it was taking every last morsel of energy she had to focus on their faces. "Oh, yeah, that's right. Pierce has already taken care of that. Screwing you, I mean. Everyone knows, you know." She waved her gun drunkenly at him. "Way to go, Pierce, although I think Joanne could have done a lot better."

"Get up, Jaclyn," Monty said sternly.

"Go to hell…Monty," Jaclyn replied, tightening her grip on the 9mm. "If you want to take me out, you'll have to do it here. You know what?" she mumbled. "I won't even put up a fight. Look." Jaclyn smiled and set the gun on the coffee table in front of her. "Just go for the temple." She pointed to the exact spot. "Respect my last wishes and let me die in this rat hole. I find it very apropos, don't you?" She stared at the ceiling. "If you live in the gutter, you deserve to die like the rodents that inhabit it."

"Stop feeling sorry for yourself," Monty said. "I hate to see you like this. What happened to the woman who—"

Jaclyn sat up for the first time, though it was clearly a struggle. "Don't you fucking *dare* pretend you give a shit about what happened to *that* woman," she spat contemptuously. "You didn't give a good God damn fuck nine years ago when the three of you acted like all I needed was some patching up after I'd been tortured and fu…" Jaclyn was shouting now and Pierce saw her look down at her gun. "You dismissed, practically ignored it all…told me to come back just so I could mosey on along to the next damn job."

"We were wrong to do that," Monty replied. He always hated to hear that his operatives had suffered in the line of duty, but it had been especially painful to learn in his updates from Cassady what Jaclyn had endured. And now, to hear and see it himself, how it had fractured Jaclyn, was unbearable.

"We can't even begin to tell you how sorry we are," Joanne said.

"Oh, okay. Well, in that case, why don't we call it good and go out for burgers and shakes, like a big happy…are you all fucking insane?" Jaclyn asked. "Oh, oops, we made a mistake that cost you the last ten years of your life. But, hey, we're sorry."

"You're right," Monty said. "An apology is painfully inadequate."

"Why her?" Jaclyn asked him. "Why did you have to send Cassady on this job? Was it because you couldn't stand the fact that I was happy?"

"If you're implying that I sent her there to get killed just to spite you—"

"You know what?" Jaclyn rested her elbows on her knees as she looked from one to the other. "It doesn't even matter. None of this matters." She dropped her head and ran her hands through her hair. "Cassady's dead. The only person I ever loved is gone." She rubbed her eyes. "I should have gone with her. Been there to protect her. But I wasn't, so I'm as much to blame." She looked at the gun. "What's the point?" She grabbed the Sig Sauer from the table.

"Now!" Monty yelled, and Arthur shot her in the neck.

Jaclyn looked up, a mixture of shock and disbelief on her face. "Why?" she asked as she slowly fell back on the couch. "I can't do this anymore," she said, and shut her eyes.

Monty ran to her and knelt between her legs. He removed the tranquilizer dart and cupped her face with both hands. "Cassady's alive, honey. She's alive," he said, but Jaclyn was already out cold.

About the Authors

Kim Baldwin has been a writer for three decades, following up twenty years as an Emmy-winning network news executive with a second vocation penning lesbian fiction. In addition to her *Elite Operatives* collaborative efforts with Xenia Alexiou, she has published six solo novels with Bold Strokes Books: *Hunter's Pursuit, Force of Nature, Whitewater Rendezvous, Flight Risk, Focus of Desire,* and *Breaking the Ice.* She is a five-time Golden Crown Literary Society finalist—winning in Romantic Suspense, a 2010 Independent Publisher Book Award Silver Medalist, a five-time Lesbian Fiction Readers' Choice Award winner, and the recipient of a 2008 Alice B. Reader Appreciation Award for her body of work. In 2010, she recorded an audiobook of *Breaking the Ice.* She has also contributed short stories to six BSB anthologies: The Lambda Literary Award winning *Stolen Moments: Erotic Interludes 2, Lessons in Love: Erotic Interludes 3,* IPPY and GCLS Award winning *Extreme Passions: Erotic Interludes 4, Road Games: Erotic Interludes 5,* a 2008 Independent Publishers Award Gold Medalist, *Romantic Interludes 1: Discovery,* and *Romantic Interludes 2: Secrets.* She lives in the north woods of Michigan, where she is currently working on her next solo novel, *High Impact.* Her website is www.kimbaldwin.com and she can be reached at baldwinkim@ gmail.com.

Xenia Alexiou is Greek and lives in Europe. An avid reader and knowledge junkie, she likes to travel all over the globe and take pictures of the wonderful and interesting people that represent different cultures. Trying to see the world through their eyes has been her most challenging yet rewarding pursuit so far. These travels have inspired countless stories and it's these stories that she has decided to write about. *Dying to Live* is her fourth novel, following *Missing Lynx, Thief of Always,* and *Lethal Affairs.* She has won a

Golden Crown Literary Society Award and three Lesbian Fiction Readers' Choice Awards. Xenia is currently at work on *Demons are Forever*, the fifth book in the *Elite Operatives* Series. For more information, go to her website at www.xeniaalexiou.com, or contact her at xeniaalexiou007@gmail.com.

Lethal Affairs and Thief of Always have been translated into Dutch and Russian. In 2010, *Dubbel Doelwit* (Lethal Affairs) won second place among Dutch readers in their vote for best all-time Lesbian International (translated) book.